By Matthew Lang

TWITTERLIGHT
Dragonslayer

Published by DSP Publications
www.dsppublications.com

DRAGON SLAYER

MATTHEW LANG

DSP PUBLICATIONS

Published by

DSP Publications

5032 Capital Circle SW, Suite 2, PMB# 279, Tallahassee, FL 32305-7886 USA
www.dsppublications.com

Trade Paperback ISBN: 978-1-64080-463-0
Digital ISBN: 978-1-64405-105-4
Library of Congress Control Number: 2018943359
Trade Paperback published September 2018
v. 1.0

Printed in the United States of America
∞
This paper meets the requirements of
ANSI/NISO Z39.48-1992 (Permanence of Paper).

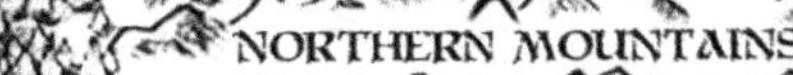

NORTHERN MOUNTAINS
AER GORAGON
GREAT NORTHERN FORESTS
BOOLIKSTAAD
R. Shelde
BLACKWATER
BLACKWATER MARSH
SPINE OF THE WORLD
SLASHERCLAW FORESTS
AERGONITE CAVERNS
R. Aergon
WAYSTATION
Kingdom of Aracao
Known Lands
CLOUD FORESTS
N

DRAGON SLAYER

MATTHEW LANG

DSP PUBLICATIONS

CHAPTER 1

IN HIS twenty-five years, Adam never thought of how he would die. Oh, he'd "died" often on the field of battle reenactments, but those had been foam weapons, carefully choreographed dramatic finishes, and a lot of rehearsal beforehand. This was different. He'd seen real battle death since arriving in this twisted hellhole of a lost world—quick, brutal, and messy—and somehow he'd managed to survive, whether through fighting or fleeing. Not this time.

Staring up the dirt track, past the veritable sea of four-armed, leathery-skinned barbarians, he saw his fate as clearly as the officious-looking elders standing on the platform of stone and logs. It might as well have been etched into the heavy obsidian blade clutched loosely in two of the burly executioner's hands—Warning: Trespassers will be Eaten. Of course, that would only work if the kanak gave warnings.

Every step was agony. The sharp stabbing pain shooting from his wrenched ankle was almost worse than the prodding from the stone-tipped spears that urged along his limping progress. His head throbbed from where he had fallen to the ground, and his left eye was swollen shut. Back in high school, Adam had read about executions and how broken prisoners would shuffle slowly toward their fate. He'd always thought they were too tired to move faster or their movements were impeded by manacles. Now he knew better. Even as much as he yearned for the pain to stop, each ragged breath that rasped into his lungs was sweet punishment. Every second he took walking up the street between the jeering kanak was a second longer to feel his heart straining in his rib cage. The oblivion of death hovered before him, more horrifically real now than any time since he'd arrived here. This had to be a windup. Part of him felt like he was sitting on his couch staring at the TV, wondering if his favorite character was about to be killed off midseason. The rest of him worried that this was really the end. And so he struggled second to second, hoping for something—anything—to happen.

One second longer for his luck to change.

Only it didn't.

The track made its way between the two largest dwellings to the center of the village. The din of the watching crowd swelled until it sounded almost like a football grand final. At least it would have if said footy crowd was clad in wraps of cured animal hide or woven vegetation and chanted along to a beat kept by the stamping of their feet while accompanied by the droning of clashing trumpet sounds—it was just like a footy crowd at a grand final.

Entering the central square, Adam passed a fire pit piled high with deadwood awaiting the touch of flame to send it roaring up into the perpetual dusk of the jungle sky. On the dais behind it was a rude throne of wood and jutting bone, and seated upon that was the kanak chieftain, easily a head taller than the rest of his clan. Although he still had the dark brown skin and ebony hair, his clothing was where his appearance differed—and significantly so. Unlike the warriors, who wore nothing bar a leather loincloth or penis-gourd and their tattoos of black and red, the chief's clothing was of finely woven reeds in red, black, and brown. Around his neck he wore a gorget of polished bone and turquoise—and infuriatingly, Adam's battered watch, glinting from a leather thong. Standing to his right was an older kanak female leaning on a gnarled staff, the goat skull and beads of bone and turquoise indicating her rank as a shaman or medicine woman of some sort. She wore a red silk wrap over her shoulders and around her waist, and an ornate grass skirt that almost reached her feet. Her expression was proud and serene as she watched Adam's approach.

All this passed through Adam's brain in the blink of an eye as his focus moved sharply to the low table—or rather two table halves—that sat on the dais between the throne and the fire pit. They were made of wood and clearly fitted together, one lip overlapping the other to create a seamless surface, barring a circular hole in the middle. It looked like the table would then be held together with thick wooden pegs, two of which lay conveniently on one of the table halves. As his stomach attempted to heave up the last dregs of bile, Adam dug his heels in, momentarily halting his guards in their attempts to drag him forward, and wrenching his ankle so hard his vision threatened to black out entirely. The chanting of the crowd was feverish, barraging his ears with a thrumming cacophony of noise. It no longer mattered that he didn't understand the language; he knew all the words.

Do not get locked into that thing, his brain screamed at him as his eyes tracked around the area, looking for a gap through which he might bolt, but found none. Then clawed hands gripped his arms, and two of the warriors half marched, half dragged him forward as he struggled to free his hands, still bound behind his back with a length of twisted creeper.

"What's the weirdest thing you've ever eaten?" Rusty asked, snuggled up behind Adam in the postcoital glow of their lovemaking.

"Raw snail. Dare in year ten," Adam said, pulling their combined sleeping bags around his neck to ward off the desert chill that threatened to seep through the walls of their canvas tent. "You?"

"Witchety grub. Tonight."

"Oh come on, you don't have any stories?"

"Not personally, no," Rusty said. "My dad was fed monkey brains, though."

"What?"

"Monkey brains. From the monkey, apparently."

"Explain, please?"

"He was in... I think it was Egypt? Or somewhere in Africa, anyway, and they served him monkey. He said they had a table with a hole in the middle—they put the monkey's head through the hole and use a knife and...."

Forced to his knees, Adam found the raw wood dug into his neck as a cheer went up from the surrounding crowd. From his new vantage point, he could see old bloodstains and knife marks on the table's surface, and the last wooden peg was dropped into the table with the finality of the last nail being hammered into his coffin.

Two months earlier.

TRAINING WAS always an issue. The Society for Creative Anachronism often attracted members who felt a romantic connection to the chivalry and courtly mannerisms esteemed in the Middle Ages, and those people were not always physically suited to the art of combat. It took a fair amount of strength to wield a sword or axe with lethal force. It took skill to make it look like you were wielding a sword or axe with lethal force without the force actually becoming lethal. Most times, practice was more along the lines of a carefully choreographed dance, with people working on timing their blows to strike shields or other foam blades, rather than the soft, fleshy parts of their fellow enthusiasts. Only a few were willing—and able—to wield real weapons, and even then, such duels were carefully monitored. When Adam joined the society in the first year of his Bachelor of Science at the University of Melbourne, he had little going for him bar his height and the natural breadth of his shoulders. Still, he knew he wanted to buckle his swash with the best of them, and in time he was able to broad his sword, quarter his staff, and battle his axe as well.

Two years, hundreds of blisters, and an ongoing stint in the Army Reserves later, Adam was now one of the SCA mentors and weapons specialists, showing eager new enthusiasts the right way to hold a staff, and trying to curb their enthusiasm for hitting each other with their foam weapons. The fiberglass core could hurt even with the exterior padding. Even so, despite his flourishes and dazzling displays of skill, his fights still tended to be as carefully choreographed as the larger battle scenes.

Today had been a good day, as he and June, one of his fellow mentors, engaged in a mock fight with their training swords. The duel resulted in several wrenched muscles, not a few bruises, and a great deal of banging on their sturdy shields. He'd also spent a bit of time showing off some of his fancier metal blades, as that always impressed the newer members. After packing away the weaponry, he said goodbye to his fellow enthusiasts and hit the showers at the university gym for the last time—end of the semester in November meant the end of their official meetings until March. Adam, who had already completed his practical assessments, now faced the prospect of a summer of casual work and sleeping in, with occasional training sessions mixed in where possible. Right at the moment, however, he faced the equally wonderful prospect of a hot, steaming shower to wash the remaining grime from his skin and the ache from his limbs.

The university showers were separated into cubicles by the same dark gray dividers they used to partition their toilets, ensuring near complete privacy. Adam selected one at the far end, hung his towel on the peg provided, turned on the water, and stood outside the cool spray until the water made it from the water heater to his showerhead. Despite the drought more or less breaking, he still felt guilty taking long showers at home. Somehow, here at the gym, it was less of an indulgence and more of an acceptable treat. Still, his shower was relatively short, taking only as long as he needed to shampoo his hair and wash himself down with whatever bodywash he had found on special in Priceline and jammed into the bottom of his gym bag—OGX or something. June would probably have admonished him for not using conditioner, but the tight soldier's crop he maintained didn't need much in the way of care—there just wasn't enough there to matter. His chest was covered with a sprinkling of browny blond hairs, although the treasure trail leading to his crotch was slightly more noticeable. Or would have been if he showed it off more.

He felt the stares on him as he strode out of his stall, towel slung low across his hips after a brief rubdown. Still, Adam wasn't really in the mood to follow up on any of the subtle offers that came his way in the locker room. Nearly a year after the "Dear Adam" email from Rusty breaking things off, he wasn't quite ready to date again. And as much as he wanted someone to come along and sweep him off his feet, he wasn't holding out hope of that actually happening.

Adam dried himself, then opened his locker and pulled a fresh pair of cargo pants from his duffel. Cargos were one of the habits from the Army that had infiltrated his civilian life—exactly how people got through the day without the extra pockets was beyond him. The lightweight variety he favored were casual enough to pass as relatively trendy, quick to dry when wet, and as a bonus, hugged his ass in a very flattering manner. After stepping into a pair of clean black trunks, he pulled the khaki material up his legs and secured it around his hips with a plain black belt. Then on went the battered "once black but washed to the point of gray" T-shirt and the cotton shirt that had become another habit, sleeves rolled up to leave his muscular forearms bare. White socks and brown walking boots were stepped into and tied with military precision. His friends often teased him about looking like a soldier, but there was a certain blessing in knowing what you were wearing each morning, along with the fact that if he added dog tags to the outfit, he instantly became a bit of a man magnet, which he had to admit was quite nice. In fact, the only decoration Adam habitually wore was his watch, a chunky heavy-duty steel model that looked perfectly normal at first glance, but with a face of pearly white polished stone that was a handcrafted, bespoke piece he'd bought on impulse at a craft fair at the Abbotsford Convent one weekend.

It happened just as he was exiting the underpass that led from the sports oval to Tin Alley—the site of numerous muggings and at least one death, despite the bright lights that illuminated it all night, every night. Adam's common sense told him it was simply too easy to block off both front and back exits and gang up on whatever poor sod was stuck in the middle. Ever since the last mugging, Adam had taken to keeping his hand on the hilt of whatever weapon he was carrying at the time, and in this case, he was fortunate he did.

There was no noise. Only a light breeze that swirled around him, tugged at his clothing and would have ruffled his hair if he had much to speak of. Sparkling motes of gold lit up his face as they rained to the ground from a glowing reddish hole in the middle of the sky. Shielding his eyes against the dust, he squinted at the greenish blue treetops that appeared beyond the hole above him. It looked like a window into a sky that was… somewhere else. Suddenly he was rushing toward it, with a strange feeling of being stretched before his feet left the ground.

CHAPTER 2

THE FIRST thing that struck him was the smells. Gone was the dry dust and smooth eucalyptus of Melbourne spring. Instead there was the reek of unwashed bodies coupled with blood and the sickening stench of rotting shit, which he later learned to identify as the scent of a disemboweled corpse. The second thing that struck him was a backhanded blow from a gargantuan four-armed man. Or sort of man. The giant stood head, shoulders, and shoulders above Adam's six-foot frame, its skin a leathery, weather-beaten brown with just a hint of scales.

The force of the blow sent Adam reeling backward, catching his foot in something knobby, warm, and somewhat damp. He hit the ground hard, the breath fleeing his lungs on impact. As he lay on the flattened grass with the hilt of his spring-steel broadsword jabbing into his neck, Adam's eyes went to the object he had fallen over—the mangled body of a man in armor of purplish leather and hard, glossy black plates. Adam's foot had caught in the hollow of the man's knee, which was cast out at an unnatural angle from the rest of the corpse, and a smear of dark crimson liquid was already seeping into Adam's boots.

The dead man had been shorter—and younger—than Adam, but had possessed hard slabs of muscle that put Adam to shame. Blood was still oozing from several wounds, but the man had likely died from the jagged gash across his throat. Adam didn't have time to dwell on his first dead body, however, as the four-armed giant turned toward him, its lower pair of arms clutching a wicked blood-tipped stone spear that spoke eloquently to what had caused the young man's injuries. The rest of the giant was naked, except for a large pointed gourd—covering what Adam could only assume to be an equally large member—and swirling tattoos in red and black, which Adam felt to be superfluous, given the prominence of the gourd. The rest of its—his—possessions were either functional weaponry or decorative scraps of wood and bones caught in the braids and dreadlocks that adorned the giant's head. Other than that, his body was completely hairless and would have made fashion photographers swoon. Adam, though, was more concerned about the two small tusks in the giant's lower jaw and the heavy spear arcing toward him.

Instinctively he rolled to his left, tugging his spring-steel blade from his gym bag and his foot from the corpse, just fast enough to avoid the spear's point, which dug into the ground scant inches from his shoulder blade. Adam didn't quite manage to roll to his feet before the giant was upon him, and barely brought the blade up in time to fend off the next attacks. The giant struck at him with the long stone knife and the wooden club in his other pair of hands. Adam parried the first blow, and in the process, sheared the stone blade in two, before moving to block the club. The impact of wood on steel brought their crossed weapons inches from his face, and the force of it left his muscles feeling like a combination of butter and overcooked pasta. But then the spear was coming again, and this time, Adam felt it scratch across his bicep as he rolled desperately away. Then the club scored a hit on his abdomen, tearing a cry from his throat and more than a few tears from his eyes. Hopelessly outmatched four hands to two, Adam could only wait for the blow that would come and end it all.

Only it didn't.

A very human yell rang through the air above him, followed by a bestial cry of pain and a slick squishing sound. Then warm, sticky liquid rained down upon him, and he realized it was blood. The giant's blood. Wiping at his face with his free hand, Adam peered up at the oversized, serrated teeth of a lizard large enough to engulf his head. Frantically his mind scrambled back to what he could remember about dinosaurs. Could it see him if he didn't move? Or was that the frogs? His body, however, scrambled instinctively to its feet, his hands bringing his sword back around in front of him. It was only then that he looked past the scaly, crested head and saw the rider. Perched on a saddle atop the middle pair of six great legs was a figure not dissimilar to the corpse Adam had fallen over, but this man's armor was worn with age and damage, despite showing signs of once being exquisitely detailed. The man's face was mostly obscured by a strange pointed helmet that was reminiscent of a beetle's carapace, with the heavy cheek guards looking like black mandibles clutching either side of the man's chin. His left hand held the reins of his six-legged mount, with a small buckler strapped to his forearm. His right hand held a curved saber that dripped with the red blood of the giant that was now crumpled over his own spear.

"Can you ride?" his timely rescuer asked.

"What?"

"Can you— Just get on," the man said. His left hand dropped the reins and reached out to Adam, just as another of the four-armed giants crashed through a curtain of creepers and into the small space at the base of a great gray-barked tree. Given the choice between the scary lizard-riding man who saved him and another of the giants that nearly ended him, Adam chose the man. Grabbing the proffered hand, he vaulted off one of the lizard's legs and up onto its back, his gym bag banging against his back as he landed.

"Hold on," his rescuer said, roughly pressing Adam's left hand to the wide belt around his hips. Adam grasped the thick leather and held on for dear life as the lizard bolted forward, wending sinuously through the undergrowth, nearly taking off Adam's feet before he hoisted them out of the way. Spears whistled around him, and suddenly he was going up as the lizard ran straight up one of the trees that grew in this area of cloud forest. Then they were running through the canopy, and Adam wasn't sure what was harder—hanging on or not throwing up.

The ride seemed to take forever, and when the lizard finally slowed, they came to an opening in the jungle, a temporary patch of sky caused by the toppling of a forest giant. Fungi and mosses had already colonized the iron-gray trunk, working slowly to turn the great tree back into the rich loam of the jungle floor. In the space cleared by its fall, small saplings were jostling toward the light in a mad bid to reestablish the jungle canopy, and the red light of the sky shone down to kiss the ground. With a slight shifting of his knees, the rider nudged the lizard into the leaf-littered hollow at the base of the tree, where the roots had pulled out of the ground. Three other lizards were already there, unharnessed and tearing strips out of the carcass of a spider the size of the greatest Great Dane. Two other people, a man in riding leathers and a woman in a regal cross-tied dress, looked up from their conversation at the sound of their approach.

"HAIL THE all-conquering Captain Darius," the second man said. "I see you've picked up another stray."

"Another?" Adam's rescuer asked, his tone neutral as he helped Adam dismount.

The man pulled a soft green robe off one of the exposed roots and slipped it on. "We found this one hiding in our shelter," he said, jumping down from his perch on a mound of moss-covered something and giving a furry bundle a kick.

Only when the bundle gasped did Adam realize it was a creature—a person—bound on the ground, albeit a person covered in short brown fur. It looked, for all intents and purposes, like a very skinny, bony version of a Hollywood werewolf, just a lot less scary for being bound in rope, struggling feebly, its fur matted and unkempt.

"I'm surprised it's managed to survive out here for so long," Darius said, striding toward the shivering form. "It must have been but a child when it was exiled from the caverns."

"Exiled?" Adam asked, the word escaping his mouth before he could clamp down on it.

The robed man's smile was not particularly friendly. "You are not from around here, are you?"

"What gave me away, my accent?" Adam asked before mentally kicking himself. Sometimes he really had a big mouth—and not in the good way. Maybe it was speciesist, but right now he was thinking that sticking with humans would be good for survival. Assuming this wasn't a very elaborate TV setup. Which he'd never consent to having broadcast.

"I think, Your Highness, we should restrain that man. He could be dangerous."

"We are all dangerous, Magister," the woman said pointedly. "And I'll not turn away potential allies so hastily. I am Esmeralda of Aergon," she said, pushing a strand of dark curly hair back from the almost translucent white skin of her face. "By what name are you called, wanderer?"

"Adam," he said, and suddenly a lifetime of geekery came to his rescue. "Forgive my ignorance, but I take it you are a princess, Your Highness?"

Esmeralda laughed, although her tone held little joy. "Yes, I am, but I am cut off from my father's caverns. Titles mean little on the surface. And in answer to your question, the bound creature is a cursed Child of Selune, she who fled the sky. All are tested, and the accursed are abandoned to the light of the uncaring sun."

"Then if you're from underground, what are you doing in the light of the uncaring sun, Esmeralda?"

"Your Highness, you cannot possibly allow—" the robed man started.

"Hush, Xavier," Esmeralda said. "*We* have spoken," she added, affecting a frosty royal tone worthy of the Queen of England. "We came to the surface seeking a mystical weapon to end my people's exile," she added.

"But we were not expecting the kanak," Darius rumbled. "Where is everyone else?"

"Not coming," Xavier said, his voice tight.

"All the more reason to keep this one… Adam," Darius said. "Flat-footed and no mount and he still survived some twenty counts with a kanak."

"Twenty counts is good?" Adam asked.

"On foot? Yes."

"We should be going back," Xavier interrupted. "It is too dangerous out here."

"Did you not hear the drop stones falling?" Esmeralda asked. "There is no way in, for all that the caves lie but a thousand paces away. It will take months just to lever them all out of the grooves in the floor, and the drop mechanisms will need repair before the tunnels are clear."

"Drop stones… seal your tunnels?" Adam asked.

"Defensive measure," Darius said shortly.

"And you don't know how to survive up here?"

"We can manage."

"Is that macho-commander speak for no?" Adam asked. "No offense, but it sounds like macho-commander speak for no."

"That is not a helpful attitude," Esmeralda said, bristling slightly.

"Neither is ignoring the facts," Adam said evenly. "You're going to need him," he added, indicating the bound creature.

"What makes you say that?"

"You said it yourselves. He's survived up here for who knows how long. And if you don't know the terrain, you need someone who does."

"Too dangerous," Darius said flatly.

"And you're not?"

"We only have four mounts," Darius said. "He would need to ride with someone."

Adam glanced around at the three others. This felt like the start of a video game. One with the dialogue options down at the bottom, usually labeled "diplomatic," "attempt to be inappropriately witty," or "get angry and probably get yourself killed." Mentally, he chose diplomatic. At least for now. "Fine," he said. "Teach me how to ride, and he can ride with me."

"What?"

"Well, I'm the one who wants him around because I think he's my best bet at surviving, and I'm not really important to any of you, right? If he plays up or mucks me around, you can ride on and take your chances without us."

Darius hesitated and then turned to the princess. "His argument makes a certain amount of sense, Princess."

"Then he can free the captive," Esmeralda said coolly. "And if he is torn to ribbons in the process, we will have our answer. If not, we can congratulate him on his clear thinking."

"Thank you," Adam said, only slightly sarcastically.

Esmeralda's expression was unreadable. "You are very welcome."

THE OTHERS had withdrawn to what they must have felt was a safe distance, and Adam could feel their watchful eyes on him as he squatted next to the mass of dark fur. Close up, he could make out the darker brown stripes that crossed its back, breaking up the richer chestnut—or at least the patches of chestnut fur that were not covered in dirt or muck. He could also count the creature's ribs and wondered at how gaunt it was. Even as he looked at the lanky-limbed humanoid lying prostrate in its bonds, its chest cavity rising and falling gently with each breath, he saw it was regarding him out of one, barely open, deep brown eye.

Adam had always heard the phrase "struck by the intelligence of the animal's gaze" bandied about, but in this particular instance, he was struck by the intelligence and humanity in the gaze that regarded, no, *measured* him. He still wasn't sure if this was some elaborate theme park full of special effects, if everything he was experiencing was real, or if he was just locked in a padded room somewhere drooling into a straightjacket, but regardless of where he might be, the person lying bound on the ground was exactly that—a person.

"Did you get all that?" he asked. "I mean, did you understand it all?"

The eye closed and then slowly opened, and the man—Adam assumed it was a man—nodded ever so slightly.

"So, um… I'm going to free you now…. Don't, like, bite or anything, okay?"

Even with the twisted leather gag in his mouth, there was the ghost of a smile and a feeble shake of the head.

Although Adam had his sword, he found the knots simple enough to undo after a bit of worrying. Several years in the Scouts had proved handy in the end—although strangely, he felt a working knowledge of bondage might have been more useful in this instance. Of course, in bondage, the typical idea was to restrain without hurting. Whoever had tied these knots hadn't had such niceties in mind. As he freed the man's lightly furred arm, Adam could see the others tensing. The feeling crackled between the three observers, and it only intensified as the man continued to lie on the ground, with Darius putting his hand carefully on his saber. Almost embarrassed, Adam turned his back and focused instead on freeing the man's legs and feet, catching an accidental glimpse under the tattered loincloth that appeared to be all the man was wearing—or all he had been permitted to retain. Only when Adam removed the taut gag and began coiling the now slack cord did the man slowly roll into a sitting position, carefully keeping his hands in full view the entire time.

"Thank you," the man said, his voice thick and dry.

"No worries," Adam said softly. "I'm Adam."

"Duin," the furred man said.

"Shall we get moving?" Xavier's voice cut in. "As much as I would love to take our time getting to know each other, we have a kanak war band somewhere back there that could sniff us out at any moment."

"Good point, Magister," Esmeralda said, stepping closer to the mottled green-and-black lizard that must have been her mount and glancing around the edges of their small clearing. "Let us ride."

"And… how do I do that?" Adam asked.

Duin raised a tentative hand. "I can—"

"No, you can't," Xavier snapped firmly.

"—show you how," Duin finished softly.

"I will show you," Darius said firmly. "Come and meet Zoul."

"Zoul?" Adam asked. "Who's Zoul?"

ZOUL TURNED out to be one of the larger lizards that had been dusk baking in the reddish light, which made him appear an angry black. On closer inspection, however, Adam discovered he was really a dark green. His scales were edged with purple in a pattern not unlike the supple leathers Xavier and Captain Darius wore, and his eyes were slit vertically in the way of reptiles. A tall crest ran from the top of his head down part of his neck, and it appeared that the giant six-legged lizard would be able to raise or lower it at will, much like the plumage on some birds. However, what Adam really noticed was the lizard's teeth—sharp, pointed, and each somewhere between two and four inches in length.

"Zoul, this is Adam," Darius said as they approached the lizard, who had turned his head to watch them with reptilian disinterest. "He's going to be riding you for a while, along with… the Child of Selune. Don't hurt him."

As if in response, a long bluish tongue flickered out, and a transparent inner eyelid dropped down over the lizard's eye.

Urged by Darius and trailed by Duin, Adam stepped closer to the lizard's flank, noting how the leather saddle was fitted almost directly above the lizard's middle set of legs, with straps securing it around the lizard's chest, midsection, and tail.

"You will need this," Darius said, taking a wide leather belt out of a saddlebag. He strapped it around Adam's waist. "It belonged to one of our champions, but… she doesn't need it now. Do not dishonor it."

"Um… I'll try not to," Adam said as Darius buckled him in, allowing two long leather straps to dangle front and back of Adam's person.

"Good," Darius said. "Now, to mount a lizard, you need to let him know you're here by gently placing one hand on his foreleg. The other can be placed on his saddle. They're used to riders, but you don't want to spook them."

Adam tried very hard not to visualize a spooked lizard and exactly how it might react with its knifelike teeth.

"Now we're on the left of the lizard, so you want to step up onto his foreleg with your left leg and swing yourself over so you're sitting in the saddle. Your Highness, if you wouldn't mind demonstrating?"

Obligingly, Esmeralda vaulted into her saddle with the grace of one who had grown up riding lizardback, then attached the heavy metal clips on her riding belt to catches in the saddle's pommel and cantle.

"Now you, Adam."

Adam found himself boosted by a helpful hand on the small of his back, and before he had time to panic, he was astride the great beast, clipped into the riding saddle, with reins in his hands and Duin clinging on behind him. Then came a quick reminder to keep his feet up on the strange leather protrusions on the side of the saddle—so designed to keep a rider's feet from scraping on whatever surface the lizard was scrambling over, but they made Adam feel as though he was being spread out over a leather mount so he could be, well, mounted himself. All it needed was a B grade soundtrack and a dodgy camera angle and it could be streaming live over the internet for three dollars a month. He tried not to think about it. He tried not to think about Duin's furry body pressed up against his, or the strange smell that was part dirt, part strong mammalian musk, and part something altogether different that he couldn't quite pin down. He especially tried not to think of the wolfman's sharp teeth mere inches from his own ear. And then, with luggage stowed in the tough netting that was bundled over the lizards' rear haunches, Darius ordered them all to move out and prodded Zoul into a skittering amble. Almost immediately Adam was far too busy trying not to fall off to think about anything else.

Chapter 3

For what seemed like an eternity, Adam's world narrowed to the time between each lizard-induced jerk and crotch-crushing jolt he was enduring. Grimacing in pain, he tried to work out how Darius or Xavier could possibly ride as comfortably as they seemed to be doing, when Duin came to his rescue.

"You need to brace yourself with your legs," he murmured. "Squeeze the saddle with your knees to keep your body raised above it. If you need to, you can lean forward and brace with your hands on the saddle horn or even on your lizard's neck. It is also the position to be in if you need to fit through a narrow tunnel—or avoid being knocked in the head by a low-hanging stalactite."

"Right, thanks."

Adam did as Duin suggested and found the entire experience suddenly very much like his first, and only, attempt at riding a horse at anything greater than a sedate walk. All his concentration had to go into keeping his balls from being squished, and that was supposed to be done by moving with your mount to prevent said ballsack ever coming into contact with the hard leather of the saddle. Twelve-year-old Adam never quite managed to master the canter, and twenty-five-year-old Adam still suspected he'd looked like a cartoon character bouncing on the back of a galloping horse when the instructor urged them into a run. Worse, his leg muscles had quickly given up hope of supporting his body properly and left his testicles to their own, very limited devices. Now his legs protested but took their share of the burden, which was a big improvement. However, he found it to be very much like bracing himself in a plank position at the gym—meaning every muscle in his body was probably going to be sore later.

Of course, this new posture also meant Duin's crotch was riding against his ass each time Zoul's six-legged gait made its up-and-down cyclical movements. In other circumstances, this would either be cause for embarrassment or celebration, but Adam had other things to worry about than potentially awkward contact between intimate body parts. As it was, he spent most of the ride hanging on for dear life and occasionally remembering to tug on the reins. Thankfully, Zoul proved largely self-powered and self-motivated, following the others with barely any encouragement from his rider.

Even with the lizard's autopilot switched on, movement through the wet forest was difficult. Adam had to make a conscious effort to remember to duck to avoid being swiped by tangles of vines and broad arrow-shaped leaves of blue and green. Small boat-shaped pods dangled like skeletal fingers from trees here and there, and bright pinkish flowers grew from rosettes of long, fleshy leaves that he was certain were growing directly on the branches, rather than out from them. There were no signs of habitation, human or otherwise, and the entire experience had a surreal lost-world flavor to it, although this was aided by the lizards' philosophy of movement, which their riders had obviously embraced since early childhood: go straight from point A to point B, and if anything gets in your way, go over it.

Zoul turned out to be at equal ease traversing flat ground as he was climbing near-vertical escarpments or over fallen trees in order to cross a wide gorge or river span. More than once, they climbed through the canopy to avoid herds of what appeared to be large dog-sized beetles foraging in the swampy ground by a river bend. Sometimes the group's passage through the treetops would stir up small flocks of flying creatures that were strangely rhomboid in shape, sunlight glinting off feathers as small and fine as scales as they fled into the reddish sky.

Many bumps and swipes from branches later, the group finally emerged at the top of a cliff, next to a thundering waterfall. The break in the vegetation was so sudden that Adam reared back, tugging at the reins frantically as the lizard thundered toward the brink, causing Zoul to turn and chirp at him quizzically. At the sound, the others reined in just ahead.

"Come, we're nearly there," Darius said, raising his voice to be heard over the sound of the waterfall cascading over the edge of the precipice.

"Nearly where? It's a sheer drop!" Adam objected, forcing himself to relax his death grip on the reins long enough to rub the sweat from his eyes, leaving a muddy smear across his forehead.

"We have a waystation at the foot of the cliff," Darius said patiently. "It's used by our scouts, so there will be supplies there."

"And we're going to what? Walk straight off the cliff?"

"Not off. Over," Xavier said, urging his mount forward. "Just hold on tight and make sure you're clipped in."

With that, the magister leaned low over his lizard's back and disappeared over the edge of the cliff, the others in tow.

"Did they just…? They didn't just…? But that's…."

"They're cave lizards," Duin said, his voice low and strangely gentle. "Look at Zoul's feet. He will not fall, and if you do not panic, you will not fall either. And if you do not panic, I will not fall with you."

Adam glanced down at the great lizard's feet and noticed for the first time that they were sprawled like outspread hands and, instead of claws, ended in bulbous toes more reminiscent of a frog's than a lizard's. Pausing to check that he was still securely fastened into his saddle, Adam took a deep, steadying breath.

"Hold on tight, all right?" he said.

"As if my life depends on it," Duin replied gravely.

"It sort of does, you know."

"Yes, I know."

Adam laughed at that, a short sharp laugh, tinged with hysteria at the edges. "This is crazy. I can't believe I'm seriously about to ride off the edge of a cliff."

"Not off, over," Duin repeated. "Or down, to be more precise."

"I don't know how you can be so calm about this."

Adam felt the furred man shrug. "It was a normal part of growing up," Duin said. "I rode a hatchling up and down the cavern walls for hours on end when I was younger—before I was cast into the light, I mean."

"Cast into…. You mean here, the surface?"

Duin nodded. "Yes. Trust me, we will be fine."

Some of the furred man's calm must have rubbed off on him, because Adam's legs trembled only slightly as he squeezed his knees gently, urging Zoul into a slow walk that took them step by reptilian step closer to the edge. For a moment, Adam saw only the lack of ground that was fast approaching, and then the view opened up, with the red of the sky and the sun hanging over the horizon in the exact same place it had been when they started their trek. Below them, a sea of never-ending foliage stretched out to meet the dusk, the wending curves of the river disappearing into the mass of green. Strange bellowing cries rang out from the forest below, and small flights of the rhomboid fliers were flitting through the foliage. Then the pressure of Duin's body on his reminded him that gravity would soon be coming into play, and he dropped down so he was nearly flat against Zoul's back.

"That view was beautiful," he murmured as Duin's grip on his belt firmed and the man's body pressed more closely against his own.

"It was? I… suppose it was. I never thought of it that way before."

"Maybe you just see it too often," Adam suggested.

"No," Duin said slowly. "I do not think I ever have. When I look at the land, I see ambush sites, hunting grounds, places to forage, and cover where I can travel without being seen. I have never stopped just to look at the view."

"Oh."

"Thank you."

"For what?"

"Helping me see it."

Adam smiled tightly. "Keep me alive long enough to keep seeing it and I'll consider us even."

Duin's replying chuckle was music to Adam's ears. "I will make it my official job, if you like."

"I would like," Adam said. "I would very much like. Seriously, though, I don't have a clue where I am or what I'm doing here."

"I know," Duin said softly. "But then, as you pointed out, up here, neither do they."

Adam looked down the cliff at the small figures of Darius, Esmeralda, and Xavier, easily twenty or thirty meters below them and descending with practiced ease.

Adam snorted. "If they did, I probably wouldn't be here, would I?"

"I... do not know," Duin said. "I am unsure if I really know them or their ways anymore."

"Just how young were you when you were exiled?" Adam asked.

"I was a child still. The Rite of the Red Sun is the last test we face before we are accepted as adults."

"I meant how old were you?" Adam asked. "You know, in years."

"I do not understand. What is a year?"

"The time it takes for the world to travel around the sun."

"And... how long is that?"

"Three hundred and sixty-five days."

There was a slightly awkward silence. "What is a day?"

"Okay, now you're screwing with me," Adam said. "Day, you know, time it takes for the world to turn... twenty-four hours, one day and one night."

"Night?"

"Yeah, when the sun goes down and it gets dark and the moon is in the sky. Seriously, drop the clueless act."

"There is no moon."

"What?"

"There is no moon," Duin said, his voice strangely bitter. "I am told that once there was a moon that lit up a dark sky when the sun had gone to bed and did not shine her light upon us, but if there was, I have never seen it. Here we have this unchanging twitterlight, not these days and nights."

"I have them—you know, where I'm from."

"Truly? You are not just saying that?"

"No. Why would I do that?"

Duin shook his head. "I have no idea, but I would suggest not speaking of it to Magister Xavier. He would not take it well."

"Okay, but you'll have to tell me why later," Adam said. "Wait, are you saying the sun never moves… it never sets?"

"Have you seen it move through the sky since you arrived here?"

"Actually, no," Adam said. "I was wondering about that."

"I am told that if you travel toward the light, there is a lifeless land without water, just dust and rock as far as the eye can see, and the brightness of the sun burns your flesh," Duin said. "And if you venture into the dark, there is a frozen land where the only things to grow have no eyes and feed on muck." Once again Adam felt the man shrug. "I have never wanted to test the truth of either story."

"And this here is what you call 'twitterlight'?" Adam asked.

"Yes. It means that between light and dark, or something, according to the… them."

"I just want to go home," Adam said with a sigh, his temples beginning to throb as the exertion and dehydration caught up to him.

"Sometimes, so do I," Duin said. "But mine do not want me back, and…. I do not know where you are from?"

"A place called Australia," Adam said hopelessly. "I don't suppose you've heard of it?"

"No, but I never bothered with surface maps. My family were tunnel hunters."

"That would still be a useful skill up here."

"I like to think it helped," Duin agreed, and Adam thought he felt Duin grin.

THE GROUND was a lot closer now, and the tail of the lizard in front of them was just disappearing into the thick waxy leaves of the canopy below. Once Zoul followed, Adam blinked repeatedly, his eyes struggling to adjust to the lack of light, so densely packed was the foliage. As they made their way down the final stretch of cliff accompanied by the roar of the water hitting the rocks below, Adam took in tree trunks as thick across as his beat-up old car was long, and the great cavernous spaces between them, pierced here and there with dappled shafts of reddish light, giving the entire area the feeling of an old vaulted cathedral that was beginning to molder. The rich smell of loam filled his nostrils, and from the corner of his eyes, he saw a flash of movement as something leapt from a nearby tree into the safety defined as "away from the big lizards." He couldn't say he blamed it at all.

The forest below the cliff was thicker than the one they had left, and the air inside the bubble of its canopy was still and heavy with age. Thick beards of moss hung from tree branches, and Duin reached out to grab a good handful as they continued their journey down.

"What's that for?" Adam asked.

"Tinder," Duin said.

"Oh, right."

The ground was surprisingly free from the dense undergrowth that had dominated at the top of the cliff, covered instead by a squishy layer of damp, rotting leaf litter and a network of sprawling roots that twined across the surface, creating uneven terraces that Adam was certain he would trip over, given half the chance. Thankfully, Zoul was much surer on his feet and had no trouble rejoining the others on the level surface.

"Are we there yet?" Adam asked, only half in jest.

"Almost," Darius said, ushering them around a large boulder and up toward a great fissure in the rocky cliff face just large enough for a lizard to clamber through. It had been covered by a curtain of thorny creepers, which Xavier and Esmeralda were carefully moving aside to allow passage through them.

"They look nasty," Adam said.

"They are," Darius said absently, one hand on his saber as he kept a watchful eye on the jungle around them. "And they keep out anything that might lair in the cave."

"Clever."

"Necessary," Darius said with a shrug. "We'll enter once Xavier has made light."

"Made?"

But then he saw Xavier was sprinkling a coarse powder into a stone bowl that was already half-filled with something greenish and lumpy. And then, as Xavier urged his mount into the narrow gap, Adam could see a pale greenish light shining outward from the bowl, casting a dim illumination on the rock face. Princess Esmeralda, looking tired and just a little bedraggled from the rigors of their journey, followed him in.

"Go," Darius said to Adam. "I'll bring up the rear."

As Adam pushed forward, trying to stay close enough to the light source, he was relieved to see light shining from behind him, and realized Darius must have a similar contraption to the one Xavier was carrying. The crevice opened into what had probably once been natural caverns, now shaped by human hands into something more habitable. A number of creaky bunk beds, or rather bed frames, had been constructed by lashing lengths of bamboo together. There were no mattresses, just shorter lengths of bamboo lashed in place, but Adam was ready to fall onto one and pass out. There were lizard stables of a sort, which consisted of large individual stall-like spaces with nests of dried grasses where the lizards could be tethered. Obviously with their climbing abilities, a partial door would have been useless in keeping them in.

Before settling into the main room, the three cave dwellers started unpacking the few belongings they had brought with them, including some bedding and foodstuffs that had been packed into Zoul's netting. The stone bowls of light were placed in niches in the walls, casting their dim, unwavering glow around the room, and after being handed a smaller light dish, Adam and Duin were sent to investigate the storerooms, along with strict instructions from Magister Xavier not to let Duin hold the light bowl or the bamboo equivalent of a crowbar. Adam resisted rolling his eyes, then turned and led the way around the corner into a room of tightly sealed barrels and wooden crates. Many of them proved to be empty, but there was a fair amount of dried fruit and meat of some sort, several cloaks, a few pairs of leather boots, and two sets of armor. The boots and armor were largely made from what Adam now recognized as lizard skin. They also featured some of the thick blackish shell that Darius wore.

"What is this stuff?" Adam asked.

"Spider or beetle carapace," Duin said, pushing his matted brown hair out of his eyes.

Adam stopped and stared at his companion. "Wait a minute. Weren't you… furry?"

Duin smiled ruefully, the very human expression strangely out of place on a person Adam had previously associated with a short muzzle.

"This is what I was like before…. Outside of light cast by fire or the sun… I look just like you… well, like the others."

Indeed, Duin now appeared to be a scruffy, dirty man who had been crawling along the forest floor. Or rather, a near-naked, scruffy, dirty man who had been crawling along the forest floor. Beneath the smears of mud and matted hair, patches of pale skin covering a lean, muscled body showed through. Here and there, Adam could see scars, one particularly noticeable one running across the man's torso from what must have been a vicious slash. His face was long, and his features strong, if delicate in appearance. He also appeared much younger than Adam would have expected—except for his eyes. Duin's brown eyes still held the same look of worldliness that Adam had first noticed back up the mountain.

His skin was still marked with the same tiger stripes that adorned him when he was furred, although the pattern was much lighter and seemed more like an intricate set of tattoos than natural pigmentation. Of course, Duin's sudden lack of fur also made Adam painfully aware that all Duin wore was a decidedly skimpy loincloth. Somehow, the knowledge that even with fur Duin had been just as naked barely five minutes ago didn't help.

"Adam?"

"Sorry," Adam said. "I just…. I didn't know."

"I take no offense. I imagine there is a lot you do not know about here."

Adam snorted. "You can say that again."

Duin paused as if considering Adam's words. "Well, yes, I could. But why would I?"

Adam smiled. "It's a figure of speech, Duin. Never mind. Let's keep looking—if nothing else, you're probably going to need some clothing now."

Duin smiled, although the expression did not quite reach his eyes. "I gave up clothes a long time ago, Adam."

"Maybe," Adam said. "But the princess might take exception to your nudity in her royal presence."

"We shall see," Duin said. "They did not keep much here, did they?"

Adam brushed his hand over the thick layer of dust that lay over the lid of a barrel of bone-dry meat. "I guess they didn't use it much. I'm not sure I'm going to be able to stomach that stuff, although I know I'm going to have to."

"You soak it first," Duin said with a grin. "Something tells me there's going to be a lot of water gathering."

Adam looked at wooden buckets that had been stuck in the corner. "Well, I guess that answers the question of what those are all here for."

When they walked back into the main chamber to make their report, Esmeralda, as Adam expected, had wrinkled her nose and given them instructions to fetch enough water for drinking and cooking, as well as "cleaning *him* up while you are out."

"I knew it," Duin said with a rueful grin as they exited the short tunnel into the sunlight, each carrying two buckets, and Adam with his gym bag slung over his shoulder. He'd noticed Xavier's interest in it, possibly either for the fabric or color, and he wasn't about to leave it behind. Darius escorted them up the tunnel with his lizard and a number of sharpened bamboo spears, and Adam assumed he was going off to hunt.

DUIN'S SMILE was shy as he stepped out into the red light of the surface, and this time, Adam was watching as the fur literally sprouted from Duin's skin and his face elongated into the now familiar muzzle. It was especially strange to watch Duin's ears migrate up the sides of his head to their perch on top of it, twitching slightly as they swiveled in response to sounds Adam clearly couldn't hear.

"Are we going to be safe?" Adam asked, suddenly conscious of his broadsword being the only weapon they both carried. "Shouldn't we bring Zoul?"

Duin sniffed the air. "I think we'll be all right," he said as he led them through the leaf litter toward the pool at the bottom of the waterfall. "There aren't any signs of kanak, and I don't smell anything dangerous nearby."

"Kanak," Adam said. "Those are the four-armed tall people who seem to want to kill us on sight, yes?"

"Yes."

"Why exactly do they want to kill us?"

Duin shrugged. "Prestige, I think, although whether from kills or looting I am not sure. I never ventured near enough to a kanak settlement to find out—mostly because I have no wish to get eaten."

"They'd eat you?" Adam asked, nearly dropping his buckets.

"They would eat you, given the chance," Duin said, pushing past the few scraggly bushes that ringed the wide pool.

"And you're sure there's none around?"

"If they lived near here, they would use this lake for drinking, washing, and bathing, and there would be a path through the jungle by now. I see no consistent path, no broken branches to keep it clear along the way, so… I think we are safe."

Adam sighed, his muscles relaxing and releasing tension he didn't know he'd been carrying around. "Okay, but if we get eaten, I'm telling on you."

"How can you tell on me if you get eaten exactly? Or are you speaking of an afterlife?"

This time Adam did laugh, just a bit. "That was a joke, Duin. Don't worry about it."

Duin shook his muzzle. "You are a very strange man, Sir Adam," he said, wading out into the lake and ducking himself under the surface.

"Just call me Adam, Duin," Adam said. "I'm hardly a sir."

"If you say so, S—Adam," Duin said. "Would you be offended if I asked you about your land?"

Adam shrugged and squatted to lower the buckets down on the large pebbles that covered the bottom of the pool and spilled out around to the dry shore area. "You can certainly ask," he said, dropping his now battered gym bag onto the shoreline next to them. "But I don't know if I'll be able to explain it to you properly." He stared at the green-and-white bag. Or the once green-and-white bag. Suddenly he was bone-tired and wondered just how long his unending day here had really been. Adam reached into the left pocket of his cargo pants and pulled out his phone. Amazingly it still worked—and somehow the screen wasn't cracked. The rugged outdoor case Rusty had bought him years ago clearly did work in extreme environments. Hitting the Power button, he stared at the screen, on which two words were written in neat capital letters: NO NETWORK.

Suddenly the enormity and sheer unreality of his situation came crashing down on him. Adam felt a tightness in his chest and weakness in his limbs as tears welled unbidden in his eyes. He very nearly dropped the phone, only maintaining enough presence of mind to turn it off to conserve the battery.

"Adam?"

"I want to go home."

Dripping water as he walked back to shore, Duin knelt next to where Adam had slumped to the ground and gently took Adam's hand in his. "Tell me about this land of Australia?"

CHAPTER 4

"I'm SORRY," Adam said, blinking at the tears threatening to spill down his cheeks. "I don't do this at home, any of it. I live in a city, I go to uni, I go to work, and I study chemistry. I don't ride through the wilderness on giant lizards fighting monsters and collecting water. I just…."

"What's your sky like?" Duin asked.

"What?"

"Your sky. What color is it?"

"Blue," Adam said. "Well, mostly blue. It's gray if it's cloudy, black at night, and red like yours at dusk or dawn."

"And your city, it is above the ground?"

Adam bit his lip and nodded. "Most of us live above ground in houses or apartments. I live in an apartment, just a small little place, but it's big enough for me. One bedroom, a bathroom, kitchen, and an area to eat and relax or watch TV. God, I'm going to miss TV."

"What is tee-vee?"

"Moving pictures… stories. Do you have theater here?"

"I know what it is."

"Imagine theater, but recorded, so you can play it back whenever you want, and that's television. Kind of."

"Magic?"

"Not really, but… might as well be, I suppose. Look, Duin, I'm a lazy sod of a city slicker. I buy my food, clothes, entertainment, and…. What the hell am I doing here, and how the hell am I going to survive? I have no skills here. None."

"You saved my life," Duin said. "I may not know much else about you, but you are a great negotiator."

"Yeah, I can talk," Adam said. "Woo-hoo. That'll get me far."

"It has got us both here, alive, and probably fed shortly," Duin pointed out. "And apparently you can hold your own in a fight."

"Not as good as I'll need to be, unless I have Darius looking over my shoulder."

"So you train," Duin said. "You improve and you survive. But first, you bathe. You will feel better once you're clean."

"And we should get back with the water before they send Xavier out to turn us into toads?"

"Turn us into something," Duin agreed. "Probably not toads, though. Come, the water is quite refreshing."

"Let me get out of all this first," Adam said, tugging at the knots of his shoelaces.

Duin wrinkled his nose as Adam peeled off his shirt and T-shirt. "You might want to clean those as well."

"I stink, I know," Adam grunted. "I've also got a bag of clothes to clean here as well."

Duin grunted, the sound a peculiar combination of canine and human. "Let me get the muck out of my fur and I will help you."

Adam grinned. "Thanks. I appreciate it."

When Duin considered himself clean enough and came over to lend a hand—or paw—he marveled at the softness of Adam's modern fabrics, and Adam spent a few minutes helping him read the care labels that were still inside, although he had no answers when Duin asked exactly what *viscose* was and how it was made.

"It feels like really soft, stretchy silk," Duin said. "I wish I had clothes like this."

"You can borrow them if you like, once they're dry."

"Adam, look at me. Do I look like I need clothing?"

"Well, back in the cave maybe," Adam said with a grin. "You should at least wear a pair of my trunks. I'm not sure Esmeralda needs to see you naked."

Duin sighed. "No, if I wear those, Magister Xavier will want them because they are new and different. Best keep them for you. Come," he said, his breath huffing out in a drawn-out sigh. "It is time to fill up those buckets and make our journey back."

"Oh, my favorite part of the day," Adam said, his voice flat. "Still, I do want to eat tonight. Can we wait until we've got the water to put clothes back on?"

"That is probably a good idea," Duin said, throwing one of Adam's T-shirts over a nearby bush to dry out a little. "We are unlikely to catch cold here."

Adam smiled, enjoying the warm air on his skin. "Not unless we try really hard, no."

Feeling slightly better about his predicament, Adam was able to admit that this place, at least, met the definition of jungle paradise. The rock face they had climbed down earlier that day rose sheer and majestic behind the tall trees, and the waterfall thundered into the riverbed, kicking white spray high into the air. The stones around their feet were round and smooth, and the entire pool would easily be Olympic-sized, had it been deeper. It was also nearly completely hidden, with low shrubs and ferns growing right up to the water's edge, some of which Duin indicated were edible.

"I knew we should have brought Zoul," Adam said. "We need someone to haul this food back."

"We can come back," Duin replied with a shrug. "I sort of like being outside."

"I can tell," Adam said. "You smile more out here."

Duin stilled and turned to face Adam, framed perfectly by the thundering falls in the deeper end of the pool. "You treat me like a person."

"Well… you are a person," Adam said. "I think the fur's kind of cool, and… well, I'm looking forward to seeing what you look like inside, now you're clean."

Duin snorted. "Much the same as anyone else, I would imagine." Then his eyes narrowed. "Adam, stay very still."

"What? Why?"

"Because if you move, you might just spook it."

"It?"

"Shut your eyes."

"What?"

"Shut your eyes."

"Duin, you said we were safe here."

"We are," Duin said. "Trust me. Close your eyes."

"Fine," Adam said, closing his eyes. "You do realize I'm standing naked in a pool by a waterfall in what could be called a tropical paradise?"

"If you say so." Duin's voice came after a short pause. "Although I am not sure I understood the significance of that. Do not move. Not a muscle."

"Okay," Adam said, his mind racing with the possibilities.

It was amazing how much the absence of one sense heightened the others. While the roar of water on rock still dominated, he could just hear the soft *swish* as Duin moved through the shallows at the edge of the pool, and fancied he could feel the man's presence as he moved closer, closer and—

There was a loud splash, a wave of cool water splattering his shins, and a cry of triumph from Duin.

"Got it!"

"Got what?" Adam asked, opening his eyes.

Duin stood before him, his lower jaw open in a canine grin, one hand raised and clasped around a wicked-looking crustacean. It was a brownish purple in color and about a foot and a half in length, with eight segmented legs sprawling out from beneath its armored body, waving helplessly in the air as its flattened tail section flapped in an attempt to get free. It looked, for all intents and purposes, like a strange cross between a lobster and a trilobite. Adam started and nearly lost his footing on the smooth stones as he recoiled from the spindly legs and large waving claws.

"What the hell is that thing?"

"Dinner, I hope," Duin said. "I do not know what they would call this, if anything at all, but w—I have always called them *chtick-tick*."

"Chtick-tick?"

"That is what the kanak say when they catch them," Duin said with a shrug. "It is as good a name as any."

"And why did I have to close my eyes?"

"It was about to crawl over your feet, and I did not want you to scare it off."

This time Adam did jump, and would have fallen if Duin hadn't grabbed him with his free hand. "What was it doing down there?"

"Looking for food, I believe," Duin said, nodding at the grape-sized tadpoles that swam here and there throughout the entire pool. Just like us."

"Just like us," Adam echoed. "I'm surprised there aren't any fish, to be honest with you."

"There are flitterfish," Duin said. "But they do not live in the water."

"Where would you find them?"

"Up there," Duin said, pointing into the nearby trees, where the rhomboid fliers Adam had seen earlier were hanging from the underside of the branches, their scales a silvery-blue shimmer and their wing-fins a metallic blue-green.

"Oh," he said. "Are they edible?"

"If you can catch them, yes."

"Right," Adam said. "Okay. Water?"

"Water," Duin agreed. "I will find something to bind the chtick-tick."

"And then we'll probably have to make a second trip for the foodstuffs you found."

"Or for more water," Duin added as he tore off a section of trailing roots curtaining down from a low-hanging tree branch and expertly trussed the chtick-tick up so it couldn't use its claws.

"If we are, I'm bringing Zoul."

AND PERHAPS unsurprisingly, that was exactly what happened. By the time Adam, Duin, and Zoul fetched enough water, fern fronds, and caught a few more chtick-ticks and other small shrimplike crustaceans, Esmeralda and Xavier had collected a fair amount of firewood, which appeared to surprise Duin.

"I suppose even a princess has to pitch in at times like these," Adam murmured.

"I am more surprised the necromancer does not find wood gathering beneath him," Duin replied quietly.

"Necromancer?"

Duin nodded. "Magister Xavier."

Any further comment Adam would have made was interrupted by the return of Darius with a twitching bundle that turned out to be a brace of spiders, each one the size of a large dog, hairy legs twitching slightly as they hung off his saddle.

"Spiders? Does that count as a successful hunt?" Adam asked Duin carefully.

"You would not want to hunt one of the larger lizards alone, so yes," Duin said, smiling slightly.

"I'll take your word for it," Adam said.

Duin's tinder was put to use creating a cooking fire, and Adam and Duin were allowed to take charge of the cooking of the spiders, which as far as Adam could tell, consisted of cutting the head and poisonous fangs off the spider before charring the hairs off the rest of it. According to everyone who wasn't Adam, spider was very good eating, but the spider's hairs were known to cause an unsightly rash on human skin. The chtick-ticks and shrimplike marin, as Esmeralda called them, were boiled in a large cooking pot with the fern shoots to create a rather plain soup that Adam would probably have seasoned liberally with salt back at home, but with hunger pangs gnawing at his stomach, he dug into his food with gusto. Spider, it turned out, had a texture much like shellfish, although there was a smoky aftertaste to the meal that he wasn't completely sure about. Still, with five mouths to feed, not counting the lizards, who had a mix of fresh spider and dried fruit, the meal was very soon over. There had been little conversation, bar some grumbling from Xavier about missing his creature comforts, but that stopped when Esmeralda pointed out they couldn't return to Aergon, so complaining about things wasn't going to achieve anything.

Despite wanting to ask question after question, Adam was too tired to do more than eat his fill and help with the little cleanup that was necessary. Afterward, Esmeralda, Darius, and Xavier took turns bathing, guarded by their vigilant mounts, and Adam couldn't quite shake the feeling that the three were very careful never to leave him and Duin alone at camp, with Darius and Xavier especially careful not to leave them alone with the princess. Still, when he was finally able to seek his allocated pallet of hard bamboo, folding up a soft cloak for use as a pillow, none of this was at the forefront of Adam's mind. He sank gratefully into a deep sleep and didn't wake when the others sought their own bunks.

CHAPTER 5

ADAM AWOKE with the distinct impression he'd overslept. His entire body ached, and he felt as though he had gone several rounds of boxing at the gym, and then been severely beaten in a quarterstaff fight. Of course, the reality of his situation sank in rather quickly when he looked around his bedroom and found the last day or so had not, in fact, been a dream.

Turning his head caused enough pain to make him whimper, his ribs and inner thighs protesting most strenuously. In the dim light of the room, he could just make out Duin sitting cross-legged in front of his bunk, dressed in a loose shirt and leather trousers. His shaggy brown hair still fell like a mane around his shoulders, but it was a bit less scraggly, and it looked like someone had attempted to drag a comb of some sort through it—and most likely given up. He appeared to be cracking open roasted nuts, placing the kernels into a small leather bag.

"How long—" Adam coughed, clearing his throat. "How long have I been asleep?"

"Long enough," Duin replied. "You looked like you needed it, though."

"I feel like crap," Adam groaned. "I don't want to move, but even without moving, everything hurts."

Duin's low chuckle filled the room. "Magister Xavier thought you might need this," he said, reaching for a small stoppered gourd bottle. "He said it should be rubbed into your muscles when you woke up."

"What is it?"

"Something to help with the pain," Duin said. "Past that, I cannot say, but Esmeralda has agreed it should help."

Adam groaned. "I'll risk it. I'll try anything right now."

"So, where exactly does it hurt?" Duin asked.

"Everywhere."

"I am being serious, Adam."

"So am I."

"Oh," Duin said. "Sorry. In that case we will have to get your clothes off again."

Even chuckling hurt. "You know, normally when a nice man asks me to get naked, it's for a completely different reason."

"It is?"

Adam groaned as he rose into a sitting position, nearly hitting his head on the bunk above. "Never mind," he said, pulling his shirt over his head to hide the flush on his face. "I'm rambling."

"You had better come here," Duin said, patting the mat of soft woven rushes he was sitting on. "I think the bunk might be a bit cramped."

Adam grunted agreement and very slowly lowered his pants and trunks inch by painful inch down his legs. After a moment, Duin came over to assist and folded the garments before placing them back on the bed. Then he helped Adam to the floor, maneuvering him so he lay on his front. As Adam paused to adjust himself so he wasn't crushing his privates, he felt a slight shift in the mat as Duin knelt next to him. Adam heard the sound of the cork popping from the gourd container, and immediately a subtle aniseed smell reached his nostrils. Then hands were spreading a warming oil over his back, the calluses on Duin's fingers catching only slightly on his skin. Surprisingly, Duin proved to be a good masseur, expertly seeking out the knots of tension in Adam's muscles and easing them into relaxed compliance, lingering long enough to be sensuous before moving on. Either that or he was guided by the loudest groans, cries of pain, and the amount of flinching Adam did every time he found a new ache. After a while, Adam was in considerably less pain— either the oil did have its promised pain-relieving effect, or the massage itself was doing him the world of good. He was also feeling a good deal warmer, his skin tingling slightly, almost as if it was being pressed up against a vibrator. His lips quirked at the thought of a full-body vibrator, but as Duin's hands moved down his spine to knead his ass, the feelings of warmth, sensual touch, and the buzz on his skin created an altogether different sensation, which he had honestly thought he would be too sore to experience. His groans became softer, and he caught himself arching into Duin's touch and gasping in pleasure when Duin's fingers brushed past his balls as the man massaged his legs.

"Are you all right?" Duin asked.

"Oh, um, yes," Adam said quickly. "I feel so much better. I don't know what's in that oil, but it's fantastic."

Duin's hands worked down each of Adam's legs in turn, kneading each thigh and calf before rubbing gently at Adam's feet, manipulating his ankles and releasing spots of tension he wasn't even aware he had—as well as many he wasn't aware could be soothed through massage.

"How is it that you're so good at this?" Adam asked.

"Back in Aergon, before I… left… I sometimes worked in the baths. We—they—have hot water from underground lakes or something. There's a word for it, but I can't remember what it is. Anyway, there are big public baths, and massage skills were highly prized. It was a very good way to get money, although I was mostly there to keep the place clean or wash towels."

"I thought you were a hunter."

"My father taught me to hunt, yes," Duin said. "But all Aergonites are expected to learn a second skill as well as apprentice to one of their parents. It is meant to prevent us—them—from losing skills as a people. I had almost forgotten I knew how to do this, truthfully. I wasn't doing it long before… the rite."

Adam heard a rustle of fabric and turned his head to see Duin pull off his shirt and lay it to one side before using his forearms to apply pressure up and down Adam's back in an almost scissoring motion.

"If you're going to do that, you might want to take your pants off as well," Adam suggested slyly. "I'm not sure you want to get too much of this oil on them."

Duin paused for a moment and then grunted his agreement. Out of the corner of his eye, Adam was treated to the sight of the man peeling off his trousers and smallclothes and returning to the mat in glorious nudity. The throbbing in Adam's groin grew more insistent, and he sighed with guilty pleasure as Duin knelt again, warm fingers slowly turning Adam's muscles into putty.

"Why does Aergon have a court necromancer?" Adam asked, in an attempt to quiet his lustful feelings. "Isn't a necromancer someone who animates the dead or something?"

"Yes," Duin said. "And that is exactly why Aergon has a court necromancer. They're not a numerous people, Sir Adam—"

"Just Adam, please."

"Of course… Adam," Duin amended. "The Caverns of Aergon are a dangerous place—safer than here, perhaps, but still dangerous. Not all of the lizards are tame, and there are cave spiders as big, if not bigger, than the lizards. Good eating, but not safe. And the kanak know where the entrances to the caverns are, as you saw. Sometimes their raids are not as impressive, but too often a hunter will not come home or a forager's basket is found torn into pieces. Sometimes children sneak up to the surface and never come back."

"Or are sent above and lost to society?" Adam asked.

Duin's hands stilled. "I had not thought of it that way, but I suppose there is that too."

The turn of conversation had caused Adam to deflate somewhat as he pondered the society Duin had left behind—and the society that Princess Esmeralda and the others were so desperate to save. "That sounds rough."

"I am not sure," Duin replied. "Compared to life alone in the light, it is not that bad. Time to turn over, I think."

"Hmm? Oh right," Adam said, rolling over onto his back and, funnily enough, staring at the ceiling properly for the first time. The stone here was a deep earthy brown, and there were enough ridges and broken points in the rock to catch the light to show where the stalactites had been hacked off in order to clear space inside the cavern. Given the position of the light behind Duin, his features were hidden in shadow, so much so that he appeared to be a silhouette, all long lines tapering in to a narrow waist, with the only highlighted details being the contours of his shoulders and the hollow of his neck.

As Duin worked his hands slowly over Adam's chest, calloused fingers brushed over sensitive nipples, and Adam found his body responding to the touch in its usual, predictable fashion. It was not long before Duin noticed the effect his ministrations were having, and his hands slowed mere finger-widths from Adam's pubic bush.

"Adam... you... I...."

Smiling in the dark, Adam covered both of Duin's hands with one of his own, and then cupped the man's chin with his free hand. Sitting up, he pressed his lips to Duin's surprised mouth. The man was slow to respond, but then he parted his lips, allowing Adam's tongue to invade his mouth, slicking up against his tongue. Duin half melted into Adam, his upper body following Adam back onto the mat, and he pulled Adam close with a ferocity, passion, and fervor Adam hadn't expected. In the near darkness of the lonely cave, teeth bumped against teeth and hands sizzled over skin, Duin now gripping at Adam's skull through his hair as he pressed his mouth more firmly against Adam's own. Adam sought Duin's crotch, gripping a cock as hard and proud as his own and eliciting a soft whine. Adam took the opportunity to roll them both over so Duin was on his back and Adam on top, grinding their oil-slicked bodies together.

Then he kissed his way along Duin's jaw and down the man's chest, where he teased Duin's nipples with teeth and tongue, the peppery sweetness of the unguent sticking to his lips as Duin twitched and bucked beneath him. The tingling of the oil only added to the sensations of skin on skin, and Duin's hands roamed over Adam's body, seemingly determined to touch every square inch of him. Adam kissed his way down Duin's taut abdomen and brushed his day-old stubble across the sensitive head of Duin's cock, eliciting a groan as Duin's fingers dug into Adam's shoulders. Adam chuckled and paused, holding off doing anything for so long that Duin looked at him, eyes as wild as his hair and lips moist and parted. Plastering on his most devilish grin, Adam held Duin's gaze as he slowly sank his lips over Duin's manhood, fighting the urge to close his eyes as he enjoyed the sticky sweet taste of precum. Duin's responses were pure, uninhibited, and a sudden thrust caused Adam to gag.

"Adam?" Duin was cradling him in a flash, touching his face with concern. "Did I do something wrong?"

"You went in too deep," Adam gasped, wiping at his eyes. "Gag reflex."

"I cannot believe you did that."

"I like it," Adam said. "Didn't you?"

"Oh yes, very much."

Adam turned and kissed Duin's cheek. "Exactly. I like that you like it. Making you feel good makes me feel good. Plus your precum is tasty."

"Precum?"

Adam laughed and reached out to swipe a glob of the fluid off Duin's member. "See?"

"That?"

Adam nodded and licked his finger, and then pressed his lips to Duin's again before Duin could react. "What do you think?"

"I'm not sure," Duin said. Then he pushed Adam flat on his back and pinned him to the mat. "I think I might need a bit more to taste—and I still have not finished your massage."

"Screw the massage." Adam gasped as he felt Duin's mouth engulf his prick and then pull off with a popping sound.

"No," Duin said. "Or you will be stiff and sore when we ride out."

"So you can massage me again," Adam suggested as Duin rubbed more of the oil onto the front of his legs.

Duin chuckled. "Only if we get privacy like we are right now."

"Ah, good point," Adam said as he ran his hand along Duin's back to his ass. "I suppose we might have to be quiet as well. Just in case they come to investigate."

Duin paused, grinned, and took Adam back into his mouth, and Adam had to stifle his own groans as Duin held his hips down to ride out Adam's involuntary thrusts.

"I think I like yours better," Duin said.

"Funny, I don't," Adam replied, his fingers ghosting over Duin's testicles, causing him to shiver. "Come back here, you're too far away."

Duin grinned and started to worm his way back up Adam's body, then paused to tease Adam's nipples in the same way Adam had teased him. Adam growled in mock irritation, pulled Duin up, and kissed him savagely. As their bodies ground and thrust together, Adam felt his orgasm rising, his balls clenching as his oil-slicked member thrust against Duin's. Wrapping his arms around Duin, Adam kissed him desperately, feeling his heart hammering against his ribs as his balls clenched, his cock swelled, and then he was shooting between their bodies, and Duin's hands were digging into his shoulders, and the man was whimpering into Adam's mouth as he shot his own pleasure, mingling their seed together as they both came down from their orgasmic highs.

For a time they were still, the only sound being their breath, heavy with their exertion. As he lay on the mat, feeling Duin relax against him, Adam turned his head and kissed Duin's temple, his right hand gently stroking the striped skin of Duin's side.

"I think that was officially the best massage I've ever had," Adam ventured.

"That's not normally how mine end," Duin said.

"Normally?"

"Perhaps a few times."

"Seriously?"

"No," Duin said. "Some people in the bathhouse did, but I did not know it was happening until I was nearly old enough for the rite… and, well…. Look, it happens, but I never wanted to…. People looked down on those who did, and…."

"I get it," Adam said. "And I want you to know that I don't think any less of you now," he added, emphasizing his feelings with a lingering kiss.

They lay in silence for a few blissful minutes, and then Duin got up and laughed a bit at the mess they had made. "There's still some water left that we can clean ourselves with," he said. "It was meant to be used after your massage but…."

"Duin, this *is* after my massage," Adam pointed out.

"True," Duin said.

They used a rag to wipe themselves down, giggling like two naughty schoolboys and not doing too good a job, but the oil appeared to have absorbed easily into their skin. When they were clean enough, they dressed and ventured out into the light, Duin again going through the strange transformation from near-naked man to one clothed in chestnut striped fur. This time Adam appreciated how much Duin's physical stature grew when the transformation occurred, with the man adding a good three inches in height and a fair bit more in terms of raw muscle. Suddenly the leather pants that had been hanging low around his waist were sitting snugly on a muscled backside, and the shirt that had seemed so baggy and voluminous now threatened to burst at the seams. For more than a few seconds, Adam watched, mesmerized by his friend's new physique, and then hurried to catch up when Duin turned around, one brow raised quizzically.

"You grew," Adam said hastily, feeling a slight heat on his cheeks.

"I know," Duin said. "It is the blessing—or curse—of Selune."

"Just as long as you didn't think I was perving," Adam said with a grin.

"Since I do not know what that means, I can honestly say I was not thinking that at all," Duin said.

"Good."

"But I can make a good guess from context."

"Less good," Adam said.

Duin smiled. "I'm not sure I mind."

"Okay, now you're just being a tease."

THEY FOUND Xavier, Darius, and Esmeralda sitting outside around the remains of last sleep's fire pit, with all four of the riding lizards tethered nearby. Darius was checking his weapons, and Xavier was grinding up some leaves and roots in a small mortar and pestle. To Adam's surprise, Esmeralda had a needle and thread and was mending a number of ripped garments—including Adam's long-sleeved shirt. Noting Adam's gaze, she smiled serenely at him.

"We all have to help where we can," she said. "It is good to see you back on your feet."

"Thank you, Your Highness," Adam said. "I apologize for slowing your journey."

"It is of no matter," Esmeralda said. "Safe resting places may be hard to find in the coming sleeps, so we should indulge while we can. I trust you have not suffered any ill effects from our journey so far?"

"I did, but I'm all right now. I don't know what is in that oil, but it was amazingly effective."

"You'd have to ask Magister Xavier about the specifics," Esmeralda said. "He's the one who made it."

"Thank you, Magister Xavier," Adam said as formally as possible, although he resisted the urge to bob his head in a pseudo bow.

"You're welcome," Xavier said. "It's nothing out of the ordinary. A few herbs and roots, and an extract from the heart of a jeweled jumping spider. Not too much, of course, as they can have some interesting side effects."

"Xavier, it is *rumored* to have those side effects," Esmeralda corrected.

"What side effects?" Adam asked.

"Some people believe it works as an aphrodisiac if ingested," Esmeralda said primly. "I doubt that personally."

Xavier winked at Adam over her head. "Well, as the princess said, only if ingested. Keep the unguent. You'll probably need it over the next few sleeps if you're riding for the first time. It would be nice if we had more time to rest here, but Darius feels it best to press on."

Darius nodded. "There's little sign of kanak, but they could see smoke from our fire and come to investigate—and there's signs of slasherclaws in the area, and they're best avoided."

"Slasherclaws?" Adam asked.

"Two-legged lizards about as big as, well, you," Darius said, the ghost of a smile touching his lips. "They're pack hunters with sharp toe-claws—one slice would gut you like a flitterfish."

"Oh, like a deinonychus."

"What's a dino—whatever it was you said?" Xavier asked.

"Something we used to have where I'm from," Adam said. "They hunted in packs, were about as big as me, and had large claws on their feet. They died out a long time ago."

"Really?"

"Yeah. A comet fell from the sky and wiped them out," Adam said. "Wiped out a lot of things, actually."

"That's… incredible." Xavier paused for a moment and then shook his head. "I can't imagine what that would be like."

"I don't really know," Adam said. "It was long before my time."

"So you've never seen one alive?"

"No, only their bones. But as much as I'd like to see a real one, I'd rather not see them up close, if that's all right with you."

"We can hope, but just to be safe, let's fit this to you," Darius said, lifting the pieces of armor Adam had found in the storeroom yesterday—or rather, yestersleep, as the locals might call it.

"That was way too small for me," Adam said.

"Yes, it was," Darius said with a grin. "I have modified it. It won't be a perfect fit, but it's the best we can do."

Curious, Adam walked over, noting in passing that Duin had hauled out his bag of nuts and was back to cracking them open between two flat stones. Darius had used a leather jerkin as the basis for a new suit of armor, with stitching removed along the sides and new panels sewn in to accommodate Adam's larger frame. The beetle-black armored plating was then secured over the stop with straps and buckles. The backplate and breastplate appeared to be made with the flattened wing cases of an insect that must have been a good three or four feet in length, and there were shoulder guards to match. The leather straps went under the shoulder guards and around the sides of his chest, buckling in along the sides in a second concession to Adam's frame.

"How did you take it apart so easily?" Adam asked.

"I didn't," Darius said. "A full set of carapace armor comes in three pieces. The sides of the cuirass are riveted to the padding you'd wear underneath, as are the rerebraces. The shoulder guard, breastplate, and backplate are separate. When properly fitted, you'd need a precision strike to find a weak point, and the kanak aren't known for finesse."

"I got that impression, yes," Adam said wryly.

"You'll also need these," Darius said, lifting two smaller curved sections of padded armor, with more straps.

"Bracers?" Adam asked.

"Yes," Darius replied. "I suggest we try them once you've got used to wearing the armor. You're already bearing a lot of extra weight."

"And you'll probably be sore again when we stop to sleep," Xavier piped up.

"Thanks," Adam said dryly.

"You are welcome."

"So where exactly are we planning on moving on to?" Adam asked when he sat back down next to Duin, absently reaching for a nut and getting his hand slapped for his troubles.

"An excellent question," Esmeralda said. "Darius, have we worked out which direction we need to travel in yet?"

Darius shook his head. "North dark or north-north dark is my best guess. I'm sorry, Your Highness, but I haven't had much to go on."

"I gave you the best I had!" Xavier said defensively. "The texts I'm working with are not exactly clear, and most of my scrolls were lost when we were ambushed!"

Adam turned to Esmeralda. "I'm sorry, but I have no idea what any of that meant, Your Highness," he said.

Esmeralda laughed. "We're seeking Wyrmbane, the sword of Fernando Aergon."

"Don't tell me; let me guess. It kills wyrms?"

"According to legend, it cuts through dragon hide like a soft-boiled egg," Darius said, a steely glint appearing in his eye. "King Conrad is failing, and the princess… that is, we all believe it is time to return to our home on the surface."

"So… once you get this weapon, you're going up against a dragon, then?"

Darius glanced at Esmeralda. "Perhaps," he said. "We still do not know who is destined to wield it."

"Destined?"

"There are some prophecies," Esmeralda said simply. "But they are a little obscure."

"It doesn't matter," Xavier said. "The point is, we came to the surface to find the sword, and by the time we find it and return, the caverns should be open to us once again."

"Assuming we can find the ruins of Fernando's Keep," Darius corrected. "The directions Xavier had were on our map, but that was one of the important things to go… missing."

"And you can't remember them all?"

"Not all the fine detail, no," Xavier replied. "A lot of the directions were conjecture in any case, based on what I and my predecessors could decipher from journals and documents Fernando's people kept during the Long March to the Caverns of Aergon. I do not have all of those documents—they were too precious and fragile to bring along. Unfortunately they also referenced landmarks we may not see now, given that journey was undertaken some four or five generations ago."

"So what do we—or rather you—know and remember, then?"

"North-north west?" Xavier said helplessly. "Or north-north dark in the current parlance. I remember there was talk of the statues of our ancestors, a tree of stone, and roads leading south from Blackwater, but I have little hope that those roads still exist."

"Blackwater?" Duin asked, speaking for the first time since he and Adam left the cave.

"That is what his keep was called, yes. It was built near a large area of peat bogs, and I understand that the people were not overly creative when it came to naming their lands."

"I know where there are peat bogs to the north dark," Duin said.

"Do you now?" Xavier said sarcastically. "And why should we trust you to lead us safely?"

"Because you don't have a choice?" Adam suggested coolly. "It's in the right direction, and your other options don't seem too great at this point. Oh, and because you're going to apologize for tying him up and treating him like dirt?"

"I'm what?"

Esmeralda cleared her throat meaningfully. "I see your point, Sir Adam, but that would be my responsibility. Goodman Duin, we apologize for the way in which you have been treated by our people and, should you aid us in our quest, pledge to henceforth do everything in our power to see to your safe return to civilized society. Do you accept our apologies and pledge your commitment to our cause?"

Duin rose from his rock and bowed low. "I do, Your Highness."

"Thank you," Esmeralda said formally. "When should we start, and how long is it going to take?"

"It would take me many sleeps on foot, Highness," Duin said. "However, I believe it should be no more than five or six at the pace of your riding lizards."

"We can leave once we've restocked our provisions," Darius said. "And the sooner, the better."

After a little discussion, Adam and Duin went to harvest more of the young fern shoots and refill their waterskins for the journey ahead, and Darius packed all the dry supplies they would take from the waystation.

"Shouldn't we leave some for the next scout to come this way?" Adam asked.

"No," Darius said simply. "We need the provisions, and either we will return in time to direct a resupply mission, or they will be out in force looking for us when we do not return."

And with that cheery response, Adam wished he hadn't brought up the topic at all.

CHAPTER 6

DESPITE XAVIER'S continued misgivings, their little band of adventurers, as Adam liked to call them, adjusted readily to Duin's direction and were soon moving along at a brisk pace. Over the next few sleeps, he learned a lot more about his companions and the society they came from.

Darius was captain of Esmeralda's personal guard and a surprisingly uncomplicated man, proud to serve the royal family of Aergon. He was not large by modern standards, standing around five foot seven inches in height, but he was solid muscle all the way through, with a body that most men would have killed for. He was a serious man who spoke little and smiled even less than Duin, but serving royalty had given him manners and courtly graces Adam did not expect in a soldier—especially given his own time in the reserves. Darius was also a consummate rider and huntsman, proficient in many weapons, from the curved saber he indicated was a standard weapon for lizard riders, to the spear and blowpipe, which were cruder hunting tools he had fashioned from surface-growing bamboo. He topped the spear with a flint point and made darts for his blowpipe from sharpened slivers of bamboo, fitting them with the fluffy seed stalk from wild grasses that plugged the narrow blowpipe sufficiently to allow for a smooth flight and a clean shot. Darius had tipped his darts with the poison from the spiders he had killed for their dinner the first sleep and created a quiver from a section of bamboo, covered at the top with netting made from palm husk, which stopped the darts falling out when his mount ran down a tree or across the underside of a rocky ledge.

Magister Xavier turned out to be witty and urbane in mannerism, possessing a powerful and surprisingly rich store of surface lore. Xavier had been one of two apprentices to learn under Magister Nickedemus, who had apparently been a man of great power and learning. Of all the three Aergonites, he was also the one with the richest knowledge of their people's history, and Adam learned more about Aergon from his conversations with the necromancer—including the all-important *why*.

"Defense" had been Xavier's simple answer. "Obviously I studied the healing arts, but there is precious little that can be done with sorcery to aid healing."

"I don't know," Adam disagreed. "That unguent of yours seems pretty magical."

"Hardly," Xavier said with a chuckle. "Just the right balance of herbs and other ingredients. It is one of our master's oldest formulae."

"Our?"

"Her Royal Highness and I," Xavier said, his voice taking on a slight mocking tone.

"Esmeralda studied magic?"

"Yes," Xavier said shortly. "And she fancies herself something of an expert, despite her lack of practice."

"Mmm," Adam said noncommittally. "How exactly is necromancy defense? I mean, do you really raise zombies?"

"Yes, I do," Xavier said. "It is a lot of work to prepare the body for zombification, especially if you want a zombie that has some skill in battle—and one that isn't going to be lost to rot in a month or so."

At this point the conversation deviated to timekeeping, and Adam learned that Aergon did indeed have a calendar, although it was based around sleeps rather than days, with weeks of seven sleeps and ten months of thirty sleeps. That settled, they turned back to the topic of the undead, and Adam asked the question he wasn't certain he wanted an answer to. How did Xavier stop the corpses from rotting?

"Salt," Xavier said. "There is a great underground sea which we tunneled into, and we have been extracting salt for years. Once we found that preserving bodies in salt made it more difficult for rot to set in, defending our people became much easier."

"And they're really that effective against the kanak?"

"Ha! Hardly," Xavier said with a dark laugh. "But that is not why we have them. They are fantastic sentinels, especially against the cave spiders, who find them unpalatable, but mostly they defend us against the dragon."

"The dragon this sword is meant to kill?"

Xavier nodded. "Her name is Khalivibra, and she has caused us more damage than all the kanak combined."

"How's that?"

"She drove us from our homes on the surface," Xavier said. "It happened a long time ago, back in the time when the sun did not hang motionless in the sky as it does now...."

INSTEAD, ADAM was brought to understand, this world once had a day-and-night cycle, with the sun rising in the morning, setting in the evening, and the stars and moon coming out to shine down on the land during the night. The ancestral Aergonites lived on the surface, much in the way Adam had always envisaged an idyllic feudal existence. They were ruled from the city of Aer Goragon, capital of the Kingdom of Aracao and known far and wide as the Golden City on the plains, for it was built of a yellow stone that gleamed in the morning sun. There were also seasons—times of growth and greenery and times of falling leaves and snow.

In the days of King Henricus the Third, tragedy befell the land, and as Magister Ignatius Solmento foretold, the light of the moon was darkened by the flight of great bat-like wings. The dragons came in the hundreds, and the great serpents fell on a people unprepared for their onslaught. Their fire burned crops, livestock, homes, and people. Their wings brought terrible storms to lash the land and flood the fields. Where the dragons landed, the ground shook and ruptured beneath their feet, collapsing buildings, castles, and mountains alike. No one knew how many people died in those early years, though in time the Aergonites learned to fight back, harnessing great magic to strike down the wyrms and stabilize the land. Some even struck bargains with the dragons for protection of their lands, although the protection was not a guarantee of safety for those living near the borders where another dragon lurked.

However, the people of Aracao soon found themselves facing a far greater challenge—the dragons had cast the moon from the sky. At first the people missed only its glow, striving instead to adapt to a lifestyle of subterranean cultivation in their attempt to hide their food stores from the dragons. Most of them, of course, had taken to living beneath the ground in cellars and tunnels to hide from the dragons for so long some had not seen the sky in cycles.

And then the cycles stopped.

Slowly the days and nights became longer, the seasons stretched and lengthened, but no one knew why. At first most common folk simply welcomed the times of sun and shivered through the times of ice, but soon they were alternately cursing at or pleading with the gods, and some even threw themselves into depraved dragon cults in desperation. But neither the gods of old nor gods of new were listening, because some years after the dragons first came, the world stopped turning—or so says the Book of Solmento.

As one side of the world burned, the other side froze, and the dragons fell to fighting for what food they needed to support their vast bodies. They were forced into the band of twitterlit land between light and dark, just like the rest of all living creatures. Soon there were only two that claimed Aracao as their territory, and they preyed on the people there. Some say they farmed the people as the Aergonites today farm spiders now for silk and meat. Any pretense of cooperation had vanished with the dragon wars, and the king could do little but acquiesce to the dragon's increasingly bold demands for power, food, or both. When their demands were not met, the dragons simply took what they desired, so after a few years, all of Aracao lived their lives in fear of the dragons' raids. Until Prince Fernando.

Fernando was the youngest of the royal family and about as far down the line of direct succession as one could get. His estate, if you could call it that, was known as Blackwater Keep, for it sat at the edge of a large peat bog. The peat tilled into his fields made his lands fertile, and his status as the least of the royal family had given him enough latitude to pursue his passion for the magical arts. And when the great golden wyrms raided his lands for the seventh time, he turned his attention to the creation of a weapon that would end their incursions—a weapon that would come to be known as Wyrmbane.

"Forged from the light of a fallen star and strengthened with folded moonsilver, Fernando set the blade with stones sacred to the moon goddess, Selune, in the hopes she might lend her aid against those who had cast her from our skies—and perhaps she did," Xavier said. "In a mighty confrontation, Fernando, in his fifty-first year, slew the great dragon Khaled, mate of the dragon Khalivibra, who hunts us even now in retribution for the deed. For the killing blow struck by Prince Fernando should have been the start of our grand revolution; instead it was a dirge. Straight and true was the thrust of his blade into the dragon's breast, the serrated edge of Wyrmbane digging deep—so deep that it stuck, wrenched out of his grasp as the great beast's body fell back into

Blackwater Keep. Its death spasms brought the structure down around it as it died, killing the prince and fully half of the keep's inhabitants.

"It is said that in death the drake Khaled uttered a curse so powerful it caused the fire in his belly to burn his blood and blacken the land. Blackwater burned, and the peat in its marshes caught fire, and the people of Blackwater had no choice but to flee—south from their home, harried by Khalivibra herself, and leaving burning Khaled in the ruins with Wyrmbane lodged in his chest, and surely leaving behind any hope of our salvation with it."

"That's a bit dramatic, isn't it?" Adam said. "Isn't recovering hope of salvation the entire point of this outing?"

Xavier laughed. "That is most certainly true. I do apologize, Sir Adam. I do like a good oration, and that ending is the traditional one as it would be told in the Caverns of Aergon. Mayhap we shall change the ending of the tale, no?"

Adam had laughed along with the magister and continued riding.

HE CONVERSED little with Esmeralda, although that was partially because he felt unable to approach or talk to her, never quite certain if it would be rude to talk to a princess uninvited. On those rare occasions he did speak to her, however, she was refreshingly down to earth.

"I never expected a princess to be so skilled," Adam said at one point during their ride.

"When you say 'skilled,' I assume you are referring to practical survival skills, rather than singing or embroidery?" Esmeralda asked.

"Well… yes."

Esmeralda shrugged. "I am the only child of a dying king who rules a shrinking kingdom," she said. "I understand that once a princess' tasks were limited to chatter about gowns and hairstyles or some similar nonsense, but there is no neighboring prince waiting to wed me and lead my people. As far as we know, there are no other kingdoms left free from the dragon's tyranny."

"So… you're doing this in part to find a suitable husband?"

Esmeralda looked at him for a long, unsettling moment before bursting into peals of laughter. "You know," she said, "that is a very good way to put it."

"And why can't you just rule Aergon yourself?" Adam asked.

"I am just a woman, Sir Adam."

"So?" Adam said. "Wait, was that a 'I'm just a woman so I can't rule a kingdom,' or 'I'm just a woman and men won't *let me* rule a kingdom'?"

"Is there a difference?" Esmeralda asked. "I am precluded from ruling by my sex, and I do not have the skills or training required to rule."

"And some man whose claim to greatness is wielding a magic sword to kill a dragon is?"

"He would command respect."

"And you can't?"

"Not as immediately, no."

"Well… that's stupid."

Esmeralda laughed again. "You are a delightful man, Adam. Is it truly like that where you are from? A woman can do anything a man can?"

"Pretty much," Adam said. "There's still some things women generally choose not to do, but it's more their choice than them being barred from it."

"It sounds like a very nice place," Esmeralda said, her tone thoughtful.

"Well, I like it," Adam said. "Of course, it could be said that I'm biased."

RIDING THROUGH the lowland rainforest was a very different experience for Adam. Unlike the cool heights of the mountains, the air below the tree canopy was thick, still, and humid. After only an hour's riding—according to his still-functioning watch—he was soaked with sweat, and the Aergonites weren't faring much better. The red light that slanted here and there through the canopy was barely enough to see by and gave Adam the impression of walking in the darkened pits of hell. They had taken to using torches in order to light their way, collecting swollen taproots full of sap that burned brightly enough to give them some visibility in the darkness—the wan light of the Aergonite bowls having proved too dim to cut through the murk.

It was interesting to see that Duin, true to his word, reacted to the fire much the same way as he did to the sunlight, which really made perfect sense when Adam thought about it. His furry friend kept away from the fire if given the chance, bothered by the way the flickering light caused fur to sprout and vanish. More often than not, Duin scouted ahead, wearing the leather pants and loose shirt he had acquired at the waystation, but even so, his muzzle would occasionally lengthen or hair would begin to sprout along his arms. The first few times this happened had been unnerving for Adam, but after a while, it became normal.

It was amazing what became normal. The constant buzzing of insects and biting flies became normal, as did smearing their exposed skin with thick mud in an attempt to prevent the bloodsuckers finding a meal, at least until Duin found a certain plant, its mass of orange-brown roots hanging from an overhead tree branch looking for all the world like the remains of a massive food fight. Breaking open the roots revealed a pungent-smelling clear fluid, which turned out to be a much better insect repellent than heavily caked mud, although Duin cautioned them against getting it into their eyes or mouths.

The forest was also teeming with life, from small lizards and rodents who scuttled away as they approached, to dragonflies as long as Adam's arm that zoomed through the air, hunting the flying flitterfish that lived even here. There were also large herbivorous tortoises, although the one they encountered was *merely* the size of a horse, and Duin warned they got at least three times as large.

"Their eggs are good eating if you can find a nest—and dig through it," he said.

There was, however, a distinct lack of larger mammals, from what Adam could see. No birds either. There were plenty of reptiles and insects, as well as spiders and scorpions big enough to make sleeping within four feet of the ground a very dangerous proposition, but aside from a few rodent-like creatures and what appeared to be a herd of wild goats that they spotted in the distance, the only mammals Adam really saw were the humans themselves, who were often outclassed by the other creatures of the jungle. On more than one occasion, they had to climb up the trunk of the nearest tree to wait out the passing of an army ant swarm, where each individual ant was a good six inches in length.

Indeed, the biggest obstacle to their progress was the sheer amount of waiting they had to do—be it waiting for the ant swarm to pass or, more commonly, waiting for the rain to ease. Adam had vague recollections of learning about the water cycle in geography in high school, but he had been completely unprepared for the deluge that occurred every twelve hours or so. Sometimes it seemed they had gone barely any distance at all before Duin squinted through the canopy, sniffed the air, and declared that they needed to set up camp—and by camp he meant construct a platform in a tree with a roof. The first time he mentioned it, Magister Xavier had scoffed.

"The lizards aren't tired, and we aren't tired. Besides, the distance we traveled can hardly be called a full sleep's march!"

"I know that, Magister," Duin said evenly. "But in a short while, you will not be wanting to march anywhere. Humor me this once, and if you want to ride on in the future, I will defer to your judgment."

Grumbling, the necromancer gave in, helping to haul lengths of bamboo up a tree, where they were lashed together with jungle vines and erected into a roof of stretched oilskin covered with large banana plant-like leaves for extra protection. Aside from the cutting of the bamboo, it took the five of them remarkably little time to create a shelter large enough to provide cover for them and their mounts. Duin was also adamant that any fire for cooking needed to be done quickly, and was to be started well before the shelter was complete. "I do not see what the rush is," Xavier muttered as they roasted the catch of the day—a couple of large snakes—over the glowing coals.

Duin looked at what little sky could be seen from the forest floor. "You will."

"Is it just me, or is it getting dark?" Adam asked. "I didn't think it got dark here."

"The sun remains still," Duin replied. "But that does not stop clouds from blocking out the light. Is that snake cooked?"

"Yes," Darius said. "But we still need water."

"Stamp out the fire and get inside," Duin said. "We can get that later."

"The stream isn't far, Duin," Adam said. "We could nip over and be back in a matter of minutes."

"We could," Duin agreed. "But we will not have to. Trust me."

Shrugging, Adam mounted Zoul, Duin leapt on behind him, and the great lizard scuttled up the tree just as the first drops of rain trickled through the canopy.

At first the rain just bounced off the leaves and trickled down stems and branches, but then the drops became splatters, and then splatters became a heavy deluge as the foliage above proved insufficient to prevent the torrential downpour that hit the forest. Gripping one of the buckets they had taken from the waystation, Duin reached outside their little shelter and in mere moments pulled it back in, full to the brim, although inside, they had barely enough light to see anything.

"If you would be so kind to provide us with some light, Magister?" Duin asked politely.

Wordlessly, Xavier brought out the covered stone bowl and sprinkled a bit of powder into it, along with a small amount of rainwater, and the greenish glow brightened noticeably.

"What exactly is that stuff?" Adam asked, leaning in for a closer look.

"Careful," Xavier said, holding Adam back. "You'll block the light."

"Sorry."

"No harm done," Xavier said. "In answer to your question, this is a water slime that grows naturally in the Caverns of Aergon that we have used to light our homes for generations. All it requires is water and some fertilizer and it glows for us."

"What's that powder that you throw on it?"

"Bone ash," Xavier replied. "It has proved to be the most effective fertilizer of all those we have tried."

Adam stared at a smear of white powder on the rim of the bowl. "Suddenly I wish I hadn't asked the question."

Xavier laughed. "Come, let us eat, and then we might as well use the rain to get clean. I do not know about you, but I am tired of swimming in my own sweat."

Esmeralda wrinkled her nose. "I, for one, am certainly tired of the smell."

Adam grunted and started unbuckling his armor. "This stuff really doesn't help with that."

"It does keep the bugs off, though," Darius said, starting to remove his own armor.

After a moment, Duin came over to help Adam. "Thanks," Adam said as Duin's nimble fingers made short work of the buckles keeping the breastplate tight around his chest. "I'm really not used to this sort of thing."

"When we get a moment, you and I should train," Darius said. "From what I saw earlier, you are good with your weapons, but I believe we could hone your skills further."

"Sure," Adam said, wincing as Duin helped lift the breastplate and backplate over his head and deposited it in the corner of their little shelter. "Just as long as we don't run out of that pain-relief oil of Xavier's."

Xavier laughed. "I will make some more next time the good captain brings us back some spider for food."

"If we need to, we can set up earlier next time," Duin suggested. "It will give us time to hunt and recuperate."

Esmeralda pursed her lips. "How long does the rain last?"

"Long enough to catch a bit of sleep," Duin said with a shrug. "I am sorry, Highness, but I have never been able to keep an accurate measure of time here."

"Then let us rest now," Esmeralda suggested. "Given we spent this long on a shelter, we may as well use it. And we can see how long the rain lasts—assuming the time of rain doesn't vary?"

"It shouldn't," Adam said. "If this is anything like the rainforests back home, the heat of the sun is evaporating water from the forest, which forms lots of clouds and fog. When there's too much moisture in the air, it falls as rain. Given how long we rode today, I figure we probably have ten or twelve hours between each downpour."

"And if we had a portable candle clock with us, that information would be very helpful," Xavier said. "With no way of accurately measuring time, how can we possibly know when rain is imminent?"

"Duin knew," Darius said softly, peeling a section of snake off the bone with his knife. "He should be able to give us fair warning."

"Sleep," Esmeralda said firmly. "We may not have done a full march, but in these conditions, I think we could all use the rest."

The companions finished their simple meal of snake and rainforest fruits and tossed the remains down to the rainforest floor beneath them, hoping no predators would be attracted by the bones—or if they were, that said predators wouldn't think of looking up a tree to find them. They took turns "showering" in the rain on the small ledge that they'd built outside their shelter, and Adam was surprised at the casual attitude to nudity that the Aergonites shared. Perhaps it was the bathing culture that they appeared to have, or perhaps they had never developed the puritanical morals that still pervaded life back home. Still, he couldn't help but be a little shocked when Esmeralda stepped back into the shelter, stark naked, reaching for a towel to dry herself off with. Hastily, he averted his eyes, only to find Duin staring at him, an unreadable expression on his face.

"Everything okay?" Adam asked.

"Yes," Duin said. "Fine."

Although Duin was still happy to apply the medical oil to Adam's sore muscles that rest, it felt completely different with the others in the same small room, and Duin's strokes were cursory and businesslike, leaving Adam with the vague feeling he'd done something wrong. Still, there was little he could say with everyone in such tight confines, and he resolved to bring it up at a later time if the opportunity arose.

CHAPTER 7

THE RAIN let up after a few hours, but as Esmeralda predicted, the companions chose to rest a bit longer before moving on.

"It's such a waste," Darius said as they loaded the lizards again and resumed their trek.

"What is?" Adam asked.

"Creating that structure only to leave it."

"I don't think we can carry the bamboo with us. Do you?" Adam asked.

"Oh no," Darius said. "I agree we have to leave it. I just wish we did not."

"You need a mobile hut on wheels that the lizards can tow."

Darius was quiet for a while, and Adam could almost see him turning the idea over and over in his brain. Finally he shook his head. "No," he said sadly. "It would work until we needed to run up a tree or cliff."

Adam smiled. "As you say."

After their third rest, they encountered the river again, here a wide brown expanse that cut through the forest, winding its way to an estuary somewhere downstream. At the bank of the shore was a large, strangely shaped rock pillar, overgrown with vines and mosses, ferns and small trees growing out of cracks and crevices farther up the rock face.

"And we have to get across that?" Xavier asked as they sat looking out over the expanse of murky brown water.

"Yes," Duin said. "The most direct route would be to cross it here and again when it loops back, but I normally only have to build a raft for one—an unmounted one."

"Well, it's too far to swim," Adam said flatly.

"You don't want to swim," Darius said. "There could be cokudrillos in there."

"Cokudrillos?"

"A water-dwelling lizard twice as long as Zoul and with jaws big enough to rip your head off," Darius said, his face grim. "They lurk under the surface with just their eyes and nostrils poking above, looking just like water-soaked logs."

"Right," Adam said once it was clear there was no punch line coming. "So how long would a detour around the river take?"

"Another seven or eight sleeps or so, I think," Duin said.

"We can afford an extra week, right?" Xavier said, eyeing the water nervously.

"Or we could just build a really large raft and go with the river current," Adam suggested. "I don't know about you, but I'd be quite happy to not ride for a while."

"What do you mean?"

"Well, Duin just said that we'd have to cross the river twice. Why don't we just build a large raft and float it downriver until we reach the second crossing point? I don't know if it'll save us as much time as going cross-country would, but it'll save a lot of effort."

"We'd have to gather more food," Darius said speculatively.

"And we wouldn't have fire," Xavier pointed out.

"We can if we bring a flat stone to keep it on, and wet the bamboo around it to stop any burning," Darius said. "And we can do without if we must—silver scarabs can be eaten raw when fresh caught."

"Silver scarabs?" Adam asked.

"A swimming scarab," Darius replied, although the description did little to help Adam. "Good eating, and they're found here as well as in Aergon."

Despite Xavier's continued misgivings, they set about building their raft, using several layers of long bamboo to create enough deck space and buoyancy to keep them out of the water once fully loaded with people and lizards. They also managed to construct a small lean-to at the back, which could be used for sleeping, and a larger shelter for the lizards and their provisions.

Adam was cutting creepers for cord when he found something. "Hey, what's this?" he asked, pulling vegetation away from the rocky surface.

"A boulder, surely," Esmeralda said irritably from where she was weaving tough coconut husk fiber into netting for carrying extra provisions.

"Maybe at one point, but seriously, look," Adam said, stepping back to reveal a large stone face, pitted with age and covered in a beard of moss.

Esmeralda gasped and ran over so quickly, she nearly tripped. "I don't believe it! That must be the statue of King Teodoros the Wise! It was said to be twenty feet tall and carved in granite from the quarries of Atacosca!"

Adam stared up at the vine-covered effigy in front of them. "Well, it probably was twenty feet when the head was on it," he said.

"King Teodoros on his throne," Esmeralda said, her voice soft with awe. "Magister Xavier, is this not one of the landmarks mentioned in the Book of Solmento?"

Xavier paused. "Why… yes, Your Highness. I do believe it is."

"Then we are on the right track," Esmeralda said, her eyes sparkling. "Come, we should hurry."

Adam took one last look at the statue before him, fancying he could see the detail now he knew what he was looking for—an ancient king on his throne, proudly welcoming those crossing into this domain. A rocky protrusion became a hand, and a swell in the ground became a foot—more so when he scraped away the layers of moss and humus. How much power the man must have had to have this statue erected with no other purpose than to stoke his own ego. How many men it must have taken to carve this tribute to a king's vanity. And now both the king and sculptors were gone, leaving only this headless statue to be reclaimed by nature as a base for her plants or a nest for her birds—or not-birds, as was the case in this strange land. Sighing, Adam gathered his vines and turned back to the raft construction.

The progress of their build was interrupted by the rain, and the companions spent a few cold hours huddling under their lean-to while they waited for it to abate. Then, loaded with coconuts from nearby palm trees and their dwindling supplies of dried fruit, they launched their raft into the rippling waters of the river, poling it out into the current and allowing the water to carry them where it would.

The middle of the river flowed deceptively quickly, and soon the five companions found themselves moving at a fair pace, watching the vegetation-choked riverbanks pass by on both sides. Looking at them now, Adam found it hard to believe that the inside was as open and spacious as it was. From the raft it looked as though the trees came all the way down to the banks, merging into a mass of rushes and grasses that yearned toward the water and the red of the sun. Insects flitted here and there across the water, seeking out food of rotting meat or fresh blood, or even other insects, as Adam found when a dragonfly as long as his forearm swooped down to carry off a waterbug. Every so often, Darius cast one of the pieces of luggage netting into the water behind them, then, after a while, pulled in a number of silver scarabs, which turned out to be a long, smoothly helmeted crustacean with crablike swimmerets. They tasted much sweeter than Adam would have expected, and when he threw the remains of one such meal overboard, there was a rush of water as a reptilian head rose to snap up the carcass in powerful jaws.

"Cokudrillos," Duin said as their raft bobbed in the ripples caused by the creature's sudden appearance. As the giant swam off, Adam caught a glimpse of a flipper and a long rudder-like tail.

"Maybe we should have taken the long way around," Adam muttered. "I don't like the idea of what would happen if one decided to try to overturn our raft."

"It's never happened to me before," Duin said.

"Obviously not, you're still here," Adam said, grinning to take the sting out of his words. "But have you ever spent this long floating down the river before?"

"Now that you mention it, no," Duin said. "Still, hope for the best, prepare for the worst, right?"

"How do we prepare for the worst in this case?" Adam asked.

Duin reached out and picked up one of the long bamboo lengths they were using for poling. "We might want to consider getting into shallower water, for a start," he suggested.

DESPITE ADAM'S constant fretting, the river ride passed uneventfully, and a few sleeps later they disembarked after selecting a landing spot and prodding the shallows carefully to ensure no cokudrillos lurked nearby. The lizards scrambled happily onto the land—all four of them had been ill at ease on the raft, although they had been content with the diet of scarabs that had been offered to them. However, just as they were getting ready to set off again, a loud roar shook the jungle, and a dark shadow appeared over the river.

"Quickly! Into the jungle!" Darius hissed, leading the way farther into the foliage. "We don't want her to see us."

"Who's she?" Adam asked as he followed the captain away from the riverbank.

"Khalivibra herself," Darius said, his voice low and awed. "I didn't think she flew out this far."

"How would you know how far she flies?" Xavier hissed. "You know she raids as far south as the Caverns of Aergon."

"True," Darius muttered. "I was just hoping we wouldn't see her."

"Or rather that she wouldn't see us?"

"Yes."

"She must guard the sword," Duin said. "I know if there was one weapon that could kill me, I'd want to make sure it was well defended."

"Well, that's a twist," Xavier said. "To get the sword to kill the dragon, we have to get past the dragon."

Adam meanwhile had been staring upward, trying to catch a glimpse of the mythical creature. He was vaguely aware of Esmeralda chanting something in the background, but he was mesmerized by the downbeat of the massive wings. Through a gap in the trees, he caught a flash of a golden hide, gleaming reddish gold in the light of the sun.

"It'll see the raft," Adam whispered. "She'll see the raft."

The earth shook as the dragon landed, splashes and the sound of waves indicating she'd found an open spot in the river. Peering back the way they came, Adam finally caught more than a glimpse. The dragon was not what he had expected, with a much shorter neck and a more densely muscled body than the fantasy depictions of Earth. Its massive bat-like wings were more familiar, but sprouted at a point equidistant between her fore and hind limbs, rather than up above the fore-shoulders. Its face was wide and stout, looking almost heart shaped, with two short horns protruding from its skull, but its teeth were as long and sharp as any Adam could have imagined.

A wave of nausea washed over him, and he doubled over in his saddle, trying not to heave up his last meal. The only way he could describe it was like the comedown after a night of vodka Red Bulls—but more so. Then the feeling was gone, and Duin was grabbing at Zoul's reins.

"Run!" he said, his voice shrill with terror.

And run they did, fleeing deeper into the forest just as a blast of flame shot out toward them, turning the green rainforest to clouds of choking smoke. It might have been worse, but the rain-sodden vegetation was too wet to catch fire. Surprisingly soon, the companions were beyond the smoke and flames, Darius riding close to the princess and guiding her mount over the uneven terrain of the forest floor. Only then did Adam realize she was still chanting, one outstretched hand holding a glowing shard of rock that looked a bit like a milky quartz.

"What happened?" Adam asked. "The dragon's not following us?"

"No," Darius said tightly as he urged them onward. "Her wings would get tangled unless she came in on foot, and she won't risk that."

"Why not?"

"Because she does not know if we are accompanied by zombies," Xavier said, looking over his shoulder at the clouds of smoke drifting upward into the canopy. "And thanks to Esmeralda—Her Royal Highness, Princess Esmeralda," he corrected when Darius glared at him, "she does not know exactly where we are, even if she were to come in."

"Okay, I get the magic thing the princess is doing, but where do the zombies come into things?"

"Did you not feel it?" Xavier asked. "The dragon is not dangerous because she is a great fire-breathing lizard. We could deal with one of those. We *have* dealt with those in the past. Khalivibra is dangerous because she attacks your mind."

"You mean the feeling that your brain is about to dribble out of your ears?"

"That is just the start," Xavier said. "In some cases that passes, and then you serve her will. To everyone else you appear perfectly normal, but in the past... we have had people lead their families to the surface to be taken by her, herders leaving their flocks out for her to eat... once a sentry even let an invading band of kanak into our tunnels."

"And how did you find out about it, then?"

"Observation," Xavier said. "And postmortem examination in some cases. In others the people confessed after being caught. We have always known that dragons possessed the ability to influence people, but never on such a great or insidious scale."

"And you defend against this with zombies?"

"They have no will but their maker's," Xavier replied. "And you can leave them with simple commands that prove very handy."

"Like 'fire this ballista at any dragon, kanak, or giant spider that comes within range,'" Darius said tightly.

"And then hit the alarm gong," Xavier agreed.

"And Esmeralda—Princess Esmeralda—is defending us from the dragon right now?" Adam asked.

"Yes," Darius said. "But we need to guide her while she concentrates. We need to keep safe until the next downpour—Khalivibra doesn't like to get her wings wet."

"We're going the wrong way, though," Duin said. "We should be going north dark along the riverbank."

Darius shook his head. "Too dangerous. The bank is too exposed, and she'd pick us off one by one."

"We can manage," Xavier said confidently. "We can pick our way deeper into the forest and then cut back toward the river once the rains come."

"If we travel when it rains, she should lose our track completely," Darius agreed.

"I knew you were going to suggest that," Xavier said. "I asked myself what the most unpleasant plan you could come up with would be, and of course you suggest it."

"Well, I'm not very keen on it either," Adam said. "But it sounds like the best plan we have."

"We'll be fine," Darius said confidently.

"I'm not so sure," Duin said, his body tensing. "I think we have entered slasherclaw territory."

Chapter 8

Darius paused and looked around. "What makes you say that?"

"On your left, there are claw marks on the trees. The gouges suggest the alpha male of a slasherclaw pack, and the white splatter would be its spoor."

Darius's eyes swiveled left. "Up the trees, all of you," he said, urging them into the lower branches of the rainforest giants.

"These slasherclaws," Adam asked as Zoul easily climbed up a large tree trunk. "Can they jump?"

"Oh yes," Duin said. "At least as high as you are tall, if not a little bit more."

Adam glanced over the edge of the thick branch. "How far would you say that drop is?" he asked.

Duin smiled. "At least twice your height, Adam."

"Good. Wait, can they climb?"

"You know, I really have no idea."

"Oh. Great."

Once again Adam found himself guiding Zoul through the three-dimensional maze of the forest canopy, going from branch to branch in a long, slow meandering course above the ground, which eventually took them back to where they could hear the sound of the river, and Duin indicated the rain was about to come.

Venturing to the forest floor to find wood and bamboo for a shelter had never felt so nerve-wracking. Adam and the other men worked together, alternating between keeping watch for slasherclaws and cutting and hauling supplies. Luckily they were able to gather food among the canopy, snagging various fruits and large nuts that had a spongy inside reminiscent of nougat. They also managed to catch some flitterfish by hanging netting between two branches and chasing the flying creatures into it. They weren't quite ready when the rain started, and they were soaked through by the time they'd got the roof up. It wasn't until the rain was falling in sheets around them that Esmeralda stopped chanting, the light fading from the stone in her hand, and she slumped forward, her chest heaving as she gulped in great breaths of air. Carefully, Duin unbuckled her from her saddle and helped her down, supporting her trembling frame against his own.

"Are you all right, Your Highness?" he asked.

Wearily, Esmeralda nodded and accepted the waterskin he offered.

"Get out of your wet things," Duin suggested, holding out a blanket to her. "I'm sorry, but we did not build a fire."

"Fire would have drawn the slasherclaws to us," Xavier pointed out.

"Slasherclaws?"

"We haven't seen any yet," Xavier hastened to reassure her. "But we have seen signs that there is a pack in the area."

"A fire might also have brought *her* attention back to us," Darius said.

As one they all looked out in the direction of the riverbank, invisible behind the sheets of rain dropping down from the sky. "Do you think she'll come back?" Adam asked.

"Almost certainly," Esmeralda said, now rugged up in a blanket and taking a bite of a juicy red fruit. "She knows roughly where we are now, and I am almost certain she knows why we are here."

"How did she find that out?"

Esmeralda shrugged and wiped at her eyes. "I do not truly know. She may have gleaned it out of our minds before I could shield us."

"Let's get some rest," Darius suggested. "We're going to need it, I think."

Esmeralda yawned and nodded. "We will need to start out just about as soon as the rain eases," she said. "Selune's teeth, why did you set up camp so close to the river?"

"We needed the bamboo," Xavier said. "And with the slasherclaws around, we dared not carry it too far."

All in all, none of them got much sleep that rest time.

ADAM WAS woken from a light doze by a hand clamping over his mouth.

"Mmph?"

"Shh," Duin whispered in his ear. "There are slasherclaws beneath us, and you looked like you were about to start snoring."

Adam wanted to protest that he didn't snore, but was honest enough to know that he did. Instead he nodded his understanding, and when

Duin released him, he rubbed the sleep from his eyes and crept over to the edge of their tree house and peeked down to the ground below.

It took him a while to pick out the creature from the trees and the leaf litter, especially in the poor light, but he saw below the first true feathers he'd come across since tumbling into this strange world. The beast was a cross between lizard and bird, and at first glance he thought he was looking at a small emu. It was only when he caught the glint of a yellow reptilian eye, sharp teeth, and the large sickle-shaped claw on the big toe of each of the creature's two feet that he was convinced it was not a bird at all. Other than a bright red crest, its feathers were mostly a reddish brown with darker arrow-shaped markings, the pattern being most pronounced on the head, elbows of the much smaller forearms, and along the long, stiff tail that shot out behind the creature, probably for balance, poised as it was for perpetual sprinting. Adam could envision it pouncing, biting at the neck of some poor unsuspecting person while the claws came around for the kill. Then the slasherclaw raised its head and gave a mournful hooting cry that was answered by a vibrant chorus, and Adam saw that it was not alone.

The slasherclaws hopped onto the large, bulbous roots and the rocky boulders that littered the ground, their heads bobbing in a fashion that reminded Adam of a turkey—a nearly man-sized turkey capable of ripping his guts out and having him for lunch. The slasherclaws had congregated in a loose circular formation, darting quickly here and there, lifting their heads in turn to give out their hooting cries. After a short while, Adam noticed a marked dimorphism in the creatures gathered below. Most of them were fairly drab in color, their tan feathers accented in blacks and rainforest leaf green. The ones doing the majority of the strutting and hooting had crests of feathers almost as long as their jaws and colored a bright red. The males—or at least Adam decided they were males—were craning necks up tall and raising crests in a battle of plumage. Only once did the display devolve into snapping, and even then it was only a brief lunge when the slightly smaller male edged in too close. As sharp teeth snapped inches from the skin of its neck, the slasherclaw gave a yelp and scrambled away, running back into the dubious safety of the root network with his crest flat against his neck.

"It's a courtship ritual," Xavier breathed softly. "We may be the first people to witness something like this."

"The first people to witness it and live to tell the tale, you mean," Adam said, unable to shake the nagging feeling he should be Instagramming the display. "That's assuming of course we do live to tell the tale."

"They're blocking our way," Darius said flatly. "We don't want to ride through that."

"Can't we backtrack around them while they're busy?" Adam suggested.

"I'm not sure," Darius said. "We don't know how long they'll be here, and it will take several slow cycles of your 'watch' for us to go back. There are too many fallen trees here for my liking."

With the traditional candle clocks not being practical, or more importantly, available, the Aergonites had been quick to take advantage of Adam's kinetic watch to keep track of time and progress. They had already established that there tended to be six hours—or slow cycles— of Adam's watch in which they could travel, allowing for two hours to break and set up camp to avoid the four hours of heavy rain that came nearly on the clock. Xavier and Esmeralda were particularly perplexed by the timepiece, especially since Adam kept insisting that the watch was not a magical artifact. One rest, Esmeralda insisted on checking it for magic, and had been sorely disappointed when her tests—which involved a discarded feather dipped in a pot of boiled water infused with what, to Adam, had been a collection of random leaves and seed pods— yielded no result.

"Of course, one should remember that many of the most powerful magics do not register to that field spell," Xavier had remarked sardonically from the sidelines. "Perhaps it is hiding its aura from you."

"You know, Xavier, you were never very funny as a child," Esmeralda had said icily, "and you aren't any more amusing as an adult."

NOW ESMERALDA was looking down around the landscape with increased scrutiny. "Is it just me," she asked, "or has anyone else noticed that the fallen trees look like they fell to unnatural causes?"

"What do you mean?" Xavier asked.

"Well, all the uprooted trees we found prior to yestersleep have been rotted through the core, or smothered by other plants, or struck by lightning or something."

"Yes, what's your point?"

"The fallen trees here were all broken. Some of them had their trunks snapped; some of them were perfectly healthy, other than being uprooted."

"And almost all of them had deep gouges in their trunks and branches," Duin said slowly.

"Exactly."

"Wait, what are you suggesting?" Xavier asked.

"That someone drove us here," Esmeralda said slowly. "To this specific tree above the courtship grounds of the slasherclaws."

"Oh, come now," Xavier scoffed. "Who could possibly have the power to do something like that?"

Adam and Duin exchanged a glance and bolted from the edge of the platform, rushing to load Zoul with his share of the provisions and their—or rather, Adam's—personal luggage. Moments later, Darius and Esmeralda joined them.

"Seriously, what could—"

From behind them came a low, rumbling roar and the sound of huge wings beating somewhere out in the fog.

"Oh," Xavier said softly and ran toward his mount.

"Backtrack?" Adam asked Darius as he passed the captain, holding two bedrolls.

"No," Darius said curtly. "She knows where we are."

"Besides," Duin said from the far edge of the hut. "That's where she's coming from."

Back along the line of trees they had traversed earlier, Adam could just make out a great dark shadow growing larger and larger along with the beating of those massive bat wings, blowing the post-rain fog toward them.

"Ride hard!" Darius cried, all thoughts of stealth forgotten. "Let's hope the slasherclaws will be as surprised as we are."

Duin reached Zoul about three steps before Adam did and hesitated.

"Get on!" Adam snapped, hefting Duin into the saddle. "You can drive just as well as I can, I'm sure."

Scrambling up behind Duin, Adam only then realized the major problem—Duin wasn't wearing the riding belt.

Cursing, he gripped the saddle horn with both hands as Zoul scuttled across the platform, nearly losing his balance as the great lizard descended headfirst down the tree. Then he all but squashed Duin against

Zoul's back and held on for dear life until he reached the almost level ground of the forest floor.

Captain Darius's hope that the slasherclaws would be put off by the dragon Khalivibra's appearance, looming through the trees wreathed in the smoke and flames from their overnight shelter, proved to be a futile one. The smaller feathered lizards stared at the five riders in curiosity for an all too brief moment, their crests rising and falling as they cocked their heads in eagle-like thought. Then the largest male bellowed a hoot with significantly more snarl to it, and the beasts rushed toward them.

Zoul responded with a dash of speed that just kept them clear of their hunters, although a cry off to the right indicated Darius had been less fortunate. Then there was a bolt of darkness as Xavier made a throwing motion, and the slasherclaw was writhing on the ground, yelping in pain as its body was wracked with magical energies. Darius spurred his mount onward, blood oozing from a gash on his thigh.

"Ride hard!" Darius cried as his mount shot forward, fear surely lending swiftness to its feet as much as the thumps of Darius's heels in its sides.

Zoul was off and running, but Adam could see the slasherclaws keeping pace, two of them on either side, disappearing among trees and falling behind only to pop out of the root maze to trail them once more. For once, Zoul's ability to literally run up the sheerest of surfaces was of little help. For every boulder scaled and every tangle of roots navigated, the feathered reptiles were either able to wriggle through or leap over, and in some cases Adam felt they must have leapt over six feet in the air, hitting the ground running in their relentless pursuit.

As they passed a narrow passage between two enormous tree trunks, Adam and Duin were treated to a demonstration of the slasherclaws' abilities. Suddenly even the dim red light was being blocked out, and the feathered body of a large male was descending upon them, a leap from higher in the tree bringing him in for the kill. Adam cried out a warning and frantically ripped his sword free from its sheath across his back, trying to maintain his grip with his knees and free hand. For the first time, he was grateful for the armor, its thick bulk suddenly becoming a bulwark against the sharp teeth and claws that landed just behind him. The animal snarled, and its breath was fetid and stank of carrion. Up close it looked more terrifying than before, a cruel cunning lighting its large reptilian eyes. It lunged at Adam's back, and its yellowish teeth snapped just short of his head, small forearm claws raking at the backplate of his armor.

Half turning, Adam shoved hard at the slasherclaw, and would have sent it tumbling if its feet hadn't been tangled in the netting covering their belongings and food. Arguably, however, that same netting had just saved his life, preventing the predator from latching on to his neck and bringing its wicked scything claws into play. Still, Adam knew the woven fibers wouldn't be strong enough to hold the beast captive forever. As it worked one foot free, Adam swung his sword as hard as he dared, biting deep into the slasherclaw's feathered shoulder and neck. The force of his blow toppled the beast backward, foot still caught and its body now being dragged alongside as Zoul struggled with the additional weight. Frantically, Adam hacked at the animal's foot as well as he could, twisting across his torso as he tried to maintain his grip on Zoul.

However it wasn't until Duin guided Zoul close to a rocky outcrop that the slasherclaw was torn away, the force of the impact also ripping a great section of the netting across Zoul's back. As a good portion of their provisions tumbled to the ground behind them, Adam glanced back and saw the rest of the slasherclaw pack stopping to investigate the oilskin and forest fruits, as well as starting to devour their injured pack member. The weak, it seemed, were akin to food for a slasherclaw.

"Go, go, go!" Adam hissed, and after a quick look behind, Duin guided Zoul up over the boulders, and only when they were far away did they urge Zoul to slow down, Adam reaching forward to soothe the trembling lizard.

"Can you see the others?" Adam asked.

"No," Duin said after a moment. "And I can't smell them either."

"Did you see which way they went?"

Duin shook his head. "Sorry, I was too busy trying not to get us eaten."

It took Adam a moment to realize his friend had made his last explanation without a trace of irony or sarcasm. "Given the circumstances, I'll forgive you," he said dryly. "It's a pity about our food, but on balance, I'm just as happy being alive."

"Let's climb a tree or something," Duin said, his eyes already searching the canopy above them. "Maybe we'll have more luck spotting them from a height."

"Sure," Adam said. "Let's just get the riding belt onto you."

"We can swap if you prefer?" Duin said.

"No, that's all right," Adam said as he unbuckled the riding belt and slipped it around Duin's waist. "I'm happy enough to stay where I am"—*and possibly humping your ass,* his brain added, and Adam would have laughed at the inappropriateness of it all had he not been so shaken.

Once they were properly strapped in, with Adam's hands resting on the thick belt around Duin's waist, they picked the tallest tree and urged Zoul into a slow walk. Even so, Adam found himself trembling as they rode up the tall gray trunk spotted with lichens and small epiphytic orchids. *Adrenaline,* he told himself, *it's just the adrenaline and the fight-or-flight response kicking in.*

"Are you all right?" Duin asked over his shoulder.

"Yeah," Adam said. "I'm fine—or I will be fine."

"Good," Duin said. "We just survived an attack without serious injury. Don't fall apart on me now."

"I won't," Adam promised. "How far up should we go?"

"Probably no more than this," Duin said with a grin. "Look over there."

Now at the level of the lower boughs, Adam peered through the maze of branches he had come to think of as the aerial highway. Off in the distance, in the direction Duin was pointing, was a small plume of woodsmoke.

"They made it," Adam said, breathing out a sigh of relief.

Duin grinned at him. "Let's catch up with them."

"Sounds like a plan," Adam said. "Let's hope none of them were injured."

"I'm sure they're fine," Duin said as he nudged Zoul across the boughs and back down to ground level.

They rode comfortably for several minutes, and it was perhaps because of their relief at being safe that they failed to notice the warning signs and blundered out of the undergrowth at the edge of the clearing into… the village in the clearing. It was made of longhouses, each raised high above the ground on tall wooden stilts. A few goats—the first mammals larger than the six-legged striped rabbits he had seen disappearing from their path over the past few sleeps—cropped at the short grasses. The most impressive of the longhouses stood in the center of the village, ringing a large open space. They were ornately carved, and the walls painted in pictorial art that reminded Adam of Aztec carvings he had seen in old back issues of *National Geographic* at his dentist's. The other houses lined a dirt track that wound its way to the edge of the clearing closest to the distant river.

Small four-armed children, naked or wearing scraps of leather and rag cloth, darted between the house stilts, throwing balls of woven grass or chasing after flitterfish and other small creatures—some of which were then clubbed to death. Others helped the women of the village weave baskets and prepare food. The women were dressed in skirts of grass and wore strings of beads around their necks, torsos largely bare to the sun. The men wore even less than the women, most standing tall, muscular, and naked other than a large gourd secured over their genitals with leather cord. A few wore scraps of Aergonite armor or leather wrappings, but they were more decorative than anything, the rainforest climate not being conducive to heavy clothing. Clothing would also have obscured the swirling tattoos that covered their bodies, many with regular raised patterning that didn't seem like natural skin. Their hair was a uniform black, worn in intricate braids or dreadlocks, and their four arms grasped a large variety of tools and assorted weaponry.

"Kanak…," Duin breathed.

The kanak at the edge of the village had stopped their activities and were staring at the mounted pair as if they couldn't believe their eyes. One of the warriors was the first to react and brandished a spear at them, bellowing a challenge.

"Run?" Adam suggested, but Duin had already turned Zoul and urged him into the reptilian equivalent of a gallop along the edge of the village. Unfortunately the kanak had missile weapons. The children threw whatever they could get their hands on—fruit, pebbles, and in some cases, goat dung. Dodging the smaller missiles was bad enough, but Adam was worried about the flurry of actual weaponry that was bound to come. Zoul's path took him to a cliff rising up on the far edge, and Duin guided the lizard straight for the rocky surface.

"Try following us now!" Duin crowed.

A spear hit the cliff beside them, the force of the throw driving it several inches into the crumbling rock surface, causing Adam to start. More spears followed, and then the air was filled with tiny darts that clattered all over the cliff face and bounced off Adam's armor. Except one. Wincing, Adam reached up and plucked the small feathered dart out of his neck. The top was splattered with blood—his blood—and a strange black smear. Absently he noted the feathers on the dart meant the kanak must have brought down a number of the slasherclaws. Then his vision began to blur.

"Oh shi—" he said as he blacked out, and his fingers slipped from Duin's waist.

Thankfully, he was unconscious before he hit the ground.

CHAPTER 9

ADAM AWOKE to pain. He was in a sunken wooden pen, hands bound behind his back and a thick rope tethering his left leg to a large protruding root. He was on his front, his face mashed into the dirt. As he raised his head, his gaze focused on a large black ant that reared backward, antennae waving as it considered whether or not to crawl up his nose. Despite the pain, Adam pushed himself into a sitting position away from the ant and its fellows, trying to put as much distance between his flesh and the insects' overly large mandibles. Closing his eyes against the spinning of the world, he tasted blood in his mouth and wished—for the first time, truly wished—to be sitting on his couch back home. Spitting onto the earthen floor, Adam huddled in the corner and looked around his prison.

The pen was made of thick bamboo and shaded by a tree with foliage so blue it was nearly black. Aside from the ants, and a hairy spider he hoped wasn't poisonous, Adam was the only inhabitant of the small cell. Experimentally he started to rise, only to fall back down as his left leg protested vociferously. Gingerly testing his calf, he concluded nothing was broken, but given his lack of firm medical training, it was more of a hope than an actual diagnosis. Taking further stock of his situation, Adam found he had been stripped of his armor, although he still retained the leather leggings Darius had insisted he wear, along with his hiking boots, and he immediately wished he had continued to keep a knife in his boot.

Wincing, Adam knee-walked over to the wall of the pen, which stood, palisade-like, in the ground. At one point, a mixture of mud and grass—at least, he hoped it was mud and grass—had been used to fill the gaps between the poles, but the twice-daily rainstorms had washed most of that away, allowing Adam to peer out into the village proper. It was much as he remembered outside, but the goats were huddled under the longhouses, and there were no villagers in sight. Frantically he searched for something sharp—a blade, arrowhead, stone, anything, but he came up empty and resorted to twisting his wrists to loosen the rope that bound his hands. Or he tried to. The air was hot and muggy, and soon sweat dripped down off his brow into his eyes, causing him to blink and curse, eventually closing his eyes entirely. It wasn't as though he could see what he was doing even with them open.

In the distance, thunder rolled and sounded again, much closer. Then the heavens opened and the rain descended as he had become used to… only this time he was not in the safety of a well-crafted shelter. Now he was out in the middle of it, and although the rain was warmer than that he might have experienced at home, it still leeched the warmth from his body after a while, reducing him to huddling by the tree for what little protection the leaves gave him. Hours later, when the rain finally eased, he was numb with cold and barely looked up as sounds of activity filtered through the fence.

Leaning against the wall, he nonetheless caught bleary, unfocused glimpses of the village outside, and he got his first lengthy look at the kanak. The one he saw carrying a baby clutched to her breast was obviously female and wore the grass skirt he had seen earlier and a string of brown, red, and ivory beads. After a moment, Adam was surprised to notice that the kanak females only had one pair of breasts on their upper pair of pectorals, the lower pair having nipples but no mammaries. The baby was clutching at her with three of its four hands, the last holding the long necklace of beads she wore around her neck. The children resumed their games, and a few of them scrambled up the side of the wall and stared down at Adam with their wide yellow-green eyes, whispering and giggling among themselves, some of them ducking back behind the fence if Adam met their gaze. A few of the more daring ones threw pieces of twig and small pebbles at him, and he wasn't able to stop himself from flinching, causing the children to squeal with excitement. Then one of the larger kanak warriors came to the fence and stared down into the pen, grinning when he saw Adam looking back at him. Turning away, he bellowed something in the guttural kanak tongue, and activity around the camp stilled, and then started again in a frenzy of noise and bustle.

Sometime later a gate at the far end of the pen opened and four males entered, two of them armed with long ceremonial-looking spears. Staring at the large, muscular warriors, the fight drained out of Adam. Logically, he knew his chances of not going with them were next to nothing. His left leg protested again when he was hauled to his feet, and again when large hands grabbed his neck and limbs, holding him near immobile. The rope around his foot was removed with a swift cut by an extremely sharp saber—looted no doubt from some unfortunate Aergonite scout—and Adam was hauled out of the pen with quite a bit of ceremony.

The path from the animal pen to the center of the village was lined with kanak of all shapes and ages, and a heavy drumbeat rang through the air as he was pushed along. With his limited vision, Adam was unable to see much, but could make out that the path between the longhouses led toward the central gathering spot he had seen earlier, with a large fire pit piled high with deadwood awaiting the touch of flame. Seated on a throne of wood and bone was a large kanak male wearing a richly woven loincloth and a gorget of bone and turquoise, as well as a headdress of red-and-brown slasherclaw feathers—and infuriatingly, Adam's battered watch glinting from a leather thong around his neck. Standing to his right was an older female leaning on a gnarled staff, the goat skull and beads of bone and turquoise indicating her rank as a shaman or medicine woman of some sort. She wore a red silk wrap over her shoulders and around her waist, and an ornate grass skirt that almost reached her feet. Her expression was proud and serene as she watched Adam's approach. Behind them was a carved totem, rising tall above the longhouses, carved and painted with horns, claws, teeth, and scales of yellow, and what looked like the suggestion of bat-like wings and fire breath. Before them was a low table, or rather, two table halves, which looked like they fitted together, barring a small circular hole in the middle. He stared at it for a good twenty seconds before he realized what he was looking at and started to struggle.

ONE YEAR, Adam had taken a bludge subject typically reserved for international students, which had included a camping trip to Uluru in the middle of the vast Australian desert. Basically a glorified tourist outing. Adam had ended up sharing a tent with a hunky American exchange student named Rusty—who had made it very clear he was interested in what Adam had hidden in his pants, and the feeling was definitely mutual. Rusty's father had, prior to retirement, been a businessman with some big multinational company, although exactly which one was escaping Adam's memory just now. They'd just been treated to an outback barbecue, with kangaroo and emu both on the menu, and then the tour guide had broken out the witchety grubs—long, roundish moth larvae that were a squidgy white and yellow, looking for all the world like someone had squished balls of chewed gum together and covered it with a thin, semitranslucent membrane.

Toasted over the fire they tasted a lot like peanuts, or at least, so it was said. However, the thought of eating grubs had almost proved too much for "processed hot dog and sliced cheese" Rusty.

"I can't believe you made me eat that," Rusty had said, turning over to face Adam when they crawled into their tents after a few beers.

"It's good for you," Adam said as he pulled on the clean T-shirt he was planning on sleeping in. "Besides, aren't strange foods like that meant to make you more virile?"

"Virile? You and your dictionary words. What's that one mean?"

"Extra horny," Adam said, grinning.

"Now, I don't need help with that. And the moment I don't want to barf thinking about what I just ate, I'll prove it to you."

"Is that so?" Adam said, lying down next to his friend.

"Well, I've heard it gets cold in the desert at night."

"I've heard that too."

"Don't you think the best way to keep warm is sharing body heat?" Rusty suggested. "Not with a T-shirt that reads 'Mister Clever'?"

Adam laughed, ripped off his shirt, and joined his friend, quite literally, in the sack.

Later, when they were drowsing off in their now zipped-together sleeping bags, Rusty snuggled up against Adam's back. "What's the weirdest thing you've ever eaten?" he asked suddenly.

"Raw snail. Dare in year ten," Adam said promptly. "You?"

"Witchety grub. Tonight."

"Oh come on, you don't have any stories?"

"Not personally, no," Rusty said. "My dad was fed monkey brains, though."

"What?"

"Monkey brains. Fresh from the monkey, apparently."

"Explain, please?"

"He was in… I think it was Egypt? Or somewhere in Africa, anyway, and he was served monkey. He said they had a table with a hole in the middle—they put the monkey's head through the hole and use a knife and…."

ADAM HAD wondered if Rusty, or possibly Rusty's father, made up that story, but now, staring at a table of two halves with a hole in the center, he was beginning to think he might be experiencing something similar firsthand—and from the wrong end.

A great roaring cheer rose as Adam struggled uselessly against his captors, only to be forced to his knees as the wooden table snapped around his neck, the rough wood pricking into his skin. From his new vantage point, he could see old bloodstains and knife marks on the table's surface, and he bucked his shoulders and tried to rise to his knees, struggling to dislodge at least one half of the table, even after heavy wooden pegs dropped through two sets of matching holes that lined up, one over the other, to lock the tables together.

"Fire! Fire!" Adam yelled, on the basis that someone was more likely to respond to a call of "fire" than a call for help. He got his feet under him and heaved up, but found the table was far too heavy for him to budge.

He didn't know how long he struggled, shouting and yelling as the sunlight steamed down in its unwavering blood red. But then the shaman began a chant, which slowly crescendoed with the boom of drums and the stamping of many kanak feet. A wicked-looking stone knife was placed on the table in front of him, and his eyes nearly crossed as it lay before his sweating face, the point facing directly toward him.

I'm going to die, his brain said quietly. *I'm going to die a horrible, painful death in some fucked-up jungle, and no one at home is going to know where I've gone. Fuck my life. Heck, fuck my death.*

Adrenaline had long worn off. He had been jerking to get free for so long, slamming his neck around the wood of the table so much that he was certain he had rubbed his flesh raw by now. As the chanting reached a fever pitch, the chief picked up the stone knife, then raised it above his head. The blade glinted dully in the sunlight, and Adam saw flecks of dried blood on the blade. With a desperate heave, Adam threw himself backward, and the table rocked, teetering slightly before settling back, trapping him firmly beneath it. With a toothy grin and what sounded very much like a chuckle, the chieftain brought the knife down hard.

Adam screamed.

The crowd laughed as the stone bit into the wood barely a centimeter from Adam's face. Grinning, the chief wrenched the knife out of the wood and raised it above his head again. Adam looked up in defeat. Maybe it wasn't this stroke. Maybe it wasn't the next, but eventually one of them would connect, cracking his skull open and hopefully ending his life before the kanak brought out their spoons, or whatever implements they ate with.

He didn't even register the bellow and the rush of footsteps as anything unusual until the chieftain toppled over, borne to the ground by some great furry snarling thing. The kanak fell heavily against the table, knocking it over and knocking out one of the pegs. Adam's neck twinged as he was thrown forward and to the side, his nose stopping mere inches from the ground. With a final push of desperation, Adam shouldered the table halves apart and pushed himself out through the resultant gap. Gritting his teeth against the pain of his sprained ankle and more than one complaining rib, he ran forward, dodging around the shaman, who tried to block his way. The drums had stopped, and a babble of panicked voices rose to fill the air in its absence.

In a few moments, the warriors would grasp their spears or bows and charge at him, and Adam darted instead for the only open space he could see—the area on the far side of the fire pit, where the two largest longhouses stood. Arms still bound, he bolted underneath the first house, finding the taller kanak had left him ample headroom. The uneven ground on the other side of the longhouse nearly threw him, and he grimaced as he jarred his ankle in a pothole. Then a hand closed around his arm, and he struggled weakly, barely mustering the energy to scream. Then the hand was steadying him and urging him onward, and a welcome voice growled in his ear.

"Run," Duin said, and Adam gasped at the reprieve, finding a burst of energy as they dodged around the totem. Duin helped steady him as they ran out into the forest beyond the village perimeter. The first sounds of pursuit picked up behind them, and Adam forced himself onward, his lungs burning, even as a crashing off to the side indicated he and his improbable rescuer were being flanked. He veered away, pushing into Duin's fur as he did, but their pursuers moved much faster than he and Duin could go, and Adam suspected someone had been lying in wait for them. And as a great six-limbed form plunged out of the foliage, with yellow-green eyes and a maw full of sharp teeth, Adam realized just how true that belief had been.

"Zoul!" he exclaimed, gasping with relief.

"Did you really think I'd have made it back without him?" Duin asked, plucking a knife from the saddle and cutting swiftly through the rope that still bound Adam's hands.

"Right now, I'm not really thinking," Adam said tersely, as Zoul raised his crest and chirruped happily at them, long forked tongue flickering out.

Duin sprang into the saddle. "Fair point," he said. "Well, don't just stand there," he added, holding out a hand. "Get on!"

Taking the proffered hand, Adam swung himself back into the familiar position and helped clip Duin into the saddle.

"Hold on tight," Duin said, urging Zoul into a fast run.

"Always," Adam rasped, his throat raw with exhaustion as Zoul zipped easily through the trees and headed toward a different cliff, down into a lower valley, rather than upward as they had tried before. This time they were able to vanish quickly into the canopy of the forest below, and the roars of the kanak faded behind them as Zoul headed off into the trees, and Adam found himself wiping his forehead in relief as well as a result of the thick humidity at the bottom of the valley.

"Thanks, Zoul," Adam said, reaching forward and patting his lizard on the midshoulder. "And thank you," he added, hugging Duin tightly and kissing the man's furry cheek. "Thank you so much."

Duin smiled. "You are welcome," he said. "It's nice to be able to repay this debt."

"What?"

"Well, if you had not intervened back at Aergon, I might not be here. You saved my life."

Adam hugged him again. "Consider us even," he said.

"Oh, and you might want this back," Duin said, handing Adam his watch, which he must have grabbed from the chieftain on his rush through the village.

"Oh, Duin, I love you, love you, love you, love you," Adam said, securing it back on his wrist. "I feel almost m-myself again."

"You should put a shirt on," Duin said as Zoul slowed to a walk.

"Do we have to?" Adam murmured, pressing his face into Duin's warm fur and rubbing suggestively at Duin's belly. "You r-run around naked all the time."

"I have fur to keep me warm," Duin said.

"I have you to k-keep me warm," Adam said with a giggle.

"Adam, are you all right?"

"Of c-course I am," Adam said, a little bewildered by the chattering of his teeth. "W-why wouldn't I be?"

"When did you last eat? Or drink?"

Adam shrugged. "The d-day before we r-ran?" he said.

Duin grunted. "All right, you can play with my fur later, if you promise to rest and eat something first," Duin said.

"All r-right," Adam said, snuggling deep into Duin's shoulder. "I do feel v-very tired."

CHAPTER 10

A DAM WAS only dimly aware of being held tightly as Zoul shifted from horizontal to vertical to horizontal again, and then being lifted onto a soft bed. Later, he felt the bed shift, and a warm, only slightly hairy body slipped in next to him and a blanket was drawn over them both. When he woke some time later, he was alone in the bed, which turned out to be made of dried grasses and a bracken-like fern. His head was still pounding, and all the aches and pains from his ordeal were clamoring to make themselves known. Almost before he could look around, Duin was there, handing him an opened coconut, and Adam gratefully drank the sweet liquid inside, his stomach clenching almost painfully at the first nourishment it had had in far too long.

"Not too fast," Duin said, placing a restraining hand on Adam's wrist when Adam would have taken another large gulp. "You won't keep it down if you take too much."

"Sorry," Adam said. "I'm just starving and…."

"I know," Duin said, squatting next to him and placing a damp cloth on Adam's forehead. "I know, but you need to take it slow."

Adam winced. "How bad is it?"

"Nothing too serious," Duin said. "You wrenched your ankle, pulled some muscles in your neck and chest, and you got pricked by a dart, but the sleeping poison should be out of your system by now."

"Sleeping poison?"

"From the root of the *Lapen* grass," Duin said. "It's the kanak's primary hunting strategy, when they want to bring down prey they can eat later. In small doses it's harmless."

"I don't recall any darts being used in the battle I was in when I first arrived," Adam said, his brow wrinkling under the cool cloth.

"Well, blowguns are fairly unwieldy," Duin said. "They are normally used in ambush and abandoned in favor of attacking with spears. After all, a kanak can usually overpower a person in close quarters much more efficiently than by slowly aiming a hollow piece of wood at a moving target."

"Then why did they use them on us?"

Duin grinned. "Because we were escaping."

"Ah, right. Good point," Adam said drowsily. "Wait, did you put that root stuff in the coconut?"

Duin's sly chuckle was both comforting and frustrating. "Of course I did," he said soothingly. "Rest, Adam. I'll be here when you wake up."

THE NEXT time Adam woke, the last of the jungle rain was dripping down into the ground below from a much more substantial roof of banana leaves and palm fronds—or at least, the plants he had started thinking of as banana plants and palm trees—and Duin was sitting by him neatly eating a flitterfish.

"Welcome back, Adam," Duin said.

"Thanks," Adam rasped. "Sorry," he said, and made a weak gesture at his throat.

"I know," Duin said, lifting a coconut and slicing the top off with a few whacks of a saber. "You have slept through two rains."

Adam drank, the cool liquid easing the dryness of his throat, and he sighed happily. "Sorry you've had to sit here for so long."

"It's no trouble," Duin said. "And I have kept myself busy."

"So I can see," Adam said, looking around the much more substantial walls of the tree house. "This almost looks like you're building a permanent structure."

Duin shrugged. "We are out of sight from the ground and hidden by leaves," he said. "There are no threats nearby, and you are going to need time to get well."

"Actually, I really need to go," Adam said.

"Need to go? Go… ah, right. We will have to take a ride down on Zoul for that."

A quick trip to ground level to the toilet trench and a wash in the jungle rain later, Adam was feeling much better, especially after Duin rubbed his injured leg with some of Xavier's medicinal oil that they still carried. Unfortunately, circumstances didn't lead to a repeat of their first session. Duin's hands were tender, true, but they were also swift and clinical.

"Duin," Adam asked as the man went to plug the bottle. "Have I done something wrong?"

"Of course not," Duin said. "It's at least as much my fault as yours that we blundered into the middle of that kanak village. I too was expecting to find our traveling companions up ahead."

"No, I meant with us," Adam said, gesturing at the distance between them. "Back at the cave, I thought we connected and... well...." His voice trailed off uncertainly. Perhaps airing relationship issues with the guide wasn't the smartest of ideas.

"I promised to aid the Princess Esmeralda on her quest," Duin said, averting his eyes.

"What does she have to do with anything?"

"I thought you and she... I mean...." Even in the dim light, Adam could see Duin was blushing.

"Me and.... What makes you think I have any interest in Esmeralda?"

"She's beautiful, powerful, nice... and she's a princess."

"She's also a woman," Adam said. "I'm not interested in women."

"You... truly?"

Adam shook his head. "I like men. And right now, I really like you."

"Oh."

"Unless... of course... well... if you don't, I mean...."

Duin reached out and gently took Adam's hand in his own. "I do. I just never thought... I mean, really, look at me."

"I do that every day," Adam said. "I mean, all the time."

"Adam... I'm a monster."

"Look at yourself now," Adam said. "No, really, right now."

Duin did, and perhaps for the first time, saw what Adam was seeing. The structure he had built was walled on one side by the tree trunk, and on another two by a wall of bamboo, leaving the last wall partially open to allow them to access the platform outside. Shielded as they were by the tree's branches, only a small amount of light filtered in from the doorway—certainly enough to see by, but inside the shelter Duin resembled nothing more than a fairly hirsute man. His arms and torso were dusted with a smattering of chestnut hair, which Adam would forever think of as fur, but his face still looked as human as Adam's, with only a soft accumulation of downy hair on his cheeks and chin. His hard muscles rippled visibly as he moved and inspected himself, and Adam felt himself harden with desire as Duin ran his hands over his own form.

"Not a monster," Adam said softly, reaching out to draw Duin toward him.

Slowly, carefully, Duin lowered himself to the makeshift bed, his body pressing up against Adam's. His fingers traced Adam's stubble-lined jaw, and then his lips met Adam's with a desperation and relief so sweet Adam thought he could taste it. Moaning into his lover's mouth, Adam brought his hands up to clasp Duin's head, and was surprised to find his thumbs encountering wetness on Duin's cheeks.

"Duin? You're crying."

Duin wrapped his arms around Adam and pulled him close. "I am not a monster," he whispered against Adam's mouth. "I'm not a monster."

Adam smiled. "No, you're not a monster," he said. "Never have been and never will be."

With trembling fingers, Duin helped Adam to remove his underpants, which was all he had worn since returning to their treetop abode. Adam gasped as Duin kissed the hollow of his neck and paused to lick and bite at his chest, while his hands returned to play with Adam's straining cock. They stroked him tenderly, and Adam arched into Duin's grip as Duin's mouth trailed over his abdomen and down one leg to his right thigh, ignoring Adam's leaking cockhead. Adam felt his lover alternatively kiss and bite at the tender flesh that joined his leg to his groin, and he moaned as a hot tongue reached out and swiped a pearl of precum from the very tip of him.

"I-I thought you said you hadn't done this before," he said as he ran his hands over Duin's head and stroked the back of his neck encouragingly.

"I haven't really," Duin said. "But I worked in the baths. I know what's meant to happen."

"You do? Oh, you do…." Adam gasped as Duin's mouth enveloped him, one hand tugging the foreskin back from Adam's cockhead and allowing Duin's lips and tongue to tease the sensitive ridge of his glans. Then the hot, delightful wetness was sliding lower and lower, and then… Duin was pulling off him, coughing and spluttering.

"I don't think that was supposed to happen," he said when he had regained his composure.

Adam laughed. "It's not unheard of," he said. "Gag reflex."

Duin groaned and rubbed his head against Adam's thigh. "I wanted to be good at that."

Adam smiled and rolled them over. "Practice, my impatient friend, practice."

Shifting Duin back up onto the mattress, Adam licked and nibbled his way down Duin's body, using just the very tips of his fingers to brush over his skin, tugging teasingly at Duin's body hair as he drifted his hands over Duin's hard cock, allowing Duin to feel the heat of his hand but not his touch. Then he moved his fingers lower, teasing the heavy sack of Duin's testicles before slowly rubbing lower and lower, his fingers already slick with the sweat from Duin's body. Pushing up at the base of Duin's cock, Adam lowered his head to his lover's cock, tasting the salty-sweet flavor he remembered from their first encounter and using his tongue to seek out more of the clear fluid. This time it was his turn to nearly gag as Duin groaned and thrust into Adam's mouth, and Adam was forced to use his free hand to hold his hips in place.

"Oh yes…." Duin groaned. "Adam, that feels so good."

Adam pulled off Duin's cock with a smack. "It tastes really good too."

Diving back down, Adam held Duin firmly by the root and swallowed, feeling Duin's thickness invade his throat before pulling back to the ever growing symphony of Duin's whimpering. Smiling, he reached up with his right hand and inserted three fingers into Duin's mouth. Duin responded like a starved beast, sucking eagerly and coating Adam's fingers with saliva, which Adam transferred to the tight opening of Duin's ass.

"Adam… are you going to…?"

"Just relax," Adam whispered softly as one digit slowly entered the hot, tight space.

"How can I relax when you're—oh Selune, that feels good."

"Just enjoy it," Adam said, before sliding his lips back down over Duin's hefty prick, using his tongue to tease its head.

Withdrawing slowly, Adam soon had two fingers worked into his lover, and crooked his fingers to rub at the sensitive spot inside that always made him go wild.

Duin writhed on the makeshift bed, and only the fact that Adam was waiting for this exact response allowed him to ride the wave of Duin's reaction as Duin arched up, trying to press into Adam's mouth and back against his fingers at the same time, his hands clutching at Adam's hair.

"What—what was that?" he asked.

"This?" Adam asked, rubbing at Duin's prostate again, getting another drool of cock-honey as a reward.

"Mmmmm-hmmm…." Duin almost purred, one hand reaching back to spread his asscheeks wider for Adam's fingers.

"The part that makes it feel really good when another man is in you," Adam replied, his own cock hardening as he pictured that very act.

"Gods, I wish I had done this sooner." Duin sighed. "I didn't know it would feel so…." He shuddered as Adam pumped his cock slowly in time with the slow circling of his fingers inside. "So… so good. Adam, will you… please… enter me?"

Adam paused. "Duin, I'd really like to, but… we don't know that it's safe."

"Safe?"

"We could… catch something."

Duin's bark of laughter was short and sharp. "Adam, my condition is not something you can catch. I know there's stories of people being bit and—"

"No," Adam interrupted. "I meant there are diseases that you can catch sexually if you're not protected."

"You didn't worry about this last time," Duin accused.

Adam leaned up and kissed Duin softly on the lips. "What we did wasn't that risky," he said. "But me in you, or you in me, is potentially dangerous."

"You won't catch anything, then," Duin said impatiently. "You'll be the first person who… I've ever… you know what I mean."

Adam kissed him again. "I know, lover, but how do you know I don't have something?"

Duin growled and hauled Adam's face down. "If my choices are trusting you and having you inside me or not having you at all, I will take my chances."

"And how do you think I'd feel if I gave you something?"

Duin snorted. "Do you have anything that I don't want to get?"

"I don't know," Adam said. "I don't think so, but you can never be completely sure. If we were back home, I could… wait…."

"What?"

"Don't go anywhere," Adam said, gently withdrawing his hands and heading back over to his battered but still intact gym bag. He fished into the side pockets and pulled out part of his stash from the free condom packs he picked up at just about every gay festival he attended, thoughtfully individually ziplocked with a small packet of water-based lube.

"Back home we have these," Adam said triumphantly, showing Duin the clear packet.

"Shiny squares?" Duin asked quizzically.

"Protection," Adam said, lying back down next to Duin and kissing his lover passionately. "And more importantly, it means that yes, I can and will make sweet, sweet love to you, my furry lover."

Duin moaned into Adam's mouth and whimpered as Adam slid into position between his legs, watching with slightly unfocused eyes as Adam ripped open the foil packet with his teeth and rolled the latex condom down over his shaft, before tearing open the lube and applying it liberally to both his cock and Duin's opening.

"Ooh, that's cold," Duin moaned as Adam slid first one, then two fingers inside him.

"Is it?" Adam murmured, bringing his hard member to rest in the crease of Duin's ass. "Let me warm it up for you."

The first push was gentle, and Duin yelped into Adam's kiss when the head of Adam's cock popped inside.

"Scales!" Duin swore. "That feels so much bigger than I thought it would."

"Do you want me to stop?"

"No, just… go slowly."

"Okay," Adam murmured, kissing Duin's forehead. "Just let me know if you want me to stop."

He slid in deeper, slowly, and felt Duin's cock stiffen between them when his cockhead rubbed against the right spot. With a grin, he pulled out a little before sliding all the way in, relishing the clench of Duin's muscles around him as he slowly dove into his lover's body.

"Oh yes," Duin groaned, grabbing Adam's thighs and pulling him in so Adam was buried to the hilt. "That's so nice."

Cradling his lover in his arms, Adam moved his hips slowly, relishing the way Duin's body moved with him, twining together in a jumble of limbs and hot, sweet kisses. He kissed Duin's collarbone, up his neck and back down along his jawline, before losing himself in Duin's lips, all the while moving, thrusting, and finally, climaxing with a cry that he muffled in the hollow of Duin's neck. As his hips slammed against Duin's ass, he felt Duin spasm, and the wetness of his creamy load filled the space between their bodies.

"I don't want to move," Adam said, panting slightly as he lay atop his lover's recumbent form.

"Then don't move," Duin mumbled, kissing the side of Adam's head and wrapping long arms around Adam's body.

"I'm not too heavy for you?" Adam asked.

"Not that I noticed," Duin said. "Although I sort of think you're… um… oh… yes… sliding out."

Adam chuckled. "Feels different, huh?"

"Ah, yes, I would say it does," Duin said as he watched Adam peel off the condom. "What do you do with that now?" he asked.

Adam paused, looking at the semen-filled rubber. "At home we usually throw them away."

"A material that stretches but does not burst like that and you throw it away? Surely it can be cleaned and reused?"

Adam stared at the wrinkled and very unsexy bundle he held in his hands. "I'm sure it could be," he said reluctantly. "I think they were originally reusable, but apparently the more you use them, the greater the chance of them breaking, which isn't very safe, so we don't reuse them back home."

Duin sighed. "All right, but it should be buried like everything else—we don't want to leave clues to our whereabouts."

"Yes, sir," Adam said with a grin. "At least it's biodegradable—eventually."

"What?"

Adam smiled. "It will rot eventually," he said. "On the other hand, these won't," he added as he rolled to the side of the mattress and picked up the foil packet that the condom came in and the empty—but mildly sticky, lube packet. "I guess I'll keep them with me on the off chance that I'm ever able to return home and dispose of them properly."

Adam could feel Duin's eyes upon him as he rose and moved over to his gym bag once more, grabbed one of the plastic bags he used to keep his dirty laundry in, and dropped the litter inside before tucking it all away in a pocket. He turned to see Duin lying on his side, supporting his head with one hand.

"Is that what you'd want to do?" Duin asked. "Go home?"

Adam stilled. "Eventually, yes," he said. "I don't belong here."

"So this… you here with me now… what is it exactly?"

Sighing, Adam came back to bed and snuggled up next to his lover, holding Duin close enough that their foreheads touched. "You and me right now is you and me here, right now," he said. "I don't know what tomorrow is going to bring. I don't know if I'm ever going to be able to get home, or if you or I will die before that becomes an option, but to not be with you because I'm afraid of what the future might or might not be seems a bit silly, don't you think?"

Duin smiled weakly. "I don't know, Adam. Now I feel that if I don't lose you to Esmeralda, I will lose you when you return home."

"Assuming she's still alive and there's a way for me to get home," Adam said.

"If I hope her dead, I have failed her, and if I wish there is no way for you to return, I fail you," Duin said. "But part of me wishes I could wish both. What does that make me?"

Adam smiled and kissed his lover's cheek. "Human," he said simply. "It makes you very, very human. Anyway, you're not going to lose me to any woman, and assuming there's a way back, you could always, you know, come with me."

"Me?" Duin said. "Go with you?"

"Sure," Adam said. "There's a moon in my world," he added. "And as far as I know, no real magic, or curses, or anything of the sort. You'd be you, just you. No more Duin the Wolfman."

"Wolfman?"

"Sorry, is that rude?" Adam asked. "I just can't help thinking that you're a bit like a wolfman. A werewolf or something."

"What's a werewolf?"

"A person who, under the light of the full moon, can transform or must transform into a wolf—a hairy creature with a muzzle and a tail and that hunts in packs and scares the living bejeezus out of people," Adam said. "Of course, according to popular legend, the werewolf often has an in-between form that is really powerful where they stand on two feet like a man but have the fur, head, and claws of a wolf—and often the tail as well. TV writers really like that one."

"I see," Duin said. "What else do these recorded theater stories say?"

"That if you're bitten by a werewolf, you can become a werewolf, like you mentioned earlier," Adam said. "And that they can only be killed by silver and cured by belladonna, which is poisonous to people, so I don't want to think about how many people must have died trying to cure lunacy."

"We have much the same legend here," Duin said. "Although I have never heard of 'wolves.' I am told that once this curse was a gift of the moon goddess, Selune, and of course we had three forms, the man, the *haerunwoln*, and that which was in-between the two."

"Haerun… what?"

"Haerunwoln," Duin said. "The sacred forest tiger that my form imitates. They're very rarely seen now, but if we come across one, I'll introduce you."

"You can speak to them?"

"Not really, but we usually understand each other, in a fashion," Duin said. "I am told, of course, that only silver could slay a haerunwoln or chosen of Selune, but I have not wished to put that to the test."

Adam hugged him close. "And I for one am very glad you have not. I like having you here, even if I don't exactly know…." Adam sighed and closed his eyes, breathing in the reassuring scent of Duin, the funk of sex, and the lingering smells of crushed bracken.

Duin sighed. "I do not really know what the future will bring either."

"So let's not worry too much yet, then," Adam said. "We have each other, and let's enjoy it while we do."

CHAPTER 11

ADAM AND Duin stayed in their makeshift love nest for a few more sleeps than strictly necessary for recuperation, but eventually they decided they should press on toward Blackwater. Duin wasn't certain if he had given Darius clear enough directions on how to get there—or even if the man yet lived—but both he and Adam agreed their chances of survival would be higher if they could find the rest of their little group. Returning to Earth, or even the relative safety of the Aergonite caverns, would, after all, be nearly impossible without Esmeralda's patronage, and Adam had to hope the princess had survived.

Finally, with their packs replenished through judicious foraging and their belongings mended as best they could manage, Adam and Duin set out again, heading back toward the marsh that they hoped would be Blackwater. For once, the jungle they traveled through was benign, and they passed without incident, their biggest worry being avoiding the occasional giant centipede or spiderweb. More than once, though, they avoided the spiderweb only to hunt down the spider with a spear of sharpened bamboo. The hunting process itself was one that Adam soon grew proficient at, although the first time he had to kill for his supper was not one he relished.

"You'd have thought this was your first hunt," Duin noted when Adam scrambled to the ground, dry retching into the grass.

"It is," Adam said.

"Oh. Sorry."

Their conversations in that time of relative peace were light, and they both refrained from discussing anything of major significance, wary of invoking a future neither of them could be certain of. Similarly, neither offered much insight into their pasts. For his part, Adam could certainly understand Duin not wishing to dwell on his period of exile from Aergon, and Adam himself lacked the words to explain his home to Duin in any way that would make sense. After a brief attempt to explain the concept of electricity as "tame lightning," he had given up and instead mined Duin's knowledge of how to survive in the landscape they passed through.

Adam also spent a fair amount of time practicing his swordplay, for although he had lost his favored spring-steel long sword during their flight from the kanak village, he still had a heavier broadsword and the curved Aergonite sword Darius had been teaching him to wield. His foam swords had been lost to the slasherclaws, and he hoped they'd tried to eat them. He wasn't sure what happened when a dinosaur tried to eat fiberglass, but he hoped it wasn't good.

The more Adam thought about everything that had happened, though, the stranger the dragon's persistent attacks on the traveling group had been. While he could certainly appreciate the possibility of it coming across them at random and attacking opportunistically, for it to have gone ahead to set up such a carefully thought-out ambush made Adam uneasy. How could it have known which direction they were heading when they themselves barely knew? Was the dragon truly so clever as to be able to pluck such knowledge directly from Duin's mind? And how was it that they had escaped without it attempting to use its brain-crippling thought magic against them?

At camp that night, Adam found himself staring moodily at the coals of their fire, glowing red against the red of the sun, worrying the questions back and forth in his mind.

"Are you all right?" Duin asked. "You've been very quiet today."

"I'm fine," Adam said. "Thinking is all."

"They must be some very deep thoughts," Duin said. "I think the water beetle has been well and truly cooked."

Adam stared at the oversized beetle leg he was holding over the fire and smiled sheepishly, leaning over to kiss Duin's cheek. "Sorry," he said. "I'm just worrying needlessly."

They encountered the river again that day, running much wider and shallower here than when they had set off on their raft, and while it had proved much too shallow for the cokudrillos, it was still full of silver scarabs. It was also inhabited by water beetles nearly as large as Adam himself. Some of them were herbivores, but Adam saw others feasting on the scarabs. The beetles had proved remarkably easy to catch and subdue, and had a vaguely peppery taste, especially when eaten with a purplish watercress that Duin had indicated as being safe—and rather tasty.

"I think I'm full," Adam said. "But I hate to waste all this food."

Duin chuckled. "I know what you mean. I'm about full up to here," he said, indicating his throat level. "And even Zoul probably couldn't manage another bite."

On the far side of the fire, the lizard hissed indignantly before haughtily taking a tiny bite out of the remains of the second water beetle they had brought down after it had shown slightly too much interest in their first hunt.

"Don't be a greedy guts, Zoul," Adam admonished. "I know you'll eat even if you're not hungry, but then you could get ill, and where would you be, then? Neither Duin or I know much about lizard illnesses."

Zoul ignored him and pulled off another bite.

"It always amazes me the personality that lizard has," Adam said. "And his vocalizations. I never thought I'd hear a lizard chirp."

"What sound is he meant to make, then?" Duin asked.

"I don't know," Adam said. "I've never really thought about it, but I've always associated chirping with birds."

"The small feathered slasherclaws you have in your land that fly like flitterfish?" Duin asked.

"Yeah," Adam said uncomfortably. The entire notion sounded really silly when Duin said it like that. Sometimes he felt as though Duin was just humoring his crazy insistence of being from another world with condoms, cars, birds, and a day-and-night cycle. Sometimes he wondered if he wasn't just deluded. Of course, then he stared at his gym bag for a while until he felt better.

Then Duin was rising carefully to his feet, his eyes glued on a clump of tangled shrubs on the other side of their camp. "Stay very still, Adam. Don't frighten her."

Adam froze, remembering the giant crablike creature Duin had pulled from the waters at his feet all those sleeps ago. "Is it... is she dangerous?"

"Probably not," Duin said slowly. "But she will run if she thinks you'll attack her."

Swiveling only his eyes, Adam looked into the shadows where Duin was crouched, his hands held carefully in the air before him. Slowly, and displaying great reluctance, a lean four-legged animal crept into the light.

It looked like a short-furred wolf, with the build of a greyhound and fur to match Duin's own. Like Duin, it had dark brown stripes over its back, and its tail was long and thin, tapering to a sleekly furred point. Making a comforting crooning noise, Duin slowly reached down and picked up an uneaten section of the beetle and held it out to the creature. Never taking her eyes off them, the animal reached forward and then with a sudden lunge, grabbed the meat and retreated back to the edge of the shrubbery's gloom until she was just a silhouette and a pair of glowing eyes. Then, to Adam's amazement, there was a soft chorus of mewling, and a number of pups crept out to gnaw at the carcass.

Carefully, Duin backed away, pushing the remainder of the beetle over toward the mother and pups.

"That's a *haerunwoln*," he said softly, coming back and wrapping an arm around Adam's shoulders.

Adam, however, was still staring at the almost mythical creature he had only ever seen in grainy black-and-white footage padding around a concrete cage, or in art like on the label of his favorite beer. Okay, there was that one time it was fighting monkeys on the television, but that had been an ad for said beer and probably didn't count. "That is what your other form is?" he breathed.

"Yes," Duin said.

Adam turned and buried his face in Duin's shoulder and held him tight. "Thank you," he said.

"My… pleasure," Duin said uncertainly. "I did not know it meant so much to you."

"I didn't either," Adam said, looking up into Duin's eyes. "Do you know what we call them where I come from?" he asked.

"What?"

"Thylacine," Adam said. "And as far as we know, there's none left."

"None left?" Duin asked. "What do you mean, 'none left'?"

"I mean, to the best of our knowledge, every last thylacine in the world is dead."

"Dead," Duin echoed hollowly.

"Yeah," Adam said softly. "For nearly a hundred years, I think. I've always wished I could see one alive, but well… I never thought it would be possible."

Duin smiled. "Well, I'm glad I was able to show you one, then."

Adam sighed. "Me too. Do you think she'd let me touch her?"

"Probably not," Duin said, shaking his head. "Most haerunwoln won't come near humans at the best of times. Aergonites will kill them on sight for their fur, although supposedly they started hunting them in retribution for Selune abandoning our skies."

"Some things never change," Adam muttered.

Slowly, Adam reached out to his gym bag and pulled out his phone. The thylacine glanced up at the new light source but went back to her food as Adam brought up his camera and started recording some video, Duin watching the small glass screen in amazement. After a few minutes, Adam stopped the video, and he and Duin sat there long after the coals of their fire had died down to ash, just watching the thylacine and her pups. Then with a long look in their direction, the mother led the way off into the forest, her litter of three following her into the undergrowth. As soon as he could no longer see them, Adam was over at the bushes they had been hiding in, combing through the litter carefully.

"What are you doing?" Duin asked.

"Looking for fur," Adam muttered, pulling bits of it off twigs and leaves where it had snagged.

"Why? Do you really need that to remember?"

Adam shook his head. "No, but if I do get home… people in my world have been trying to bring thylacine back—cloning them. If I can bring them some intact DNA from a real living thylacine…." Adam stopped and looked up at Duin, his eyes shining. "Okay, bottom line, we could have them in our forests again."

"And fur will help you do that?"

Adam shrugged. "Maybe. It couldn't hurt. I just need something to carry it back in so we won't lose it."

Duin laughed. "I told you we should have kept that… what did you call it? A condom?"

Adam shook his head and then paused. He still had the little ziplock bag the condom had been packaged in. "Duin, you're a genius," he said, springing to his feet and kissing his very surprised lover on the muzzle. It took almost no time to grab the bag, and soon the precious fur was safely stowed away.

"What is that?" Duin asked finally, pointing at the phone Adam still clutched in his left hand.

"My mobile phone," Adam said. "It doesn't work here, but it normally lets me talk to people very far away."

"But you were not talking to anyone else just now."

"Um… it's also a camera," Adam said. "It can take—record—both still and moving pictures for… memories. Keepsakes."

"Like your tee-vee?"

"I guess," Adam said. "Just… I use it for personal records."

"You recorded her so you could remember the experience later?" Adam nodded.

"So you have other pictures and moving pictures on your… phone?"

"I do, yes," Adam said.

"Can I see them?"

"Sure," Adam said. "Just… not for too long. I can't charge the battery here, so I've been trying not to use it."

It was easier to explain his life at home with the help of his phone, even if most of his apps didn't work. Adam ended up turning on flight mode to help the battery along, and the built-in clock told him it took two hours to go through the photos of the last several years of his life.

"We should stop," Duin said, squeezing Adam's hand.

"It's all right," Adam said, swallowing hard. It was a simple photo of his birthday party, with his mum and dad having a barbecue in the backyard of their suburban home.

"I didn't mean to upset you."

"You didn't. I just… miss them. And I don't know if I'll ever see them again."

"I know," Duin said, turning Adam's hand over and kissing his palm. "We are in the middle of the forest, and I think we should wait until we are somewhere safer before looking through the rest."

Adam nodded and turned his phone off again before allowing Duin to lead him back to their raised camp to sleep.

THEY REACHED the boundary between the swamp and the forest a few sleeps later, and Adam was surprised to find it really was a boundary. Rainforest turned into a series of overgrown glades and water meadows, with long, tough—and in some cases serrated—grasses reaching up above Adam's head. This in turn gave way to areas of marsh, swamp, and slowly moving water. Duin's muzzle extended until it was almost a canine-like snout as he stepped into the full brightness of the reddish sun, and his ears twitched as they took in sounds well above what Adam could hear himself.

"Well, here we are," Duin said. "I hope this is the right place."

"Is there a keep here?"

"There are ruins everywhere," Duin said. "But I think there is one here too."

"You think?"

"I don't normally come here," Duin protested. "The place is full of snakes—and mostly poisonous ones at that."

"Great," Adam muttered. "And how about cokudrillos?"

"Occasionally," Duin said. "But usually the bigger ones don't venture too far out of the deep water."

"So if we stay on dry land, we should be safe?" Adam asked.

"Yes," Duin said. "But that in itself can pose a problem."

Before they left the edges of forest, Duin had them cut some stout poles of bamboo, and now, dismounting from Zoul's back, he probed at the ground before them, and in short order found a spot where the pole disappeared down below the surface.

"What the fuck?" Adam swore.

"Most of this isn't solid," Duin explained. "The plants grow on mounds of other plants, and sometimes there's enough dirt for trees to grow on floating islands of... stuff. We'll need to walk ahead and lead Zoul."

Adam stared down at the solid-looking ground that wasn't. "That's probably a good idea."

It was amazing how stressful entering the swamp was after having become used to the rainforest. Gone was the protective embrace of the jungle canopy, and instead Adam found he could see for vast distances in all directions, the flat emptiness broken here and there by small stands of trees growing on what must have presumably been higher ground. Higher actual ground. Progress was slow as they inched their way forward step by cautious step, and they had to stop more than once to dry off when Adam missed his footing and fell into the muck. Plunging through the mat of vegetation into the fetid black water below was perhaps the most disorienting thing Adam had ever experienced. The water stung his eyes, and the roots grasped at his limbs, the vegetation and dirt preventing him from reaching the surface, even as he exhaled the precious air from his lungs. Then a hand reached down, grabbed the back of his shirt, and pulled him up enough so he could breathe. Blinking, he saw Duin's furrowed brow as his lover helped him tear away the roots and decaying matter that impeded his progress.

"Thanks," Adam gasped when he had finished coughing and spluttering. "Let's keep going."

Duin shook his head. "No, we have to get you dry. The last thing you want is to be wandering around here in wet clothing and shoes."

"Why not?"

"Your feet will rot," Duin said simply.

Adam paused and stared at him. "How do you know that? You don't wear shoes."

"I used to," Duin said. "So did the others who were exiled with me."

"Others?" Adam said. "What happened to them?"

"Not here," Duin said shortly.

"Right," Adam said. Suddenly he didn't feel like continuing the conversation.

They struggled on until they found a stand of trees and constructed a small sleeping platform high enough to get them away from the insects that scuttled over the ground, and a fire to dry out Adam's feet and boots. Unfortunately, the clouds of mosquitoes that inhabited the swamps followed them everywhere incessantly. Smoke kept them at bay for some time, but the moment Adam stepped outside of the smoke column, they attacked with a vengeance. Adam spent a fair amount of time slapping ineffectively at tiny bodies. Duin, being furred, had less of a problem, and simply rolled himself in some thick mud to keep them off, and Adam was tempted to follow suit, but he was worried about gangrene. Once the insides of Adam's boots were dry, they went hunting, eventually finding a small cokudrillo in a shallow pool. With the ease of practice, Adam distracted it until Duin could jump onto its back, hold its jaw down with his bamboo pole, and dispatch it via a blade to the brain, then jumping clear as it spasmed in the throes of death, tail and all six flippers thrashing madly and throwing up clouds of silt.

They had then cooked and eaten cokudrillo tail steaks, and Adam had been able to use the fat from the creature as a form of insect repellent. It was amazing that it worked, but it did. Zoul had then crunched through the rest of the carcass, looking very pleased with himself. Adam wasn't entirely happy with the smell of the raw fat, but given the options, he was happy not to be constantly scratching at his skin. Of course, the biggest problem Adam found was that the cycle of rainfall he'd become used to in the forest didn't happen out on the bog. There was certainly some rain, but overhead the clouds blew west toward the distant mountains without a drop of water falling, and as such, the sky never became so dark that he felt comfortable sleeping. He tossed and turned on their sleeping platform next to Duin, trying to catch a few winks, but for the most part, sleep eluded him, and he grew increasingly irritable as they continued onward through the marsh.

It was some sleeps later that they finally came to a larger expanse of solid ground, and Adam caught his first glimpse of the ivy-choked keep, only about half of which was still standing, the rest long having crumbled in upon itself, looking as if it had been demolished just as told in the tale, by a great beast falling into it and disappearing beneath the ground. It was with some relief that Adam stepped onto the first large expanse of truly solid ground they had traversed in a long time.

"Is this it?" Adam asked.

"I don't know," Duin said. "It's the only ruined keep that I know of in this swamp, but I don't even know if it's the right swamp."

"But is it a peat swamp?" Adam asked.

"Dig into the turf and see?"

Adam did as Duin suggested and soon hit a solid brown mass of compressed vegetation that had a rich, earthy smell to it and a crumbly texture.

"I sometimes come here to get fuel for fire," Duin said. "I keep a store of it hidden in the territory where I usually live."

"And where's that?" Adam asked, lifting a sizable chunk to take with them.

"Off toward the north light," Duin said, gesturing vaguely east. "Many sleeps into the forest."

"What were you doing all the way out at Aergon?" Adam asked.

"Foraging," Duin said promptly. Too promptly. At Adam's sidelong glance, he eventually added a further explanation. "I was… bored. And sometimes I go back to see if they've thrown someone else out."

"Xavier said it happens regularly."

"Yes," Duin said. "But I don't know when, and sometimes the children… not everyone is suited to life on the surface."

"I see," Adam said. The pained look on Duin's face made him change the subject. "Let's find some shelter and then water."

Surprisingly, or possibly not surprisingly, clean water had been the most difficult thing to find in the marsh. Adam and Duin had taken to boiling their water each time they made camp, but after the constant rain in the forest providing a near endless supply of clean water, Adam felt as if he had never been dirtier, smellier, or more dehydrated. When they had some dry land, they dug into the ground to allow the sand to filter the water, but that had provided mere mouthfuls at best. There had also been fewer trees with boughs full of succulent fruit to bite into, and all in all, Adam found himself yearning for the convenience of the rainforest.

"Do you think they're here?" Duin asked as they trudged up toward the still standing battlements.

"I don't know," Adam said. "You'd think if they were we'd have seen some evidence of their passing by now."

"Maybe we got here first," Duin suggested.

"Possibly," Adam said. "You're the one with the directions in his head. Do we wait and hope, then?"

"For a while," Duin said. "I'm not sure this will be the safest place to stay if the dragon does patrol here."

They entered the keep by clambering across the fallen outer wall, where the big blocks of stone that had been used to construct the keep had toppled into the once-filled moat, which was now dry and choked with grass. The drawbridge of the keep had probably been lowered, but now it was just a few rusted chains hanging from an empty portal, the planks long having rotted through. Adam fancied he could see lengths of the twisted metal that had once held the planks of the drawbridge together lying among the grass. They found themselves in the middle of an overgrown courtyard, with the main buildings of the keep mostly intact against the far wall. The courtyard itself had once been paved with flagstones, but a large section of it had collapsed into the ground, with a massive triangular-shaped section of it a gaping hole, mostly filled in by the resulting rubble, fallen wall blocks, and the occasional twisted tree that thrust its way out of the debris.

Unlocking the main doors of the keep proved unnecessary, as they had already been cracked open. They did have to strain to push it open wide enough for Zoul to get through, as the hinges had long ago rusted stiff. The shriek as the hinges gave was worthy of a horror film, and Adam and Duin were overwhelmed by the smell of guano, sitting in large reddish brown mountains that covered the floor of the once great hall. They ducked back outside as the noise echoed around the hall, rousing the bats that roosted far above in the ceiling, some of which came swooping out the door in their bid to escape. As the shrieking mass of leathery wings fled into the sky, Adam wondered if the bats in this strange land even used sonar, given that there was always light for them to see by.

When the shrieking and flapping ceased and the last stragglers exited the lair, or decided the strange sounds weren't worth leaving the roost for, Adam and Duin tiptoed inside, only to cause another flurry of egress as they brandished their makeshift torches of sap-laden tree root to light their way. This time, they ducked inside rather than out, shielding their heads from the bats that scurried overhead. Zoul, for his part, was happy to grab the occasional unwary bat that came too close to his toothy maw. The flames lit up the vaulting of the great room for the first time since people had fled to the dubious safety of the Aergonite caverns, and Adam marveled at the stonework and the tall ceiling, as well as the great fireplaces along one wall that would have warmed the room with a cheery heat. On the other side, there still remained stained traces of frescoes painted into the walls and the tattered, moth-eaten remains of what must have been richly embroidered tapestries.

"This place is amazing," Adam said, his voice only slightly muffled by the rag he had thrown over his mouth in an attempt to filter out the worst of the bat smell. "And it's so long. Easily as long as a footy field."

"A what?"

"Never mind," Adam said, treading carefully around the edge of the room to the other long wall to stare at the painted frescoes. "I wish I knew what these pictures were—they have to mean something."

"It's the Leaving of Selune," Duin said, pointing at the central image where the sky changed suddenly to red from blue, and a stylized depiction of dragons sweeping down from the sun on wings of gold and peasants fleeing from their fields to the sanctuary of the keep's walls.

"And look before it," Adam said, moving toward the left. "See, I told you."

"What's that?" Duin asked.

"Day," Adam said, pointing to the sun that moved across the sky in the idyllic pastoral scenes of hunting, jousting, and medieval-like farming. "And night," he added, indicating another scene that showed stars in the night sky as flocks slept peacefully in the field.

Adam fumbled to pull his phone out of his bag to take some pictures. No one at home would believe this. Assuming he got home. He would get home. Pushing aside the cycle of thinking that would send him into a tailspin, he focused instead on Duin, who was regarding the images with a strange expression on his face.

"Penny for your thoughts?" Adam asked.

"Hmm?"

"What are you thinking?"

"Oh. I just… I always thought it was made-up," Duin said, staring at the image of night. "Look, there's a haerunwoln—thylacine—in the moon."

Adam raised his torch to light the large painted globe, easily ten or twelve feet in the air above them. "So there is; look, it's curled up and sleeping on its forepaws."

They shared a smile and walked back along the wall, looking at scenes of a man, who must have been Fernando, forging a sword and doing something magical in an arcane-looking laboratory with strange-colored flames and liquids in misshapen glassware. Then the largest panel showed him confronting a great dragon, standing dramatically on the edge of the keep wall as the dragon reared before him, great fangs gleaming and a curl of flame threatening to burn the prince to a crisp. The last panel was… empty, although flecks of color in the mortar of the plain wall suggested a scene of feasting and revelry.

"They never finished," Adam said.

"Well, if Prince Fernando died fighting Khaled and they had to leave, they wouldn't have."

"But they finished the previous panel?"

Duin shrugged. "You've met some Aergonites. Maybe they figured they couldn't lose and finished it in advance."

"Or hoped they wouldn't lose," Adam said softly. "Living on hope. Seems like a thing here."

"Yes," Duin said with a sigh. "It must be nice. I wish the moon was still around."

"Come on," Adam said, ducking again as a bat winged its way just over his head. "Let's go see what the rest of the place is like."

By unspoken agreement, they went upstairs rather than down, forcing open the doors at the top of the great stone stairs, and found the interior of the castle had withstood the elements much better than the great hall. The windows had remained protected by their heavy wooden shutters, although the linen in the windows looked like it would crumble to the touch, and in some cases had been eaten away by moths. Adam had initially expected to find beds and couches ravaged by mice, but the rooms were completely devoid of bedding, and the carved hardwood furniture was amazingly intact, if somewhat uncomfortable. Still, it looked inviting after spending a fair amount of the last few sleeps on rude platforms up trees in an attempt to keep out of the reach of whatever biting bugs and snakes slithered along the ground. Only last sleep, he had awoken to Duin pinching ticks from his chest hair, and Adam had wanted to return the favor.

"Have you seen how much fur I have?" Duin had said. "Wait until we get into the keep proper."

"We don't have the stone glows," Adam pointed out. "Even inside we'll need fire for light, and that'll cause you to fur up."

Duin shrugged. "Yes, but less so than out here."

"How do you cope when you don't have someone to groom you?" Adam asked.

Duin smiled. "There are hot springs near where I live. I soak in there for some time and the old fur and ticks just float away."

Adam snorted. "The original spa experience! I like it."

"Spa?"

"I mean the natural version of your baths in Aergon," Adam said after a moment's thought.

Now they pulled together a makeshift bed in the middle of the room, using a number of benches to create a platform, although they weren't able to find much for padding, other than the luggage netting they had used to carry their belongings. Then they found some candles left at the bottom of a cupboard and lit some for light, and used ancient metal candle holders that Adam half expected to fall off the walls at any time.

"Where did all the beds go, do you think?" Adam asked as he sat crossed-legged on the floor, inspecting Duin's body for signs of any blood-sucking ticks.

"They probably took them when they left," Duin said, sighing contentedly as Adam rifled methodically through his hair.

"Portable beds?"

"Well, ours were," Duin said, grunting as Adam pulled a bloated bug from the back of his neck and drowned it in a small cup of water.

"Really?"

"Well, not 'ours' as in my family's," Duin said. "But the ones at the baths were. They had straw mattresses tied on and everything, and I remember hearing someone say they were just like the ones we brought with us from the surface. Apparently the king sleeps on one of the originals."

"Lucky him," Adam said enviously. "I'd kill for a soft mattress right about now."

"Well, unfortunately I don't know of much we can use for that here," Duin said. "The grasses will be full of bugs."

"It's all right," Adam said. "I'm just missing my creature comforts."

Duin laughed somewhat bitterly. "So am I, Adam, so am I."

Despite being warm, dry, and safe for the first time in a very long time, neither Adam nor Duin were inclined toward passion that sleep. Instead, after installing Zoul comfortably in a nearby room, they caught a number of crabs for dinner, as well as raiding an overgrown garden for potatoes and spinach leaves large enough to use as fans if they had been more rigid. They ate better than they had for many meals, especially when Adam found some strawberries that had grown into a wild ground cover, the fruit small as his thumb but sweeter than anything he'd ever found in a supermarket. Sated and somewhat cleaner after a wash that didn't end with them crawling back into the dirt, they were more than happy to blow out the candles, crawl onto their pallet, and sleep in the first real darkness since leaving the rainforest.

CHAPTER 12

ADAM WOKE to a strange sensation of stillness. For a moment, the dark and silence that surrounded him caused him to panic slightly, uncertain of where he was. Then the events of the last sleep caught up with him and he relaxed into Duin's embrace, allowing himself the luxury of a brief sleep in. As he closed his eyes, Adam felt Duin snuggle closer, and felt Duin's morning wood press against his behind. Experimentally, Adam clenched his ass around the hardness, feeling it twitch in response. As he continued to massage Duin's cock, he felt Duin's breathing change, and the arm that had been thrown around his chest tightened, pulling him back against his lover.

"What are you doing?" Duin murmured, his voice thick with sleep.

"Seducing you, I think," Adam said. "Honestly, I just woke to you poking me—what else was I supposed to do?"

Duin's laugh was a low rumble, and he kissed Adam gently on the back of the neck. "I do not know, but I'm not complaining. I'm not sure I'm going to be able to move much, though."

Adam grinned and turned over, pushing Duin flat on his back. "That's all right, I don't think you're going to have to," he said, turning around on the bed so he was facing the object of his desire. "And I think I'm in for a very tasty prebreakfast snack," he added, sliding his lips over Duin's cock.

AFTER A pleasant start to their waking time, Adam and Duin checked in on Zoul, who wasn't in his room. Finding the shutters opened, they peeked out into the outside world, only to see the lizard down at the bank of the nearest bog, happily tucking into what appeared to be a large dead octopus.

"Zoul!" Adam scolded.

The great lizard looked up at them, raised his crest, and chirped pointedly.

"Well, that puts us in our place," Duin said.

"I didn't think we were that loud," Adam said.

"Or took that long."

"I guess we should look at getting fed ourselves?" Adam suggested.

"Probably," Duin said. "Do you think Zoul would share his catch?"

"I doubt it," Adam said. "But I'd be happy raiding that vegetable patch again."

"You go ahead with that," Duin said. "I'll see if I can get us some meat."

Grinning, Adam went out and gathered more strawberries and pulled up what looked like overly large carrots, only to find them far too woody to eat. Investigating other plants, he chanced across some more potatoes, which he gathered happily, and moving farther in found oversized pea pods, which he snacked on while he picked more giant spinach leaves. By the time he had started building a fire pit out of loose rock and flagstones, and a fire from peat and deadwood, Duin was coming back, dragging a catfish longer than his arm along behind him.

"How on earth did you get that?" Adam asked, eyeing the monster.

"I used my fingers as bait," Duin said with a grin. "Thankfully, the leather gloves we got at the waystation work quite well for fishing," Duin said, dropping the catfish by the fire and holding up his hand, the leather somewhat torn around his fingers.

"I think I'd prefer not to know," Adam said as Duin gutted and scaled the fish. "Do you think we should try to find somewhere to store the rest of that?"

"Well, we can see if they left anything in the kitchens," Duin said.

"They must have left something," Adam said. "Come on, Zoul!" he called to the crested lizard. "Let's go find the kitchens."

"Don't forget a candle," Duin said.

Adam grunted and grabbed two of the candles and a cracked dish they had found the night before for a candle holder.

The kitchens were, as Adam had suspected, down the stairs from the great hall, and Adam ducked below the flurry of wings he had come to expect as he entered, and this time Zoul appeared too full to snap at the bats that flew past. The kitchens themselves were swathed in shadows, only the dimmest glimmer of light making it through the grimy, vine-covered windows that had once looked out over the overgrown garden. From the inside, Adam was surprised to see there had once been a door leading out into the garden; although in retrospect he probably shouldn't have been. However, it had long been overgrown outside, and now the only entrance was from the great hall. Setting the candle down on an ancient wooden bench, he looked around the kitchens. As he expected, much of the contents were missing—presumed taken when the inhabitants of Blackwater left all those years ago. Rusted hooks hung from the wooden beams overhead, pots, pans, and ladles long gone. The shelves that ran along one wall were largely bare, bar dust and cobwebs, although Adam could see a few stacks of heavy serving platters that had been left behind. The huge fireplaces were as bare as the shelves, missing even the grating and fireplace tools that would have been used to tend the fire or spit roast a whole boar—or spider, as may well have been the case.

A search of the walk-in larder was equally fruitless, turning up only a few cracked ceramic jars. However, descending into the scullery, Adam found a large copper wash pot, which would easily double as a cooking pot, and a number of clay bowls hidden in the corner which must have been overlooked, along with some ancient whittled spoons that had probably been used by servants long gone.

"Are you coming?" Adam called as he moved back toward the kitchen door, and a chirp from the distant recesses in the ceiling answered him as Zoul wound his way back down the wall and out into the outdoors, Adam being careful to pull the door shut behind him.

"Any luck?" Duin asked, looking up as Adam walked back to their campfire.

"Some," Adam said, showing Duin the fruits of his labor. "They cleaned the place out pretty thoroughly when they left."

"Nothing dangerous lurking inside?"

Adam shook his head. "No. The place was deserted. No large spiders, no insects really, not anything."

"Strange," Duin said. "I guess closing those doors up tight behind them worked better than I imagined."

Adam heaved the copper pot onto the coals of Duin's fire and filled it with water from one of their waterskins before helping add the catfish meat, potatoes, and other vegetables into the soup. Given time and more seasoning, it could probably have been a stew, but they were too hungry and too impatient to let it simmer. As soon as they were able, they dug into the pot with their bowls and tucked in, Adam savoring the first meal he'd been able to eat from a bowl for quite some time. Duin, in contrast, appeared to be having a bit of trouble remembering how to use cutlery other than a knife, and eventually he gave up on the spoon entirely and grasped the bowl in both hands and raised it to his lips to drink. They polished off the entire pot of soup in short order, and after a pause to wash up and stash their belongings in their upstairs room, they decided to explore the rest of the keep, Zoul padding along behind them.

This time they headed to the far end of the great hall, where they found the stone stairs leading down into the bowels of the keep and forced the swollen wooden door open. It moved surprisingly easily, given it was bloated with moisture from years of exposure to the bat guano, and as they squeezed into the long corridor beyond, Duin laid his hand on Adam's shoulder.

"Is it just me, or was that too easy?" he asked.

Adam turned, watching hairs sprout across Duin's face as the candlelight from the saucer he carried shone more directly on his face. "I don't know," Adam said. "I've never actually forced a door open before. Why do you ask?"

Above them, Zoul skittered across the ceiling as Duin turned to face the door. "That door should have been stuck into its frame," he said. "Look." He pointed at the doorframe. "You can see the black line of the mold and the brown of the wood where they've torn past each other."

Adam stepped closer and peered at the section Duin was indicating. "Well, yes, isn't that what would happen when you push through a stuck door like we did?"

"I guess so," Duin said. "Except we should have heard it splinter and tear. I just heard it grate a little."

Adam paused to think about it. "Now that you mention it…. What do you think that means?"

Duin growled somewhere deep inside his chest. "It means that someone's gone through here ahead of us."

Adam turned and stared back down the passageway that stretched out ahead of them. "But I don't see any footsteps in the dust."

Duin pointed to the ceiling, where Zoul had craned his neck to stare at them, his eyes glinting in the candlelight. "You wouldn't have if they were mounted."

"Why not the floor?"

"Habit, maybe? In Aergon, the floor is reserved for people on foot. It makes the tunnels less crowded. I'm told there are also magics for those who want to pass without leaving tracks, although I have never seen it in person."

"Either way, this is good news, isn't it?" Adam asked. "It means they're here."

Duin wrinkled his nose. "I don't know. Why would they have gone ahead without us?"

"Maybe they thought we didn't make it."

"Maybe," Duin said doubtfully. "I think Esmeralda would have waited."

"How do you know she didn't?" Adam said. "Between me getting caught by the kanak and… recuperating… we came here rather late. I mean, if the others had come straight here, they'd have arrived days—I mean, sleeps—ahead of us."

"I hope you're right," Duin said as they started off along the stone corridor.

"What's the dire alternative?" Adam asked lightly.

"I'm not sure," Duin said after a brief pause. "This just feels wrong."

BLACKWATER KEEP had been built with a dark gray granite, and layers of grime on the stone made it look nearly as black as its name suggested. Here and there, growths of slime crept up the walls, and small formations of dirty white crystals had formed at the base of the walls.

"Those are pretty," Duin said. "I wonder what magic made them."

Adam looked behind him at the stairs that circled back on themselves, leading back to the great hall. "I'd say the bats did," he said. "That's the residue from their guano seeping through the floor into the corridor. I reckon we're right underneath the great hall."

Duin looked at the plain, unassuming stone arches that supported the ceiling above them. "Why would there be a corridor from the lord's rooms under the hall?"

Adam shrugged. "I don't know. Maybe so he could raid the pantry? I think a better question is, what's through that door?"

Duin stared at the banded wooden door that stood in the square lintel, a dim greenish glow spilling into the corridor through the crack beneath the door. "That looks like—"

"I know," Adam said with a grin. "Shall we?"

Duin smiled and rapped on the door. "We made it!" he called out as the door swung inward on surprisingly smooth hinges.

"Hello?" Adam called into the silence.

Sharing a glance, they slowly edged inside, Adam unsheathing his broadsword and Duin warily entering with a makeshift bamboo spear held out before him. The room they entered was partially destroyed, with the far end crushed by fallen masonry. The section that remained, however, still had all the markings of an arcane study. And somehow, when all the other rooms had been stripped bare, this was remarkably well preserved, collapsed end notwithstanding. It still had a barely moth-eaten rug, bookshelves piled high with tomes and scrolls, and jars of strange dried plants and animal parts. There were bowls of copper and wood, brittle quill pens and pots of ink, and a stack of crucibles and stained mortars with their associated pestles.

What Adam could clearly see was that the room had been ransacked thoroughly. One of the Aergonite stone bowls stood on a lectern dragged into the center of the room recently enough to leave tracks on the carpet, and precious glassware had been swept onto the floor, shattering into fine shards to prick unwary feet. Books and parchments lay scattered and open on the benches in haphazard piles, and more than one jar of dried flitterfish wings or something equally unusual had been spilled, with no attempt made to clean it up.

"Look," Duin said, nodding toward a number of clear boot prints in the thick dust on the floor. The prints showed a pointed boot, tightly fitting around the foot, and appearing to have little in the way of a sole. "Aergonite boots."

"Xavier," Adam said, looking around the wreckage of the room.

"Or Esmeralda," Duin agreed. "She'd be almost as interested in this room as he would be."

Adam shook his head. "Somehow I can't see her being this… disrespectful, though," he said. "I mean, this must have been Prince Fernando's study, surely?"

Duin pointed over to the rubble at the far end of the room, where the tip of an anvil was just visible beneath the dust and dirt. "I'd say you're probably right."

"So the question is, what was Xavier so hell-bent on finding here?" Adam asked as he started picking through the books.

"I have no idea," Duin replied. "What makes you think he was after a book?"

Adam shrugged. "They're the only items that have been properly rummaged through."

Duin sighed. "I can't read very well, Adam."

"Well, I'm not too bad," Adam said. "Besides, did you have anything else planned for today?"

Duin smiled. He seemed to be getting used to Adam's earth colloquialisms, although it was still strange to Adam that any word incorporating *day* or *night* would be colloquialism. "Surely it might be easier finding Xavier and asking what he took?"

"Maybe. I'd prefer to ask Esmeralda why she didn't stop him ripping this place apart," Adam said as he pulled up a chair and flipped open the closest volume.

"Maybe she couldn't," Duin said, then blew out the candle and hesitated before reaching for the smallest scroll he could find.

Adam stilled. "You mean maybe she didn't make it."

"Well… yes."

Adam sighed and turned the blank front page of the leather-bound tome over to reveal an illuminated capital letter and the scrawl of spidery handwriting. "I don't really want to think about that."

Duin looked down at the scroll, and his lips moved slightly as he read some of the words. Adam caught something about "potatoes" before he put the scroll aside and regarded Adam with a level gaze. "You know, since the light bowl is here, Xavier probably isn't too far away."

"I know," Adam said. "But given your hunch, I'd rather know what he's up to first."

Duin unrolled another scroll and put it down almost immediately, and Adam saw an illustration of an out of proportion flower before the scroll rolled itself shut. "If I didn't know you better, I'd say you didn't trust him."

Adam shrugged. "I don't know I do," he said. "I don't know if I trust any of them—except possibly Darius. He just seems to want to get the job done."

"And the other two?"

"I don't know. But I'm sure they have ulterior motives we don't know about."

"Ulterior motives?"

"They want something else they're not telling us."

Duin stilled. "You're probably right," he said, his shoulders slumping slightly.

Adam reached over and grabbed Duin's hand in his. "Hey, I'm not going anywhere."

Duin refused to meet his gaze. "Except home."

Adam snorted. "Maybe. I'm yet to be convinced of that."

When Duin pulled his hand away, Adam sighed and returned to his book.

"... for the Lady and Lord Arman of Reyes, and the aforesaid persons: bread 1 1/2 quarters, wine, 4 skins; beer, already reckonned. Kitchen. Goats from Aer Nero, 6, 1 crested haradyn and 3 lizardlings and 8 lbs of fat, 12 sv. 2 bits; alfo eggs, 20 bits; 6 dozen flitterflish, dried, 3 sv; flour, 6 bits. Bread for the kitchen, 3 bits. Marshalcy. Feed for 50 riding beasts, jerky, 3 quarters and a half..."

Adam placed the book onto the pile of discards, and then picked up another.

"... canne caufe paralysys of the flefh to sett inn withyn two candylmarcs." Startled, Adam looked back, only to find the book was talking about diseases of the haradyn, which appeared to be a domesticated six-legged herbivorous lizard the people of Blackwater had used for eggs and meat.

Adam flipped through book after book, putting aside bestiaries and books on animal husbandry or the benefits of letting fields lie fallow or the use of peat as fertilizer. Zoul had long created a nest in the corner and gone to sleep, while Duin was slowly going through the scrolls, looking at the ones with pictures first, then reshelving them in the small square boxlike shelves that he identified as a scroll rack. For a moment, Adam wondered if he should give up the idea altogether as a lost cause—none of the books seemed particularly insightful or interesting, but then a passage caught his eye.

"... is importaint to consydor the mystical energies captured by each of the elements you plann to use. The redcap toadstool, fore all its poison, is a potente source of katalytic energies—iff ye are trying to cast enchantments of decaye. Atteympting to use thee redcap in a poultice of healing or balm to turn the blayde of thy foes, wille nott worke. However, harnesfyng the strengthe inherant in claye, or etched stone will yield positive rysults. Alfo importynt are quantities, wych muft be in proportion

to each other iffe the enchantment is to work. For example, the throwing of a balle of flame has allways been much prized by practitioners of the magickal arts, but the preparation of such a spelle is never as symple as they would have you believe. Whilft there are many wayes to achieve the desired effect, moft of the spellf I know of perfonally include the noxious smelling, yellow brimstone. Thys is combined with the Salt of Petreus, or catalyzed through the firey amber, but for best effyct, no more than twice the weight of brimstone than amber should be ufed, and no less than seven parts Salt of Petreus to one parte of brimstone iffe the El Quikaes school of thought is to be believed."

"What have you got there?" Duin asked.

"A book on magic," Adam said. "I think."

Duin grimaced. "Beyond me, then. I don't know how people keep that in their heads."

"It looks a lot like science," Adam said. "Chemical reactions and all that—just with a different understanding of energy and catalysts and—" He glanced up at Duin's uncomprehending stare. "—alchemy," he said after a brief pause.

Duin laughed. "I don't understand that either. I mean, turning lead into gold?"

"I don't think that's possible," Adam said. "At least not without having a solution of gold ions or something that had gold in it that you could extract with an electric current, and that would probably cost more than the gold itself, especially now, but... sorry, I'm talking my world again, aren't I?"

Duin smiled. "Yes, but I do not mind as long as you don't expect me to add to the conversation."

Adam grinned. "This is what I study back home," he said. "The alchemy at least, not the magic. Still, the fundamentals seem remarkably similar."

"Great," Duin said. "You keep going with that, and I will get food. I'm famished, and I know you must be too."

"Actually, I should be okay for a bit longer," Adam said. "Are you sure you don't want some help?"

"No, I can manage," Duin said. "And I'm not much help with reading. It is hard enough working out what the words say, but when the pages are torn out of the covers...." Duin shrugged.

"What?" Adam asked, rising to his feet.

"This book," Duin said. "Someone's torn the pages out."

"Someone?"

Adam and Duin shared a long, thoughtful glance. Wordlessly, Duin picked up the battered cover and handed it over.

At first glance, the book looked much like any other that was sitting in the pile—slim, unassuming, and bound between thin sheets of cloth-covered wood.

"The Book of Solmento," Adam read. "Who's he again? That name sounds familiar."

"According to legend, magister to King Henricus… or one of the King Henricuses anyway," Duin said. "He foresaw the events of the Fall of Selune and the Long March. When the dragons first came from the skies, he was possessed by the gods, crying out horrible prophecies about the end of Aracao."

"Did he?" Adam asked skeptically.

"So I'm told," Duin said. "A number of them have come true. Selune has abandoned us, and we hide from the skies like children under the bed."

Adam blinked at the simile, coming as it did from someone who used the plainest speech possible most of the time.

"His words," Duin said. "That's about all I can remember being taught when I was a child."

"You said he was 'possessed by the gods,' is that the same as being crazy?"

"I… do not know, but if you are saying his speech made no sense and he sounded like a madman, then yes, I believe so."

"Then who wrote down what he said?"

"Mennos, the high priest of Selune, I think."

"Okay. Why would Xavier want that book?" Adam asked. "If the book is that important, don't the Aergonites have copies?"

"I… think that is something we should ask when we find him."

A loud crash from the other end of the room dragged their attention back to the present, and a guilty-looking Zoul was backing away from a barrel of yellow powder, most of which had clumped together into a solid mass. Or had been before the lizard toppled it, causing a fair amount to spill onto the floor. Suddenly the great lizard turned away and sneezed, a complicated, multipart movement that saw his eyes squinch shut before his head jerked violently down, the ripple of the sneeze passing through much of his body, even pulling his foremost pair of legs off the ground entirely for just a brief moment.

"Zoul…," Duin began.

"I love you, you big scaly beast," Adam breathed, staring at the caked yellow powder.

"What?" Duin said.

"That stuff," Adam said, "is going to make everything a lot easier."

"It is?"

Adam grinned and threw his arms around Duin's neck, then kissed him soundly. "I hope so," he said. "Just trust me. Go and find us some food. I have work to do."

When Duin returned with a meal of barbecued cokudrillo and apples, Adam was pouring the last of a fine mixture into some of the small clay containers, then plugged them tightly with bunched rags.

"You reek of brimstone," Duin complained, wrinkling his nose as he entered the study. "And you're as filthy as if you'd been crawling around in the muck all day."

Adam stared down at his stained clothing and nodded. "I suppose I am."

"And you were doing what, exactly?" Duin asked.

"Alchemy, I hope," Adam said. "Come on, we should finish up and go find Xavier."

"Yes," Duin agreed. "I suppose we should."

Neither of them mentioned Esmeralda—or Darius.

Duin continued to badger Adam for details throughout the meal, and especially when they packed the small round rag-plugged pots into a makeshift carry-harness for a less than enthusiastic Zoul. However, his questions stopped when they pushed along the corridor, past the turnoff to the kitchens, and down to what would have been a guard barracks. The barracks was the last door they were able to enter, the passage, and a good two-thirds of the room having been lost to the cave-in. It also stank. In other circumstances, this would have been something they would have expected—after all, water trickling into the once lush furnishings would cause rot and decay, especially as the room was now far from watertight.

However, while there was certainly mildew, rot, and the first evidence of vermin Adam had expected to see throughout the rest of the keep, the former barracks smelled not just of rotting billets and slime, but of blood, death, and putrefying flesh. It also contained two dead bodies. Just inside the door, barely at the edge of the light being cast by the other stone light Darius and the others had been carrying, lay the corpses of a crested riding lizard and one captain of the guard. Both bodies were mangled and showed signs of battle. Darius's corpse lay facedown with his right hand still on the hilt of his blade, and even to Adam's inexperienced eyes, the lizard's corpse bore the slashing wounds more likely to have come from the captain's blade than anything else. A lizard's bite would normally create a u-shaped series of puncture wounds, like the ones that could be seen through the holes in Darius's shirt. Adam wasn't sure where his armor was, but it appeared that the lizard's attack had taken him by surprise.

Farther into the room, the scene was even stranger. Esmeralda was backed up against the far intact corner. She had slumped to her knees, but both of her hands were raised above her head, palms out, a sphere of scintillating silvery white energy surrounding her form. Inside, Adam could see her arms trembling with effort, and her long dark hair was plastered against her forehead and hanging limply around her face.

Magister Xavier stood closest to the light bowl, one arm stretched toward Esmeralda and the other stretched out toward the collapsed wall. Tendrils of fiery orange light played over everything, seemingly drawn from the rubble and across Xavier's body before arcing out to strike against the globe encircling the princess. The magister himself was soaked with sweat, his pale green spider-silk robe stuck to his form, clinging to each muscle as his body strained under the magic he was channeling. His eyes widened when he spotted them in the doorway, and he called out to them.

"Help me!" he cried. "Something… it's trapped her. We have to get her out before she fades."

Adam hesitated, reassessing the situation. Duin, however, reacted instantly. As fur sprouted out across his body and his muzzle lengthened, Duin hurled his bamboo spear directly at Xavier, who managed to dodge the unwieldy weapon, its nonaerodynamic design doing little to help it fly true.

"What was that—" Adam started.

"He's lying," Duin growled, regaining his human features as the glow from the orange energy faded from the air.

"Who's a clever moonchild, then?" Xavier snarled, getting back to his feet. Raising his hands once more, he made a pulling motion, the muscles in his arms straining as he tightened his fingers into fists. In response, blocks tumbled from the wall, and a shower of dirt and pebbles rained down onto them. A large ivory-colored claw thrust into the room, pushing aside giant stones, and Adam's eyes widened as the tongues of orange fire danced across the old dragon bone.

For a moment they stared, transfixed, and then Adam, Duin, and Zoul scattered in three different directions to avoid the burst of energy that Xavier sent hurtling toward them. Adam ran into the room, Duin scrambled to the left, and Zoul ducked back into the corridor outside, all avoiding what appeared as filaments and strands bunching together into a tangled weblike mass that splattered into the ground, missing them. Adam had expected it to burn, to set something on fire, but instead, the energy twined its way across the floor and soaked into the corpses of Darius and whichever lizard had wound up dead on the floor. Whichever lizard. Adam didn't even know its name.

Then both Darius and the lizard twitched, shuddered, and jerked to their feet, eyes and mouths weeping flame. Darius's fingers once more gripped his sword, and he slashed at Duin, who leapt for the fallen stone blocks. Despite his pluck and hunting experience on the surface, Adam knew Duin was not a trained fighter and that he relied on being able to outwit, outmaneuver, and when all else failed, outrun his opponents. Being stuck in an enclosed space with only one exit and friends in danger would be a recipe for another dead body, and Adam found his own route barred by the mass of the dead lizard, its mouth slavering for the first time since Adam had known it. His broadsword, ever an extension of his arm in practice and duels, suddenly seemed inadequate. Resolutely he struck forward and scored a blow across its snout. He would have expected it to have been able to dodge the blow—Zoul would have certainly—but perhaps the old zombie shuffle had some basis in fact. *Fact. Zombies. Right.*

Even against a larger opponent, the drills he'd gone through back home, the mock battles, and the recent training with Darius came to him as naturally as breathing. Still, he felt the only thing keeping him from being snapped like a twig was the clumsy lack of control that Xavier was exhibiting. Adam had thought the magister would have played the corpses like puppets, but then Xavier screamed and the dragon bones stopped their push into the room, the tip of a snout and teeth now poking out of the rubble, allowing Duin to swing out of reach of Darius, who faltered momentarily. The once proud lizard too, collapsed in a heap, shaking uncontrollably, and Adam risked a glance over its form to Xavier, who was directing orange fire down to the shards of ice that had thrust out of the ground. Esmeralda had got to her feet and was leaning up against the wall, one hand gripping the stone and the other pushing upward through the air; her face strained with effort. Then her shield wavered, and Xavier lashed her with a torrent of flame—and this time, it burned straight through her defenses and wrapped around her. Gritting his teeth against Esmeralda's scream, Adam darted past the reanimating lizard and swung his sword down hard at Darius's corpse, the force of the blow jarring his blade, his muscles numbing as the vibration traveled up his arm.

"You missed?" Duin said incredulously.

Darius, or rather Darius's corpse, turned its head and lashed out at Adam with its right hand. Or rather, its right hand stump, Adam's initial attack having sliced off Darius's hand at the wrist. Grinning, Adam kicked the sword away, only to be punched in the chest, the blow sending him reeling backward, as much from the heat as from the force of it. The flames coursing through Darius's form were quite literally that—flames. Luckily for Adam, his stumble took him out of the path of the lumbering lizard, and he was pushed farther back as it barreled past, forcing Duin to jump even farther up the rubble pile, narrowly avoiding being crushed as a second great claw knocked more rubble into the room. Adam himself was scorched by the heat of the lizard's passing and fell back against a warm scaled form. With a cry that was very nearly a scream, he whirled to face a very surprised Zoul, who let out a high-pitched chirp, his crest rising as he backed away.

"Zoul! Don't sneak up on me in battle," Adam said, realizing immediately how ridiculous that sounded. Then he whirled around, worried about his exposed back, only to find both zombies were trying to knock Duin off his perch. And if the riding lizard worked out how to use its feet properly, or Xavier managed to draw the dragon bones far enough in or got enough power out of them to incinerate the lot of them….

Zoul hissed menacingly and butted Adam, the clay bottles clinking gently in their padded bag.

"Zoul, no!" Adam said sharply, pressing his free hand back against the lizard's snout.

Xavier glanced over at Adam, gesturing with his right hand, and the now one-handed Darius turned and stumbled toward them. "That is the first smart thing you have done so far," Xavier said, his chest heaving. "You know her quest has nothing to do with you," he said, jerking his head in Esmeralda's direction. "And I know as well as you do that all you really want… is to go home."

"You don't know that," Adam said, pushing Zoul back step by cautious step, trying to keep both Darius and Xavier within his sight.

"Of course I do," Xavier said. "I saw it inside your head—back when her magnificence Khalivibra first flew over us."

"You?"

"Of course. Someone has to lead us back to glory, and do you really think it's going to be someone like you? Or her?" he said, sneering in Esmeralda's direction. "As she said herself—it's not like she's qualified to lead a disparate people."

"And the dragon is?"

"Well, with the right guidance, yes."

"The right guidance… being you?"

"She has shown me the future and asked for my help. Does it not make sense?"

"Yeah, well, unless that future was 'roasted,' I think you've been had."

"I have seen the proof of her ascension, and with her power and my guidance, we will lead the people into the light."

"So why kill everyone?" Adam asked, his free hand bumping into the padded fur pouches he and Duin had tied onto Zoul's back. "Unless by people, you mean zombies."

Xavier smiled. "Well, I can't have anyone—woman or cursed beast—who's going to try to work against her golden glory."

"What, you're saying Duin's a threat?" Adam asked.

Xavier shrugged. "Not for very much longer." Overhead, the dragon's jaw pushed through the wall, toppling the block Duin was standing on, and he was forced to jump to another, scrambling to stay out of range and avoid the fiery energy that crackled over the dragon's skull, its lower jaw falling to the floor with a clatter.

Adam lunged forward, pressing one end of the formaldehyde-soaked rag he'd used as a plug against Darius's face, shoving hard enough to send the corpse shuffling backward. "Catch," he said as he lobbed the jar in a wobbly trajectory toward the necromancer.

Xavier stepped back, easily avoiding the jar. "You really sh—"

Then Adam's impromptu grenade exploded, sending shards of glass and pottery and smoke in all directions, and for the second time, Xavier faltered. As the zombies collapsed into quivering heaps, Duin jumped, rolling as he hit the floor. One clawed hand grabbed Darius's fallen sword, and then he was on his feet with the blade sliding through Xavier's chest. Xavier gasped and stared down at the blade protruding from his breast, slick with his blood. Then he toppled over, his knees collapsing as he hit the floor.

Chapter 13

THE SUDDEN silence was deafening. As the light faded back to pale Aergonite green, Adam walked slowly into the room, barely noticing Zoul following him in. Duin paused just long enough to slit Xavier's throat before stepping over the sudden pool of blood to help Esmeralda to her feet. As he brought her into the circle of light, Adam could appreciate how vicious the magical battle had been. Esmeralda's eyes were dark with lack of sleep, her clothing largely in tatters, and her skin covered in welts and burns where Xavier's attacks had scored.

"Are you all right, Your Highness?" Adam asked tightly.

Esmeralda nodded. "Yes," she said, her voice weak. "Thank you."

"Yes," Duin agreed. "What was in that flask?"

Adam shrugged. "Gunpowder. I mean, exploding powder and whatever shards of debris I could find to improvise a bomb with. Not really enough force to kill outright, but enough to cause some damage and a lot of distraction."

"Duin certainly distracted Xavier," Esmeralda said grimly.

Adam looked down at the twisted body of the first person he had ever tried to kill. Then he ran to the corner and threw up his lunch.

"Sir Adam?" Esmeralda asked. "Are you unwell?"

Adam shuddered, gratefully taking the waterskin Duin offered him to clear the taste of bile from his mouth. "I'm not used to this real battle stuff, all right?"

"You fought well," Esmeralda said. "You have nothing to be ashamed of."

"Except the part where I've just been instrumental in killing someone?" Adam suggested.

"If you had not been, we would be dead right now ourselves," Duin pointed out.

"I know that," Adam said. "But that's cold comfort, don't you think? I mean, is this the life of a quest? Ride, travel, eat whatever crap you can find, kill people, and move on?"

"No," Duin said stiffly. "That is trying to stay alive when—"

"I know, I know, sorry. I'm being a shit," Adam said. "I've never…. I'm not coping, and you're here for me to lash out at. Just… give me a bit of space, all right?"

Stiffly, Duin nodded and turned away, walking back toward the central light to help the princess tend her wounds—and to have his own scrapes checked over. Wiping his mouth with his sleeve, Adam sat down on a fallen stone block beneath the still-protruding dragon bones. Part of him wondered how safe it was, tempting fate by sitting so close to a recently collapsed wall. Part of him didn't care what the risks were. Shortly, Esmeralda came over and joined him, her usual grace marred by a slight limp.

"He means well," she said softly. "And if he hadn't—"

"I know," Adam said. "I know, I know, I know."

"But he's forgotten what it's like if you've never…. It's a different world, even for me."

"I know."

Esmeralda sighed. "I am sorry, Sir Adam. Goodman Duin and I will find somewhere else to be for a while. He says you were in Fernando's study earlier? Come find us there when you are ready." She looked up at the vacant eye socket of the dragon skull. "Legend has it that Lord Fernando thrust Wyrmbane into the heart of the dragon Khaled," she said. "It's strange, but I almost wish Xavier had brought through more of the skeleton before you defeated him. Of course, we could all have died if you had not acted when you did. But I fear we have no hope of retrieving the sword now. So much for the grand quest."

"What happens now?"

Esmeralda smiled sadly. "I do not know. But we will have to work something out. Xavier was right about one thing—even if I can be a leader, it does not help much if there are no people to lead." Esmeralda reached out as if to pat his shoulder, then pulled her hand back. "But those are my troubles, and I should not burden you with them."

ADAM HEARD Esmeralda's footsteps move away from him, pause, and then continue, almost as if she'd stopped to pick something up. With the sound of her footsteps receding up the corridor and the *pad-pad-pad-swish* of Zoul's six-legged gait following, Adam was left in the silence of the dead. There was little blood, most of it having been consumed by

Xavier's flames, along with the bodies of Darius and whichever lizard it was that had attacked him. Indeed the entire room smelled more like a burned roast than an abandoned mortuary. Absently he wondered if he should close Xavier's eyes or possibly move the necromancer's sprawled form into a more dignified pose. Everyone deserved dignity in death, and in giving that to Xavier, Adam could demonstrate that he was the better person. Of course, that would require him to actually be a better person, which he wasn't. He considered giving Darius some dignity in death, but he couldn't actually bring himself to touch the body. Or rather the ashes that had once been the body. Had once been Darius. Bile rose in his throat, but there was nothing left to throw up.

When his stomach stopped heaving, he climbed back up the rubble pile to stare at the bones. Unlike the fossilized bones of dinosaurs he had always been fascinated by, these bones weren't the smooth black of fossils. These were the heavily stained brown of old bones buried in the dirt while various creepy-crawlies ate away the flesh one scale and muscle fiber at a time. He pushed at the lower jaw with his foot, the reptilian V of the bone as long as his torso, and the entire maw easily big enough to swallow him whole. He reached down, plucked one of the large fangs from its socket, and turned it over and over in his hands, looking at the grooves in the still-sharp teeth that in other circumstances could probably be sharpened further into a serviceable blade. Looking at the rest of the skull, he noticed the eye sockets were big enough for him to fit his head into, and in a fit of pique, he clambered up farther and attempted to stick his head in. Then he revised his estimate of the size to *nearly* big enough to fit his head into.

Adam had assumed the dragon had been crested, just like Zoul and the other lizards were. Thinking back, he couldn't recall if the dragon Khalivibra had a crest or not. Somehow he'd been too busy focusing on other things when he'd seen her—like the great wings, sharp teeth, and the running away really fast. The blackened spike he had taken for a crest-bone was actually the pitted blade of a sword, and reaching under the skull, Adam closed his hand over the hilt of an ancient weapon. Yanking hard, he tumbled to the floor, falling flat on his back and narrowly avoiding cracking his head open.

The sword itself was a bit of a let-down, the blade scarred and rusted from its unexpected burial, and even if the years of grime was cleaned off, Adam doubted it would be battleworthy again. The hilt was in similarly bad shape, the corroded metal of the grip flaking in his hand, although at one point, it must have had leather wrappings over it, slender as it was. The crossguard had been gilded, which hadn't tarnished, but some of the coating had worn away, exposing the steel below to the ravages of the elements. The pommel, however, was as brilliant and beautiful as if it had just been crafted. It was an ovoid chunk of jade, only slightly smaller than Adam's fist, and it gleamed in the light, a deep green worthy of any emerald, and little veins of paler green that made Adam think of the posters for the *Alien* movies. The stone itself was semitranslucent, and in the light of the stone bowl, it almost appeared to have a light of its own.

As Adam sat up and turned the sword over, lifting it high to get a better look at it, he felt that there should have been something more at that moment. If he'd been a real hero on a real adventure, there surely would have been. Some sense of awe or reverence for the blade, or for the people who had invested so much of their hope in it. How proud they must have been to see it raised in the hand of their Lord Fernando, and how they must have exalted as he thrust it into the brain of the dragon Khaled, killing it. How profound their despair as the death throes of the mighty beast destroyed their home and their lord, forcing them to flee to the mountains of the south. Adam should have felt something more than the cold of adrenaline draining from his system. At the very least, there should have been an uplifting, inspiring soundtrack swelling behind him as he raised the sword experimentally, surprised at the lightness of it. It felt as though the blade itself was no weightier than the plastic toys of Adam's childhood, which he had brandished as he ran through the corridors of his parents' house to the cries of "Don't run indoors, Adam!" trailing after him. It was with these plastic blades that he had slain the monsters of his own imagination, and on one or two occasions, the evil villains represented by his childhood friends. Even then, at the back of his mind, battle music sounded as each fight reached its climax, and he could almost hear the ringing of the trumpets and the crash of the drums. At least, he could have heard it then. Now there was nothing except a chirp from Zoul causing him to drop the sword back onto the floor.

"Zoul! How many times have I told you not to do that!" Adam scolded, retrieving the blade and scrambling to his feet.

Zoul made a dismissive sound and butted Adam with his head.

"Okay, just the one and with the qualifier of 'when in battle,'" Adam said, reaching out to rub at the ridge above Zoul's eyes. "Well, just don't do that when I have a weapon in my hand, all right?"

Zoul chirped agreement, his tongue flickering out of his mouth as he gazed at his rider with unblinking reptilian eyes.

"What are you doing here, anyway?" Adam asked. "Didn't Esmeralda take you with her?"

Zoul chirped again and then scuttled back toward the door. Halfway there, he turned and stared at Adam once more, lowering his head until it was resting on the ground.

Adam grinned and bent to retrieve both Wyrmbane and his own modern sword. "All right, I get the message," he said as he followed the lizard back to Lord Fernando's mystical study.

When Adam walked into the room, his eyes went straight for Duin, who stared at him, one hand holding the remnants of a torn book and one with a sheaf of paper that Adam thought were crumpled pages. For a long moment something crackled through the air between them, broken only by Esmeralda's cry.

"You found it!" she said, rushing to Adam's side.

"I'm not sure it's any good, though," Adam said, laying the ancient weapon on one of the cleared tables. "I mean, look at it. I don't think it's going to be much use even if we can clean it up—and I don't know about you, but I don't have any idea how to forge weapons—even if the forge wasn't buried under a ton or two of unstable rubble."

Looking toward the back of the room, Adam saw that the movement of the dragon skeleton had affected other rooms and more rubble had fallen in, and the forge was now buried completely.

"But you found the sword," Esmeralda breathed, her eyes shining as she looked at the ancient relic with the reverence Adam had not felt clear on her face. "If I can work out what Fernando did to enchant it, perhaps we can...."

As Esmeralda spoke, she reached out and gripped the blade, then lifted it up, only to stop as the pommel stone fell off with a thud and rolled its way toward the edge of the table.

"Oh my," Esmeralda said, dropping the blade with a loud clatter and a shower of rust.

Adam reached out and grabbed the stone just as it would have tumbled off the edge and onto the hard ground below.

"Whatever glue held that together must have failed," Adam said, looking at the narrow top of the ovoid where the egg-shaped stone had fit into the rest of the metal hilt. "I guess it's a wonder it survived this long in any case."

A tremor shook the building, and Duin glanced nervously at the ceiling. "That's a mystery we should discuss somewhere else, I think. I'm not liking the sound of that."

"That's just dirt moving," Esmeralda said, waving her hand dismissively. "We'll be fine if we get up top, and I need to sleep."

"And what's the plan for when Khalivibra arrives?"

"What? She's coming?" Adam asked, jumping out of the chair.

Duin shrugged. "Do you really think Xavier didn't tell her we were here? Or that she won't care that he's stopped reporting in?"

Adam groaned. "Just how good at this mind-reading thing is she?"

"I don't know," Duin said. "But do you want to risk our lives on the hope that the answer is 'not very'?"

For a long, tense moment, they stared at one another. And then there was a flurry of activity as Adam pocketed the pommel stone and whistled for Zoul.

"Where are your mounts?" Duin asked.

"We made camp in the north," Esmeralda said. "They should still be there."

"Go," Duin said. "Adam, can you get the bowl in the barracks?"

"On it," Adam said and ran out of the room, Zoul close on his heels.

They caught up with Esmeralda just as she was exiting the great hall, and Adam swung her onto Zoul almost without the lizard slowing. It proved to be a short ride over firmer ground into the fringes of an evergreen forest, the heavy pine trees casting long dark shadows in the surface light. The small camp had been constructed much the same way as the camps they had built in the rainforest, with a sleeping platform high in the branches, and only the broken tethers and the odd piece of beetle carapace gave away the location. Adam's stomach sank, and he reined Zoul in to a walk when the great lizard chirped happily, crest rising in excitement. Then two heads poked out from the shadows below the sleeping platform, and Adam sighed in relief. Esmeralda was already scrambling down to greet her mount, and Duin was climbing the tree to gather any supplies that had been left behind.

Soon they were packed and mounted—Esmeralda on her lizard, Anu, and Duin on Darius's former mount, Hele. This time Adam had ensured he knew their names. "Are we going back to Aergon?" he asked.

"No," Esmeralda replied, her eyes scanning the horizon. "We must travel to Duin's people."

Adam stared in shock at Duin, who appeared to be having trouble controlling his new steed. "You have people?"

"Duin is not the first to survive being cast to the sun," Esmeralda said.

"That's not the point," Adam said, turning toward Duin. "You lied to me. Why?"

"Because Xavier could not know," Duin said. "I'm sorry, Adam. I wanted to tell you. I really did."

"And what else don't I know?" Adam asked, crossing his arms over his chest.

"Adam, we don't have the time."

"Take the time," Adam said through gritted teeth.

Duin pointed back over Adam's shoulder. "No, I mean we really don't have time."

The impact as Khalivibra barreled into the keep shook the ground, great talons tumbling masonry blocks from the walls as fire set the peat of the marshes ablaze. Khalivibra's cries echoed through the marsh, although whether they were of rage or disappointment, Adam couldn't tell.

"North," Duin said shortly, reaching out to the reins of Esmeralda's steed, the princess already clutching the strange milky stone she used in her shielding magic. "We'll have to hurry…. I don't know how long she can protect us."

Caught somewhere between terror and anger, Adam hurried to keep pace, and they slipped deeper into the darkness of the forest, leaving the dragon behind.

THE CLOUDS continued to drift past without showering them with rain, and they made good time scrambling through the pine needles on the forest floor. Adam kept looking behind to see if the dragon's fire would catch the forest, but luckily it appeared the sodden ground of the swamp was preventing too much damage, or at least, if the peat had caught fire, the flames hadn't spread north to the forest—and Adam hoped the prevailing westerlies would keep it that way. Esmeralda was near comatose when they finally stopped to rest, the white stone falling from her fingers as they helped her off her mount. In the pine forests, Duin and Adam constructed tents from branches and the oilskin, rather than one of their treetop platforms.

"Slasherclaws?" Adam asked.

Duin shook his head. "They only hunt in the rainforest."

"What are the dangers here, then?"

Duin shrugged. "Spiders and scorpions, mostly. The wild lizards don't usually bother us here."

Us. Suddenly everything came crashing back, and Adam worked on in silence until it was time to cook up the meal of tree serpent and pine nuts. "Tell me about your people?" he asked finally after Esmeralda had retired to the tents.

Duin sighed. "There is not much to tell. Others have survived here, and they—we—have a stronghold of sorts in the trees to the north. Boolikstaad, it's called. We've learned to live off the bounty of the forest—such as it is—and try to find those exiled from Aergon, but it is a difficult journey—as you know."

"And how does Esmeralda fit into all of this?"

"She cared," Duin said simply. "She disagreed with sending children to the surface, and she started riding topside with her guard to give them supplies."

"How did she manage that without getting caught?"

"She left caches of goods in the forest for the Children of Selune in advance, either on pretense of a joy ride or a trip to gather supplies. As long as she was guarded, she could do as she chose, and so we began to speak with her."

"And Xavier?"

"Esmeralda suspected he was working against her father, the king," Duin replied. "You would need to ask her for the details of that. All I know is that she believes it possible to kill the dragon, restore the golden city, and return Selune to our skies, and end the curse of the Children. The elders of Boolikstaad agree with her, and that is why I'm here."

"They must hold you in high esteem to give you such an important mission," Adam said.

"No, I'm just expendable," Duin said, wrapping his arms around himself.

"How so?"

"The elders don't trust Esmeralda entirely, so they refuse to send someone valuable to them—and it's no secret that I… will not be contributing to the next generation."

Something unlocked deep in Adam's chest, and he breathed easily for the first time that sleep. "So… you'd still be willing to come home with me?"

"Are you sure you still want me with you?"

Feeling slightly weak at the knees, Adam crossed the camp and sat down next to Duin, then wrapped his arm around him. "The thought that you might be staying here… that was the scariest moment of my life."

"Scarier than facing Xavier?"

Adam pretended to think about the question for too long a moment. "Yep," he said eventually. "Not quite as scary as thinking I was going to die at the kanak village, though." He kissed Duin's furry temple. "Thank you for coming back for me."

Adam felt Duin's fingers firmly grasping his own. "You would come back for me."

Adam smiled into the forest gloom. "Always," he said. "Bed?"

And for one sleep, that was all that needed saying.

CHAPTER 14

ADAM DIDN'T see the stronghold of Boolikstaad until they were virtually at its gates. As they worked their way deeper and deeper into the forest, Adam found the trees getting larger and more gnarled with each passing minute. Eventually they came across a dense mass of trunks and branches, each trunk easily as large as a small house and trailing strands of tree mosses reaching down to brush against his face.

Duin reined his riding lizard in. "We're here," he said.

"We are?" Adam asked.

Esmeralda laughed suddenly. "Of course. Ingenious really."

"What?"

Esmeralda pointed upward.

"What?" Adam said again. "There's just a lot of branches up there."

"Yes," Esmeralda said. "And they don't all have the same leaves."

Duin led them around the trunk of the nearest tree, then along bulbous barky protrusions that would have acted like an irregular but serviceable staircase for someone on foot. As they passed what Adam later thought of as "first floor" and continued into the foliage, he gasped as the vista opened before him.

The great branches of the trees had been shaped and guided into their current forms with ropes—some of which were still guiding smaller branches to interweave. It looked much like a collection of interlocking giant bonsais. The great pines formed a superstructure, but in their nooks and crannies, other plants grew, and smaller branches rose to be woven into protective walls of living greenery that both hid the haerunwoln from below and cascaded down from the heights in a dense curtain that surely would hide them from above as well. The air inside this cultivated canopy was clean and fresh, and a light breeze blew through the treetops, although quite how that had been engineered, Adam never found out. Houses had been made in empty hollows or built on platforms secured among the branches, and the green Aergonite glows lit the faces of hardworking men and women, all with only a trace of the thylacine features Adam would have expected in full torchlight.

It felt odd pushing past the people going about their day-to-day—or sleep-to-sleep—lives, and the hush that followed in their wake was odder still. Crossing numerous trees, Adam was aware that they were now in the center of the old pine grove, winding their way up the largest and tallest tree. They passed small family dwellings, treetop gardens planted with edibles, and carved benches for sitting. He saw fletchers creating arrows from wood, flint, and flitterfish fins or lovingly securing slasherclaw feathers to a precious steel-tipped projectile, and men and women he presumed were hunters riding up the trees with giant spiders, beetles, and lizards strung between them. All paused and stared as they passed.

They stopped sooner than Adam thought they would, some distance before the branches would have become too flimsy to build upon, and by now a good hundred people were following them, keeping a slow, respectful distance and sprouting fur as the sunlight played upon their features. In the green light ahead, Adam saw a small, simple dwelling in the trunk of the tree. Unlike some of the others, which had doors, carved window shutters, and were surrounded by ornate railings, this one looked like the hollow of a tree, and had it not been for the light inside spilling out of the crack that, to all intents and purposes, served as a door, he wouldn't even have noticed it. Stepping through the door was an elderly woman, her long white hair caught in a single braid and her feet still nimble as she descended gracefully down some ornate stairs to the large open platform they found themselves on. Her robe was of fine silvery silk and her bearing regal. Advancing toward them, she held her hands out in ritual welcome.

"Duin, Child of Selune, we welcome you back to the arms of the all-mother."

Duin stretched his arms out toward the woman and inclined his head. "Jirsca, Mother of Boolikstaad, blessed are we to stand in her light. I bring before you Princess Esmeralda of Aergon and Sir Adam of Australia."

Jirsca raised her arms toward each of them in turn. "Your Highness, Sir Adam, welcome to Boolikstaad, the refuge of the Children of Selune. Be welcome in her light. The circle of elders will hear you when you have rested."

Without waiting for thanks or acknowledgment, the old woman turned and climbed back up the stairs to her small cottage, and a younger woman stepped forth toward them, her nervousness only betrayed by a slight tremor in her voice.

"Your Highness, Sir Adam, I am Martinia. If you would please follow me, we have rooms prepared for you. Your mounts will be cared for."

"Wait, what about Duin?" The words were out of his mouth before he could filter them diplomatically.

"Duin has his own quarters. He will be able to visit later if he so chooses."

"Could he come with us?" Adam asked. "I'd feel more comfortable if he did."

"Sir Adam, Duin has been away for many sleeps. I'm sure he'd like to ensure his home is as he left it."

Adam decided to go for broke. "Only if he doesn't mind, but… Duin, please?"

Adam could feel heads turning, and murmuring started among the crowd before hushing down to near silence. Duin, his cheeks flaming, glanced nervously at Martinia's carefully expressionless face before locking eyes with Adam. "Of course, Sir Adam," he said formally. "I would be happy to see to your needs."

Adam opened his mouth to protest that wasn't what he meant but then thought better of it. He caught a flash of disapproval on Martinia's face before she got control of her features, and as he dismounted to follow their host into the inside of the great tree itself, he made a note to ask whether that was linked to Duin's sexuality.

THE BEDCHAMBER Adam was shown to was small but comfortable, with curved walls of living wood. The headboard was curved to match, and indeed, every piece of furniture tended toward a rounded shape, although there was no fireplace or bath. Wordlessly, Duin ensconced himself in the small servant's bedroom that adjoined Adam's room, and Martinia advised that their belongings would soon be delivered.

"Although what they will make of your bang powder I have no idea," Duin said softly after the door closed.

Adam laughed. "Neither do I. Did I just get you into a lot of trouble?"

"Not really," Duin said. "You have just given me some status here—for as long as you are here at least."

"Is that why they wouldn't let you stay up here with us?"

Duin glanced pointedly at the open window and tugged at his ear before answering. "Not exactly. Staying here is not my… place in society."

"Well, I think—"

Duin put a finger on Adam's lips. "I know."

In a sudden onslaught of impishness, Adam grabbed Duin and hugged him tight around the waist, marveling still at the man's smooth alabaster skin. "Fur, the ultimate sunscreen," he murmured.

"What?"

Adam shook his head. "Never mind. Didn't you mention something about hot springs nearby?"

Duin smiled and walked into the small servant's room, then returned with two towels and some simple silk robes. "Yes, I did. We should change into these, though—leave your clothes. I think everything we've been wearing could use a clean."

In this fae-like place, Adam was half expecting elaborate embroidery, as might have featured in a *Lord of the Rings* movie, but although everything from the clothing to furniture was incredibly well-made, there were none of the embellishments he would have expected. A quick glance around as Duin led him back down the stairs confirmed that this was true of the entire city. Durable and serviceable, but not ornate or ostentatious. Either the haerunwoln valued natural forms or they were too busy trying to survive to create works of art.

"How have you kept this place secret from the dragon?" Adam asked.

"By being very careful who we let in," Duin said. "And… listen, can you hear it?"

Adam paused and listened as the sounds of the city filtered in… as well as a harmonic chanting that looped around and around, repeating over itself as if the singers were indeed singing in the round. "The singing?" he asked.

"It is a prayer that protects us and this place from mind magic and turns the dragon's mind from us should she get too close."

"And when you venture out? Who protects you then?"

"Selune," Duin said with a smile. "We are… resistant to that sort of magic, and so far we have not been too unlucky."

"I thought she cursed you."

"That is the thought of the Aergonites. We here in Boolikstaad learn to see our condition for the blessing it is. How can we not when it protects us so?"

Adam smiled somewhat wistfully. "It must be nice to have that sort of faith."

"Who do you pray to?" Duin asked.

"I don't, generally," Adam said. "The universe, I guess."

"You do not fear the wrath of the gods?"

"I have enough to deal with the wrath of man," Adam said. "I'm not sure about the gods or whether they exist in my world as people believe they do here."

"People believe they do?"

"Well, to be fair, I haven't personally met one yet."

"Neither have I, but I think the mark of Selune is fairly obvious, don't you?" Duin asked.

"I would accept that you have a physical condition that causes you to morph bodily between two forms," Adam said slowly. "I would also accept that it is known as the mark of Selune. I currently have no evidence that the physical condition is caused by divine action, and therefore cannot rationally accept it as proof of the existence of a goddess." He grinned at the startled look on Duin's face. "Sorry, you're talking to a scientist over here. We're trained to be highly skeptical of everything from a young age."

"So I see," Duin said dryly as they walked along a wide branchway, passing a group of women carrying baskets of freshly picked yellow fruit and cooked shrimp, trailed by youngsters carrying baskets nearly as large as themselves.

"Large family," Adam commented.

"We care for the young collectively," Duin said. "Given that we have many orphans even without the children we rescue from Aergon, we have to."

"So childcare involves manual labor?"

"How else will they learn?" Duin asked. "Is it that different where you come from?"

"Actually, yeah, it is," Adam said. "Don't know if it's better back home, though. I didn't learn to cook until a few years ago. Wait, how do you cook here?" Adam asked. "I can't imagine a lot of fire being used."

"Almost none," Duin agreed. "We can't afford the risks of a forest fire or discovery, so we use the hot springs to cook food or preserve it where possible."

"I'm just looking forward to being properly clean for the first time in days," Adam said. "Not to mention safe."

Duin looked around the tree city, its unwavering green phosphorescent lights playing across his face as they walked. "I still look around and wonder what would happen if Khalivibra does find us here. How long do you think it would take her to reduce this place to ash and dust?"

"I don't know. A few hours?"

Duin snorted suddenly, the corners of his mouth turning up in a grin.

"What?" Adam asked.

"Has Esmeralda worked out the magic behind your 'watch' yet?" he asked as they descended another staircase of roughly shaped roots and into a thicket of younger trees.

"I've told you; it's not magic."

"As you say," Duin said blandly, leading the way to a small, secluded pool of steaming water.

"You do all your cooking here?" Adam asked, refusing to rise to Duin's needling.

"No, there's larger communal pools on the other side," Duin said. "These are reserved for guests and elders."

"Do you get many guests?"

"To be honest? I think you and Esmeralda are the first."

After slipping out of the robe, Adam was only too happy to sink into the hot water of the pool, letting the heat seep into his muscles. He was even happier when Duin brought over some soft tree bark which, when rubbed against itself in the water, produced a soapy froth that helped wash away most of the dirt and grime of their travels.

"So how many people are watching us right now, do you think?" Adam asked quietly as Duin gently scrubbed at his back.

"Probably a lot," Duin said, squinting up at the branches overhead. "I'm sure there's some gaps in the branches people can see through—and definitely hear through."

"I don't think I'll be able to get used to that," Adam said, reaching back beneath the water to stroke Duin's thigh.

Duin gave Adam a quick hug. "I know."

Adam sighed and sank down into the water until he was nearly able to float, with his hair fanning out around his head. Before long, matted patches of hair were floating off to the side, and he chuckled ruefully as he gathered them up and dropped them onto the ground.

"That is officially the biggest hairball I've ever seen," Adam said with a wry smile.

"Only because I'm not currently furry."

"Lucky you. Any chance of getting a haircut? I think I need a haircut and shave," Adam said, tugging at his scraggly beard. "You look good with fur on your face, but I don't like it on mine."

Duin laughed. "I'm sure that can be arranged."

CHAPTER 15

ADAM AND Duin found their packs in the suite when they arrived, although the foodstuffs and cookery gear had been taken somewhere else. Adam was relieved to find his gym bag in the room, along with his personal electronics. Part of him wanted to take a few more pictures of the city, but another part of him worried about the implications if someone other than Duin saw him doing it. Most of their meager clothing supply had been taken away, but Duin helped dress him in a pair of leather trousers and a soft silk shirt dyed in forest green. Duin himself dressed in a similar pair of pants, but his shirt was the undyed cream of raw silk, which to Adam's mind, only highlighted Duin's pale skin and angular features.

Their next meal was a feast such as Adam had never seen before, with piles of crab and shrimp and delicately prepared flitterfish cured in lemon juice with a fiery chili pickle that reminded Adam of kimchi. There were steamed nut breads and dumplings and a dark, bitter brew that tasted vaguely of cinnamon sweetened with honey to wash it all down, alongside flagons of light, fruity wine. There were speeches and promises of support from both Esmeralda and Elder Jirsca, a vision of a united New Aergon for both human and haerunwoln alike. And while Adam was surprised that there was no mention of Wyrmbane's recovery, he kept his peace and concentrated on filling all the nooks and crannies of his belly that had been on survival rations for far too long. It was only when he, Esmeralda, and Duin were summoned to a council with the elders that the significance of his discovery became clear.

They were ushered into a cozy meeting room with carved chairs and a view overlooking an edible garden on the level below, overflowing with purple berries and greenish blue marrows. Three of the eldest haerunwoln joined them—Elder Jirsca, who had greeted them on arrival, Elder Faas, an old stooped man who spoke little, and Elder Thera, the youngest of the three, her hair still being mostly auburn with only touches of white.

"I thought there would have been more of you," Elder Thera said without preamble after they all sat down.

"We were ambushed by kanak," Esmeralda said simply, her voice even. "We lost most of our number and were likely betrayed."

"Likely?" Elder Jirsca asked sharply. "You do not know?"

"Who knows what hold Khalivibra has over the kanak?" Esmeralda asked, spreading her hands.

"They worship her," Adam put in. "Well, Duin and I saw a totem in the village we… passed through after we were separated at the river," he said when they all turned to look at him. "Sorry, I thought I'd mentioned that."

"Well, there you are, then. In any case, I was about to say we can't interrogate our necromancer to see if he did betray us because he's already dead."

"Necromancer?" Elder Jirsca said, frowning. "I was not aware Magister Nickedem—"

"No, it was Xavier, his pupil," Esmeralda said. "Although I cannot say for certain that Magister Nickedemus was not beholden to the wyrm."

"The implications of the treachery are troubling, Your Highness," Elder Thera said. "Your father's rule has clearly been compromised, and I question how you can expect us to throw our lot in with your people."

"Because if we defeat Khalivibra, her hold will be gone from everyone," Esmeralda said evenly. "I can't promise it will change the culture of my people, but without making the attempt, I don't see how life for the Children will ever improve."

"Have you not seen our city, Your Highness?" Thera asked. "Our life is hard, but we thrive in spite of your people's attitudes. What do we gain by helping you reclaim your ancestral losses?"

Esmeralda's jaw was hanging open, and her cheeks flushed with embarrassment as she stumbled over an answer.

"I… you…."

"I didn't think so," Thera said pointedly, sitting back in her chair.

"Clearly not," a voice said, and Adam realized it was his own. "You have a wonderful city here in the trees—and of course, provided Khalivibra doesn't find it, it will continue to be a wonderful city regardless of what you decide."

"That sounded like a threat, Sir Adam," Thera said, her eyes narrowing.

"It wasn't," Adam said evenly. "It's a statement of fact. You're doing fine now, but if your population grows—and it is growing—you'll need more food. You'll need to farm or forage more or hunt more widely. And you can't protect everyone all the time. Eventually someone will get seen. Eventually someone will be tracked. Eventually Khalivibra will come, and your city of wood will burn like… well, a city of wood." He looked around the table at everyone's startled expressions.

"Of course," he continued, "you might not need to worry about this. It could be generations before that happens. You'll probably have died of natural causes. Of course, haerunwoln youth will still be exiled from the Aergon caverns in the meantime, and many of them won't make it safely here. Many will die on the way, and you won't be able to find a good portion of them. Some will probably take their own lives in despair rather than face a horrible death on the surface… but that's not a reason to help the Aergonites leave the caverns either. I mean, it's not like you need to help anyone if you don't want to—"

"All right, Sir Adam, you've made your point," Elder Jirsca said softly.

"No, I don't think I have," Adam said. "Princess Esmeralda has worked for some time to ensure that haerunwoln children are safe. The next time you want to ask why no one stands up for you, maybe you should ask when the last time was that you stood up to aid anyone else."

"Even so, there are matters we cannot help directly with," Elder Jirsca said, her voice as rich and melodious as Adam remembered from yestersleep. "We are not numerous enough to fight as an army, nor would we be welcome if Aergon sent theirs."

"Army?" Adam asked.

"Of course," Elder Thera replied somewhat caustically. "You didn't think Khalivibra has just been sitting on her hoard of gold for all this time, did you? She commands an army of thralls, armed with whatever weapons existed in the city when she first warped their minds. You will not break them, and even if they fight with fists, you'll have to cut through them all to retake Aer Goragon."

"Unless we kill the dragon first," Esmeralda said softly.

"And how will you do that without an army?"

Esmeralda took a deep breath. "We found Wyrmbane. Adam?"

Reaching into a pouch hanging at his waist, Adam brought out the rounded stone and placed it carefully on the table before him, lest it roll off to the side.

"Where is the rest of it?" Elder Jirsca asked. "Surely that cannot be the sword?"

"The sword proved to be just a sword," Esmeralda said, pushing an errant strand of hair back behind her left ear. "The power of the Dragonslayer was vested in that stone."

"Then we need a blade," Jirsca said slowly.

"Yes," Esmeralda said, "and my people will forge it."

"Then until they do, we shall keep the stone safe," Thera said, reaching out toward it.

"Like hell you will," Adam said, snatching it back. "No offense, Elder, but I don't trust you with it at all. We give it to you and there's no way you'll give it back to us."

The woman's cheeks colored. "You doubt my word?"

Adam smiled tightly at her. "No, I don't. That's the problem. Did you hear the words that were coming out of your mouth not five minutes ago?"

"It's all right, Adam," Esmeralda said, leaning forward and resting her elbows on the table. "If she wants to take it, let her take it. I am sure we can trust her integrity."

Adam glanced at Duin, who shrugged, and then back to meet Esmeralda's gaze. She was staring at him intensely, and for a moment, he thought he caught the flicker of a smile. Grudgingly he put the stone back onto the table and tried not to wince at the triumphant smile that broke out across Elder Thera's face as she reached and snatched up the stone.

There was a loud sizzling sound, a cry that was almost a yelp, and the stone dropped back to the tabletop, rolling this way and that across the table. Thera was on the floor, clutching her hand amid the remains of her broken chair. Even from across the table, Adam could see her skin was blistered and burned where she had touched the stone.

"Sorcery!" Thera gasped. "She wants the stone for herself."

Esmeralda sat back with a soft smile. "Of course I do," she said easily. "I want its power just as much as you do. Even if I never used it to slay Khalivibra, if I could harness it… but I cannot. No one can. The stone chooses."

With a sense of timing that Adam had hitherto only associated with screenplays, Wyrmbane rolled to the edge of the table and dropped itself into his lap. Despite the searing it had given Elder Thera, it proved to be quite cool.

"And it has chosen Sir Adam," Esmeralda finished.

Adam looked up at the ring of faces once more staring in his direction.

"It's done what?"

"THE PROPHECY is true, then," Elder Faas said, his voice low and so soft Adam had to strain to hear it.

"I believe so," Esmeralda said solemnly.

"What prophecy?" Adam asked.

By this point several servants were helping Elder Thera to her feet again, and one was bandaging her burned hand. "Congratulations, Sir Adam," she said sweetly. "You get to slay Khalivibra."

"What?"

"You did not tell him?" Elder Jirsca asked.

"There wasn't time," Esmeralda said. "By the time we were safe, we were on the way here already."

Elder Jirsca folded her hands into her lap. "I think we shall have to work with Princess Esmeralda's plans," she said. "You seem to hold all the cards, Your Highness."

"No, she doesn't," Adam said firmly. "I haven't agreed to any of this."

"But you found Wyrmbane," Elder Jirsca protested.

"And who said I was going to use it?"

Duin coughed and reached inside his tunic to retrieve a battered book, which he placed on the table.

Adam gave him a sour look. "You too?"

"You asked the question," Duin said apologetically. "I picked these up at Blackwater."

"What are they?" Adam asked warily.

"The Book of Solmento," Duin said. "The one we found in Fernando's laboratory. Xavier had the missing pages. I thought you might want them."

"You knew?"

"I guessed," Duin said. "I do not *know* any more than you do."

"Is that an original work?" Elder Faas asked.

"I believe it is, *Waur* Faas," Duin said. "It does not appear to be altered as ours is."

"I thought you didn't read well," Adam said.

"I don't," Duin said. "But I have a good memory. I know it is different to the stories Waur Thera taught us."

"Then perhaps we may all learn something today," Elder Faas said softly. "Princess, would you be kind enough to read the relevant sections?"

"Relevant?" Adam asked.

"There are over three hundred pages, Sir Adam," Esmeralda said. "And we still do not know what half of the writings pertain to."

Skeptical, Adam sat back wordlessly as Esmeralda opened the leather cover and sifted through the loose pages Xavier had torn from the start of the tome. Finding the correct place, she cleared her throat and began to read.

"I see the times where the world does not turn, and this shall be a sign to the heir of Aergon that the times of testing is nigh. Mark the calendar of old for the sacred times of our Lady Selune, and at the height of her power, return to the pillars of the moon and cast the symbols. Bring with you the catalyst of the sun and the gifts of the moon, and the chosen will be revealed unto the worthy. For only one who has seen the moon can continue this great journey, for it is in the light that we were born, and in the light that we shall return, should our world ever be rewon.

"As above, so below, and the Children of the Moon must..."

"Darn," Esmeralda said. "It's torn right there."

"... not dwell beneath the ground," Elder Faas supplied. "That is the passage that forced us out of Aergon."

"Despair not," Esmeralda continued. *"For the light of Selune shall not be lost, and the great wyrm will be cast down. And when breath is lost and the night is at its darkest, only then shall the path back be clear."*

"What the hell does that mean?" Adam asked.

"Selune only knows," Elder Faas said calmly. "You must understand, Sir Adam. Ignatius Solmento was a great man driven mad by what he saw. We do not know the meaning of every passage—nor can we know that every passage has meaning."

"You're saying this could all just be the ravings of a madman?"

Elder Faas smiled sadly. "Would that they were. Magister Solmento is the only raving madman to have predicted the Fall of Selune and the arrival of the golden wyrms. When those events came to pass, our people took more heed of his words—thankfully, Mennos, the high priest of Selune, had the foresight to record them just in case."

Elder Thera made an indelicate noise. "You mean he wanted to be certain he had the key to his riches and survival should Selune truly abandon us for our excesses."

"What excesses?" Adam asked.

"We can discuss that another time, Sir Adam," Elder Faas said. "If you would continue, Princess?"

"For the hero who finds the Eye of Fernando and sets it anew shall cast down the wings of gold that wound the city under the red sky that never changes."

"The Eye of Fernando?"

In his lap, the pommel stone glowed a warm green.

"Not possible," Adam said. "Even if you go by that gibberish, I can't set the stone in a sword. I don't know how. What am I meant to do, pick it up and push it into the pommel?" As he spoke, Adam picked up his broadsword and pressed the green stone against the plain steel end of his modern sword.

Strangely, it sank easily into the metal until it reached what Adam would have thought of as a perfect midpoint, and then with an audible click, it refused to budge farther. When Adam again took his left hand away, it was fused into the metalwork of his blade, looking for all the world as if it had been set there deliberately, an oval gemstone encased in steel.

"I guess so," Esmeralda said mildly.

"That wasn't funny."

"It was from over here."

"I still don't see how I'm in any way qualified to kill a dragon. I'll get killed. Worse, I'll get you all killed too."

"But you are the chosen," Esmeralda said. "I knew it when you first arrived—one who has seen the face of Selune. The ritual worked and—"

A cold certainty stole over Adam's body. "Ritual? What ritual?"

"The ritual to reveal the chosen," Esmeralda said more slowly.

Adam folded his arms across his chest and stared at her impassively. "Do go on."

"I have known for some time that something was not right, that Xavier might have betrayed us," Esmeralda said, her eyes scanning his face. "Down below we mark time carefully, using candle clocks. The magisters—and I—have some that are precisely calibrated so we know when the solstices are, or should be now that the sun no longer chases after the moon. It has been important, because each solstice is a time of power. In summer, the sun is at her strongest, and her followers are mighty, but in winter, Selune is at her peak, and we can still call upon her for aid. And we need that more than ever if the balance is to be returned to the world."

"But that's impossible," Adam said. "You get solstices because the angle of the world's tilt affects how the sun shines onto it at any given moment in the planet's orbit around the sun. If your world doesn't turn, the angles with which the sunlight falls would always be the same, so solstices would not occur."

Elder Jirsca shook her head. "How is it that you know so swiftly what it has taken our people a hundred cycles of living topside to work out?"

Adam shrugged. "I'm a scientist. It's my business to know."

"I see," Elder Jirsca said carefully. "Well, one of the first of Selune's Children to be exiled to the surface was apprenticed to Magister Paulus. We call her Bonita, lady of the skies, and it was she who first traveled to the dark way out in the west, to the frozen lands that still see the stars of old."

"Well, yes," Adam said. "They don't go anywhere. You just can't see them for the light of the sun."

"So Bonita said," Jirsca agreed. "And she took with her maps of the heavens she had copied from the library of Aergon before leaving, and returned to tell us something none of us had known—our world is still moving. According to her observations of the stars in the dark, we...." Jirsca paused and stood up, then walked over to the sideboard and picked up a rounded yellow fruit. "Where you come from, Sir Adam, the world must turn like so," she said, turning the fruit in her hands. "And the day passes into night as the light from the sun falls over us, even as the shadow of night falls upon the other side?"

"Yes."

"When Selune left our skies, this world stopped turning," Jirsca continued, stopping the turn of the fruit. "Although, as you pointed out, the world would still orbit around the sun," she added, walking slowly around the table. "But Bonita has shown that instead of staying perfectly still, our world is, in fact, doing this."

As she took her next step, Jirsca moved the fruit so it rolled gently up and down. "It's slow, but it's noticeable, and when our scouts made contact with Her Highness here, we worked out that it takes one full cycle—which I think you call a 'year'—for it to move down and up."

"Which means we have solstices, based on the movement of the world relative to the sun, and they work well enough for our purposes," Esmeralda said.

"Wait, when you made contact with Esmeralda?" Adam asked.

"Ah, yes," Esmeralda said. "In Aergon we have used the solstice—the old winter solstice—every cycle in an attempt to find the chosen of Solmento's prophecy. We go to the surface and invoke Selune's ritual at the sacred stones, but it never worked, and I began to suspect that Xavier might have been doing it wrong. It was not much at first, especially given how advanced he is—was—in the magical arts compared to myself, but he would mispronounce words or leave them out. Sometimes I felt the runes he drew on the menhirs were not quite formed as they should be. Little things. So I started looking at options. It was easy to access his chambers—they are cleaned every sleep, after all. And it came to me that the best way to find out about the rituals of Selune would be to maintain contact with the Children who were being sent topside, and so I did." Esmeralda's eyes grew soft and distant at the memories. "My first attempt was laughable, of course. What would I know of the things people needed on the surface? I gave them clothes, some perishable foods, candles without thinking of the need for ways to light them, mostly practical, but silly."

"And that is when our scouts met her," Jirsca said. "Ever since the start, when the treetop city was first built by the Children, we have returned each year to collect those left behind. And once we saw what she was doing...."

"We spoke when we could," Esmeralda said. "And the lorekeepers of the Children agreed with my thoughts and came up with a way to ensure that finally, we would succeed despite Xavier's interference. The haerunwoln provided us with the missing piece of the ritual, the catalyst, and our ritual worked for the first time this cycle—it brought you to us. And you have found Wyrmbane, and the Eye of Fernando has accepted your blade."

"And I want to help you because…?" Adam asked. "Don't get me wrong here, Princess, but since my arrival here, I've been shot at, sliced, battered, nearly eaten, and if it wasn't for your meddling, I'd still be at home living a life without dragons, without magic, and most importantly, without near-death experiences occurring nearly every day. You didn't ask me if I wanted to come save your kingdom, and frankly, I'd much rather not be here right now. So why the hell should I put my neck on the line for you?"

Esmeralda's eyes widened at Adam's outburst. "W-well, I thought the honor and the glory of… of…."

"She can get you home," Duin said softly, his voice expressionless. He was as still as Adam had ever seen him, gaze fixed firmly out the window. "Elder Thera believes the ritual can be reversed if it is performed at the temple of the sun in the city of Aer Goragon."

"It can?"

"We first thought to banish Khalivibra, but to do so, we would have to defeat her anyway," Elder Jirsca explained.

"I see," Adam said, his eyes narrowing. "You've known about this since I've met you, and we've been alone together for how long, and you didn't think any of this was worth mentioning?"

"I'm sorry," Duin said. "I don't know if I believe it any more than you, but I don't know any other way to get you home. I didn't want to tell you because I—"

"Didn't want me to know until it was too late?" Adam asked. "Until I'd found the stupid rock so you could say I was all 'chosen'?"

"I didn't know," Duin said, turning back. "And if this was all a big mistake, would you really want to be told you were expected to battle Khalivibra? And what if it's wrong now and you go against her and get killed? What was I supposed to say? Welcome to Boolikstaad; if you're the hero, you get to kill a dragon. If you're not, you're stuck here forever, because until someone does kill the dragon, we can't get you home?"

"You could have told me the truth."

"And then you'd have been upset and angry and possibly dead if you started yelling about it while kanak were around."

"You will not stay, Sir Adam?" Elder Faas asked.

"Stay?" Adam asked. "Why would I stay?"

"To rule."

Adam laughed darkly. "Elder Faas, I am in no way qualified to rule anything."

"But the Wyrmbane has chosen you as Fernando's heir."

"Good for it. Consider this my resignation notice—what do you call it, abdication?"

"And if we are unable to send you back?" Elder Faas asked.

"Then you can find a way, or you can slay your own bloody dragon." Scowling, Adam drove his sword point first into the table and stormed out of the room.

CHAPTER 16

THE PROBLEM with being a new face in a small tight-knit community is that it's almost impossible to stay hidden for any length of time. All but running down the steps that wound through the tree fortress, Adam found himself in the relative privacy of the hot springs he and Duin had soaked in just hours before, sitting moodily on one of the springy chairs there—a living sapling trained into a sturdy seat as it grew. At any other time, Adam would have marveled at the skill behind its creation; now he barely worried if the chair would break under his weight, given the creaking of the wood as he rocked back and forth on its springy branches. Around him the sounds of haerunwoln life filtered through the canopy, quiet as it tended to be. Through the screening bamboo, he could hear the sounds of bathing, laundry, and cooking as water was retrieved for boiling or stones were heated to bake or grill on. Above him, he heard the noise of a crowd trying to be silent filtering through the hanging curtains of sweet-smelling moss that enclosed the outdoor baths.

"Go away," he shouted, grabbing a small stone and throwing it upward into the canopy. There was a muffled squeak and a shuffle of feet, but somehow he doubted he'd get any privacy. Fuming, he stormed back up the stairs to the lower platforms, noting in satisfaction the large numbers of people scurrying away from him as he approached. Adam grabbed one of the slower ones, a young boy probably no more than thirteen. "Where are the stables?" he demanded.

The boy gaped at him. "The… the… stables?"

"Stables, yes," Adam growled. "Where you keep the riding lizards."

With a trembling hand, the boy pointed across to one of the large trees on the perimeter of the fortress complex.

"Thanks, now go and don't follow me," Adam said, turning on his heel and heading toward the tree.

THE STABLES turned out to be a series of hollows in the great trunk, although Adam suspected these had been artificially shaped rather than naturally grown. A few lizard heads poked out from the hollows, and Adam noticed most of them were tethered to something inside their stalls to keep them from wandering too far.

Spaced at irregular intervals, the individual lizard dens were accessed by a series of platforms and sloping walkways. Peeking into one, Adam retreated hastily at a baleful hiss and a pair of unblinking reptilian eyes. Catching himself on the railing, he took a deep, shuddering breath, and stared up the tree trunk. Only about thirty more to search. Then he walked around the trunk and stared at the other side of the tree, and he revised the estimate to closer to sixty.

Putting two fingers to his mouth, he whistled, and was relieved when an answering chirrup came from a stall two levels up, and a familiar crested head pushed its way out of the entrance. From there, it was but a few minutes work to saddle up his mount and ride out of the haerunwoln fortress, ignoring the shouts of the guards.

Outside, the forest enveloped him in its own form of silence, and he was surprised to find he had missed it. Here the near silent *pad-pad-pad-pad* of Zoul's feet rang loudly in his ears, and the swish of the great lizard's body through the fallen leaf litter even more so. Leaning forward comfortably in the now familiar saddle, Adam rested his right hand on the lizard's warm neck and sighed. He wanted to go home, he did. But leaving Zoul behind was going to be tough. Still, for now the lizard allowed him a means of escape, and in wandering the forest, Adam found himself guiding Zoul closer to the sound of a forest stream.

Flowing gently east—or light as the locals said—the stream had carved a sunken gully into the soft forest floor, and its clear water was stained brown with the murk of decaying leaves. Here and there the long, hairy stem of a tree fern angled its way across, and large flat rocks lay here and there, looking for all the world like giant pads of greenish blue moss and yellow lichen.

Adam reined Zoul in, dismounted, and removed the lizard's saddle and bridle. "You really don't need me to tether you, do you?" he asked.

Zoul chirped in reply and butted him gently with his head, pushing against Adam's hand until he reached up to scratch the lizard's eye ridges.

"Now I'm thinking I should have brought something to eat," Adam said with a sigh. "But I just had to get out of there. Thanks for coming along," he added.

Zoul gave him a long, slow blink, cocking his head in a fashion that Adam had always considered as the reptilian equivalent of "you're nuts, you know?" With a long yawn, Zoul wandered down to the river, staring intently into the water in search of silver scarabs or whatever other aquatic edibles might be present.

Adam, for his part, selected a large protruding rock and clambered his way onto it, his feet slipping somewhat on the damp moss. Pulling up his knees so he could rest his chin on them, he sat in silence, watching the water trickle around the rock below. He couldn't tell how long he stayed there—although later he supposed he could have checked his watch if he'd a mind to—but in the strange unwavering red light of the motionless sun, Adam sat, huddled on the boulder, gazing into nothingness as he chased the same thought around and around his head.

He was going to have to fight a dragon.

He was going to have to fight a dragon to get out of this place alive. It was like Xavier had said when they'd first talked about going to Blackwater. *To get the sword to kill the dragon, we have to get past the dragon.* Only Xavier had likely been trying to sabotage their journey even then. If it really had been pointless, Xavier would have let them get Wyrmbane. He wouldn't have killed Darius.

The loss hit him then. Properly hit him for the first time since he'd seen Darius's burned body lying on the floor where it had fallen. Darius was dead. He wasn't going to show up suddenly with a brace of spiders or flitterfish after a successful hunt, smiling broadly at his accomplishments and happy that he was able to feed their camp. He wouldn't push Adam harder in training than he'd ever been pushed at the SCA, and show him techniques he hadn't dreamed possible. Darius was gone, his ashes lying unburied in the basement of Blackwater Keep, and Adam had ridden off and left his friend behind. If anyone would have been able to fight the dragon, it would have been Darius. He would have smiled grimly at the challenge, but there would have been a glint in his eye as he sized up the best way to—

Was there actually a best way to do something this crazy?

HE SHOULD have noticed the change in the air. He should have noticed that the strange squalling calls of the flitterfish had risen to a panic and faded into the distance. He should have noticed the change in the light.

He did notice the thick net of webbing that dropped suddenly over him, but by then it was too late. His cry of surprise turned into a scream of terror as the giant spider bore down on him, its head easily as large as his torso, a bloated abdomen pointing skyward. A long strand of silk as thick as his forearm reached up into the heavens, clasped by four of its chitinous legs. The other four were clutching the corners of the net that had dropped over Adam, sticky strands catching him even as sharp mandibles snapped inches from his face. Desperately, he reached for his weapons, only to find them gone, and he cursed himself for leaving them in Boolikstaad. Instinctively he lashed out at the spider with his feet and scored a lucky hit on its face, the sole of his sturdy hiking boot mashing into one pair of close-set eyes. As the spider recoiled, a heavy object fell out of his boot and whacked him on the chin, and he thanked his lucky stars for his reinstated boot knife, which he quickly applied to the sticky webs that bound him. It didn't make the webs cling less, but it at least allowed him some movement.

Before he could get free, however, a leg slammed against his head, and he fell back onto the mossy stone, his vision blurring. Blearily, he stared up at the spider, swaying above him and staring at him with its remaining six eyes. This time the mandibles would not miss.

A bamboo spear ricocheted off the spider's carapace and spun down into the stream, causing the arachnid to recoil, and Adam rolled off the rock and into the gully below, nearly braining himself again as he fell onto a bed of partially submerged stones. Rising to a crouch, he turned to face the spider, which was twisting around on its silken thread, legs gouging into the moss of the rocks as it scrabbled for purchase. Out of the corner of his eye, Adam saw the spear lying in a tangle of fallen tree ferns and lunged to grab it, then turned it around to face the spider just as the giant arachnid found its footing and leapt.

Desperately, Adam jabbed the stone-tipped spear repeatedly at the spider's face, but its eight legs crowded around him, knocking him off his feet, and curled around his body, creating a living cage, and when it lunged… something was ever so slightly off. From above him, there was a thump, and the spider fell to one side, the spear plunging through its mouth and into the gooey center of it, and Adam found himself staring cross-eyed at a glistening fang, the point nearly touching his nose.

"Adam?" That would be Duin.

A toothy maw chomped down on one of the spider's still twitching legs, and the spear was yanked out of his hands as the corpse was dragged off him. The feeling of the spider's feet skittering over his body was one Adam hoped he'd never have to repeat, but the fury in Duin's eyes was worse than any of his physical injuries.

Duin stalked toward him, covered once more in his chestnut fur and forest-brown stripes. His fists were clenched, and the muscles in his neck were taut as a bowstring. "What in Selune's name did you think you were doing?" he snapped.

"Getting away?" Adam said, wincing as his bruised ribs and battered skull made their pains known to him. "It was stifling in there. I just wanted a place where I wasn't going to be stared at as a curiosity and have my every move scrutinized."

"Why didn't you just say so? I know lots of places that aren't home to moon spiders." Sighing, Duin squatted next to Adam in the water, his hands checking Adam's body for injuries. "Your shirt's torn."

"I fell on rocks. What does it matter anyway?" Adam asked. "I'm dead no matter what I do."

"We all are, in the long run, Adam," Duin said, his hands surprisingly gentle as he helped Adam to his feet. "That doesn't mean you need to go seek it out."

"And what do you call fighting a dragon, then?"

Duin shrugged. "Suicide."

"Well, thank you very much," Adam said, pulling away.

Duin's grip tightened as Adam wobbled. "Adam, you can always say no."

"What? How the hell can I do that? If I don't play nice, your elders will skin me alive."

"So we leave," Duin said with a smile. "We mount up Zoul and Hele, and we leave. Find a secluded part of the forest away from everything, build a tree house, and leave the religious fights to those who care about it."

"You'd do that?"

"I've considered it before."

Adam squinted up at Duin through a rapidly swelling eye. "Really?"

"Back before all this, I mean," Duin said. "And I don't want to go back to living the way I was before I met you. I… can't."

"You'd really leave home for me?" Adam asked.

"I would leave home for *me*," Duin said. "But I'd hope you'd be around if I did."

Adam smiled and winced as the throbbing in his head worsened. "Don't take this the wrong way, babe, but I kinda hate your world sometimes."

Duin gave him a light squeeze. "I know."

THEY ARRIVED back at Boolikstaad—two men on lizardback, towing a giant spider carcass behind them with only two feet of spear handle protruding from its mouth—to a chorus of hushed whispers. Gravely, Duin turned the carcass over to a tall hook-nosed man and passed the reins of the lizards to a waiting groomsman. When he would have aided Adam up the stairs, Adam gave him a fierce glare. "Don't you dare," Adam hissed.

"What?"

"Heroes have to walk themselves home," Adam whispered, pushing away Duin's proffered arm and squaring his shoulders. "I'll explain later."

It was a long and painful climb up to his rooms, and Adam's head was spinning by the time he pushed through the door and allowed himself to collapse onto the bed. Duin rushed in after him, lips taut, and started methodically removing Adam's clothing.

"I don't think this is the time, babe," Adam said shakily. "Need sleep."

"What you need is a healer," Duin said firmly, tucking a pillow behind Adam's head.

"Wha? No, 'm fine," Adam mumbled, staring down at the red line scored across his chest.

Duin's face swam out of focus, and his voice dropped away into static nothingness. "I don't think that was from a rock...."

CHAPTER 17

WHEN ADAM next woke, he felt as weak as the proverbial kitten, and Duin was applying a cool cloth to his forehead.

"How long was I out for this time?" he asked, squinting against the brightness of the light.

"A few sleeps," Duin said, tugging the cloth down over his eyes. "Keep your eyes closed—moon spider venom makes things bright for a while."

"I noticed," Adam said, coughing. "Water?" he asked plaintively.

"Here." A trickle of water reached Adam's parched lips.

Adam drifted in and out of consciousness for another two sleeps, waking long enough to have some soup and use the chamber pot. Funnily enough, now that he was in a city, as opposed to roughing it out in the wilds, he found he missed the convenience of modern plumbing even more. Either the lack of constant danger allowed him to miss his creature comforts, or his illness made him wish it wasn't a trek down a few hundred steps to get to the bathing facilities. Or that it made him near incapable of enjoying the sponge baths Duin gave him—even if it was less sponge and more rough towel.

"What have I missed?" Adam asked when he was finally able to stay awake for more than a few hours.

"A lot of talk, mostly," Duin said. "Princess Esmeralda and the Council of Elders are discussing strategy. Hunter Joeri wants to train you—or train with you—as soon as you're able. I'm not sure which one."

"Do I want to train with Joeri?" Adam asked.

Duin shrugged. "If I had to pick someone to take on Khalivibra, it'd be Joeri," he said. "I would have bet on Darius, but…."

"I always thought it'd be him doing the fighting," Adam said. "And here I am. Running from kanak, fighting with slasherclaws, taking on a… moon spider?"

"You know, running away is still an option," Duin said.

"Is it?" Adam asked. "Is there anywhere here so safe that we can grow old together and not risk it all if a kanak scout wanders past at the wrong time?"

"If we go underground, yes," Duin said. "But that's not what you meant, is it?"

"If we stay here, just you and me, all it takes is one mistake and it's over for one or both of us. No healthcare—healers. And realistically, if we'd gone out and fought that moon spider by ourselves, would I be here talking to you right now?"

Duin picked up the tray from Adam's lap and shoved it over onto the bedside table. "I—maybe," he said. "I could always come back, ask for help."

"And if they said no?"

"Can we not talk about that?"

"I think we have to," Adam said softly. "Either we take our chances against the dragon and form some sort of life here or… there afterward," he said, glancing at the still open windows, "or we cut ourselves off, and if we make one mistake…."

"You're saying it would be better to take our chances with the dragon?" Duin asked. "You're saying it's better to go into battle and risk dying now even if running away means we're guaranteed to live longer?"

"Longer isn't always better," Adam said. "And if we're doing this, you and me—I want everything, and I'll be damned if I'm going to sit by and watch you die if I fuck up at life here."

"And if you 'fuck up' when fighting the dragon, I get to watch you die?"

Adam shook his head. "If we fuck up when fighting the dragon, I think we both die. I just… I just figure we've got a better chance at beating the dragon with everyone else fighting alongside us than making it on our own if we take on everything else plus the dragon if she ever swings by."

"You've worked that out?"

"Not really," Adam said. "I just figure with everyone else around, there's more targets to hit that aren't us. Basic probability."

Duin shook his head. "See, this is why you're the hero."

"What? A callous disregard for everyone else's safety and a drive to survive?"

A small lopsided smile lit up Duin's features. "I just call that bravery."

"If you say so. Can I have a hug now?" Adam asked.

"But—" Duin started, glancing at the windows.

"If they were listening in, it's a bit late. Please?"

Duin smiled, and Adam was happy.

HUNTER JOERI turned out to be the lean hook-nosed man who had taken the moon spider's carcass from Duin all those sleeps ago, and he cut an imposing figure in supple armor of purple-green lizard leather and black spider chitin. Like most haerunwoln, his skin was a pale alabaster, marred only by the raised lines of old battle scars. Coupled with his large brown eyes and thick mane of black hair, he put Adam in the mind of a woodland spirit, an impression accentuated with the way Joeri slipped through the landscape, seemingly leaving no trace of his passing.

In their first official meeting, neither said much; instead they sized each other up the way a hunter would prey. Later, Adam could never be certain what Joeri saw, but eventually the man grunted.

"I have something for you," he said softly—Joeri said almost everything softly, as if to avoid startling the person he was conversing with. "You are the first person in many years to have brought down a moon spider."

"I had help," Adam said.

"I know," Joeri said, his grin showing even white teeth. "But even so, it was an impressive feat. I know none who have escaped its net alive."

"In your words, Adam, take the compliment," Duin said from where he was sharpening a set of elegantly curved daggers.

Joeri looked between them, and his smile widened. "You two do not behave like master and servant."

"Duin's not my master," Adam said, his eyes twinkling.

"Adam, that's not what he… oh. He enjoys sarcasm, Joeri."

Joeri shook his head. "I do not understand, but I'm sure you have good reason." He reached into a carry-sack and brought out a suit of armor not unlike his own, but with the chitinous plates a bony brown color, accented by a white crescent on the chest piece, with the pointed ends of the moon motif pointing down toward the ground. "This is for you, Sir Adam. A trophy, if you will, but one that may also keep you safe on the field of battle."

Adam reached out to touch the cool surface of the breastplate. "Thank you, Chief Hunter," he said, running his fingers over the delicate work. "It's beautiful—all these patterns...."

"We didn't do those," Joeri said quickly. "Princess Esmeralda insisted on working some enchantments into the carapace."

"What enchantments?" Adam asked, fingering the subtle weblike patterns that shone dimly in orange and blue.

"I don't know, Sir Adam. You should ask her."

"Where is she anyway?" Adam asked. "I haven't seen her since before… before I rode out."

"Battle planning," Duin said, coming over to inspect the armor. "At least that's the official story. Unofficially she and the elders are butting heads over the best way to reach the Golden City, how large an escort to send, and how to coordinate the armies when the Aergonites eventually do show up."

"If they show up," Joeri said.

"What do you mean, 'if they show up'?" Adam asked.

"The cave dwellers have lived beneath the rock for generations," Joeri said softly. "And they cast out their unwanted to the surface. How many, do you think, really have the courage to face the light of Helene?"

"I think they'll come," Duin said quietly. "They may be frightened of the sky, but they will come if their princess asks it of them."

Joeri shrugged, a surprisingly economical movement. "I wish I had your faith, Duin."

"I grew up there, Joeri," Duin said. "We—they—fear the surface, but they also want to live here again, the way they used to."

"They'd better come," Adam said. "If we're going to liberate their city, the least they can do is turn up to lend a hand. Crap, liberate a city. How many people do you think we're actually going to have to fight through?"

"One thing at a time, Adam," Duin said soothingly. "Let's see how well your armor fits you before we worry about what it's going to have to stop."

"When did you take the measurements?" Adam asked as Duin and Joeri strapped him into his armor, starting with the tough leather leggings.

"When you were feverish from moon spider venom," Duin said, strapping on Adam's greaves before helping him into the leather jerkin, to which the breastplate, backplate and pauldrons attached. Vambraces, leather riding boots, and an open-faced helm styled like the spider's head completed the ensemble, and it was only after putting the helmet on that Adam realized the cheek guards really were the spider's mandibles.

"I feel like I'm looking out from inside the spider's mouth," Adam muttered.

"You look very imposing, actually," Duin said as he finished buckling on the left vambrace.

"I suppose that's something," Adam said, stretching to test the fit. "I have to say, it's a lot lighter than I'm used to."

"You are used to metal armor, true?" Joeri asked.

"How did you know that?"

"You move as one used to carrying more weight. I assumed that would be the effect of metal armor. We will have to change the way your body thinks—our armors are softer than the steel of Aergon, and you will not be able to rely on your armor to stop every blow."

Duin grunted. "From what I saw, the Aergonites have started making carapace armor as well, though."

Joeri nodded. "They would. Even where the ore is plentiful, the fire to make steel would be risky for them."

"And better used in blades?" Duin suggested.

Joeri nodded and picked up a couple of heavy quarterstaves. "Come, Sir Adam. We should seek out a place to practice."

JOERI'S IDEAS for training locations were wildly varied, and each one found a new way to test Adam in completely unexpected ways. First there was a heavy patch of dense bamboo through which he was expected to creep soundlessly, or closer to soundlessly than he thought physically possible. Then there were the slime-and-moss-covered stepping stones half submerged in a fast-tumbling stream that he had to navigate while avoiding blows and missiles from a sure-footed assailant, and finally the thin, swaying branches at the very top of the willowy pine trees in which the haerunwoln lived. Even after seeing and touching the thick spider-silk safety net below them, Adam had stood paralyzed in fear for a good ten minutes before daring to venture out onto the limb, and lasted barely one more before falling off when Joeri unexpectedly jarred the branch he was standing on. It was a bit like trying to walk on a tightrope, a skill he had never attempted before, but suddenly the close-fitting soft boots made sense, even if his wooden tightrope was gnarly, uneven, and swayed in the slightest breeze. It took him several sleeps to adjust to a more acrobatic way of moving, let alone fighting, and that didn't even begin to cover the lessons he received on fighting from lizardback. Adam fell into bed stiff and sore at the end of each sleep's training, even after a strong massage from Duin.

"Sometimes I hate you," Adam grumbled after falling into the safety net for the thousandth or so time.

"For a groundsman, you're doing well, Adam," Joeri said. "I'm sure I'd struggle learning your fighting style too."

"Maybe," Adam replied. "I just wonder how much more time we'll have to train like this."

Joeri smiled bleakly. "At least until the generals stop bickering about the armies and get them here, which could be many months."

"I don't want to wait that long."

"Better to wait and train than be dead," Joeri said. "Hunting is a lot of waiting, Adam. Sitting and waiting for the perfect moment and hoping you don't go hungry next sleep."

Adam rolled to his feet, springing across the net with the ease of practice, and climbed back to the treetops. "So let's go hunting and see how good I really am."

"I don't think so," Joeri said. "I'm teaching you how to fight, not hunt."

Adam grabbed his staff, bounced himself to a higher branch, and swung at Joeri, who easily leaned away from the blow.

"Adam, you're being rather rash in your—"

With his legs locked around the upper branch, Adam waited until the branch whipped back up to bring his staff crashing into the back of Joeri's legs, sending the hunter tumbling into the net. After inching back toward the main trunk, Adam dropped onto the sturdier branch below and stared down at Joeri, who was still lying in the net. "So, can you teach me how to hunt now?"

Joeri bounced to his feet in one smooth motion. "When you can do that on the first strike, yes."

"Spoilsport," Adam said. "All right, come on and let's do this."

Movement gave way to combat and weapon training, and soon Adam and Joeri were dueling with staves on the stepping stones as they attempted to drop each other into the river. Adam learned quickly that speed and momentum were everything to the haerunwoln style of fighting, and he worked hard to unlearn the habits of blocking or parrying strikes that he had picked up with the SCA back home. To the haerunwoln way of thinking, it was better to not be where you could be hit in the first place, especially if you could ready your own attack while avoiding the incoming blow. Adam did find, though, that he often won by blocking or deflecting a blow that Joeri expected him to dodge, and lashing back when the hunter wasn't expecting an attack.

"I think I need to learn your fighting style," Joeri said after the third time Adam dumped him in the river.

"Maybe," Adam said. "More importantly, who are we really going to be fighting? I somehow doubt the dragon fights like you or me."

"I think the real question is, how do the people under the dragon's control fight?" Duin asked from the riverbank.

"Like madmen," Joeri replied. "I've only faced them once, but they attacked with no regard for their own safety—and fought on long after other people would have fled."

"Great," Adam said, reaching down to give Joeri a hand up. "The attack of the living zombies."

"The what?"

Duin laughed suddenly. "Actually, that's a very good description."

"We could use some of those ourselves," Joeri said. "The real ones, I mean. They'd be a great help against the dragon's thralls."

"Yeah…," Adam said slowly. "They would have been."

"What do you mean 'would have been'?" Joeri asked sharply.

Adam and Duin shared a long glance.

"The only necromancer I know they had was Xavier," Adam said. "Princess Esmeralda never mentioned him taking on an apprentice."

"Not to mention Khalivibra got to him," Duin said. "The last thing we want is two lots of zombies attacking us."

Joeri sighed. "Shards, I was hoping we'd have them to bolster our forces. No wonder the elders have been bickering for so long."

"Are you allowed to say the elders are 'bickering'?" Duin asked.

"Probably not," Joeri said. "But everyone is saying it. Come on, let's go eat."

CHAPTER 18

THE PEOPLE of Boolikstaad rarely took meals in their homes, having no fire to cook with—or at least, not having fire in their homes of living wood. What fires there were tended to be kept tiny by necessity, lest a smoking section of the forest give away their location. Instead there were great communal eating plazas just above ground level, close to the hot springs where the haerunwoln did most of the cooking and bathing. Not for the first time, Adam marveled at a society that ran without currency, with each individual giving what they could and receiving what they needed. He had, of course, seen evidence of barter for specific items and commissions, but by and large, every haerunwoln contributed to their city in whatever way they could, and always lent a hand to a neighbor in need.

The plaza was always busy, and today was no exception, with a number of people already seated at the long communal tables. Joining the queue, Adam, Duin, and Joeri helped themselves to a rich seafood—or more accurately riverfood—soup of crab, watercress, pepperberry, and a sour berry that looked a bit like a tomato. There were also chewy balls of bland tapioca and hot chilies floating in the soup, and a barbecue of coal-baked spider. With plenty of fresh fruit for the taking, the meal was simple but delicately flavored, and Adam was still thankful for a meal he didn't have to catch and prepare himself. They found seats off to one side, near a planter box of flowering succulents, and were halfway through their meal when the buzz of conversations quieted down.

Looking up from his wooden bowl, Adam saw Esmeralda heading purposefully toward them, and he rose smoothly to his feet.

"Your Royal Highness," he said, with what he thought was a formal bow. "How kind of you to grace us with your presence."

Esmeralda smiled winsomely. "Thank you, Sir Adam. I trust I am not intruding."

"No, of course not," Adam said, rising from his bow. "Please have a seat, Your Highness," he added, pulling out a chair for her.

"Thank you, Sir Adam," Esmeralda said, sitting demurely at their table. "Why exactly are we doing this?"

"Adam's decided the safest thing to do is attempt to kill Khalivibra," Duin said.

"And that's turned him into a court fop?"

"Hey, sitting right here," Adam protested.

"So is he," Duin said meaningfully, glancing over at Joeri.

Adam and Esmeralda exchanged a glance and then looked over at the chief hunter.

"Please, continue to speak as if I am not here," he said, smiling slightly. "I understand."

"You do?" Esmeralda asked.

"Of course," Joeri said. "Adam does not consider himself a hero but has decided to kill Khalivibra; as such he is acting as a hero should to get support for your war effort, Your Highness. The more support you have, the better his chances of success." Joeri smiled. "I suppose true love must be a strong motivator."

Adam's blood ran cold. "True love?" he asked, trying not to squeak.

"And how he blushes," Joeri said, his grin widening. "They will sing songs of you when you claim your bride, Sir Adam the Innocent."

"Bride?" Adam asked, staring at Esmeralda. "Ah…."

"No need to act surprised," Joeri said. "Everyone knows the reward for slaying a dragon."

"Sir Adam and I have agreed to discuss that, should we succeed," Esmeralda said smoothly. "Any promises made before that would be premature."

"And very distracting," Adam said honestly. "Let's not count our chickens before they hatch."

Joeri frowned. "Excuse me, Sir Adam, but what is a chicken?"

"Small, feathered, lays eggs… think tiny feathered lizard that's kept for meat and eggs, okay? With wings."

"Really? Where can we find some of those?"

"Oh, I'm sure they'll be around in a few hundred million years," Adam said. "Look, can we just forget about the chickens? To what do we owe the pleasure of your company, Esmeralda?"

"Mostly I just wanted to talk," Esmeralda said. "I haven't seen you in quite some time."

"You look good, though," Adam said. "Boolikstaad's been good for you."

"The rest and food have been good for me," Esmeralda said, rubbing her temples. "And the fact that I do not have to call upon magic every sleep has definitely helped. As for Boolikstaad… well, I suppose the elders are no worse than my father's doddering old councilors back in Aergon. Just when I think we've reached an agreement, one of them raises another objection and we're talking in circles for what seems like hours."

"They're scared," Joeri said. "If you succeed, the people who cast them out will return to the surface; if you lose, the dragon will probably raze Boolikstaad. Either way, our lives change forever."

"What do you think about it all?" Adam asked curiously.

"I think it's about time," Joeri said. "We've been here for generations—a lot of us were born here, even me. We're too comfortable here."

"Too comfortable?" Esmeralda asked.

"We forget how fragile this haven of ours is," Joeri explained. "If one of the large kanak tribes decided to leave the rainforest and move into the area and we didn't scare them off or destroy them quickly, we'd be dead in short order. And as you said, Sir Adam, if just one of Khalivibra's thralls finds out where we are, she'll know. And if she comes for us…."

"I still don't get why she would," Adam said.

"She's a creature of Helene," Joeri said. "We are the Children of Selune, and until Selune forgives us, we will be hunted by the wrath of her sister."

"And according to your religion, it's all right to kill the instrument of the wrath of the gods?" Adam asked.

"Isn't that normally how you pass the trials of the gods?" Esmeralda asked.

"I don't know. I've never been tried by the gods as such," Adam said. "I'm just glad there won't be religious fanatics on this side wanting to stop us from winning."

Joeri shrugged. "If there were, they'd have left by now and we'd be dead."

"That's a depressing thought," Adam said.

"True, though," Duin said.

"Would you like something to eat, Your Highness?" Adam asked in a louder tone of voice.

"I'm sorry?"

"Everyone's trying to listen in," Adam hissed.

"Thank you, Sir Adam, but I already ate," Esmeralda said. "Actually, I also came to tell you that I will be leaving in a few sleeps' time."

"You're what?"

"Leaving Boolikstaad. I need to get back to Aergon if we're going to get anything done," Esmeralda said. "You know that."

"I thought you were still arguing strategy," Adam said.

"We were," Esmeralda admitted. "But whatever we choose to do, the unchallenged fact remains that I am the only one the Aergonites will listen to. I have to go."

"They didn't want you to?"

"If they have me here, they have leverage to make sure that my people treat them fairly," Esmeralda said. "That's why you're staying here."

"What?"

"Well, you're the only other person they can hold on to."

"It does give you more time to train," Duin said, his voice carefully neutral.

"Look, not that I'm anxious to retrace our steps and go through everything we did twice more, but... you won't make it by yourself. We barely made it here."

"With a traitor in our midst and kanak on our heels," Esmeralda pointed out. "I won't have those problems going back, and Elder Faas has agreed to provide me with an escort."

"How much of an escort?" Adam asked.

"Four warriors," Esmeralda said. "We made it with fewer, and any more would make us easy to spot."

"Just like that?" Adam asked. "This is all happening rather fast, don't you think?"

"We've been here for six weeks," Esmeralda said. "That's long enough, don't you think?"

"And when you return?"

"One of my generals will come to Boolikstaad, and we'll coordinate a strike on the Golden City," Esmeralda said. "We've already started sending out scouts to see where the weak points are. The idea is to create a diversion. We lure the dragon away, slip you into the city, and you destroy the dragon's power source. Then, when she comes back to investigate, you strike her down."

"Wait, what's this about a power source?" Adam asked.

"Do you remember during our journey how I mentioned that Khalivibra has much more mental power than any other dragon known historically?"

"Sort of," Adam said. "There was a lot going on when you were explaining."

"Well, as I said, all dragons we know of have had the ability to influence people's minds. Just never on this scale."

"And you think Khalivibra's using some sort of magical MacGuffin to boost her abilities?"

"Macwhat?" Duin asked.

"Item, artifact, thing… never mind. It's a my-world thing."

"Xavier said she'd shown him the future," Esmeralda said evenly. "That she'd shown him proof of power beyond our wildest dreams."

"Yeah, standard crazy nutjob talk. What of it?"

"What else could she have shown him that would convince him to turn against Aergon? It had to be something he could use."

"I never knew him that well," Adam said. "And I don't know magic, so don't ask me what would make him turn against your people."

"Power," Duin said. "He wanted power."

"What makes you say that?" Adam asked.

"When you're on the receiving end of it, you know what it looks like," Duin said in such a matter-of-fact way that Adam felt his chest tighten painfully. "He thought he was better than everyone and was happy to use his power to prove it."

"So if Khalivibra offered him that power, why wouldn't he take it?" Esmeralda concluded.

"That is pure speculation," Adam retorted. "We have no idea if it was an artifact, let alone one we can get to and destroy."

"Which is why you're going to find it," Esmeralda said. "It's our best chance."

"And if you're wrong and it doesn't exist?"

"Then cause a big enough commotion that she has to come back and you can ambush her."

"That's actually a good plan," Adam said. "You know, except for the part where I wouldn't know what a magical artifact that boosts mental abilities would look like."

Esmeralda smiled. "Put on your helmet."

"What?"

"Put on your helmet. Just do it, Sir Adam, please?"

Adam sighed the sigh of the put-upon and put his helmet on. "Okay, now I look like I'm being eaten by a spider. Now what?"

Esmeralda reached into one of her pouches and withdrew a small piece of milky quartz. Adam had seen it before, but now it blazed a white-blue across his vision. Blinking, he averted his eyes and was surprised to find he wasn't seeing afterimages.

"You see it, do you not?" she asked.

"Yes, I do," Adam replied. "Is that what you did? These patterns?"

"In part," Esmeralda said. "I have also worked in protective enchantments to help you be resistant to fire, but such magics are not foolproof; you can still get badly burned."

"Or bitten in two, but I'll take what I can get," Adam said. "Thank you, Your Highness. I think this...." Adam let out a long slow breath. "I'm beginning to think we might have a chance."

"Maybe you should start training with Wyrmbane again, see how it feels," Duin suggested.

"I don't know," Adam said. "Last time we fenced with it, it sheared through Joeri's practice blade. Whatever else it does, I think it was designed to cut through dragon scale. Wait, how tough is dragon scale?"

"You could probably use one as a dinner plate," Esmeralda said. "I've only seen a few, and we used them for magic—as catalysts or a power source. But the ones we had were about as big as... your hand, and quite thick."

"Right," Adam said. "Well, good thing I have a blade that can cut through metal. Let's hope it works on bone or horn or whatever it is that dragon scale is made of."

"So we are really going to do this?" Duin said. "We are going to go fight Khalivibra?"

"You don't have to come," Adam said. "I'm the idiot who picked up Wyrmbane."

"The hell I don't," Duin snapped. "You go, I go. You know that."

Adam's hand twitched toward his lover's knee, but he managed to stop himself. "Thanks," he said.

"You'd do the same for me," Duin said.

"And if it was me, I hope you gallant gentlemen would come to my rescue," Esmeralda said with a grin.

"You managed fine for sleeps without us," Adam said. "What makes you think you'd need rescuing?"

"I did last time," Esmeralda said.

"Xavier got the drop on you," Adam said. "Would he really have won if you and Darius were prepared for him?"

"Honestly? I have no idea. I would like to think not, but I cannot say for certain. In any case, Sir Adam, I think it is reasonable to suggest Khalivibra is more powerful and more dangerous than Xavier was."

"Probably," Adam conceded. "But I don't think she'll be sneaking up to stab you in the back."

A nervous cough stalled any further discussion, and they turned to find a child, probably no older than ten, loitering awkwardly by their table.

"Your Highness, Waur Jirsca sent for you. The first of the scouts has just returned."

"Of course," Esmeralda said, rising to her feet. "Thank you, Puck."

The boy smiled a gap-toothed smile and scurried away.

"You should come with me," Esmeralda said to the three of them. "You will all want to hear this."

ESMERALDA LED them to a council room larger than the one where they had met the elders. All in all, it looked like a war room, with a three-dimensional map of the area standing in the middle of the empty floor. There was a notable lack of document piles on tables and weapons mounted onto walls, and Adam had to remind himself that the haerunwoln were a people unused to the notion of full-scale war against another people. Instead, the walls were hung with woven tapestries and hunting trophies, and Adam realized this great, cavernous tree hall had probably been co-opted into use as mission control, as it were. Now it was at the heart of their efforts to take back a city, slay a dragon, and hopefully, Adam added privately, to go home. The three elders were there, of course, sitting in padded chairs and doing their best to not look tired. There were also three other men who rose when they entered, who Adam did not recognize.

"Your Highness, good of you to join us," Elder Faas said, straightening in his chair as they walked in. "And Hunter Joeri. Sir Adam, these are Captains Wendell and Roelof," he said, indicating two large men who were more muscular than the average haerunwoln male, "and Hunter Stephan. Stephan led our first scouting team to the city of Aer Goragon."

Stephan, a lean man in his thirties, bowed his head slightly, and Adam could see there were streaks of gray in his reddish brown hair and laugh lines in the corners of his eyes.

"The city ain't much like it's told in stories," he said, walking over to the map. "The forest goes north more further than we've gone, and the trees've grown right up to the walls."

"And the houses outside the walls?" Esmeralda asked.

"Gone or overgrown, for the most part," Stephan said. "There are some by the north and dark gates that folk still live in, but I didn't dare go too close."

"Dark gate?" Adam asked. "Oh wait, that's west. Yes?"

"That's right," Esmeralda said. "If you would continue, Hunter Stephan?"

"Yes, ma'am, uh, Your Highness. The walls are still standing, but there are some weak parts. That yellow rock's crumbled somewhat with tree roots and all, and the southlight corner's been reduced to rubble. The houses inside are more intact than the ones outside, and you could get in through the gap, but it'd be hard to do sneaky like."

"Any other weak points?" Adam asked.

"There's a few pines growing next to the southdark wall," Stephan said. "A good climber could drop onto the parapet from there. Also, the keep inside the north wall has a large hole in it, though you probably don't want to invade there. I'm guessing that's where the dragon sleeps."

"Of course it is," Esmeralda said sourly. "She probably fancies herself Queen of Aracao now."

"And that's your job, I take it?" Elder Thera asked somewhat tartly.

"It is my right by birth," Princess Esmeralda said evenly. "Although if you want that title, I'm sure we could come to some arrangement."

"We must all play the hands we are dealt," Elder Faas said smoothly. "Selune knows that coveting your neighbor's wealth leads only to strife and unhappiness."

"We should go in by the south," Adam said. "People don't look up, and there's probably less chance that those walls will be patrolled, right?"

"Don't think so, Sir Adam," Stephan said. "There's chunks missing in lots of places, so's you can't walk around it all without getting down off it at some point."

"The southlight would be the slums," Esmeralda said. "Surely Khalivibra would have people living there."

"Wouldn't the slums be the first area to crumble?" Adam asked. "People would be living in the rich houses because they'd be the sturdiest."

"Hm… that would be the northdark, historically."

"That fits with the troop concentrations Hunter Stephan saw," one of the captains said—Adam thought it was Roelof.

"Then any feint would need to come from the north or dark," probably Captain Wendell said. "Provide a distraction from the south."

"Light," Joeri said softly.

"I beg your pardon?" almost certainly Captain Roelof said, his deep voice quizzical.

"If you attack from the light, you have the sun at your backs," Joeri explained. "They will be staring into Helene's face, which is never a good way to fight."

"The city's fourteen sleeps northdark of here," Stephan said, "Longer for an army, I'd guess."

"According to the old military journals, yes," Esmeralda said. "They had to bring their provisions with them."

"We can forage as we go," Wendell said.

"Not always," Adam said. "If you have a few thousand people, you're going to run out of food very quickly. If this becomes a protracted campaign—"

"It won't," Esmeralda said. "If it becomes a protracted campaign, the dragon kills us all."

"Ah, right. Sometimes I forget that."

"That's about it from me, Waur Faas," Stephan said. "I know it ain't my place, but I think we should get someone into the city next time. Look around some."

Elder Faas inclined his head. "Thank you, Hunter Stephan. Please eat and rest. You have done well."

Bowing his acknowledgment, Stephan exited the room, leaving a thoughtful silence behind him.

"So events move on," Elder Jirsca said thoughtfully. "Are you ready, Your Highness?"

"I am," Esmeralda said. "We will go once Captain Wendell's men have had time to say goodbye to their families."

"We will leave after nextsleep," Captain Wendell said. "Until then, Princess."

"Captain," Esmeralda acknowledged with a curtsy. "Wauren, I will come to you before I leave. Your hospitality has been gracious and more generous than I would have had the right to expect as a representative of Aergon."

"Your words are kind, Princess," Elder Faas said. "But we are all the children of the gods. Sometimes that is too easy to forget."

CHAPTER 19

"YOU WOULDN'T want to get married, would you," Esmeralda said, more as a statement than a question.

They were walking along the upper walkways of Boolikstaad, the constant rotating chanting of the haerunwoln priests and priestesses filling the air around them.

"No," Adam said simply. "I don't mean to insult you, Esmeralda, but you aren't my type."

"I know," she said. "You are not attracted to women at all."

"No."

"And your home, where you come from, this is… accepted?"

Adam smiled. "Yes."

"And if it were allowed here, would you want to stay?"

Adam shook his head. "No."

"Even for Duin?"

"Duin's coming with me," Adam said as they wandered through the treetop gardens of epiphytes and baby herbs.

"Is he?"

"You've seen how they treat him here," Adam said. "They didn't even acknowledge his existence in that room. Once I leave, what happens to him?"

"I… had not noticed that."

Adam shrugged, reaching out absently to pick up a lantern berry and pop it into his mouth. "Tell me about Aer Goragon?" he asked.

"What about it?"

"What was it like?"

"I do not know," Esmeralda said. "None in Aergon has ever seen it."

"Then why do you want it back so badly?"

"Because it is mine," Esmeralda said. "Or rather my people's. It is our home, and it was taken from us by the dragons, and we need to take it back. We need to stop hiding from the past and build a life we can be proud of here, on the surface."

"So, you don't have any idea what it was like?"

"Some," Esmeralda said. "But only what I have read in books and diaries."

"Tell me?"

"Why do you wish to know?"

Adam shrugged. "I'm going to be fighting there soon. I guess I'd just like to know why."

"You do not have reason to fight?"

Adam laughed humorlessly. "We both know my reason for fighting, and as far as I care, it could be here, in the swamps, or on the walls of your city of gold. The location for me only matters on a tactical level. For everyone else… there's something more to it, and I want to know why. I mean, why is it even called Aer Goragon?"

Esmeralda smiled and sat down in a garden hollow, a space against the tree where a small bench had been grown and nearby planters held flowers that gave off a soft, delicately sweet perfume. "It means the Golden City," she said. "I think it was named because it was the heart of the kingdom, and all the wealth flowed there. Also it's made of a yellowish stone, which is said to 'reflect the golden rays of Helene,' which shows what they know."

"Why do you say that?" Adam asked.

"Helene's rays are red."

"Here, yes," Adam said. "But if you went far enough east, they wouldn't be—you know, assuming your sun is anything like mine."

"Then Helene has turned her back on the city that spurned her," Esmeralda said. "And sent her serpent to punish those of us who made it so."

"And the city?" Adam asked.

"It sits on a small hill, surrounded once by the fields that fed its people. There are four main gates that lead towards a great park in the center of the city, which housed the King's Menagerie and the great monument erected in honor of the royal family. His castle is to the north, surrounded by the manors and palaces of his jarls, at least, those jarls that keep a palace in the city. East of them is the trading hub of the merchants, where traders from across the empire come to sell their goods—fine silks from far Backera or the sparkling wines of Freeport, all would pass through the markets of Aer Goragon. The Temple of Helene rose in the east, and you could walk down the Thoroughfare of the Gods to greet the priests of her sister at the Temple of Selune in the west, and there was balance between both of the sisters as they danced across the sky."

"Where's that from?" Adam asked quietly.

"Inel," Esmeralda said. "One of the finest playwrights of times past. That was the opening of her epic, *Fall of Aracao*, although I don't think it was ever finished."

"What happened?" Adam asked.

"Who do you think?"

"Oh."

Esmeralda nodded. "I am sorry, Adam, but I cannot tell you what to expect when you get into the city. I cannot even tell you where you should go."

"What was on the eastern side of the city?" Adam asked. "It had to be more than just a temple."

"I am not sure," Esmeralda said. "I think it was where the craftsmen lived mostly—the farriers and the blacksmiths, the candlemakers and the butchers. Inel did not speak much of them. Personally, I think she was more interested in the foibles, trysts, and goings-on of the upper classes."

"Just like everyone else, then," Adam said. "I'd say she wanted people to come to her plays."

"And that required ignoring the poorer people?" Esmeralda asked.

"Of course," Adam said. "The poor don't want to hear about themselves. They're living it. The rich don't want to hear about the poor because then they'd have to wonder if it's fair that they have all they have while others have nothing. But everyone wants to hear about the rich, either because they want to be rich or to see the rich tumble and fall."

For a while, Esmeralda just stared at him. "You are a very complex man, Sir Adam," she said finally. "And it is a great shame you refuse to be king."

"I don't want to rule anything," Adam said firmly.

"I am aware of that," Esmeralda said. "It is one of your main qualifications." Rising to her feet, she brushed off her skirts and smiled down at him, her face slightly eerie in the greenish light of the algal lamps. "Sleep well, Sir Adam. I will see you in the morning."

WHEN ADAM returned to his rooms, Duin was sitting in the corner, cross-legged with his eyes closed and hands resting on his knees. Moving as quietly as he could, Adam sat on the bed and pulled off his boots and helmet, before starting on the buckles of his vambraces.

"I can hear you, you know," Duin said, his eyes still closed.

"I know," Adam said as he took off his arm guards and started on the breastplate. "You probably heard me approaching the door."

"I did."

"Are you mad at me?" Adam asked. "Because you sound like you're mad at me."

"I'm not mad at you."

"But you're upset."

"What's going to happen after we win?" Duin asked.

"You mean *if* we win," Adam said.

"No, I mean after."

"We go home," Adam said. "You know, if you're not so angry with me that you still want to come along."

"Joeri says you're going to rule the new Aracao."

Adam set the breastplate off to one side and wondered if he dared taking off the leather jerkin without removing the backplate. He was sure it was possible, but he'd always had help before. "Joeri doesn't know me very well. Do you really think I'd want a crown and a throne?"

"I think Aracao would be lucky to have a king like you."

"And I'd consider myself lucky not to be the king of anything," Adam said. Giving up on the backplate, he walked over to the corner and knelt at Duin's side. When Duin finally opened his eyes, Adam smiled and kissed him soundly, cradling Duin's head gently in his hands. "I'm not going to abandon you, love," he said softly. "Ever. You do believe me when I tell you that, right?"

"Yes, but—"

"No buts," Adam said firmly. "If you believe me, then there's no buts." He slid his hand down Duin's spine to his firmly muscled ass. "Well, okay, maybe one or two."

"I thought you said someone might overhear," Duin objected.

Adam brought his lips right up to Duin's left ear. "Then we'd better not make any noise," he whispered with a grin. "None at all."

"Adam, I don't know if I can—"

"You have to," Adam whispered as he brought his hands around Duin's flanks to hover over his lover's groin. "I'm going crazy not touching you, and clearly you need reminding exactly who and what I want here." Grinning, he rocked back on his heels. "Now will you please give me a hand with the backplate on this thing?"

Rolling his eyes, Duin got to his feet, stretched, and maneuvered Adam so he could reach the backplate. Once the backplate was off, Duin removed the greaves and cuisses of shaped spider carapace from his legs. Standing, he helped Adam unbuckle the jerkin and pull the heavy garment off his shoulders. Then he unceremoniously toppled Adam onto the bed.

"Hey!"

Grinning, Duin all but pounced onto Adam, fingers going to the waistband of his breeches. "What? I'm helping."

Adam's chuckle turned into a gasp as Duin unbuttoned the front flap of his pants and slid the lizard leather off his legs, leaving him clad in nothing more than his smallclothes. As one of his hands tugged on the knots that kept them together, Duin leaned over Adam's form and kissed him soundly. "I thought we were going to be quiet," he whispered.

Adam had to choke back a cry when the cloth fell away and Duin's warm hand clutched his rapidly rising cock. Then his lover's mouth was taking him in and swallowing him down, leaving him grasping at the sheets as teeth delicately scraped over the head of his cock. Somehow, the necessity of keeping quiet made his body sing, each touch eliciting a burst of heat and a quiver of need. His lover's mouth let his cock go with an audible pop, and hot kisses were dropped up his stomach and chest before lips pressed against his mouth with urgency. Opening his mouth eagerly to accept Duin's invading tongue, Adam nearly groaned as his lover ravaged his mouth with a passion that held just a tinge of desperation. Adam grabbed the hem of Duin's tunic and yanked it up, forcing his lover to break the kiss as he pulled the obstructing cloth out of the way. Duin's leggings were easier to remove. Once Adam untied the cord that served as a rudimentary belt they all but fell away, leaving just the smallclothes, which took only a few moments to untie. Then they were lying together again in glorious nudity, and for a moment that was enough. Adam looked up into Duin's eyes, seeing the sense of wonder he was feeling reflected in their amber depths. Then Duin's mouth descended on his again, and he was lost in the haze of their passion, all the while trying to remember that he was meant to be keeping quiet.

As THEY basked in the postcoital glow of their lovemaking, Adam pulled Duin to him and wrapped his arms around him. "I've missed this," he whispered, nuzzling into his lover's neck. "You should sleep here tonight—this sleep."

Duin sighed and kissed Adam's bicep. "I can't, you know that. And we should get cleaned up or the whole room will smell like rutting."

"Can't we just stay like this a bit longer?" Adam asked. "I don't know how long it's been since I've been able to just hold you."

"Maybe afterward," Duin said softly. "But not for too long. If we stay like this for too long, I'm not going to want to sleep in my own bed."

Adam tightened his grip around Duin ever so slightly. "Then maybe we shouldn't go anywhere."

"Adam, if I stay here and you get into trouble, I'll never forgive myself."

"And is this trouble going to be because I love you or because they think I should marry Esmeralda?" Adam asked softly.

"Both."

Adam sighed. "I am going to take you home to a place where we can be together like this and no one will care—at least, no one who matters. And when we get there, I'm going to hold you close and you're not going to need to pull away."

"Is that a promise?" Duin asked, his voice so quiet it was barely discernible.

"That's a promise," Adam whispered, pulling Duin closer to him. "That's definitely a promise."

ESMERALDA'S FAREWELL was an occasion of much ceremony, attended by almost all of the city's inhabitants. They gathered in the council amphitheater, the people sitting in tiered seating beneath the spreading leaves, some sprouting tufts of fur as the breeze pushed through the canopy, allowing dapples of sunshine to penetrate the otherwise greenish light of the stone glows. For the first time, Adam saw the other four of the seven elders—one for each great tree pillar that made up Boolikstaad city—five of them sitting on high-backed padded stools on the balcony overlooking the amphitheater. Elder Faas and Elder Thera, as the oldest and youngest of the seven, were standing in the courtyard below, along with Esmeralda, Captain Wendell, and three other burly warriors.

As designated dragonslayer, Adam had the privilege of a front-row seat, and managed to get Duin and Joeri into seats on either side of him. As they waited for the speeches to end, Adam amused himself by watching Duin out of the corner of his eye as his lover grew the occasional tuft of fur in the sunlight that glinted through the canopy. Once, when a particularly strong gust hit, he saw Duin's right ear creep up his head into the more pointed version he'd come to know, love, and more recently, even miss a little.

"What?" Duin whispered.

"What do you mean, what?" Adam whispered back.

"You're staring at me."

"You're sprouting," Adam said.

"Sprouting?"

"Fur."

"I know, it itches."

Adam's chuckle was quickly disguised as a cough.

In the center of the courtyard, the pace of Elder Faas's speech was quickening, and he turned to address Esmeralda and her companions.

"Princess Esmeralda of Aergon, you are charged with the solemn duty of journeying to the caverns of your people to forge an unwavering alliance between the Aergonite people and the Children of Selune in the eyes of the sister goddesses. Do you accept this quest freely and without reservation under the eyes of the goddess of night?"

"I do," Esmeralda said.

"Blessings of Selune upon you, questor," Elder Faas said. "May this ring of the living wood bring you safely home." Adam craned to see the object, which, unsurprisingly, turned out to be a small smooth wooden ring that looked like it was made of a twisted twig, right down to the small green leaf buds he could see.

"Captain Wendell of Boolikstaad, you are charged with the solemn duty of accompanying Princess Esmeralda as her guardian and protector. Her quest is your quest, and her life is your life. Do you accept this quest freely and without reservation under the eyes of the goddess of night?"

Captain Wendell stared straight ahead, pride filling his eyes. "I do," he said.

"Blessings of Selune upon you, questor. Please accept the blade of Galen Haan, slayer of the kanak chief Broken-Tooth. May it serve you as well in the trials ahead."

"Sounds like a damn wedding," Adam whispered as Elder Faas continued to the warriors accompanying Esmeralda and Captain Wendell, extracting similar pledges and giving them gifts of fine metal-tipped arrows, rather than the bone-pointed ones that were more commonly used by the haerunwoln hunters.

"Really? What sort of weddings do you have? Ours are much more festive."

"Never mind," Adam said. "I'll explain some other time, but if this concludes with a blessing for health, wealth, and happiness, I'm not going to be able to keep a straight face."

He looked over as Joeri nudged him with an elbow. "If you two are going to whisper, either stop moving your heads so everyone doesn't know you're doing it, or speak up so I can hear you."

In the courtyard in front of them, Elder Faas handed over the last quiver of arrows and stepped back to address them again.

"You have accepted your sworn duties in the sight of Our Lady and bid your families goodbye. Before you embark on your journey, is there anything else you would like to say? No? Then—"

"Waur Faas," Esmeralda said, "there is something I need to say."

The crowd stirred, and the whispered conversations died down as focus returned to the courtyard. Clearly this was not something that happened during these prequest ceremonies.

"I go home to the caverns of my people," Esmeralda said, stepping forward, her voice ringing clearly through the air. "I go so I might return to bring us to our true home, Aer Goragon, where the House of Helene faces the House of Selune, where we lived before we were divided into Children of Selune and Aergonite cave dweller.

"Together we will stand, and while I am gone, I must leave in your care the most precious of treasures—he who was foretold in the prophecies of Ignatius Solmento, hero of Aracao and bearer of Wyrmbane. I have waited many cycles to say these words, to bring these tidings, and here, now, in this place under the sight of Selune, I can say to you: we will prevail. Sir Adam will lead us through the city gates to a new life without fear of flying serpents to darken our skies. And so it is with a heavy heart that I must charge you with his safety while I am gone.

"Sir Adam," Esmeralda said. "Please stand."

"Uh… okay, verily I… uh…what do you need? Your Highness?"

"I must leave you, my lord," Esmeralda said formally. "But before I go, I give you this to remember me by—a token, if you will. It is an eye of the moon spider you defeated here—the first to fall in living memory."

She held aloft a small bejeweled pendant on a leather cord. It was either cut or naturally formed in a shape not dissimilar to a tiny soccer ball, and glittered strangely in the green light of the glows.

"Thank you, Your Highness," Adam said, kneeling so she could place it around his neck. "I will remember you when I wear it and keep it close always, until we meet again."

Esmeralda smiled and stepped back. "Duin of Boolikstaad, please stand."

"What? Me?" Duin asked, rising hesitantly to his feet, looking around nervously.

"Duin of Boolikstaad, you have stood by my side—by our sides—from the beginning. You have kept us both alive in times when we would have faltered without your aid and asked for nothing in return. Your generosity will not be forgotten when we retake our home, and I hope that on that day, I will be able to offer you more than my favor," she said, handing him a flimsy length of silk.

Swallowing hard, Duin took the silk in much the same way Adam would have picked up a venomous snake. He bowed low, then took his seat, trembling as Esmeralda turned and walked back into the precise center of the formal semicircle of the quest companions, leaving a stunned silence in her wake.

"I thank you, Elder Faas, for your indulgence."

"You are most welcome, Your Highness," Elder Faas said. "Now go with good heart, and may the grace of Selune cast the shadows from your path."

And with that final blessing, the five mounted their steeds and rode down the great tree, with the haerunwoln following them to the lowest branches and watching through the canopy as the five rode across the leaf-littered ground and off to the south.

AFTER THAT, life in Boolikstaad went back to normal, which left Adam feeling jumpy and more than a little irritable.

"Are you all right?" Duin asked from the bed as Adam paced around their small room.

Adam shook his head. "I don't like this. How can everyone just go back to everyday life?"

"Because we must," Duin said. "Would you rather we sit around worrying and forget to eat?"

"Well, when you put it that way…," Adam said.

"You have never had to wait like this before, have you?"

"No. You have?"

"When I first came to Boolikstaad, I was taken in by a hunter and his wife. They'd never had children, and in a way, they became my new parents. He was one of the men chosen to go return to Aergon and bring back any new children. He used to spend a lot of time away, and the first time I'd wait by the window every sleep until he came back. And that was fine when I was a child, because he always came back. Always. So I stopped waiting and started working and hunting the way I was supposed to."

"But he always came back," Adam said.

"Yes," Duin agreed. "Until he didn't."

"Oh. I'm sorry to hear that."

"The others he went with made it back, along with two more children. He died trying to save the rest when they stumbled upon a kanak patrol."

"Well, that's something, I guess."

"Yes, it is. My second mother died shortly after, and I've been alone ever since."

"Is that why you took the job going to Aergon?" Adam asked. "To do what your dad did?"

"That was one reason," Duin agreed.

"What were the others?"

"I was born in Aergon," Duin said. "Plus, after people here… found out about me, no one really wanted me around anyway. I figured I might as well do something useful if I was going to go court death."

"I'm sorry," Adam said. "You really do hate it here, don't you?"

Duin's mouth twitched. "Yes."

"Although I've noticed they're all tiptoeing very carefully around you since Esmeralda left," Adam said.

A truly genuine smile crossed Duin's features. "Yes. She gave them something to think about."

"I'll say. Maybe they'll stop picking on you now."

"Maybe they'll just start being very, very nice," Duin said, although his tone was uncertain.

"Is that a bad thing?"

"It's different. But it does not quite feel real."

"I've had that feeling since I got here," Adam said, rubbing at his arms. "What was his name?" he asked suddenly.

"What?"

"The man you were with. What was his name?"

Duin shook his head. "There was no man. I was caught looking at the wrong time, and the rumors started. That was pretty much the end of it."

Adam shook his head. "Duin, he knew."

"What? That's not possible."

"You said it yourself, rumors started," Adam said. "He would have heard them, and if there were rumors about you, I can guarantee there were rumors saying who you were staring at, and he'd be the first person they all got told to."

"But then, why did he never…?"

Adam stopped pacing and knelt down at the foot of the bed so he could catch Duin's gaze. "Why did he never what?"

"Say anything?" Duin twisted his hands around themselves nervously, and Adam grabbed them to still him.

"Duin, it's okay."

"He's the only one who never treated me any differently."

"Maybe he liked you too," Adam suggested. "Maybe he was just too scared to act on it—or he was waiting for you to make the first move."

"Please don't say that," Duin said.

"Why not?"

"I have you, right?" Duin said, a shy smile flickering around the corners of his eyes. "I'm not really comfortable thinking about what might have been."

Pulling Duin's head down, Adam kissed him gently. "Okay. Why don't we go and jump through bamboo thickets with Joeri?"

"I'd rather not," Duin said. "You go. I'll be fine."

"Are you sure? You can watch me fall over a few times. That's always amused you before."

"I'm sure. I'll—stay here and meditate."

"Okay," Adam said. "If you need anything…."

Duin squeezed Adam's hands. "Isn't that what I'm supposed to be saying?"

"Hey," Adam said, "I'm your boyfriend. If you need support, that's what I'm here for. You don't always have to be the strong one—even if you more or less have been for, you know, most of our time together."

Duin's smile was genuine. "Thanks. Train hard."

Chapter 20

Adam found Joeri at the archery range, practicing with a shortbow. The lean man looked up at Adam with an open smile. "Sir Adam! I wasn't expecting you."

"I need to do something," Adam replied with a shrug. "I can't cope with all the waiting around."

"I understand," Joeri said. "Where's Duin?"

"Meditating," Adam said. "I don't know if he's good with the waiting either."

Joeri looked at him for a moment, his gaze thoughtful. "I suppose he might not be, at that. Come, we should see how you are with the bow. Have you had any experience?"

Adam nodded. "Some, but I normally use a longbow."

"We tend to shoot from lizardback," Joeri said. "Longer bow arms snag."

"How?"

"You've ridden a lizard. You know how they scramble through undergrowth."

"No, I meant how can you shoot from lizardback?" Adam asked. "We ride so low that we're almost lying down. Even swinging a saber from there generally requires you to brace yourself with one arm on their back while you swing."

"That's because generally you're going to be executing a hit-and-run attack from cover to cover, preferably fleeing through a narrow opening to avoid pursuit and to avoid darts, arrows, rocks, or anything else that gets shot at you in retaliation. If you're fighting one on one, you can sit up, grasp your mount with your knees, and strike outward. Of course, you hit harder on foot unless Zoul is moving at speed," Joeri added with a rueful grin.

"Okay. And… the archery?"

"If you're not ducking for cover, you can rise up and shoot. Although we tend to shoot from cover. It's either good for hunting or for drawing enemies out of position."

"Right. Okay. Let's see what I remember," Adam said, taking a bow and a quiver of arrows. After slinging the quiver across his back, he raised the bow and tugged an arrow from the leather quiver. Or attempted to. The arrow caught on something and dropped back into the quiver.

"What the—"

"You have to pull and twist the shaft of the arrow around," Joeri said. "We put netting over the top of the quiver to stop the arrows falling out when you ride upside down on lizardback. The arrowheads sit in grooves at the base of the quiver, cut perpendicular to the netting to keep them in place."

"Does it always work?" Adam asked.

"More often than not, yes."

"Okay. So…." Adam took hold of an arrow, drew it halfway, and twisted it as close to ninety degrees as he could. After pulling it out the rest of the way, he nocked it in the bow, drew, and fired. For a moment they both stared. "I think I need a bit more practice with this twisting arrow thing," he said finally.

"Yes," Joeri agreed. "Although you hit the target, at least."

"Yeah. Well, I got nothing better to do today," Adam said, reaching back to grab another arrow.

THE NEXT day was much like the one before, although Adam managed to convince a reluctant Duin to join him in training.

"I already know how to do all this, you know," Duin said.

"More practice never hurt," Adam said with a smile. "Besides, your very presence will inspire me to acts of greater valor."

"It will?" Duin asked, his tone unconvinced.

Adam chuckled and pressed his lips to Duin's. "If it doesn't, it'll still make me feel better."

Duin had rolled his eyes and acquiesced.

On a normal day, in a normal world, it would have been evening when they finished, and they were heading down from the archery range to the stables when the commotion occurred. Urging their mounts toward the racket, they found a babble of people surrounding a young man, still clipped into his riding harness. His lizard's skin was abraded, and his left arm hung limp at his side. Sweat was dripping off him, and his eyes were wild.

"I need to speak with the elders immediately," he said.

"Bern, you need a healer," Joeri said. "That arm looks bad."

"Not until I see the elders," Bern said, his chest heaving. "Unless my party made it back first?"

"No," Joeri said slowly. "They haven't."

Bern clenched his jaw and urged his tired mount up the tree, although the beast struggled to move faster than a scramble.

"I'll ride ahead," Joeri said, urging his lizard, Tandyr, into a running scuttle. "Keep an eye on him."

Adam and Duin followed Bern to the council amphitheater at the top of the largest tree, starting a parade that collected more and more followers each level of the tree they rode past. When they arrived at the amphitheater, the seven elders were already gathered. As they rode forward and dismounted, Joeri rushed over to help Bern, one of the healers fast on his heels.

"They got Captain Wendell and the princess," Bern said, the words rushing out of him before anyone could push him into a chair.

"What? Who?" Joeri asked.

"A patrol from Aer Goragon."

"They don't have patrols," Joeri said. "They've never had patrols."

"They do now," Bern said, sinking into a chair as the babble of concerned voices rose from the watching crowd, quieting down only when Elder Faas stood and held a hand up for silence.

"Hunter Bern, perhaps you would be good enough to explain what happened?"

Bern nodded tiredly, wincing as the healer set his arm in a splint. "We were returning from Aer Goragon after infiltrating the city—we climbed the trees in the south to see if it was a good way in. On our way back, we came across the patrol overpowering the princess's party. Hunter Jaak told me to run and tell you while they rode to her defense. They were outnumbered at least three to one."

"And how long ago was this?"

"I rode straight here," Bern said. "Though normally it would have been two sleeps' ride."

Elder Faas sat down heavily, looking more like an old man than Adam had ever seen him. "Captain Roelof, please dispatch some men to check the battle site. In light of the situation, I think we must proceed as if the princess has been lost."

"Scouts?" Adam said indignantly. "We have to rescue her."

"With respect, Sir Adam, how can we know she is even alive to rescue?"

"I don't believe this," Adam said. "You never had any intention of fighting Khalivibra, did you? You just sent her out there to get killed, and now you're going to wash your hands of the whole affair."

Elder Faas clambered to his feet, his body taut and trembling. "That is unworthy of you, Sir Adam."

"If so, then this response is unworthy of you."

"Any other response is premature and risks hundreds of lives, and unless we know if Princess Esmeralda is alive or dead, we cannot know how best to react!"

"Sir Adam," Elder Jirsca interjected, stepping between them. "How well did you know the princess?"

"We're friends," Adam said tersely. "And friends do not send friends off to become dragon food."

"That is precisely the nature of my question," Elder Jirsca agreed. "How intimate was your friendship with the princess?"

Incredulity penetrated the haze of Adam's anger. "Not that intimate!"

"Then she is most likely pure," Elder Jirsca said. "And she will be kept alive—at least until Khalivibra next desires to feed."

"Feed? No, come on. There's hardly enough virginal princesses around to sustain a fully grown creature of her size if that's all it eats. She must eat something else."

"According to legend, yes," Jirsca agreed. "However, also according to legend, the dragons would once protect a kingdom in return for one ritual offering a year."

"A virgin princess?"

"The stories say princes were sacrificed as well. Often kingdoms would kidnap children of their rivals to sacrifice in their stead."

"And you think this means Esmeralda will still be alive?"

"Of course. Even with the dragon's thralls, it will take time to set up an appropriate ritual sacrifice."

Adam closed his eyes, willing the waves of nausea down to the point where he wouldn't upchuck his lunch.

"What about the others?" Duin asked.

"I imagine they will be killed," Jirsca said quietly.

"If they're lucky," Bern said somberly. "If the dragon overwhelms their minds, we could end up fighting our own brothers."

"You mean *when*," Duin said. "*When* her mind overwhelms them."

"You should have more faith in the fortitude of your brothers and sisters, Duin," Elder Thera said sharply.

"Have you felt Khalivibra's mind looking for you?" Duin asked, his eyes flashing. "Because I have. Your warriors are strong, Waur Thera, but I can guarantee the dragon is stronger, even with the protection of Selune."

"And if she gets to Esmeralda—" Adam started.

"If, Sir Adam?" Thera asked. "If or *when*?"

"Esmeralda's mind is strong," Duin said. "Strongest out of all of us, perhaps."

"Strong enough?" Adam asked. "Xavier nearly beat her—he would have beat her if he'd had another day—another sleep—or two."

"He had the skeleton of a dragon to draw power from," Duin objected.

"And she doesn't?"

"Oh, right."

"Right," Adam said, heaving a great sigh. "We're out of time, Duin."

"What exactly do you mean by that, Sir Adam?" Jirsca asked.

"We need to evacuate Boolikstaad," Adam said, to the gasps of the crowd.

"What!" Elder Thera exclaimed. "You cannot seriously expect us to flee our city just because your princess has been captured. You heard Waur Jirsca; she has time."

"She is not my princess," Adam said tiredly. "But she does know where this city is and what it looks like, and she knows that Wyrmbane is here. So do her guards, for that matter."

For a moment, the only sound was the constant trade winds whistling through the leaves overhead, carrying with it the sound of the priests' chanting. "You must take the sword away from here, then," Jirsca said.

"Yes, I know," Adam agreed. "But the dragon won't know I've gone. She'll come straight here and raze Boolikstaad to the ground— along with anyone still here."

"This is not acceptable," Thera snapped. "We did not agree to be made a target of Khalivibra's vengeance!"

"No," Elder Faas agreed softly. "Selune volunteered us when we were marked as her Children. We will not shirk the duties she has laid upon us, will we, Waur Thera?"

Thera took a deep shuddering breath, and for a moment it looked as though she would disagree. Then her shoulders sagged, and she bowed her head. "No, Waur Faas. We will not."

Inclining his own head in acknowledgment, Elder Faas went on. "If Princess Esmeralda was taken two sleeps ago, we have twelve sleeps' distance before she reaches the city."

"And if they don't stop to rest?" Adam asked.

"Seven sleeps," Joeri said. "Possibly eight."

"Plus however long it takes to fly here," Adam added.

"So, less than a sleep?" Duin suggested sardonically.

The council amphitheater, which had so recently been the scene of Esmeralda's questing ceremony, was already buzzing with frantic conversations, the noise rising to a fever pitch as the elders huddled in the middle of the open space, their voices not loud enough to carry, but their gesticulations speaking volumes to the watching crowd. Captain Roelof eased his way back through the throng to add his voice to the debate, which soon grew heated. Eventually they appeared to reach an agreement, with first one, then the next of them nodding gravely, some with defiance, some with determination, and not some few with resignation etched into their features. Finally, Elder Faas nodded solemnly, rose again to his feet, and waited until the crowd quieted, all eyes looking to him.

"Return to your homes and pack what you need. Assemble in the plazas nearest to the ground and you will be directed from there. We will also need volunteers to go ahead and prepare our refuges. Please see Captain Roelof if you wish to lend your strength for the survival of our people."

CHAPTER 21

ADAM AND Duin were quiet as they moved to repack. People were streaming down the tree like ants erupting from a leafy nest as they moved to strip the city of everything they could bring with them. Bidding them farewell, Joeri had been the first to report to Captain Roelof, and he was soon sending small groups of men and women out of the city on lizardback, each one led by a hunter and carrying weapons, shovels, and heavy axes.

"Where do you think they're going?" Adam asked.

"I don't know," Duin said. "And I think it's best if we don't."

"Don't go?"

"Don't know," Duin corrected. "What we don't know we can't reveal, no matter how good the flying lizard is."

"Right," Adam said, ducking his head as he rode Zoul over the balcony and through the doorway into their suite of rooms, with Duin and Hele close behind. "Let's be quick," he said as he unbuckled himself from his riding harness and slid to the ground, then headed straight for the netting and travel packs that had remained mostly untouched since their arrival in the tree city.

Duin had seen to it that most of their clothing had been carefully repacked once it had been cleaned, what with Adam wearing his armor more often than not in recent days. Together, they slung the pack netting over Zoul's haunches and filled it with the familiar packs of camping gear, cookware, and the oilskin cloth that had formed the roofs of many a rainforest shelter. Hele too was loaded with baggage and the large copper cooking pot they had taken from Blackwater Keep.

"Food?" Adam asked.

"Not much," Duin said. "I thought we'd have time to stock up."

"We do, don't we?"

"Can you be certain of that?"

"Point," Adam said. "Let's just get going as soon as possible. We can raid the planters on our way down for anything edible."

There was no sleep that evening—or what would have been evening if the sun ever set in this land of twitterlight and shadow.

By THE time they made their way to the lower plaza of the great tree, it was already full of people, some mounted, but most of them on foot. All carried heavy packs, and in some cases, infants slung in colorful wrappings of spider silk. From halfway up the nearest trunk, Captain Roelof was shouting orders, and while some people were moving out of the plaza, inevitably led by one of Roelof's guards, more crowded in every minute. A riding lizard hissed irritably on the far side of the plaza, and a child cried out as fangs snapped inches from its face. With all the commotion, it took Adam a while to realize what wasn't there.

"Where's the singing gone?" he asked.

"Singing?" Duin responded.

"The singing. You know, the chanting your priests do."

"That's not chanting," Duin said. "Well, okay, it is chanting, but it's a blessing. A ward to keep the dragon from finding us."

"I remember," Adam said. "The point is I can't hear it anymore."

The *pad-pad-pad* of a lizard on the move came up behind them, and Hunter Joeri clapped Adam on the shoulder.

"Adam, Duin, you're just in time. Captain Roelof's sending out groups to our hunting camps. We'll expand the most defensible and have the priests keep them hidden. None of the people know where they're going until they're on their way, so that should keep the dragon guessing if— Why are you both ignoring me?"

"Did you stop the priests here from chanting as well?" Adam asked.

"No. Why?"

"The Blessing of Selune has stopped," Duin said.

"What?"

From somewhere high above, there was the sound of heavy drumbeats, or something that sounded like drumbeats. The leaves rustled, and Adam blinked as a shower of petals, leaves, and bits of bark rained down upon the plaza. The wind whipped around them, and the reddish sunlight streamed in, causing fur to blossom over the faces and limbs of the haerunwoln below. For the first time, Adam realized the children didn't change, but then, Duin had said the Rite of the Sun only happened when leaving childhood. In the plaza, a toddler picked up a lantern berry that had fallen to the ground near her, and she carefully peeled back the brown paperlike leaves to reveal the tart orange fruit within before popping it into her mouth and chewing carefully. Then she screamed as a charred body tumbled from above, a leg catching on the woven branch railing, the foot and calf hanging there as the rest of the body wrenched free and fell to the forest floor below.

People rushed to the edge to look down at the body, and then up to see where the corpse had fallen from. A ball of fire crackled through the canopy of the interlinked trees, causing blackened cinders to rain upon the upturned faces of the haerunwoln below. Then something slammed into the city, sending people sprawling to the floor.

Adam grasped Zoul's reins tightly as wood creaked around them, the entire city groaning as the walkways shifted beneath them. One of the great trunks leaned precariously in toward the central trunk, sending stone light bowls, wooden furniture, and several haerunwoln tumbling off walkways. Some people managed to grab hold of another branch or scramble along a bucking walkway to another of the great ring of trees. Others clung to the trunk itself as it shuddered and swayed. As Adam watched, muscles frozen in shock, the sounds of green wood stretching and snapping reached his ears—a tree was falling in the forest.

"We need to run," Duin said softly.

Not only was a tree falling in the forest, but a great tree was falling in the forest. A great tree that was easily wider than his apartment block at home was falling. Adam watched in horror as the trunk angled and fell hard against another on the other side of the city's tree circle, causing the walkways leading from it to buckle and in several cases break, pulling on several of the other trees. Around the city, pandemonium broke loose as people scrambled for safety, and Captain Roelof's increasingly frantic orders went unheeded.

"We run and everyone here is dead," Adam said as he picked up his helmet and placed it on his head. After unbuckling the clips on his riding belt, he dismounted and handed Zoul's reins to Duin. "Get him out of here. Get everyone out of here."

"Adam—"

"I can distract her," Adam said. "I'll come when I can."

"You can't seriously go up there on foot," Joeri objected. "What if you fall?"

"Then I don't fall," Adam said, trying to stop his hands from shaking. "I can't bring Zoul up there. Duin, keep him out of Khalivibra's line of fire, okay?"

"Adam, this is no time to be a hero!" Duin snapped.

Grabbing his lover's face in both hands, Adam kissed Duin fiercely. "I know. I'm just going to distract her long enough for you to get everyone clear of here. Tell them it's an order or something."

"From who?"

Adam yanked off the spider-eye pendant Esmeralda had given him and pressed it into Duin's palm. "Say it's from the princess," Adam said as he started to climb the stairs, pushing against the crowd of people pouring down the stairs and walkways in an attempt to get to the ground.

THE SOUND of splintering wood grew louder as Adam ran higher into the tree, passing the lower areas where simple sleeping quarters had been hollowed out for families and then past the dormitory-style rooms that housed single haerunwoln. A fletcher and weaver were next, all with the arboreal gardens that provided much of Boolikstaad's food. As he pushed past the priests' dwellings to emerge at the council chambers, he was breathing heavily, although thankfully the press of jostling bodies had abated somewhat.

From the empty amphitheater, he could see the rest of the tree city's canopy, the leafy roof now rent and torn, allowing the red light to stream in. Charred embers fell around him, singeing his face as he stared out at the destruction. The great tree that had fallen crashed into the upper branches of the tree next over from the council tree, and Adam saw the doorways and tilted windows that had once housed Elder Jirsca and her extended family. Her carefully tended gardens had been smashed or uprooted in the fall, and the lantern berry bushes had withered in the fire that had consumed much of the dead branches, causing the fresh green wood to smoke. In the midst of it all, wreathed in smoke, was a beast. A great golden beast.

She was as big as the proverbial barn—although she put Adam more in the mind of the Union building at university, with its multiple stories, purple walls, and downstairs food court. Admittedly, the dragon was more scales, fangs, and bat-like wings, but that was the closest Adam could think of in terms of size. Khalivibra's neck was short, proportionately closer to that of a lizard than the long serpentine neck he had always pictured from *The Hobbit*. Her head was wide and triangular, making Adam think of a large-scaled toad or a squat-jawed crocodile, and her body was compact and muscled like that of a pit bull. Her golden scales glittered in the reds and yellows of twitterlight and flame. The tail was shorter than he had imagined, perhaps only half as long as her body. With four clawed arms she gripped the tree, muscles flexing beneath her skin as she reached out to claw at a branch that blocked her way with talons longer than Adam's boot knife. Her wings were folded tightly against her back as she climbed higher in a sinuous wriggle that reminded Adam of a riding lizard stalking a giant tree spider.

Looking ahead of the dragon, Adam could see a small figure climbing desperately up through the branches, striving to reach the next tree among the twisted and shattered walkways, the movement of the dragon causing the treetops to shake beneath the haerunwoln's feet. He or she was wearing a delicately embroidered silk wrap, although between the fire and sunlight, their features were far more thylacine than human, with a silver-flecked chestnut muzzle and clawed hands very much evident. As the figure darted past a still intact stone glow, Adam recognized the embroidery as that adorning the robes of Elder Jirsca.

Unslinging the shortbow from his back, Adam pulled an arrow from his quiver. He sighted along it, took a deep breath, then released the arrow on his exhale. It flew straight and true, arcing toward the dragon before clattering off its scales and falling into the foliage. Khalivibra appeared not to notice, and climbed on after the fleeing elder, her progress slowed by her attempts to remove the larger branches that blocked her path. As Adam drew another arrow, it seemed that Elder Jirsca would escape, but then the dragon reared up, drew back her head, and belched forth a stream of fire that caught the entire crown of the tree, the delicate weeping needles disintegrating into ash as they burned through, going from green to a gray-black in moments. Elder Jirsca's screams died away as her burning body fell from the branches, and the tree slumped farther down, gouging into the bark of the other.

As her tree slid several meters before being caught by a heavy bough, Khalivibra spread her wings, the shock wave from their heavy beating cracking through the air as she strove to keep her balance. Forcing himself to act, Adam drew another arrow and sent it flying. The projectile punctured the dragon's wing, and if the indignant roar she let out was anything to go by, found a chink in her scales.

The giant triangular head swung toward him, her yellow eyes glaring balefully up at him. Almost in slow motion, Adam saw her brow ridges narrow as she focused in on him, and her muscles bunched as she clawed her way back into the canopy. As her head wove back and forth, a long forked tongue flickered out toward him, and her mouth opened, revealing fangs as long as his forearms.

His brain swimming in terror, Adam reached back for another arrow, only to have it jerk from his hand as the arrowhead hit the netting at the top of the quiver. Cursing at this clumsiness, Adam threw himself to the ground just in time as Khalivibra's return volley of flame licked at the living wood around him and withered the carrot tops and the fragrant bushes that Adam had always thought of as wild peppermint, despite its slightly waxy leaves.

Crawling along behind the first row of benches, Adam grabbed for support as the tree shook again, and the fencing and planter boxes burst inward as Khalivibra scrambled into the courtyard. With a burst of speed, Adam rolled to his feet, then darted behind her. Taking hold of Wyrmbane with both hands, he sliced at her tail. The blade moved faster than any he had ever used and sank through her scales like butter, shearing through the bone and striking down to the wooden floor itself. Grunting, he yanked it from the ground and ran on, only to be swept off his feet as the dragon turned around, the tail stump drenching him in blood and slamming him into the far wall. The blood was hot, thick, and stung his eyes, and it left a coppery taste in his mouth as he spat it out. Wiping his face with his left hand, he saw the dragon rounding on him, her claws leaving sap-oozing gashes in the floor.

Adam scrambled to his feet and all but fell through the door leading to the guest quarters. Turning, he ran up the stairs just as Khalivibra burst through the door—or at least, her head did, splintering the deadwood of the door, one large hand scrabbling in to find him. Adam stood, transfixed, against the mezzanine wall as the dragon came toward him. Stale breath wafted out, bringing with it the smell of ash and overcooked meat. One more strike and the dragon would have him, batting him down like a child's toy and slicing him in two or three, depending on how many of the razor-sharp claws connected. One more wriggle and she'd be close enough.

Khalivibra lunged, and there was a loud thunk that shook the entire tree. The great claws stopped a few meters shy of him, and he looked up, shrinking away as a roar echoed around the hallway. As the dragon tried to push closer toward him, straining at the confines of the doorway, he understood and ran up the rest of the stairs and into the suite that had been his room. All he had to do was run past his bed and wardrobe and out onto his balcony and jump onto her back, which should be there if she was still trying to get through the door to him. Pushing through the flimsy balcony doors, he skidded to a halt as the great head rose to greet him, its yellow eyes sly.

"Only if I was still trying to get to you through the door." The words blasted into his mind.

Adam backed away slowly and brought Wyrmbane up defensively before him.

"Stay out of my head," he snapped.

"But it's such an interesting head," Khalivibra said. *"So many thoughts swimming below for me to fish out and devour."*

"Then come and get it," Adam suggested. "I mean, why not? I'm sure you know what this is. Can you feel it? I can feel it. Apparently some old prince created it to kill your lover."

"That is not the Sword of Fernando."

"No, but it cut through your tail like butter. What do you think it'll do to your precious wings?"

The dragon's eyes narrowed, and she pushed away from the tree, great wings unfurling and launching her into the air, the downdrafts buffeting Adam back as the tree swayed from the force of her launch. Grasping the doorframe for support, Adam stumbled back, cursing at the dragon's flight. How had Fernando done it all those years ago? Had he stood at the edge of his parapet and waited, trusting his reflexes to get one lucky thrust before the dragon's attack struck home and killed him? How could a blade, one blade, be of any use against a creature with such bloody great wings? The thought flashed across his brain in moments, and then his eyes widened, and he ducked back into the room just in time as the dragon's bulk slammed into the council tree, rocking it down to its roots. The tree groaned around him as the furniture slid against the far wall and then rushed back, nearly crushing him. Indeed, if it wasn't for the curved wall of the rooms, he would have been flattened. Then the furniture slid away and a second impact rocked the tree, sending him crashing into the door of the wardrobe, still full, he remembered irrationally, of the fine clothes he and Duin had been gifted with for the duration of their stay in Boolikstaad.

As the tree swung back, the wardrobe shifted and slid across the room, bearing Adam in front of it as it came to rest just before the still-closed door leading out into the main corridor. He could make it to the door and out into the main amphitheater. He might even make it to the stairs.

"Ah, but will you make it to the ground in time?" Khalivibra's voice rang in his mind. *"Will I pick you out of the foliage,* Sir *Adam? Or will you simply die when the trees come down?"*

The next impact threw Adam into the wall, where he hit his head and slumped to the floor. Luckily for him, he never felt the impact as the greatest tree of Boolikstaad smashed into its neighbor, both heading toward the ground.

CHAPTER 22

WHEN ADAM came to, he was in the dark, and the air was stale and heavy. He was lying on something soft—well, mostly soft—and there wasn't so much as a pinprick of light to see by. Automatically his hands went to his pockets for his Zippo lighter, only to remember he hadn't found a place in his armor to hide it yet, and it had been stashed in his gym bag and stowed among the packs on Zoul's back. His body also took the opportunity to remember the beating he had given it, and all of the aches and pains from his fight came flooding in, along with the taste of drying blood that still flecked his lips. Hopefully not his blood. Running his tongue around his lips, he felt a couple of splits, as well as a large swelling where his face had been mashed against something hard, so some of it was probably his blood.

Resisting the urge to panic, Adam felt around a bit more, finding the hilt of his sword, smooth silk fabric and the slightly scaly texture of lizard leather. Reaching above, he felt some round wooden pegs, and suddenly he knew exactly where he was. Bringing his knees to his chest, he pressed his feet to the door of the wardrobe and pushed. The door was heavier than he remembered, but when fine particles of ash and dirt spilled onto his body, he stopped pushing, coughing as he pawed at his eyes. Taking a deep breath caused another coughing fit, and he fished around until he could pull a corner of a shirt over his face. Bracing his legs against the door again, he paused.

If he was buried far underground, letting the dirt in would mean letting the air out, and quite possibly suffocating himself. On the other hand, the door was moving. Under normal circumstances, with rest, a proper inclined gym seat, and no injuries, Adam could easily leg-press over two hundred kilos, and even if these weren't normal circumstances, he was hoping two hundred odd kilos of debris wouldn't be enough to suffocate him. If nothing else, he had no idea if anyone would find him before he ran out of air. Closing his eyes, he took a deep breath through the silk and pushed with as much strength as he could muster, his legs protesting every inch of the way. Dust and ash fountained into the small space, and when Adam finally kicked the door open, he rose spluttering in a cloud of soot, forcing himself to stay standing as he coughed into the shirt still wrapped around his nose and mouth.

Staring at his surroundings, he found himself back in his Boolikstaad room, standing on the wall near the entry door. The bed lay off to one side, twisted in a broken heap, with the remnants of the mattress falling in blackened piles through the slats of the bed. It had been a simple bed, even compared to cheap Ikea or two-dollar-shop furniture standards, but Adam had found out that by Boolikstaad standards, having a frame to put a mattress on was luxurious. The majority of Boolikstaad's inhabitants had slept on mattresses of piled rushes and a bracken-like fern held together with a thick cover of woven silk. The blankets were much the same as his had been, simple silk stuffed with the fluffy seed filling of a forest tree, and his had burned to ash along with the mattress, the remnants falling over the baked end of the dragon's tail, which must have fallen in when the tree fell.

The main door was blocked by the wardrobe beneath him, and walking across to peek into what had officially been Duin's room showed that the small window there was pressed into the ground. The large doors to the balcony that he had expected Khalivibra to come bursting through however long ago were up where the ceiling would have been, and largely covered by blackened branches and leaves. Thankfully, Adam was a tall man, and the room, while plush by Boolikstaad standards, had been no larger than a small hotel room. Standing on the closed wardrobe doors, he threw his sword out the doorway and onto the now horizontal outside wall, trusting Wyrmbane wouldn't let anyone else pick it up. Then he jumped, caught the edge of the door frame, and pulled himself out onto the charred wood that had once been his bedroom wall.

The sight that greeted him was one of devastation. The proud trees of Boolikstaad were no more, most of them having been reduced to still-smoking embers or smashed into raw kindling. Here and there the corner of a planter box protruded, or the carved stone of the green glows they used for light could be seen poking out of the devastation, the dim light lost in the red that poured in through the hole in the canopy. The soft chanting that he was so familiar with rang in the air still, but it was a thin lone voice off to one side, rather than the constant chorus he had become used to.

Turning his head, Adam saw two haerunwoln sitting in the shade of a small pine, swathed in their robes of undyed silk and surrounded by vigilant guards. One protector and one spare, apparently, but somehow the two men seemed a frail shield from the ravages of the dragon. Across the former city site, men and women worked to salvage belongings and tools that had been left behind in the exodus, or dug to recover the bodies of loved ones. A pall of dust and smoke hung in the air, but worse still was the grim silence with which work progressed, all the time with lookouts keeping an eye on the skies. A shout went up when he was spotted, and by the time he carefully navigated his way back down to the ground, Duin was there, looking as furred and pointy eared as he had on their journey north, his short muzzle stained with soot.

"You really need to stop doing this, Adam," Duin said, as he pulled away from their hug. "Are you all right?"

"I don't know," Adam said, gratefully accepting Duin's shoulder in support. "I guess so. Nothing feels broken, but I ache everywhere."

"Where were you?"

"I got knocked into the wardrobe when she was demolishing the tree," Adam said. "I must have passed out."

"That probably saved you," Duin said. "She can't read your mind if it's not thinking. That and the fact that you'd have hit a lot of other trees before hitting the ground. When the others fell, there was nothing to break their fall… almost no one survived the drop."

"But you got everyone out of the lower levels?"

"Yes," Duin said. "Most of them anyway. Some panicked, but that couldn't be helped."

"Where will you go?" Adam asked.

"With you," Duin said simply. "You gave Joeri quite a shock, you know."

"How? Did he think I was going to run away like a cowardly rabbit?"

"A whattit?" Duin asked. "Wait, never mind. I probably don't know it anyway. No, he just… when you… before you… you know…."

"Oh?" Adam's eyes widened. "Oh. Right," he said, nuzzling into Duin's neck. "He can bite me; I don't give a crap."

"I don't think he wants to bite you," Duin said. "Are you sure you're all right?"

"I just fought a dragon," Adam said, reaching down to pick up his sword, which he attempted to wipe clean on the sleeve of a silk shirt to little effect. "Everything hurts, and I should be dead right now, so no, I'm not all right, but I don't think I could be any better."

Duin sat Adam down on a large flat rock by the steaming hot stream flowing from the hot springs. They were in what once had been the kitchens of Boolikstaad, by the looks of the pots and cauldrons half buried in the dirt of the forest floor. On the far side of the stream, the roots of the tree Adam had always thought of as "the one with the stables" clawed at the air, the inner network of roots a dark, sprawling cave mouth that rose out of the broken ground. Twisted root ends thrust out of soft mounds of soil like teeth in a monstrous wooden maw. Adam was propped up against a mostly intact log, and Duin carefully removed his helmet. "I'm amazed the carapace isn't more dented," he said, tugging carefully as Adam's bloodied hair pulled away from the inside of the leather helm—or in some cases pulled away from his head, stuck to the inner padding.

"She never actually hit me," Adam said, wincing as Duin put the helmet down and started on the buckles of his armor. "If she had, I'd be dead."

"I guess you got lucky, then, even with the head wound."

"I don't have a head wound," Adam said. "Most of that is blood from her tail."

"Really? You hurt her?"

"Yeah. The sword certainly works," Adam said. "But that's the thing. How can I get close enough to strike with it when she can just fly off and kill me from a distance?"

"One thing at a time, Adam," Duin said, removing the breast and backplates from his jerkin and then easing Adam out of the stiff leathers. After dipping a cloth in the warm water, he started cleaning the blood from Adam's face and hair. "You know, I hate it when you do this."

"Do what?"

"Run off without me."

"I had to," Adam said. "Zoul wouldn't go with anyone else."

"Sometimes I feel like I should have been a healer rather than a hunter, given the scrapes you get into."

"If you weren't a hunter, we'd have died before we got here," Adam said, wincing as Duin's ministrations dug at the gravel and splinters in his wounds. "Why do these things always hurt more afterwards?" he grumbled.

"Because if they hurt this much when you were getting them, you'd never last a fight."

"Yeah, I know, adrenaline and such," Adam said irritably. "Sorry, that was just me wishing it didn't have to hurt so much."

"Well, we'll have you patched up in no time flat," Duin said.

"No time flat?" Adam asked. "You never say that."

"You mean, I never did until I met you," Duin said with a smile that was only partially forced.

"So now I'm a bad influence as well? Thank you so much."

Duin shrugged and waved over a healer, who started to apply a pungent salve to Adam's wounds before the worst of his injuries were bound with clean bandages. "I should give you this back as well," Duin said, lifting the spider's eye pendant off his head.

"It looks better on you, you know," Adam said.

"This pendant was a gift from Princess Esmeralda," Duin said sternly. "And it was given to you, not to me."

"I know," Adam said, ducking his head so Duin could put the pendant back around his neck. "I was just making an observation."

Duin's smile was brief, and Adam noticed how his lover's hands trembled ever so slightly as they continued to clean his wounds. Thankfully, the thick leather trousers had prevented any major damage to his lower body, just the bruising he had taken from being knocked around. The pain of putting his cleaned armor back on, however, was much greater than he had anticipated.

"I know it hurts," Duin said sympathetically, "but it will hurt a lot more if you get caught without it on. It will take at least a sleep for the salve to do its work."

"Please tell me the salve is magical," Adam said, gritting his teeth against the weight of the breastplate and backplate that Duin was reattaching.

"Blessed, Sir Adam," the healer corrected sternly. "The favor of the goddess is a gentler balm than the brute force of sorcery, and much more effective at healing."

"Is that a tone of disapproval I hear in your voice, Healer Marcel?" Duin asked.

"Sorcery damages the fabric of the world," Marcel said. "It tears what is real to exert itself and allows chaos into the order of nature."

"Does that order of nature include a great winged fire-breathing dragon killing everything in its path?" Adam asked pointedly. "Because if it does, I say 'Yay, sorcery.'"

Marcel sighed and rubbed at his temples. "I know, but I still don't have to like it. Sorcery leaves a stain on the world, Sir Adam. I have spoken to the Elders of Selune, and we know the dragon is using sorcerous magics."

"Well, we did suspect that was the case," Adam said.

Marcel shook his head. "With respect, Sir Adam, we suspected the dragon had found a way to bolster her own powers. However, it was always a possibility that her powers were a gift from Helene, rather than those wrought through magic."

"If the results are the same, what does it matter how she got her powers?"

Marcel smiled as he tied off a bandage on Adam's arm. "Because it means her powers are not drawn from the favor of Helene. The very fact that she has them may even be a sign that Helene's favor is waning."

"Okay, but how does that help us?" Adam asked.

"I suppose you could take some comfort in the knowledge that Helene may not smite you for destroying her champion," Marcel said. "And that she may not give aid to Khalivibra in your final confrontation."

"That's a lot to put on a 'maybe,'" Adam said.

"But better than having the opposite as a certainty. Had we known earlier, we may have been bolder in the past."

"Well, you may have to be bolder now," Adam said as he stood up and then sat back down in a hurry as the world swam before his eyes. "Okay, that wasn't a good idea."

"You should probably eat," Duin said as he reached into a rucksack and pulled out some spider jerky and some fruit that Adam had never quite got a handle on, looking like small yellow bells and tasting a little like a watery guava. "Here," he said, placing them into Adam's hands and pulling out a waterskin that he placed on the rock between them. "I'll get Zoul."

ADAM HAD never tried to describe a lizard happily galloping toward him. He had heretofore never thought of a galloping lizard, and truth be told, he had never expected to see one. In Adam's limited experience, giant riding lizards didn't gallop so much as scuttle, with a sinuous motion that put him in the mind of a six-legged serpent slithering through the landscape. Apparently, Zoul did have a gallop switch, but it wasn't one he chose to use very often. His head was held high, mouth open, and crest fully extended upward as he ran across the broken ground, six large feet flailing as he all but danced around Adam, butting him enthusiastically with his head.

"Ow, Zoul, stop it," Adam said, pushing on Zoul's head to stop him from hitting him again. "I'm glad to see you too, okay?"

Zoul chirped happily and promptly settled down next to Adam, worming his way forward so Adam's left hand was resting on his head.

"All right," Duin said when he reached them, riding Hele at a more sedate walk some minutes later. "I feel a bit bad saying we need to ride now," he said, unbuckling his riding harness.

Zoul closed his inner eyelids and hissed as Duin approached.

"Do you think you could talk to him?" Duin asked Adam plaintively. "He's been like that ever since I stopped him following you up the council tree."

"Be nice, Zoul," Adam said, tapping his mount on the nose. "I needed you away from the dragon."

Zoul's chirp sounded more like a grumble, but he allowed Duin to approach and help Adam with his riding harness, even if he gave Duin the proverbial cold shoulder, or six. Despite his aches and pains, Adam found settling down into the saddle was something blessedly familiar, and he happily urged Zoul into a walk, following Duin to the edge of the city boundary and back up into the highway of old tree boughs, where they were met by Hunter Joeri and Elder Thera.

Joeri nodded as they approached. "Welcome back, Sir Adam," he said. "I wasn't sure I'd see you again."

"Me either," Adam said. "Waur Thera," he added, inclining his head toward the woman, who looked more or less the same in the deep shadows of the old forest, only a light dusting of fur covering her features.

Elder Thera inclined her head but made no other acknowledgment as the words of the blessing tumbled from her lips.

"We take no chances," Joeri explained softly. "Come, we must ride."

<h1 style="text-align:center">CHAPTER 23</h1>

THE TREETOP dwelling Joeri led them to reminded Adam of the sleeping shelters he and Duin had frequently constructed in the rainforest. Based in a stand of large hollow trees with thick elephant-like branches, there were enough haerunwoln crammed into the small area that Adam couldn't see how it could hide anyone should a patrol march by.

"We're not safe here," he murmured as they dismounted, handing the reins of their mounts over to a lizard keeper.

"I know," Joeri said as he helped Elder Thera down from her mount and handed her a waterskin. "We can't all stay here, but most of the priests were in the canopy when she attacked."

"We thought we had more time," Elder Thera said, her voice sounding hoarse and husky from overuse.

"We all thought we had time," Adam said. "How did she get there so fast?"

"Wings," Duin said shortly.

"I meant the information."

"So did I," Duin said. "She'd have a way to talk with her patrols."

"But they didn't know where the city was."

"Esmeralda did," Duin said flatly. "And she doesn't have the benefit of Selune's blessing."

"She has magic."

"So does Khalivibra."

"You're right." Adam sighed. "That brings me back to the part where we're not safe here. If she sends out another scouting party for us...."

"She thinks you're dead," Duin pointed out. "Why would she come after us again?"

"If I was dead, wouldn't Wyrmbane choose again?" Adam asked. He glanced around at them but received no answer. "What, you don't know?"

"Until you arrived, we did not know if the Wyrmbane was real," Thera said. "To the best of our knowledge, there have only been two who have ever wielded the blade—including yourself."

"But it could?"

"It is possible."

"Then she'll be back," Adam said. "Or be sending her minions after it."

"How do you know that?" Duin asked.

"The same reason she came to Boolikstaad in the first place," Adam said. "If there was one weapon in the entire world that could kill me, I'd want it destroyed, or at the very least, know where it was locked up. Preferably by me."

"Then why didn't she stay and take it off your corpse?" Thera asked.

"I don't know."

"Maybe Wyrmbane would not choose again," Thera said. "Did the princess not say she summoned you here? Summoned you as hero?"

"Yes," Duin replied when Adam's words failed him.

"Then the stone will not choose merely anyone. Khalivibra must know that."

"Especially since the ritual Esmeralda used requires dragon scale as a reagent," Duin said. "And her people have none left."

"But we have dragon scale," Adam said. "The tip of her tail is in the room I was staying in."

"I will send someone to fetch it," Joeri said, stepping aside to speak with a young guard.

"Even so, without the princess, our only hope is you, Sir Adam," Thera said tiredly.

"Yeah, well, I sort of wish I wasn't," Adam said.

"I concur," Thera said simply, her voice as carefully neutral as he'd ever heard. "Which is why I suggest we rest now and rescue her as soon as we are able."

"We'll set out tomorrow," Adam said. "After next sleep, that is—you know what I mean."

Elder Thera nodded. "I will have much to prepare."

"You do?"

"If I am to travel longer than a sleep from here, yes. Hunter Bern said it would take us near eleven sleeps to reach Aer Goragon. I will find it hard to ensure we are hidden from the dragon's mind for all of that time."

"She'll only find us if she looks," Adam said. "Wait, you're coming with us?" he added as the rest of his brain caught up with the discussion topic.

"Someone has to ensure you reach the city safely," Thera said. "And I am not entrusting that task to anybody else."

"With respect, Waur Thera, you belong with your people," Duin said.

"And if I serve them best by accompanying Sir Adam to Aer Goragon, then that is what I must do. Also, I may be able to speed our journey somewhat."

"You can?" Adam asked. "How?"

"I will speak with Elder Faas," Thera said, turning away to climb down a rude ladder into the depths of the tree's hollow. "Rest now, Sir Adam. You will need your strength next waking."

BY THE time Duin had shown him to a corner of the tree where he could rest, Adam could feel his eyelids drooping, and as soon as he and Duin had removed the carapace plating from his armor, he was in bed, clothes and all. "How come none of you have armor like mine?" Adam asked around a yawn.

"It doesn't fit properly if we go out into the light," Duin said. "You've seen how I grow and change. The scouts have smaller overlapping rows of carapace—that's the best we can do, but that is neither stealthy nor comfortable to be in."

"And my armor?"

"Master Cobus was pleased to have a chance to apply his knowledge of Aergonite plate mail," Duin said with a smile. "And working with moon spider carapace no less."

"You say 'moon spider' as if it's important."

Duin stilled. "But it is. The moon spider is traditionally a creature sent by Selune to test her warriors."

"Sent by? What, you mean she whispers around its arachnid ears and sends them off to attack people?"

"It makes as much sense as birds do," Duin muttered.

Adam sighed. "I'm sorry. I didn't mean to insult your faith. But it's hard to give credence to something I don't believe in."

Adam felt Duin's lips gently touch the back of his neck. "I don't think that matters, Adam," he said. "She might just believe in you."

Adam awoke to find things pretty much as they had been when he went to sleep. The carapace sections of his armor were piled in a heap at the side of his bedroll, and he was still sore from sleeping in his leathers, although not so stiff and sore as he thought he would have been after the injuries he had sustained from the dragon's attack. Duin was curled up on a bedroll next to his own, and Adam absently reached out to stroke the mop of tangled brown hair that adorned the top of his head.

"You love him, do you not?" Joeri's soft voice said, and Adam turned to find the hunter sitting cross-legged in the shadowed corner where the platform met the tree trunk.

"Yes," he said. "Very much."

"And he loves you."

"I hope so," Adam said.

"He does," Joeri said. "That is plain for all to see."

Adam sat up and glanced to where his sword lay between the bedrolls. "Is that going to be a problem?"

"No," Joeri said. "Take care of him, please."

"As long as he'll let me," Adam said. "Besides, mostly he takes care of me."

Joeri nodded and stood up, clearing his throat. "I'll bring some food up, and then we should talk. Waur Thera and Waur Faas wish to speak to us below."

As Joeri headed down the tree from the tiny platform they were sleeping on, Adam leaned over and kissed the back of Duin's neck. "Hey, lover, wake up."

"Mmm? Don't wanna," Duin mumbled, moving back as if to snuggle against Adam, and promptly slipped off the bedroll. It was only a few inches, but it was noisy as Duin fell against Adam's sheathed broadsword and leapt away, cursing. "Shards, that thing is dangerous, Adam!"

"I'm sorry," Adam said, snatching up the sword. "Did it burn you?"

"I don't know—I don't think so?" Duin said, turning his back and straining to peer over his shoulder. "What does it look like?" he asked.

"Fantastic?" Adam suggested, stepping close and dropping another kiss on Duin's shoulder. "A little red is all. Does this hurt?" he asked, running his fingers lightly over the patch of reddened flesh.

"Not really," Duin said. "I'll live, I think. What's going on?"

"Joeri's bringing breakfast," Adam said. "The elders want to talk to us."

"Right, of course," Duin said. "I suppose I should get dressed."

"You don't have to," Adam said. "I like the view, although you look just as sexy in your harness."

"When this is over," Duin said, "you and I have a lot of time to make up."

"I know," Adam said, reaching for his boots. "Do you really think we're going to make it?"

"We have to," Duin said. "I don't really see we have any choice now."

Adam sighed. "No, I suppose we don't."

"How are you feeling now, anyway?" Duin asked, securing his harness with a whittled wooden buckle.

"A bit stiff," Adam said. "But remarkably well, considering."

"You should get Healer Marcel to give you a jar of that ointment," Duin suggested as he came over to check Adam's bandages. "We should change those."

"I suppose," Adam said, shrugging out of his jerkin.

When Duin unwrapped Adam's bindings, they found the wounds and scrapes had all but healed, although the skin below was new and pink and the yellowish outline of where the bruises had been still visible.

"Can I go ahead and call it magic now?" Adam said as he stared at his right arm. "I don't know what he did, but that is amazing."

"I've never seen it work so well," Duin said, brushing some dried salve off Adam's arm. "Now will you admit that Selune is looking out for you?"

"Not without a clinical study into that salve, no. But look at that," he remarked as Duin unwrapped the longer bandage from around his torso. "You'd almost think I hadn't bled at all," he remarked as he looked down at himself.

"Except for the dried blood on the bandages, yes," Duin said. "And you know, my memories."

"Duin, I'm fine, really."

"I know," Duin said. "This time. But what about next time? We're going to head into her city, Adam. Surrounded by her people. What are we going to do?"

"Stick to the plan," Adam said. "And hope that she does think I'm dead."

"The plan required her to not be in the city," Duin said.

"So we improvise," Adam said. "You said it before; there's no other way out of this."

THEY WERE dressed by the time Joeri arrived with bowls of fruit, nuts, and coal-baked flitterfish.

"Isn't fire risky?" Adam asked as Joeri placed the platter down before them.

"Not as risky as trying to return to our kitchens at Boolikstaad. The other rivers here are too cool for our normal cooking methods, so our choice is either risk a fire or eat things raw." Joeri smiled, showing his teeth. "And while that's fine if you have no other option, I do not think we wish to risk becoming sick if we catch the wrong scarab or hunt the wrong spider."

"Is everyone coming here?" Adam asked. "I don't think we can fit all of Boolikstaad here."

"No," Joeri said, helping himself to a lantern berry. "There are other camps, much like this one. I know of one other—Captain Roelof is in charge of that one. There may be more, but for now it is perhaps best that we do not know where they are."

They finished the rest of the meal in silence, and then Adam and Duin wordlessly followed Joeri down through the branches to the tree's hollow. The inside had been separated into floors by carving out holes in which to place support beams, overlaid with rough planks of green wood and covered in rushes. Inside a stone bowl had been set up for light. Piles of documents were scattered haphazardly in the corners, and large rectangular stones had been used in combination with some wood offcuts to make rudimentary shelving. There were also bunches of herbs and flowers hung in bundles from the planks that formed the roof overhead and a small pallet of rushes and bracken in the corner for sleeping.

Elder Faas and Elder Thera were seated in a clear space in the middle of the room with a rough, chipped rock the size of a door lying on the floor between them. It was milky white in color, or at least Adam thought it would be, given the way the green glow reflected off its surface. "Ah, Sir Adam," Elder Faas said, looking up. "I think we can get you into Aer Goragon."

"You can? How?"

"This is a fragment from Selune herself," Elder Faas said, "taken from the Temple of Selune in Aergon by the first to be cast out, and before that from the temple in Blackwater."

Adam frowned. "If they were cast out, how did they sneak that out? It's a bit hard to shove down your trousers."

Elder Faas smiled. "When the first of our people left the Caverns of Aergon, there were a fair number of us, and many held important positions in the Temple of Selune. We were still cast out, but our lorekeepers tell us that the initial exile was more… civilized. They left with supplies and some of their artifacts—such as this."

"I see." Adam nodded, and then, feeling something more was expected of him, opened his mouth. "I'm not sure how this will help us, Elder Faas."

"And until Waur Thera came up with her bright idea, I didn't think it helpful either," Elder Faas said. "Waur Thera?"

"We can use the stone to open a moon bridge between here and the temple in Aer Goragon," Thera said. "I would not have attempted this before, but now that we know Khalivibra does not have the favor of Helene, she will not be able to stop us."

"Stop you?"

"The chosen of Helene can feel us when we exercise the more… ostentatious gifts of Selune," Elder Thera explained. "Just as we can feel when they exercise their gifts, or a sorcerer knows when another is working her craft nearby. For many cycles this has prevented us from using many of the blessings Selune bestowed on us so long ago."

"Like the moon bridges," Elder Faas said, beaming.

"And what exactly is a moon bridge?" Adam asked.

"A portal that bridges the gap between sacred stones of the moon," Thera said simply. "Any raw stone can be used, but the portal size is only as big as the stone itself. As you can see, we have a stone large enough that you could even ride Zoul through to the other side."

"And the other side being?"

"The fresco in the main hall of the Temple of Helene in Aer Goragon," Thera said, smiling. "It is the only raw moonstone in the city that would be still intact. Each temple has a fresco reflecting their sister goddess, and from what Bern says, we know that the Temple of Helene appears largely intact."

"How long would the journey take across this moon bridge?" Adam asked, his heart pounding.

"No longer than it would take you to take two steps," Thera said, her smile widening. "And the beauty is, even if Khalivibra does detect what we do, she will feel us working our gifts here, rather than in Aer Goragon where you will be arriving."

"And we couldn't just have done this before?" Adam asked.

"Until Bern returned, we did not think the fresco was still intact," Elder Faas reminded him. "And if Khalivibra could detect us, we would not have wished to lead her back to Boolikstaad."

"Both are concerns which worry us no more," Thera said, as four other haerunwoln entered, leading Zoul, Hele, Thandyr, and a fourth lizard that Adam recognized as Elder Thera's mount. Rising to her feet, Elder Thera put on her riding harness and stepped gracefully into the saddle. "Mount up, gentlemen," she said. "For we ride to Aer Goragon for good or ill."

Adam double-checked to make sure all of Zoul's packs had been put on before clipping himself into the saddle, just in time to see the four groomsmen hoist the large stone into position against the far wall.

Elder Faas approached it, pressed his forehead against the rock, and stretched his arms wide to grasp its edges.

"The stone remembers," he said, his voice strangely choral, as if it were overlaid with another that Adam could hear but not quite hear at the same time. "The stone remembers all and was all one in times gone past. The stone remembers all and is all one in the time that is now. The stone is—" Elder Faas stepped to one side, and Adam was shocked to see his eyes were milky white, with no trace of the pupil or brown of the iris. "—open."

And before them, in the middle of the milky white stone, was a glittering veil of green energy, leading into an inky darkness that fell away into impossible depths. Silently and in single file they entered the portal.

CHAPTER 24

THE BLACK of the portal turned out to be exactly that—the black of the portal. It was a bit like a sheet of darkness between the two places, one that allowed no light through but allowed the passage of the four travelers. Adam watched as his arm disappeared before him, seeming to be cut off where it pierced the veil, and then he was through, blinking in the red twitterlight of the sun. The temple room they were in was open to the air, with tall pillars of sandstone reaching to the sky, embedded with what looked to be golden cubes. The temple itself was bare and empty of any decoration other than the carved moonstone panel they had just exited from, giving no indication that this was—or had been—a place of worship.

"Why isn't there anything here?" Adam asked as Duin and Joeri rode into the room, the black portal closing behind them silently.

"Good question," Elder Thera said. "There should be a great gold statue of Helene here. Not to mention her altar was also solid gold."

"Can't have been," Adam said. "That would be far too soft—look, this is still here," he said, pointing at a crude sandstone block. "They must have covered this in gold."

"And that plinth must have been where Helene's statue would have stood," Duin said. "I always remembered the story of the twelve flames of Helene that would dance on top of her temple to greet the sun—although I don't understand why the sun needed greeting. It is not as if the sun ever goes away."

"But it used to," Adam said, staring up into the sky. "Twelve dancers—twelve pillars?"

"Yes," Thera agreed. "Legends say there were twelve golden statues—one on top of each of the pillars, holding aloft their bowls of holy fire."

"Why would they all be gone?" Duin asked. "Surely as a creature of Helene...."

"These dragons," Adam said slowly. "They're big, scaly, winged, and breathe fire—do they also like having large hoards of treasure?"

"Of course," Thera said. "The tale of a dragon's hoard used to inspire great feats of bravery amongst those who went to fight them. It means little to us now, of course. Gold is pretty, but not very useful to our people."

"Then I think I know where the statues ended up," Adam said. "She looted the temple of her own goddess."

"But why not take the pillars?" Duin asked.

Adam rode Zoul closer and tapped on one of the cubes sticking out from the crumbling stone of the pillars, and then peered more closely at the pitted surface of the metal. "Pyrite," he said with a grin. "It's fool's gold—not real gold at all."

"Well, that answers my question, I suppose," Duin said. "Does this mean we can agree that Khalivibra has fallen out of favor with the sun goddess?"

"We can hope," Adam said blandly. "We still need to find Esmeralda and the dragon's magic-boosting artifact."

"Yes," Joeri said from the single open doorway in the ring of walls they found themselves in. "And the first thing we need to do is sneak out of here."

Adam dismounted, crept up to the door, and peered out to see the city that once was Aer Goragon. The Temple of Helene turned out to be atop a large ziggurat, with a wide stairwell leading from the top down to an equally wide boulevard. He could still see the original paving, although much of it was now obscured by dirt, rubbish, and overgrown mats of flowering plants that had sent their runners from the decorative garden beds and across the long causeway.

Far off into the distance, Adam saw a similar ziggurat facing them, and surmised that must have been the Temple of Selune. Toward the walls on the right, the great shape of Goragon Castle stood, its imposing form looming over the rest of the city buildings, even with the large space where the eastern side of the main hall had crumbled completely. Closer to the Temple of Helene, Adam could see the roofs of the city buildings, most of them now missing many of the slate shingles that had tiled them, as well as the wooden shutters that had covered their bare windows. Toward the castle, Adam noted the twinkling lights of fires and the plumes of woodsmoke that rose into the air and trailed off to the west—or dark—as the near constant trade winds pushed their way past the once proud stones of the golden city.

"I don't think they're using this area," Adam said. "All of the people seem to be up there, where the light is."

"Why would she let them have fire?" Duin asked.

Adam shrugged. "Maybe she likes fire. She is a dragon. Does anyone know what those giant overgrown trees are doing in the middle of the city?"

"That would probably have been the great park," Thera said. "Where King Henricus kept a menagerie before his kingdom fell to Khalivibra."

"Looks like much of it has been turned into farms," Joeri said.

"I wish it was still a park," Adam said. "We'd have more chance of sneaking through that."

"Couldn't we just walk through them?" Duin suggested. "Not through them through them, I mean, but among them. If we steal some clothing, we should be able to walk straight through the middle of the city."

"Too risky," Thera disagreed. "We don't know how many people are really here—if there aren't that many and they all know each other, they could sound an alarm. Not to mention we have to find the clothes before we can steal them."

Duin shrugged. "Find someone, rap them on the head, and take their clothes. That shouldn't be difficult."

"If the dragon isn't controlling them, yes," Thera said. "I know she may not notice the loss of one connection—or even four—but we have the element of surprise here. Let's not risk it unnecessarily."

"Our mounts may also attract attention," Joeri said, his eyes scanning the darkened buildings around them.

"Either way, we need to get to the castle," Adam said. "If Khalivibra's lair is there, that's where Esmeralda is going to be."

"We can skirt the fields to the light and north if we keep to the shadows of the buildings," Joeri said. "I suggest we go across the upper level walls to avoid detection from the ground and the air."

Adam nodded. "Sounds good. Let's move."

"I take it we are going to trust stealth and the dragon's arrogance to prevent her from finding us with her mind, rather than invoking the blessings of Selune?" Thera asked as Joeri started down the ziggurat, darting quickly into the shadows of the western side of the large squared edges.

"Well, she hasn't found us yet," Adam said. "Let's keep that for an emergency."

"You put great faith in my ability to block her out quickly, Sir Adam," Elder Thera said acidly. "I hope it is not misplaced."

"I put greater faith in the ability of people to use their ears," Adam said. "Especially if what they are hearing is an ongoing melody. That seems riskier."

"I hope you know what you're doing, Sir Adam," Thera said as she followed after Joeri.

Adam shared a pensive glance with Duin, sighed, and followed after her. Nothing more needed to be said.

THEY MADE it down to the base of the ziggurat without incident, and Joeri led them a few streets away from the farmed fields before taking to the stone walls of the dilapidated houses. It was strange walking sideways through the abandoned city, hiding in the darkness but looking out into the light. The houses were made of the same crumbling yellowish sandstone as the city walls and the temple pillars, held together with a mortar that had almost completely rotted away beneath the attentions of the wind, rain, and various climbing plants that had taken up residence where the people had moved out. They found they had to move slowly, ensuring that each sticky-toed lizardstep landed on a firmly secured stone or risk being discovered or worse. Even so, their ride through the deserted northeast quarter of the town was almost fun.

It wasn't quite a sideways walking tour of Minas Tirith, but Adam kept finding his eyes being pulled to little details on the old buildings— the elaborate carved wooden shutters that showed motifs of stylized wheat grains and what appeared to be pegasi, the various wood and stone merchant shingles that still survived, some hanging from rusted chains or others carved into the keystones over the arched doorways. The streets were wide and mostly clear of debris, bar the moss that was slowly and determinedly turning the wide bricked road into a swathe of blue-green, at least in the part where the light hit. Nothing more than slime and mold grew in the shadows, and tiny insects and lizards scuttled from light to shade and back again, feeding on the vegetation or each other. Thankfully, there appeared to be a lack of giant spiders in the area, although Adam supposed that probably came down to a lack of food and hunting from the dragon's thralls. There were flocks of flitterfish roosting in some of the buildings, however, and the first time they stumbled upon such a roost they stopped and held their breath, waiting to see if the sudden egress of the winged creatures provoked an investigation. Thankfully, after several minutes of tense silence, they were able to proceed, winding their way toward the keep.

When they got closer to the northern wall, the streets started to curve around toward the west, and tendrils of smoke drifting out of chimney stacks indicated they were now in inhabited areas. There were also fewer shadows to hide in as the eternal red twitterlight flooded most of the east-west streets. Wordlessly, Joeri first checked and then guided them into an old warehouse via large attic windows, below which a large plaque reading Garandas & Sons, Merchant Traders sat crumbling beneath layers of oxidation and flitterfish crap. Inside, the warehouse was empty bar the walls and structural supports. Adam had expected a wooden floor, separating the great building into at least two levels, but someone or someones had clearly come through and stripped out the timber, if the holes in the wall where beams should have sat were anything to go by. So instead, Joeri led them down to ground level, where they gathered amid the dust of cycles gone past.

"I don't think we can get to the keep," he said simply.

"We have to," Adam said. "Maybe we should have gone in from the south?"

"I'm more concerned about noise, but I think we can stick to the shadows."

"So we repack," Adam said. "Make sure nothing clinks."

"Yes," Joeri agreed. "You especially, Sir Adam."

"Sorry," Adam said as he unclipped his harness and swung down to the ground.

"What do you have that is so noisy, Sir Adam?" Thera asked as the rest of them followed suit.

"Best you don't know," Adam said as he started shoving his spare clothes around the earthenware jars he'd so carefully constructed in Blackwater. "Just something that I hope will help."

THE LAST leg of their journey was the most nerve-wracking for them all, taking them through inhabited streets to the keep itself. Joeri guided them down as many side streets as he could, sometimes dashing between buildings, sometimes crawling on the underside of overhangs where extensions thrust out over the streets below. From what Adam managed to see and overhear, the people of Aer Goragon lived stilted lives that bore some semblance to reality, but their existence reminded him of Sovereign Hill back home—a show for the tourists to see what life was really like in days gone by. There was the cooking of food and the eating of meals. There appeared to be the mending of clothing and the gathering of firewood. As they passed underneath a window, there also appeared to be rather enthusiastic sex happening, but Adam couldn't help noticing the absences.

There was no play, for a start. Children toiled in the fields with their parents, scavenged for wood, mended clothing, and all in all acted like serious miniature adults—if adults were robots who spoke little and never smiled or laughed. From the smell of unwashed bodies, it was also fairly clear that no one bathed—or washed their clothes. From the stolen glimpses Adam occasionally risked, he saw their furniture was crude and strictly utilitarian, and indeed, daily life appeared to go on with next to no conversation or other forms of human interaction. The city plazas remained empty of markets or bazaars, and no thieves wandered through the crowd looking for an unsuspecting mark. No guards patrolled the streets, and no houses of any repute were open for business. Shops remained empty or were now used as makeshift housing, although it appeared that weavers still worked the ever-present spider silk into cloth, and a blacksmith toiled ceaselessly to turn out tools, nails, and other utilitarian items that people came to take, leaving food or clothing as a form of payment, all completing their transactions without so much as eye contact.

"They may as well be dead," Adam murmured as they gathered in the broken shell of what had once been an inn, going by the rusted sign that still bore the faint lettering reading The Crown and the Moon. The inn had been one of many in the area surrounding the castle to be damaged, and the roof and second floor had largely collapsed into the first, leaving a pile of blackened masonry covering the still visible stone that had been the bar, although the rest of its furniture had apparently been redistributed or cut up for firewood.

"Zombies, you mean," Duin said.

"Actually I meant dead, but zombies work," Adam muttered. "I don't think I saw a single smile on any of their faces."

"If you were living under the claw of the dragon, would you be smiling?" Duin asked.

"No, but are you honestly telling me a mother cradling her baby wouldn't have love for her child? Or sing them a lullaby?"

"Perhaps Khalivibra does not see such acts as necessary to keep her chattel alive," Thera suggested.

"Yeah," Adam said. "That would make sense."

"So… now what?" Duin asked.

"We go in," Adam said. "Although I will be honest and say I hadn't quite planned this far ahead."

"Let me go," Joeri said. "I'll find a way." Before anyone could protest he had urged his mount into a quick dash up the wall and back along the shadowed western wall of the inn and what appeared to have been its stables.

"I wish he wouldn't do that," Adam grumbled.

"Did you have a better idea?" Duin asked.

"Not really, but that's not the point. I just don't like being surprised like that."

"Do you want me to go after him?"

Adam sighed and shook his head. "No need to make us more of a target."

Chapter 25

THEY WAITED in silence, staring out the ruined windows to the equally ruined keep, which sat with one side pressing against the northern wall. According to the haerunwoln scouts, the hill the castle was on fell away sharply on the far side of the wall, creating a natural defense point that the keep sat upon, watching over what had once been a great road, if the large paving stone slabs were anything to go by. From their hiding place, Adam could see the dragon's guards up on the walls in old rusted armor and bearing halberds that had probably once been ceremonial. In truth he might have missed them, if not for the breeze that blew the hem of one of their dark cloaks fluttering into the air. They stood spaced evenly along the wall, still as statues, looking out toward the north and dark west, and Adam found himself wondering if they were even allowed to blink.

"Look at them up there," he murmured softly.

"The guards?" Duin asked.

"Yeah," Adam said, slightly crestfallen. "You already saw them."

"Yes," Duin said. "But I'm impressed that you did."

"They look like statues," Adam said. "But why would a dragon even need guards?"

"Keeping a lookout for us, perhaps?" Duin said. "Bern said some of the walls were patrolled."

"If that's a patrol, I'm straight," Adam muttered.

"What?"

Adam shrugged. "Never mind. I'll explain later."

"Okay," Duin said with a grin and crawled over to the window to keep watch, absently rubbing Hele's eye ridge as the lizard curled up next to him.

Adam shook his head and crept back away from the windows. "He's calmer than I am," he muttered, mostly to himself.

Thera laid a comforting hand on his arm. "Try not to let the waiting get to you, Sir Adam. Otherwise this old lady is going to fall apart in no time."

Adam turned and smiled at the proud woman. "I sincerely doubt you've ever fallen apart in your life, Waur Thera."

"I do not think I have ever been tested so in my life until now, Sir Adam," Thera said. "So I have not previously had much cause to truly be scared." Sitting cross-legged on the floor, she smoothed the silk of her robe over her legs—a useless gesture given the raw silk crumpled back almost immediately. "I feel I owe you an apology, Sir Adam," she said carefully.

"Why?" Adam asked, sitting down next to her.

"When you first came to us, I did not think of you as a hero. I did not want you to be the one to wield Wyrmbane."

"Well, if you recall, I didn't want to be a hero either—or wield Wyrmbane," Adam said with a smile.

"Yes, but you did not wish to do so because you feared for your life—and I suspect you still do," Thera said. "I did not wish you to wield Wyrmbane because it meant an end to our way of life, one way or another."

"With all due respect, Waur Thera, that's exactly what happened," Adam said gently. "And I don't think it was for the best."

"Selune turned her back on us for reveling in our own glory and ignoring her will," Thera said. "When I tried to take Wyrmbane from you, I wanted to control it. I wanted to use it for my own people, in our fashion, not in the way that it has been foretold."

"I think I understand your meaning," Adam said. "But I don't see how that has anything to do with Selune's will."

"There is more to the writings of Ignatius Solmento than the defeat of Khalivibra," Thera said. "They end with the return of Selune to our skies. If I deny Wyrmbane and your place in the prophecy, I deny Selune her glory and my people their place as her guardians. And I would have done all that because I was frightened of change, because the risk was too great."

"I saw Waur Jirsca burnt alive by Khalivibra," Adam said, his gaze fixed on the pointed rooftop of the building on the opposite side of the street. "All the people who left Aergon with Esmeralda are dead, and I only met two of them. I don't even know how many of your people perished when Boolikstaad fell. I know I didn't meet them all before the city…. Do you really think the risk was not great?"

"It has been great," Elder Thera agreed. "But perhaps it has not been too great."

"That's a very fine distinction to put on a 'perhaps.'"

"Did you know Aergon is dying?"

"Isn't Aergon a city? Cities can't die. They're not alive."

"Of course they are," Thera said. "The people who live in them are the life of the city. Without people—well, you get places like this."

"Okay, fair enough. But how is Aergon dying?"

"They have a hard life, harder than we do, even. Khalivibra knows exactly where they are, and the kanak raid frequently—which makes sense given what you and Duin encountered in the rainforest. They lose people who forage outdoors to kanak or slasherclaws, to the spiders that prowl their caverns, and then they send maybe one in every ten children to the surface to die."

"Ah."

"Exactly," Thera said. "Every cycle, more and more of Aergon's caverns empty, and more and more zombies join the front lines of their defenses—or did, if Magister Xavier was indeed the last necromancer. Their city is dying, Sir Adam. They need this to succeed more than we do."

"So why not wait until they're all dead and you can face the dragon on your own terms?"

"That was my first thought," Thera said candidly. "But what then? Where is the benefit in that? We'd still need to face the dragon and her thralls, and even if we succeed without the Aergonites, who will greet the sun should she rise each morning, as she hopefully will? Who will speak for Helene?"

"I'm surprised that's important to you."

"The arrogance of Selune's Children led to her abandoning this world and turning our punishment over to her sister," Thera said. "What would she think if the self-same arrogance of her Children prevented her return?"

"I don't know," Adam said.

"Neither do I," Thera said. "Which is why I owe you an apology for my actions—and my thanks. I was wrong, and I need to thank you for giving our people the chance to be the Children of Selune again in deed, rather than only in name."

Adam nodded. "You're welcome, Waur Thera. But you must know I'm still scared shitless."

"And yet, you're still here," she said.

"Well, it seems my choices are possibly die now fighting a dragon or resign myself to a long slow wasted life that will probably end badly eventually if I run away from it all," Adam said with a shrug. "I couldn't live like that."

"And yet that is the life both the Children and the Aergonites have been working toward in our own fashions for generations, even if we claimed not to see it. We need a new way."

"Yeah, well, you lot can argue all of that after we win, right?"

Elder Thera nodded. "Yes. I am sure the debate will be invigorating."

THEY HAD not waited much longer when the soft slither of lizard on stone heralded the return of Joeri. "Sir Adam, I think you should see this."

"What is it?" Adam asked.

"Come," Joeri said, turning his mount around to ride back up the wall.

After climbing back into the saddle of their lizards, Adam, Thera, and Duin followed Joeri out of the inn and onto the roof of the building next door, although Adam had no idea what it might have been way back when. From the far side of the roof, he found he was looking out into the central square at the foot of the castle walls. Once it had probably been a grand space from which the king could address his subjects—possibly in the fashion of the pope in the Vatican, if the small balcony was anything to go by. Adam could all too easily imagine the square bedecked in festive bunting and crowded with people cheering as they jostled to catch a glimpse of their monarch.

For a moment he saw himself standing on the balcony, the stone of the castle around him cleaned and restored until it gleamed in the sunlight. He could see himself dressed in robes of the finest silk, boots of the softest purplish leather, and a regal crown bedecked with jewels. The cloak around his shoulders was slightly indistinct at first, but the hazy image coalesced into a heavy fur cape that trailed nearly to his feet, and his wife, the Princess—nay, Queen—Esmeralda stood at his side as they raised their hands to wave their benediction over the cheering crowd.

Adam shuddered and pushed the thought as far out of his mind as possible, although like many things once seen, it proved near impossible to unsee, the mental image hanging around the edge of his thoughts for far longer than he was comfortable with. When he finally managed to clear his head, he saw the people of Aer Goragon had been silently filing into the space. In the center of the square, a large platform had been erected through the simple expedient of pushing a number of old crates together.

From the gatehouse came a tortured squeal, followed by metallic clanking as the drawbridge lowered across a moat that was now more grass and rubble than watery defense. Two lines of guardsmen marched silently from the castle courtyard and out into the outer square in their rusted armor and black cloaks, two of them all but carrying Princess Esmeralda between them. She was dressed in a silk robe finer than any Adam had seen her in, and wore a necklace that was more a collar of gossamer filigree and diamonds than a gemstone on a simple chain. Her dark hair had been swept back to fall over one shoulder, interlaced with strings of white pearls, and her pale features enhanced with lines of kohl and the faintest of blushes on her cheeks. Her expression, however, was docile, even glassy, and Adam wondered how much of her was still inside that dolled-up form. When the soldiers carrying her reached the platform, she stepped onto it without any prompting and stood there, facing the crowd with the same stillness as that of the guards on the walls.

It didn't feel real to him. In any other crowd, there would have been a buzz, a frisson of apprehension or anticipation or impatience or anything, not just a flat, empty nothingness. It wasn't even disinterest; rather it was a sense of incomprehension, as if the drama unfolding before them might as well have been a blob of paint drying on a suburban fence in the hot summer sun.

Then came the thudding wingbeat that reminded him all too much of the sound of drums, and the walls of the city literally shook as the dragon came to rest on the old keep wall, casting a shadow over the tiny balcony Adam had so admired only moments ago. A shower of sediment rained down onto the square as the great beast folded her wings neatly against her spine, perching haughtily on the parapet as she overlooked her domain. She sat proudly on the old stone, her head swaying gently backward and forward as she surveyed the scene before her, the reddish sunlight casting her long shadow across the keep's walls.

As one the crowd raised their heads to stare up at her as she puffed out her chest and roared, the noise echoing around the square and in at least one case causing a man's hat to blow off. Again the people bore the experience with a passive indifference that was more frightening than anything the dragon could muster. For a moment, Adam envisioned the great beast flying down into the crowd and wading through the square in an orgy of bloodletting while the people stood there unheeding and unmoving.

When the dragon spoke, her voice rang inside their heads. Unlike when they'd met at the top of the council tree in Boolikstaad, here, it was smooth and melodious, powerful, rich, and wheedling.

"Sir Adam," Khalivibra said, the force of her words near knocking him from his saddle. *"Sir Adam, we should speak."*

Wordlessly, Duin, Thera, and Joeri all turned to look at Adam, who shrugged.

"I know you are here, Sir Adam, and I believe we should talk. Look at me!" Khalivibra demanded, stretching to her full height and turning so her scales caught the sunlight. *"I am life perfected. I am Khalivibra, Guardian of Aer Goragon, Voice of Helene, and Keeper of the Light in these dark times. Look at my people. I am not an unkind ruler, but I am born to rule.*

"Have they filled your mind with injustice? With the whinings of spoilt children wanting what they never had the right to keep? I alone remember the days of the Fall. I alone was there when the pride of the Children forced the hand of the Mistresses. Did they tell you to stand, quaking in your borrowed boots to fight the battles they have been too weak to attempt? That the slavering beast will only be satisfied with your last breath?" she asked, punctuating her words with a bellow that sounded suspiciously like a laugh.

"Did they forget to speak of mercy?" she went on in a calmer tone. *"Did they truly think I could not have hunted down every last one of them as they cowered in their forest warren? That I could not burn the brush out from beneath them until none of Selune's chosen remained? You have seen what I can do, Sir Adam. Do not make the mistake of seeing what I will do if angered, for Helene is as vengeful a goddess as she is merciful."*

High up on the parapet, the dragon subsided, settling into a calmer posture, her wings once more closed against her back. *"Look before me,"* she said. *"See your promised bride, Princess Esmeralda of Aer Goragon. I have kept her safe for you. Come, take her hand and rule this kingdom wisely and fairly, and I can give this realm what it needs—protection from the barbarians of the rainforests and peace from which to be born anew, a place for the Children of my Mistress' sister to live in safety without fear of persecution."*

Khalivibra's voice was gentle and cajoling, promising the unwavering knowledge that what was offered could truly be given—would truly be given. All he had to do was go down, relinquish Wyrmbane, and the world would truly be his oyster—or whatever the name of the local river mollusk was.

His mind in a whirl, Adam rode from the building and out into the square, and the people parted before him like the Red Sea before the biblical Moses. He rode on, up onto the ceremonial platform, until Zoul stood shoulder to shoulder with the slack-jawed princess, who continued to stare out into the gathered crowd.

"Are you all right?" Adam asked, reaching out to take her hand, half expecting it to be cold.

Her head turn was jerky and the pressure on his hands sudden and fierce. The slow blink of her glassy eyes was not unlike how he would have imagined the tale of Sleeping Beauty to have gone—if Sleeping Beauty had awoken to a state of languid half awareness tinged with an undercurrent of fear and a dash of panic. Then the expression was gone, so quickly he felt as though he could have imagined it—he *must* have imagined it—and Esmeralda smiled warmly at him, lowering her eyelids coquettishly.

"Accept my aid, Sir Adam," Khalivibra said, her voice now a benediction. *"May your rule be long and untroubled."*

Adam closed his eyes and smiled as visions of himself as king danced through his head. "Your immense scaliness," he said, opening them once more. "That's a decision that cannot be rushed. Tell you what, I'll get back to you," he said. "Come on, Your Highness," he added, pulling Esmeralda up onto the saddle behind him and urging Zoul into the fastest near-gallop the lizard could muster. They bulled their way past, between, and in one or two cases, right over the crowd, who stood, mouths agape and as expressive as shop mannequins, and suddenly all thoughts of kingdoms, crowns, queens, and rulership fled from his mind. In its place, a babble of confusion threatened to derail his thoughts, followed swiftly with a mounting anger.

"Gotcha, you big scaly bitch," he muttered as he guided Zoul around a building and up along the far wall, heading east away from the crowd. Keeping a tight grip on Esmeralda, he urged Zoul through the maze of buildings as a deafening scream of rage rent the air. Then the sounds of stone crumbling and the shock wave of the dragon's downbeat burst through the air, followed by the first sound of human voices.

"Adam?" Esmeralda asked from behind him.

"Hold on, Princess," Adam said as the ziggurat of Selune came into view through the gaps in the buildings. "Is she gone from your head yet?"

"Yes? No… I do not know," Esmeralda said weakly.

"Is there anything you can do to stop her getting in there?"

Suddenly Esmeralda's left hand reached up and grabbed the moon spider eye pendant she had given him back in Boolikstaad. "Actually," she said, her voice stronger, "there is."

"The pendant?" Adam asked.

"Of course," Esmeralda said. "Did you think I would send you into battle unprotected?"

"Thanks," Adam said as he pulled Zoul into a shadowy alcove as Khalivibra flew over the street they were in, her eyes sweeping over the ground. "Damn, she's close."

"Did you come here alone?" Esmeralda asked.

"No. I hope the others have sense to run away."

"Run away?"

"What are they going to do against a dragon without Wyrmbane?" Adam asked as he headed for the raised road between the two temples.

"You're headed to the Temple of Selune?"

"It seemed smarter than the castle."

"It is," Esmeralda said, and might have said more if the searching pressure of Khalivibra had not pushed against their minds just then.

"She's looking for us," Adam said, his voice tight.

"Looking is not finding," Esmeralda said with a smile and clutched him tighter. Burying her face in his neck, she began to chant softly, an arcane murmur that was as familiar as it was comforting, but with a slight edge to it he had not heard before, and the force of the dragon's thought abated. He could still feel it, but now it washed over them, past them, through them even, and emboldened, he darted from the cover of one building to the next, ducking Zoul into the disheveled squat of a family home when the sound of her wingbeats grew loud enough that he thought her about to pass overhead. Up close, it looked like a peasant hovel with rushes covering the floor, and blackened flitterfish bones and shards of carapace were scattered around the hearth. The entire room was musty and moldering, and Adam was only too glad to escape after Khalivibra had gone past, guiding Zoul in one final dash across the Thoroughfare of the Gods and up the temple steps.

LIKE THE Temple of Helene, the main structure of Selune's temple sat atop a great stone ziggurat, although the steps leading up to the temple were of the polished pearly white stone that Selune's followers favored, as were the great braziers that now held little more than dirt and weeds. The temple had once possessed heavy wooden doors, both of which lay on the floor, blackened by rot. The heavy iron bands that once held the doors together were twisted shapes that poked above the weeds here and there, held together more by rust than anything else. The floor was tiled in marble, and looking up, Adam could see the entire domed ceiling of the temple had been carved from a transparent quartz. Great pillars of sandstone lined the approach to the main altar, although these did not reach all the way to the ceiling and appeared to be decorative, rather than structural. Off to the sides, he could see doors leading to other rooms, and golden frescoes adorned the walls, depicting what Adam took to be the glories of Helene.

However, Adam's gaze was immediately drawn to the center of the temple, where a huge monolith of rough rock thrust its way toward the domed sky, supported on a stand of giant bones that had yellowed with age. They were near identical to the bones Adam had encountered in Blackwater, only much more numerous and of varying sizes, and pieced together in some macabre sculpture. A splayed stand of large leg bones decorated with small dragon skulls and edged with claws acted as a plinth, and curving rib bones as long as Adam's arms cradled the great rock, which pulsed with a dim white light, stained red where it touched the bones. The menhir was topped with even smaller dragon skulls, and assembled vertebrae were aligned into swirling patterns that cascaded over the stone's surface. And all of it blazed a bright blue-white as his pendant had when he'd stared at it all those sleeps ago in Boolikstaad.

Behind him, Esmeralda loosed her hold on the pendant and stopped chanting. "She's stopped looking for us," she said.

"She probably knows where we are," Adam replied.

"Then why is she not here?" Esmeralda asked. "She would certainly fit through the door."

"And risk knocking down her… what did you call it? An arcane booster?"

"*Focus* would be more accurate."

"Right. That," Adam said as he unclipped himself and slid from Zoul's back. "She'll send someone to get us, so let's hurry."

"Hurry with what, exactly?"

Adam grinned and started opening his packs. "Pass me every one of those sealed pots," he said. He grabbed one and wedged it carefully in among the bones supporting the monolith, then started to do the same with all the others, in some cases prying them open to scatter black powder into the spaces between ceramic and bone.

"How did you beat it?" Esmeralda asked as she pulled pots out from between the folds of Adam's clothing.

"Beat what?"

"The dragon's mind. Even with the protection I gave you, that should have been more than you could bear. I know it was for me."

"Was it?" Adam asked. "You beat her in the end."

"Only when you showed up."

Adam shrugged, taking the last two pots and cracking them open, allowing the black powder to fall freely, creating a trail leading toward the front entrance of the temple. "That's still an escape."

"And what about next time?" Esmeralda demanded.

"We'll escape again," Adam said confidently.

"Before she kills us?"

"She's not going to kill us," Adam said, brushing off his hands carefully and rummaging around in his green gym bag.

"Are you sure about that?"

Standing at the foot of the temple stairs were twelve of the black-cloaked guards, forming a semicircle around Duin, Joeri, and Elder Thera, all of whom were wearing the same vacant expression that had until recently adorned Esmeralda's face. Behind them, the dragon landed on the Thoroughfare of the Gods with a force that shook the buildings, and the people of Aer Goragon came following it like baby ducks after their rather large scaly mother.

"Don't even think about it," Adam said, drawing Wyrmbane and holding it before him as the dragon advanced, towering over her black guard and the haerunwoln as they slowly started up the stairs. "Let them go, Khalivibra!"

"Let them go?" she said, her tone surprised. *"You speak as if I have some hold on them, but I do not. They follow me out of love and devotion."*

"Bull crap," Adam said. "That's a lie, and we both know it."

"You think so? Look at your friend, Duin, is it not?" Khalivibra said as the haerunwoln nocked an arrow into his bow and aimed it directly at Adam. *"Poor lost soul. All he ever wanted was a place to be, and I gave him that. A place at my side from which he will reap great rewards. Rewards you could have too."*

"Do you even listen to yourself? 'Rule at your side,' is that your offer? 'Rule under your claw,' you mean. You don't share power. You just like to let people think you do. And for your information, Duin has a place where he belongs. He belongs with me—and you can take your offer and shove it. I'm going home, Esmeralda's going to take this kingdom and sort it out, and Joeri and Thera are going to have to rebuild both this temple and the temple to your goddess. You know, the one you defiled?" Smiling, Adam dropped the open Zippo lighter from his left hand, and the pop as the black powder ignited beneath it was music to his ears. Turning his head, he stared directly into Duin's eyes. "If you're going to shoot, hurry up and do it already," he said. "Just... I love you, okay?"

CHAPTER 26

THE BANG wasn't particularly loud, but the sound of dry bone cracking and splintering in the silence that followed sounded as loud as the explosion hadn't been. Even that was soon drowned out by the screams of the crowd, who took off in every direction, trampling each other in their haste to flee from the great scaled beast.

Khalivibra paused, mouth open and one great forelimb raised midstep. Slamming her paw down into the ziggurat, her claws gouged out deep gashes in the crumbling stone, and the black guards trembled. Some fell to the ground, clutching their heads, others staggered back as if dazed, but half of them strode forward, brandishing their halberds purposefully. In one smooth motion, Duin turned and loosed his arrow through the visor of the closest guard, and Joeri gave Thera a shove that propelled her a fair distance away from the fight before dodging a thrust from the tallest guardsman. Twisting sideways to avoid the blow, Joeri grabbed the weapon's shaft and pushed away, using the backward momentum to slam into another of the black-cloaked warriors, bearing him to the ground where he dispatched the guard by sliding a knife up under the man's helmet.

"Out of the way!" Esmeralda cried as she cannoned into Adam, pushing him to one side as the pedestal behind them finally broke down completely, sending the monolith crashing through the temple wall right where Adam had been standing, raising a cloud of soot and dust. There was a reptilian chirrup of protest, and Adam could only hope Zoul made it out of the way when a searing heat engulfed them, and his vision went white as the dragon's fire swept through the temple doorway.

Adam had never been seriously burned. The most serious burn he'd had was back in high school, when he'd attempted to heat a recalcitrant piece of limestone in a test tube before adding water in an attempt to make quicklime. Of course, Adam found himself with not only the one piece of limestone that didn't want to heat, but with a succession of test tubes that only wanted to melt, and after the third time, he'd grabbed at the hot glass to change it—inconveniently forgetting that it was indeed hot. His yelp had been heard from the other end of the science block, and he'd spent the rest of the day with his hand under a cold water faucet, and it had been blistered for nearly two weeks after that. The dragon's fire felt almost exactly like that, only over the whole of his body. Adam had heard that adrenaline could make time appear to slow and hoped it wouldn't slow so much that he felt more pain.

It was Esmeralda who pulled him out of the line of literal fire and behind the stone walls, which were starting to glow in the heat of the dragon's breath, both of them collapsing onto the floor.

"What!" Adam exclaimed, patting himself hurriedly. "I'm not burnt."

"Not yet," Esmeralda said, pushing at him. "But too much longer and you would have been. I did good work on that armor, but not that good."

Rolling off Esmeralda, Adam sat up and reached for his sword. He closed his hand around the hilt just as Khalivibra thrust her head through the door.

"*I wouldn't,*" she said in warning as he tightened his grip around the hilt. "*Put that down, slowly.*"

"Why?" Adam asked. "You'll kill us anyway."

"*Oh yes,*" Khalivibra said smugly. "*But that doesn't mean I have to kill you quickly and painlessly. That mercy is more than you deserve— and my final offer.*"

Adam stared up into the reptilian face, eyes easily as big as his head, and great flaring nostrils. As the reality of defeat rushed through his body, he felt tears pool at the edges of his eyes.

"Damn you to hell," he said, releasing the sword.

"*Now, now, Sir Adam,*" Khalivibra chided. "*Is that any way to treat your most merciful servant? Oh, I have one last gift for you,*" she added.

The sound of heavy boots clanked up the stairs as three of the black guards entered the temple bearing a body, which they deposited on the floor next to the fallen monolith, and Adam bit back a cry when he saw Duin lying in an undignified heap, his fur matted with blood and his torso shorn nearly in two.

"Where are the others?" Adam asked.

"*Oh, they're dead too,*" Khalivibra said. "*But I know you didn't care nearly as much for them. Now rise, Sir Adam.*" Khalivibra lowered her head so her forked tongue flicked over Duin's body. *"Accept your fate with dignity."*

The attack came from nowhere, and long fangs bit into Khalivibra's neck, sinking into the thick muscle just behind the dragon's skull.

"Zoul!" Esmeralda cried.

"Zoul, no!" Adam shouted, but it was too late. As the lizard's feet scrambled for purchase on the dragon's scales, Khalivibra swung her body to one side, all but crushing Zoul against the temple wall. The riding lizard barely had time to register a chirp of surprise before he fell to the ground, but Adam was already moving. Tears flowing freely from his eyes, he grabbed Wyrmbane, pushed past the startled guards, ran up the side of the fallen monolith, and jumped onto Khalivibra's neck. Her skin was hot, even through his armor, and her shock evident as his weight landed upon her, forcing her head down onto the monolith's surface. When he struck, it was like carving soft butter, so cleanly did the blade slide between her eyes until only the hilt protruded from the dragon's skull. Adam was thrown clear as Khalivibra's body spasmed, limbs flailing and wings buffeting the stone of the temple. Only when her convulsions stopped and silence returned did Adam notice the blade had gone right through the dragon's skull and into the stone below.

"Ha," he muttered bleakly. "The sword in the stone."

"What?" Esmeralda asked.

"Never mind," Adam said, sitting heavily next to Duin's body. "Just… never mind."

DUIN WAS still warm when Adam touched him. Warm, but still and lifeless. Adam stroked the rich chestnut fur as he tried to arrange his lover into a more dignified pose. "I love you," he murmured again, pressing his lips to Duin's forehead. "I'm so sorry."

"May I…," a man started hesitantly, his voice crackly as though from lack of use. "May I say—"

Adam looked up to see a black guard, armor splattered with blood that was nearly indistinguishable from rust and still clutching his halberd.

"Get out," Adam growled. "I don't care how many of you there are or how many sharp edges you have, if you try anything, I swear I will kill you with my bare hands if I have to."

For a moment the guard stood perfectly still, looking again like the statue Adam had mistaken his brethren for not so long ago. Then the halberd dropped to the ground. "My liege," he said, bowing stiffly at the waist before turning and exiting the temple, the other two guards beating a hasty retreat behind him.

"His what?" Adam demanded, staring at Esmeralda, who shrugged.

"You killed the dragon," she said simply. "By custom, that makes you king."

"Yeah? Well, I hereby name you queen and abdicate," Adam said, rising to his feet and climbing carefully over the fallen moonstone monolith to Zoul's crumpled form. "Promise me you won't turn them into zombies," he said suddenly as he reached down to close Zoul's eyes, giving the lizard's snout one final pat.

"I don't know how," Esmeralda said. "That's something I never learned. But I promise," she added hurriedly as he glared at her. "I'll make sure no one turns either of them into zombies."

"Thank you," Adam said, retrieving his gym bag. "That's all I really care about now, I suppose."

"But there's so much to do," Esmeralda protested. "We have to rally the people here, get the surviving Children into the city, and get word to my people in Aergon—"

"And I'm sure you'll do a fantastic job," Adam said. "You don't need me around for that." Adam pulled out a few more items, covered Zoul with the oilskin he had used to make more shelters than he'd ever thought he'd build, and covered Duin with the thin silk blanket he had picked up from the Aergonite waystation way back when. "You said when this was over, you'd send me home. So send me home. Now. Please."

"It's not that simple," Esmeralda protested.

"Then I guess you might want to get started," Adam said, pulling out Wyrmbane and using the blade to shear off a section of the dragon's skin. "You need scales, right?"

"Yes, but—"

"Okay, scales," Adam said, taking out his smaller belt knife and prying off a golden scale slightly larger than his own hand.

"I need my pack and my books," Esmeralda said. "I'm not going to be able to do this without them."

Adam closed his eyes. "Please tell me you have them?"

"I think so—they're back at the keep."

Adam sighed. "I hate this."

"He was my friend as well, Adam, and it would be a disservice to his memory if I did not take the utmost care of you."

"Right, fine," Adam said. "You know there's no way I can argue when you put it like that, don't you? Let's go."

"If you need a moment—"

Adam shook his head stubbornly. "I'm not going to let you walk through this city on your own," he said firmly.

"All right," Esmeralda said, shaking out her skirts, now smudged with dirt and singed by flame. "Let's go, then."

WHEN THEY finally exited the temple, they found the steps had been cleared and the bodies of nine black guards lined up at the foot of the ziggurat, shrouded in their cloaks, and Joeri and Thera lay with their hands folded over their chests. The three surviving black guards knelt at the foot of the stairs, their face-concealing helmets removed and laid to one side. Underneath, they were gaunt, pale, and surprisingly young, and Esmeralda started when she saw them.

"Sir Baltazar, Sir Edmund, and Sir Pascal?" she said.

All three men lowered their heads, although the youngest, the one Esmeralda had named Sir Edmund, flushed slightly. "Your Highness," they mumbled, nearly in unison.

"You know them?" Adam asked.

"Yes," Esmeralda said. "They were all sent to kill Khalivibra in the cycles before you."

"A task which we all failed," the one who was probably Sir Pascal said, his gray eyes tired. "We were beset by the beast and swayed by its temptations. Our lives are forfeit."

"It offered you a chance to live," Adam said with a shrug. "I might have taken that."

"But you did not."

Adam's smile was bleak. "Those weren't the options she gave me."

"And what did she offer you?" Esmeralda asked suddenly. "And how did you know how she'd respond?"

"She was grandstanding," Adam said. "Everything she was doing with all of the people—it screamed 'look at me, look at me, look at me.' And she did, she made everyone look at her, made everyone bear witness to her power. Only they couldn't really, because they were already in her power. She wanted to be acknowledged by those she did not control—and because I had Wyrmbane…."

"She wanted you to acknowledge her power?"

"Exactly," Adam said. "All I did was not give it to her."

"But what did she offer you?"

Adam shrugged. "Does it matter?"

"I… guess not," Esmeralda said, looking away from him and back to the three Aergonites, who had stayed kneeling, unmoving.

"May I speak, my liege?" the last one asked.

When the silence stretched out beyond comfort, Esmeralda looked over at Adam and coughed meaningfully.

"What? Oh, right. Sure. Go ahead… Sir Baltazar, wasn't it?"

"Yes, my liege," Sir Baltazar replied. "If our lives are not forfeit, then what is our penance?"

Adam started to laugh but stopped when he saw the earnest looks on the faces of the three men before him; none of them could have been much older than he. "Can we trust them?" he asked, turning to Esmeralda.

Stepping forward, Esmeralda laid her hands on each of the men's heads in turn before answering. "Their minds are clear," she said. "I believe they are themselves once more."

"So that's a yes?"

"Yes."

"All right," Adam said. "I charge you with the safety of the Princess… Queen Esmeralda. You will follow her directives and defend her new kingdom, whatever it ends up being called, and ensure equal and fair treatment for human and haerunwoln alike. It's a near impossible task, given that there's only three of you, and if you do it properly, most people are going to want to kill you. How's that sound?"

"It shall be as you say," Sir Baltazar said, and the other two hastily followed suit.

"Good," Adam said. "Then please escort Her Royal Majesty to the palace, where she will collect what is required next, and see to her safe return here."

Somewhat stiffly, all three Aergonites looked at Esmeralda.

"You will treat all orders from Sir Adam as if they had come from me," Esmeralda said archly. "Sir Edmund, Sir Pascal, come with me. Sir

Baltazar, please stay here and guard the temple. Keep the people away inasmuch as that is possible."

As Esmeralda walked up the thoroughfare toward the large square and the keep, the cheering began, and the crowds started to gather again, this time with the electrical energy of celebration that had been so missing from their gathering only minutes ago.

"Who killed them?" Adam asked suddenly.

"The h—the Children of Selune?" Baltazar asked.

"Yes."

Sir Baltazar fixed his eyes on the queen's impromptu procession. "It was one of myself, Sir Edmund, and Sir Pascal, as we still draw breath," he said finally, his voice careful and nearly monotone. "Do you truly wish to know more?"

Anger brought Adam back to his feet. "He was important to me, so yes, I want to know!"

Baltazar met his gaze without flinching. "Then let it be said that I killed him, my liege. If that grants me a traitor's death, it is not more than I deserve."

The rage drained away almost as quickly as it had come, and Adam turned away. "You didn't do it," he said, sitting back down on the temple steps. "And even if you had, how can I blame you for falling to the compulsions of the dragon?"

"How could you not? I do."

"Tell you a secret?" Adam said. "At least, if you swear never to tell Esmeralda this?"

"I swear on my life I will tell no one."

"Khalivibra offered me the kingdom and Esmeralda as my queen."

"That is what she offered me."

Adam turned to look back up at the temple, the body of Khalivibra still lying in its grand entrance.

"You weren't in love with another man, though, were you?"

When Adam turned back, Sir Baltazar's eyes were wide. "No, I was not."

"Well, there you are, then."

"It is said that the Blessings of Selune are manifold, and that while she looked down on her Children, they could not truly die unless it were by the touch of the gods."

"That's nice," Adam said. "Pity she's not here."

"Yes. I'm sorry for your loss, my liege."

"Thank you, Sir Baltazar, but I'm not your king. You do know that, right?"

"You are and always will be," Baltazar said firmly. "And I will be proud to serve in your name."

"In her name," Adam corrected, looking back toward the gates of the keep, which Esmeralda was nearing.

"There will be no difference in people's minds."

"That's good—I think."

Epilogue

From *The Writings of Queen Esmeralda I*, Cycle 5, The New Aracao Calendar

When I returned to the Temple of Selune, the entire city followed, cheering with jubilation as we walked from King's Square to the Thoroughfare of the Gods. Had Adam been standing triumphant over the dragon's corpse, the crowd would have swarmed the steps with a roar that would have reached the depths of Aergon itself. As it was, the cheers of jubilation diminished into the tense hum of speculation, the people keeping a respectful distance as he sat on the steps of the ziggurat, head bowed in grief. As I walked up to him, every muscle in my body trembling with fatigue, I cast my mind back to his triumphant return after facing the moon spider. "*A hero has to be seen as such,*" he had said later. So does a queen.

He rose at my approach, his face impassive, and according to the stories now spun in drinking houses across the city, he gave a grand and rousing speech, brandishing Wyrmbane to the sky and causing the heavens to open and the silvery light of Selune herself to stream down upon us all. I like that story. Sometimes I feel it is my best creation—a story of hope and exactly what the people of Aracao need in these hard times. It is said that Adam swore to return, to bring back what was lost, and since that is, after all, the official story, I will quote it here.

"People of Aergon, people of Aer Goragon, people of Boolikstaad. We are here to bear witness to the dawning of a new era. A time free from the threat of dragon wings in our sky. A time to come together and rebuild, to rediscover what was lost and forge ahead into the future. We stand in the ruins of a city cast low by pride, but one that will be rebuilt anew until it is once again the Golden City!"

After the cheers subsided, he continued, "However, it is with a heavy heart that I must tell you I am leaving you—too soon, I know, for we have only just met. But the world is not yet set to rights, and it can never be so while Helene grants us only the most grudging of light and Selune hides her face from us in shame. I leave you now to find her—to beg her forgiveness and entreat her return to our fair land. So be good to one another. Help each other. Rebuild beyond the glory that once was so that her return to her family, Children, and those who love her will be in a place she can be proud to call home.”

It is said then that the domed roof of the temple lit up with moonlight, which cast its glow over the body of the great dragon, Khalivibra, and the people of Aer Goragon in benediction. This at least, I believe to be true. When Sir Adam used Wyrmbane to strike down the dragon, he pierced both her skull and the Monument of Selune, which released the merged powers of the monument and the sorcerous magics of the dragon herself. When I opened the portal to send Adam home, I had no idea that the power was there, although in retrospect I should have. Regardless, the resulting portal was larger than anything I have conjured before, and the silver light that shone through was the first moonlight I have ever seen, and it is something I hope someday to see again. In the quartz dome, we saw the image of the night sky, just as Adam had told me about on our journeys—a sky as black as the dark with tiny pinpoints of light, and a large round circle that could only have been Selune, shimmering in iridescent glory.

Adam smiled and walked into the temple as the corpse of Khalivibra crumbled, consumed by the energies that sustained the portal. He leaned down and paused to kiss Duin’s body on the forehead, and then he stepped into the center of the silver light and was gone. The silence that followed was broken by a sudden coughing, and healers rushed to the sides of Joeri and Thera, who were breathing once more, and I am not too proud to say that I ran to them as well, crying with joy.

“But how…?” I remember asking again and again.

Some sleeps later, when they had both been nursed back to health, I finally got my answer.

“Neither silver nor fire,” Waur Thera had said, sitting up in bed as she drank some soup.

“Silver or fire?” I had echoed dumbly.

“In Selune’s majesty, it is said that only the holy metal silver or the fire of Helene will end a Child bathed in her light,” she said. “If what you say is true, then we were blessed by the light of Selune and live once more.”

“But then, Duin…?”

"I do not know," Waur Thera said. "Perhaps he went through the portal with Sir Adam."

"Perhaps," I agreed, and I hope it to be so, for we never found his body. One day perhaps they will return. One day, perhaps Selune will as well, even as the writings of Solmento tell us.

Somehow, though, I feel that I may have seen them both for the last time, and my only choice is to go on and rule as wisely as I can in their memory, and in the memory of all of those who sacrificed all that we might have victory.

This is the truth of things, and I write it here, pieced together from all who remember the reality of the past, so that it may not be forgotten by those who come after me. Those who hold power here in Aracao must know that the legends are true—or mostly so. They must know that which is not told by the bards—that our world was saved by a man who was not born a hero, did not wish to be a hero, but became one because we asked it of him. We must remember that it is this quality, more than a trick of birth, that made him what he is: Sir Adam, the uncrowned King of Aer Goragon and savior of the people of Aracao.

WHEN ADAM could no longer see the brightness of the silvery white light through his eyelids, he opened his eyes, blinking at the sudden dimness. The warm air smelled of eucalyptus and freshly cut grass, overlain by the faintest tang of car exhaust. Looking around, he found himself staring at the familiar metal poles and white streetlamps of the university, almost exactly where he'd been when he had disappeared in a shower of golden light, hard concrete under his boots once more.

"Where am I?" a familiar voice asked weakly.

"Duin?"

"A-Adam?"

Turning around, Adam found Duin lying on the pavement, a light pink scar running across his chest where the mortal wound had once been.

"Duin! Oh my God, I thought…." Adam fell to his knees and hugged him close. "I thought I'd lost you."

"I… thought you had too. Is that… Selune?"

Adam looked up. "No. At least I don't think so. It's just the moon."

"Same thing," Duin said. "She healed me."

"What, so you're really a werewolf, then? Can only be killed by silver and regenerate health in the moonlight?"

"According to legend, silver and fire, yes," Duin said. "Although I really don't know about these werewolves you keep talking about."

"I'll show you on YouTube," Adam said. "Oh my God, I have access to YouTube again."

"What?"

Adam laughed and kissed Duin's cheek. "Never mind. We have lots of time here. And hey, look at you—no fur."

"No fire," Duin replied.

Adam reached into his pocket, pulled out his Zippo lighter and flipped it open, then held the flame to Duin's face. "Nope. Still no fur."

Duin stared at the moon in wonder. "Maybe she used up all the magic in healing me, or maybe it's not Helene's fire anymore…."

"Can you change at will now?"

Duin frowned. "No. At least, I don't think so—I don't know how."

Adam shrugged. "There's no magic here, babe. I told you."

"Then how did Esmeralda conjure you in the first place? Or send us back? Why am I alive if that's the case?"

Adam pressed his lips to Duin's to silence him, breathing in his lover's scent. "I don't know," he whispered. "I don't know, but right now I'm just glad you're here with me. Right now that's enough."

"What if I change next sleep? What if it's only Helene's face that changes me, not all fire now?"

"Then we'll deal. I love you, haerunwoln or human. And what if you never change again?"

"You mean, what if I become normal?"

"No," Adam said. "You're amazing, not normal. You are much better than normal, and don't you ever forget it. Okay?"

He felt Duin smile and pull back enough so he could look Adam in the eyes. "Okay."

"Good. Can we get up now? I just killed a dragon, and my legs are starting to ache."

"I just died," Duin retorted. "But we can get up, yes."

Adam grinned and grabbed his gym bag in his left hand. "Come on, let's get you home, and we can find out what date this is and how long I've been away. If anyone asks, we were at a fancy dress party, all right?"

"A what?"

"A fancy dress party. Never mind," Adam said, grinning happily as he helped Duin to his feet and threw Duin's arm over his shoulders for support. "Just let me do the talking if there's any questions, and don't let anyone know our weapons are real."

"All right," Duin said. "Adam?"

"Yeah?"

"I like the sound of that."

"Of what?"

"Home."

GLOSSARY

Aer Goragon—The capital city of Aracao. Lair of the great dragon Khalivibra.

Aergon, Caverns of—An underground cave system in the southern mountains where the Aergonites took refuge from the dragon Khalivibra.

Anu—Riding lizard. Ridden by Princess Esmeralda.

Aracao—Human kingdom predating the Fall. Under occupation by the great dragon Khalivibra.

Blackwater Keep—The stronghold of Prince Fernando Aergon before the Fall, and the site of the dragon Khaled's death. Rumored to be the resting place of the sword Wyrmbane. Located in Blackwater Marsh.

Blackwater Marsh—A peat bog to the south of Aer Goragon. Northdark of the Caverns of Aergon.

Book of Solmento—The collected ravings of Ignatius Solmento, as recorded by High Priest Mennos. Considered prophecies telling of the days after the Fall, and possibly the return of Selune.

Boolikstaad—A tree city formed in the branches of seven interlocking giant evergreen trees. Refuge of the Children of Selune exiled from the Caverns of Aergon.

Children of Selune—Humans chosen by the goddess Selune. Before the Fall, they were able to shift between human form and that of a haerunwoln, with a bipedal bestial form in between. Now they change involuntarily in firelight. Their "condition" is seen either as a blessing or a curse.

Chtick-tick—A freshwater crustacean found in rainforest pools. It has no name in human language. The moniker Chtick-tick comes from the kanak, who have been observed catching them.

Cokudrillo—A six-flippered crocodile-like creature. Found in Blackwater Marsh and some of the larger rainforest rivers.

Darius—Captain of Princess Esmeralda's personal guard.

Dark—See Light and Dark.

Esmeralda—Princess Esmeralda of Aergon, heir to the throne of the Kingdom of Aracao. A trained enchantress.

Faas—One of the elders of the Children of Selune.

Fall, the—A mystical catastrophe where the moon fled the sky and dragons descended upon the world. Day and night ceased, and life has only survived in the band of twitterlight around the edge of the world.

Fernando Aergon—A prince of the royal house at the time of the Fall. A warrior, magician, and scholar, Fernando forged the sword Wyrmbane and used it to slay the dragon Khaled. He died in the battle, forcing his people to seek the sanctuary of the Caverns of Aergon.

Flitterfish—Flying, arboreal fishlike creatures that occupy the ecological niche of birds in our world.

Haerunwoln—A local name for the thylacine, a striped marsupial carnivore. Colloquial name for the Children of Selune.

Hele—Riding lizard. Ridden by Darius.

Helene—Sun goddess. Twin sister of Selune. The gold dragon is one of her forms and said to be an instrument of her will.

Henricus the Third—King of Aracao at the time of the Fall.

Ignatius Solmento—Magister serving in the court of King Henricus the Third. Ignatius was driven mad by visions of the Fall and events thereafter. His ravings form the basis of the Book of Solmento.

Joeri—Chief hunter of Boolikstaad.

Jirsca—One of the elders of the Children of Selune.

Kanak—Large four-armed humanoids who live in the rainforest. Known to eat people.

Khaled—A great gold dragon. Mate of Khalivibra. Killed by Prince Fernando Aergon during the Fall.

Khalivibra—The great gold dragon who, along with her mate Khaled, terrorized the Kingdom of Aracao during the Fall. Reportedly favored by the Sun goddess, Helene, Khalivibra is said to have magical powers of mind control.

Lapen Grass—A rainforest grass. Its root can be used to brew a soporific. Unknown to the Aergonites, its name literally means sleeping grass in the haerunwoln tongue.

Light and Dark—East and west. With the world never turning and the light remaining a constant, the directions of light and dark are more convenient and immediate than east and west.

Lizard, Giant Riding—Six-legged lizards used for riding. There are at least three known domesticated subspecies.

Long March, The—The journey of the Aergonite people from Blackwater to the Caverns of Aergon, led by Prince Fernando Aergon's widow.

Magister—An honorific given to a magic user or mage in service of the Aergonite court.

Marin—A freshwater crustacean somewhere between a shrimp and a crayfish, and sometimes compared to langoustine in flavor.

Mennos—High Priest of Selune in the court of King Henricus. Responsible for recording the prophecies of Ignatius Solmento and collecting them into the Book of Solmento.

Moonchild—An insult used to refer to a Child of Selune.

Moonsilver—A soft metal used in the creation of many magical enchantments. Typically used for decoration or in an alloy.

Moon Spider—A giant spider said to be sacred to Selune. Defeating one is the mark of a chosen hero of Selune.

Nickedemus—Aergonite Magister and court necromancer. Trained both Esmeralda and Xavier in the magical arts.

Rite of the Red Sun—A ceremonial ritual where pubescent children in the Caverns of Aergon are brought into the sunlight. Those that show signs of being Children of Selune are abandoned on the surface.

Selune—Moon goddess. Twin sister of Helene. No longer sighted in the sky after the Fall. The haerunwoln is sacred to those who follow her.

Silver Scarab—A swimming, schooling crustacean often eaten as food.

Slasherclaw—A feathered bipedal carnivore and pack hunter. Probably some sort of dinosaur.

Sleeps—A measure of time, as in "it will take several sleeps to reach the city." With no day or night to mark time, people use sleeps instead.

Tandyr—Riding lizard. Ridden by Hunter Joeri.

Thera—One of the elders of the Children of Selune.

Waur—A term of respect among the Children of Selune. It translates most closely to Elder.

Wyrmbane—The sword of Prince Fernando Aergon. Forged from meteoric iron and moonsilver. According to legend, it was enchanted to cut through the armored scales and tough hide of a dragon.

Xavier—A magister of the Aergonite court. Trained necromancer.

Zoul—A crested cave lizard from the Caverns of Aergon. Gifted to Adam as a mount by Captain Darius.

MATTHEW LANG likes being on the run. Sometimes for health (when he talks himself into it), but more often to see another country or culture. Preferably in person, but more frequently in his mind's eye through the written word or collaborative storytelling—as the cool kids are now calling *Dungeons & Dragons* and other role-playing games.

When not writing, he claims to be fighting for pocket equality in women's clothing, whatever that means, and talks an awful lot about quokkas. He is still likely to sing and dance in public, and more than a decade on is still loving MasterChef Australia. Matthew likes his men hot and spunky, his focaccia more Italian than British, and his vampires to combust when exposed to sunlight. Other than that, he's pretty normal. His nurses say that any rumors of him escaping his straightjacket are absolute nonsense and there is no way that he has been let loose amongst the population of Melbourne, Australia, no matter what your neighbor told you.

Matthew can be found on Facebook, Twitter, and less relevantly, on YouTube under the handle MattLangWrites. He can also be found at www.matthew-lang.com. He loves it when readers reach out to share their thoughts and is currently talking about people being able to have their own adventures in the world of Twitterlight. He said something else about "*Dungeons & Dragons*," "www.dmsguild.com," and possibly "Patreon," but it was all a bit vague and we're waiting for more detail before committing to anything. We're still not sure how he's planning on doing all that from his padded cell where he's definitely still kept. No, we don't need to look, thank you very much.

Twitter: @mattlangwrites
Facebook: www.facebook.com/MattLangWrites
Website: www.matthew-lang.com
YouTube: MattLangWrites

www.ingramcontent.com/pod-product-compliance
Lightning Source LLC
Chambersburg PA
CBHW070441120726
47910CB00003B/877